THE DANTE CLUB

Matthew Pearl graduated from Harvard University summa cum laude in English and American Literature in 1997, and in 2000 from Yale Law School. In 1998, he won the prestigious Dante Prize from the Dante Society of America for his scholarly work. He grew up in Fort Lauderdale and currently lives in Cambridge, Massachusetts. *The Dante Club* is his first novel. He can be reached via his website, www.thedanteclub.com.

Topography of Hell
Bartolomeo di Fruosino, c.1420
Courtesy of Bibliothèque Nationale, Paris

Matthew Pearl

THE DANTE CLUB

A Novel

Published by Vintage 2004

2 4 6 8 10 9 7 5 3

The Dante Club is a work of fiction. Many of the characters are inspired by historical figures; others are entirely imaginary creations of the author. Apart from the historical figures any resemblance between these fictional characters and actual persons, living or dead, is purely coincidental.

First published in Great Britain in 2004 by
Vintage

Vintage
Random House, 20 Vauxhall Bridge Road,
London SW1V 2SA

Random House Australia (Pty) Limited
20 Alfred Street, Milsons Point, Sydney
New South Wales 2061, Australia

Random House New Zealand Limited
18 Poland Road, Glenfield,
Auckland 10, New Zealand

Random House (Pty) Limited
Endulini, 5A Jubilee Road, Parktown 2193,
South Africa

The Random House Group Limited Reg. No. 954009
www.randomhouse.co.uk

A CIP catalogue record for this book
is available from the British Library

ISBN 0 099 46598 1

Papers used by Random House are natural, recyclable products made from wood grown in sustainable forests. The manufacturing processes conform to the environmental regulations of the country of origin

Printed and bound in Great Britain by
Bookmarque Ltd, Croydon, Surrey

To Lino, my professor, and Ian, my teacher

CAUTION TO THE READER

A PREFACE BY C. LEWIS WATKINS,

BAKER-VALERIO PROFESSOR OF THE CIVILIZATION AND LITERATURE OF ITALY AND RHETORICAL ORATION

Pittsfield Daily Reporter, "Community Notebook," September 15, 1989

LEXINGTON BOY'S INSECT SCARE SPARKS "RENEWAL"

Search teams safely recovered Kenneth Stanton, 10, of Lexington, in a remote corner of the Catamount Mountains on Tuesday afternoon. The fifth grader was treated at Berkshire Medical Center for swelling and discomfort resulting from the deposit of larvae by initially unidentified insects nested in his wounds.

Entomologist Dr. K. L. Landsman of the Harve-Bay Institute Museum in Boston reports that the blowfly samples retrieved from the site are historically unknown to Massachusetts. More noteworthy, says Landsman, the insects and their larvae appear to represent a species that has been thought completely extinct by entomologists for nearly fifty years. *Cochliomyia hominivorax*, known commonly as the New World primary screwworm, was classified in 1859 by a French doctor on a South American island. By the end of the 19th century the presence of this dangerous species grew to epidemic levels, causing the deaths of hundreds of thousands of livestock throughout the Western Hemisphere and reportedly some human beings. During the 1950s, a massive American-engineered program successfully eradicated the species by introducing gamma-radiated sterile male flies into the population, ending the ability of the female flies to reproduce.

Kenneth Stanton's scare may have contributed to what is known as a laboratory-assisted "renewal" of the insects for the purpose of research. "Though eradication was a wise public health initiative," says Landsman, "there is much that can be learned in a controlled setting with new observational technologies." Asked for his reaction to the taxonomic good fortune, Stanton replied, "My Science teacher thinks I'm great!"

You may wonder, referring back to the title page of this volume, how the above article could possibly relate to Dante, but you will see shortly that the connection is alarming. As a recognized authority on the subject of the

American reception of Dante's *The Divine Comedy*, I was contracted last summer by Random House to write, in return for their usual paltry fee, some prefatory remarks for this book.

The text of Mr. Pearl's work derives from the true origins of Dante's presence in our culture. In 1867, the poet H. W. Longfellow completed the first American translation of *The Divine Comedy*, Dante's revolutionary poem of the hereafter. Presently, there exist more translations of Dante's poetry into English than into any other language, and the United States produces more Dante translations than any other country. The Dante Society of America, of Cambridge, Massachusetts, boasts itself the oldest continuous organization in the world dedicated to the study and promotion of Dante. As T. S. Eliot remarked, Dante and Shakespeare divide the modern world between them; and Dante's half of the world enlarges every year. Before Longfellow's work, however, Dante remained all but an unknown entity here. We did not speak the language of Italian, nor did we teach it with any frequency; we did not travel abroad in any significant numbers, nor were there more than a sparse handful of Italians living in the entire United States.

Under the full force of my critical acumen, I found that beyond these essential facts, the extraordinary events narrated by *The Dante Club* advanced fable rather than history. However, searching the databases of Lexis-Nexis for confirmation of my appraisal, I discovered the startling newspaper notice, inserted above, from the *Pittsfield Daily Reporter.* Immediately contacting Dr. Landsman of the Harve-Bay Institute, I pieced together a fuller picture of the incident that occurred nearly fourteen years ago.

Kenneth Stanton had wandered away from the family fishing trip in the Berkshires and stumbled upon a strange trail of dead animals on an overgrown path: first, a raccoon with its navel engorged with blood, then a fox; farther in, a black bear. The boy afterward recounted to his parents a feeling like hypnosis as he faced the grotesque sights. He lost his balance and fell hard onto a jagged line of rocks. Left unconscious and with a fractured ankle, he was beset by the primary screwworm blowflies. Five days later, Kenneth Stanton, age ten, succumbed to sudden convulsions while recuperating in his bed. The autopsy found twelve maggots of the *Cochliomyia hominivorax*, one of the world's deadliest insect species—extinct for fifty years, or so it was believed.

The reawakened species of fly, exhibiting a previously unreported capability to survive across climates, has been introduced since then to the Middle East, apparently through cargo shipments, and, as I write, decimates the livestock and economy of northern Iran. It has lately been theorized from scientific findings printed in last year's *Abstracts of Entomology* that the divergent evolution exhibited by the flies originated in the northeastern United States circa 1865.

To the question of how it began there was no apparent answer—except, I now brokenheartedly believe, within the details of *The Dante Club.* For more than five weeks now, I have assigned the task of additional examination of Pearl's manuscript to eight of the fourteen teaching fellows in my employment this semester. They have analyzed and cataloged the philological and historiographical precepts line by line, noting with flickering interest the minor mistakes that are the fault only of the author's ego. With each passing day, we witness a bit more evidence of the remarkable gloom and glory encountered by Longfellow and his protectors the year Dante turned six hundred. I have waived any recompensation, for this was no longer a preface I set out to write but a warning. Kenneth Stanton's death throws wide open the closed portal of Dante's arrival to our world, of the secrets still lying dormant in our own age. Of these I only wish to caution you, reader. Please, if you continue, remember first that words can bleed.

Professor C. Lewis Watkins
Cambridge, Massachusetts

CANTICLE ONE

I

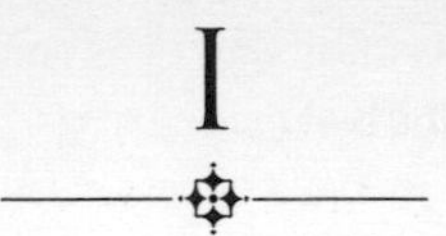

JOHN KURTZ, the chief of the Boston police, breathed in some of his heft for a better fit between the two chambermaids. On one side, the Irish woman who had discovered the body was blubbering and wailing prayers unfamiliar (because they were Catholic) and unintelligible (because she was blubbering) that prickled the hair in Kurtz's ear; on the other side was her soundless and despairing niece. The parlor had a wide arrangement of chairs and couches, but the women had squeezed in next to the guest as they waited. He had to concentrate on not spilling any of his tea, the black haircloth divan was rattling so hard with their shock.

Kurtz had faced other murders as chief of police. Not enough to make it routine, though—usually one a year, or two; often, Boston would pass through a twelve-month period without a homicide worth noticing. Those few who were murdered were of the low sort, so it had not been a necessary part of Kurtz's position to console. He was a man too impatient with emotion to have excelled at it anyway. Deputy Police Chief Edward Savage, who sometimes wrote poetry, might have done better.

This—*this* was the only name Chief Kurtz could bear to attach to the horrifying situation that was to change the life of a city—was not only a murder. This was the murder of a Boston Brahmin, a member of the aristocratic, Harvard-schooled, Unitarian-blessed, drawing room caste of New England. And the victim was more than that: He was the highest official of the Massachusetts courts. *This* had not only killed a man, as sometimes murders do almost mercifully, but had obliterated him entirely.

The woman they were anticipating in the best parlor of Wide Oaks had boarded the first train she could in Providence after receiving the telegram. The train's first-class cars lumbered forward with irresponsible leisure, but now that journey, like everything that had come before, seemed part of an unrecognizable oblivion. She had made a wager with herself, and with God, that if her family minister had not yet arrived at her house by the time she got there, the telegram's message had been mistaken. It didn't quite make sense, this half-articulated wager of hers, but she had to invent something to believe, something to keep from fainting dead away. Ednah Healey, balanced on the threshold of terror and loss, stared at nothing. Entering her parlor, she saw only the absence of her minister and fluttered with unreasoning victory.

Kurtz, a robust man with mustard coloring beneath his bushy mustache, realized he too was trembling. He had rehearsed the exchange on the carriage ride to Wide Oaks. "Madam, how very sorry we are to call you back to this. Understand that Chief Justice Healey . . ." No, he had meant to preface that. "We thought it best," he continued, "to explain the unfortunate circumstances here, you see, in your own house, where you'd be most comfortable." He thought this idea a generous one.

"You couldn't have found Judge Healey, Chief Kurtz," she said, and ordered him to sit. "I'm sorry you've wasted this call, but there's some simple mistake. The chief justice was—is staying in Beverly for a few quiet days of work while I visited Providence with our two sons. He is not expected back until tomorrow."

Kurtz did not claim responsibility for refuting her. "Your chambermaid," he said, indicating the bigger of the two servants, "found his body, madam. Outside, near the river."

Nell Ranney, the chambermaid, welled with guilt for the discovery. She did not notice that there were a few bloodstained maggot remains in the pouch of her apron.

"It appears to have happened several days ago. Your husband never departed for the country, I'm afraid," Kurtz said, worried he sounded too blunt.

Ednah Healey wept slowly at first, as a woman might for a dead household pet—reflective and governed but without anger. The olive-brown feather protruding from her hat nodded with dignified resistance.

Nell looked at Mrs. Healey longingly, then said with great humanity, "You ought to come back later in the day, Chief Kurtz, if you please."

John Kurtz was grateful for the permission to escape Wide Oaks. He walked with appropriate solemnity toward his new driver, a young and handsome patrolman who was letting down the steps of the police carriage. There was no reason to hurry, not with what must be brewing already over this at the Central Station between the frantic city aldermen and Mayor Lincoln, who already had him by the ears for not raiding enough gambling "hells" and prostitution houses to make the newspapers happy.

A terrible scream cleaved the air before he had walked very far. It belched forth in light echoes from the house's dozen chimneys. Kurtz turned and watched with foolish detachment as Ednah Healey, feather hat flying away and hair unloosed in wild peaks, ran onto the front steps and launched a streaking white blur straight for his head.

Kurtz would later remember blinking—it seemed all he could do to prevent catastrophe, to blink. He bowed to his helplessness: The murder of Artemus Prescott Healey had finished him already. It was not the death itself. Death was as common a visitor in 1865 Boston as ever: infant sicknesses, consumption and unnamed and unforgiving fevers, uncontainable fires, stampeding riots, young women perishing in childbirth in such great number it seemed they had never been meant for this world in the first place, and—until just six months ago—war, which had reduced thousands upon thousands of Boston boys to names written on black-bordered notices and sent to their families. But the meticulous and nonsensical—*the elaborate and meaningless*—destruction of a single human being at the hands of an unknown . . .

Kurtz was yanked down hard by his coat and tumbled into the soft, sun-drenched lawn. The vase thrown by Mrs. Healey shattered into a thousand blue-and-ivory shards against the paunch of an oak (one of the trees said to have given the estate its name). Perhaps, Kurtz thought, he should have sent Deputy Chief Savage to handle this after all.

Patrolman Nicholas Rey, Kurtz's driver, released his arm and lifted him to his feet. The horses snorted and reared at the end of the carriageway.

"He did all he knew how! We all did! We didn't deserve this, whatever they say to you, Chief! We didn't deserve any of this! I'm all alone now!" Ednah Healey raised her clenched hands, and then said something that startled Kurtz. "I know who, Chief Kurtz! I know who's done this! I know!"

Nell Ranney threw her thick arms around the screaming woman and shushed and caressed, cradling her as she would have cradled one of the

Healey children so many years before. Ednah Healey clawed and pulled and spat in return, causing the comely junior police officer, Patrolman Rey, to intervene.

But the new widow's rage expired, folding itself into the maid's wide black blouse, where there was nothing else but the abundant bosom.

The old mansion had never sounded so empty.

Ednah Healey had departed on one of her frequent visits to the home of her family, the industrious Sullivans, in Providence, her husband remaining behind to work on a property dispute between Boston's two largest banking concerns. The judge bid his family good-bye in his usual mumbling and affectionate manner, and was generous enough to dismiss the help once Mrs. Healey was out of sight. Though the wife wouldn't do without servants, he enjoyed small moments of autonomy. Besides, he liked a drop of sherry on occasion, and the help was sure to report any temperance violations to their mistress, for they liked him but feared her deep within their bones.

He would start off the following day for a weekend of tranquil study in Beverly. The next proceeding that required Healey's presence would not be heard until Wednesday, when he would railroad back into the city, back to the courthouse.

Judge Healey didn't notice one way or another, but Nell Ranney, a maid for twenty years, since being driven out by famine and disease in her native Ireland, knew that a tidy environment was essential for a man of importance like the chief justice. So Nell came in on Monday, which was when she found the first splattering of dried red near the supply closet and another streaking near the foot of the stairs. She guessed that some wounded animal had found its way into the house and must have found the same way out.

Then she saw a fly on the parlor drapes. She shooed it out the open window with a high-pitched clicking of her tongue, fortified by the brandishing of her feather duster. But it reappeared while she was polishing the long mahogany dining table. She thought the new colored kitchen girls must have negligently left some crumbs. Contraband—which is how she still thought of the freedwomen and always would—did not care of actual cleanliness, only its appearance.

The insect, it seemed to Nell, gurgled loud as a train's engine. She killed the fly with a rolled up *North American Review.* The flattened specimen was about twice the size of a housefly and had three even black stripes across its bluish green trunk. *And what a phiz!* thought Nell Ranney. The head of the creature was something Judge Healey would murmur over admiringly before tossing the fly to the wastebasket. The bulging eyes, of a vibrant orange color, took up nearly half its torso. There was a strange tint of orange glowing out, or red. Something between the two, something yellow and black, too. *Copper:* the swirl of fire.

She returned to the house the next morning to clean the upstairs. Just as she crossed through the door, another fly sailed like an arrow past the tip of her nose. Outraged, she secured another of the judge's heavy magazines and stalked the fly up the main staircase. Nell always used the servants' stairs, even when alone in the house. But this situation called for rearranging priorities. She removed her shoes and her wide feet fell lightly over the warm, carpeted steps, following the fly into the Healeys' bedchamber.

The fire-eyes stared out jarringly; the body curled back like a horse ready to gallop, and the face of the insect looked for that moment like the face of a man. This was the last moment for many years, listening to the monotonous buzz, that Nell Ranney would know some measure of peace.

She rumbled forward and smashed the *Review* against the window and the fly. But she had faltered over something during her attack, and now looked down at the obstacle, twisted on her bare foot. She picked up the tangled mass, a full set of human teeth belonging to the upper chamber of a mouth.

She released it at once but stood attentively, as though it might censure her for the incivility.

They were false teeth, crafted with an artist's care by a prominent New York dentist to fulfill Judge Healey's desire for a smarter appearance on the bench. He was so proud of them—told their provenance to anyone who would listen, not understanding that the vanity leading to such appendages should prevent any discussion of them. They were a bit too bright and new, like staring right into the summer sun between a man's lips.

From the corner of her eye, Nell noticed a thick pool of blood that had curdled and caked on the carpet. And near that, a small pile of suit clothes folded neatly. These clothes were as familiar as Nell Ranney's own white apron, black blouse, and billowing black skirt. She had done much needlework on his pockets and sleeves; the judge never ordered new suits from Mr. Randridge, the exceptional School Street tailor, except when absolutely essential.

Returning downstairs to put on her shoes, the chambermaid only now noticed the splashes of blood on the banister and camouflaged by the plush red carpet that covered the stairs. Out the parlor's large oval window, beyond the immaculate garden, where the yard sloped into meadows, woods, dry fields, and, eventually, the Charles River, she saw a swarm of blowflies. Nell went outdoors to inspect.

The flies were collected over a pile of rubbish. The tremendous scent caused her eyes to tear as she approached. She secured a wheelbarrow and, as she did, recalled the calf the Healeys had permitted the stableboy to raise on the grounds. But that had been years ago. Both the stableboy and the calf had outgrown Wide Oaks and left it to its eternal sameness.

The flies were of that new fire-eyed variety. There were yellow hornets, too, which had taken some morbid interest in whatever putrid flesh was underneath. But more numerous than the flying creatures were the masses of bristling white pellets crackling with movement—sharp-backed worms, wriggling tightly over something, no, not just wriggling, popping, burrowing, sinking, *eating* into each other, into the . . . but what *was* supporting this horrendous mountain, alive with white slime? One end of the heap seemed like a thorny bush of chestnut and ivory strands of . . .

Above the heap stood a short wooden staff with a ragged flag, white on both sides; it was flapping with the undecided breeze.

She could not help knowing the truth about what lay in that heap, but in her fear she prayed she'd find the stableboy's calf. Her eyes could not resist making out the nakedness, the wide, slightly hunched back sloping into the crack of the enormous, snowy buttocks, brimming over with the crawling, pallid, bean-shaped maggots above the disproportionately short legs that were kicked out in opposite directions. A solid block of flies, hundreds of them, circled protectively. The back of the head was completely swathed in white worms, which must have numbered in the thousands rather than hundreds.

Nell kicked away the wasps' nest and stuffed the judge into the wheelbarrow. She half wheeled and half dragged his naked body through the meadows, over the garden, through the halls, and into his study. Throwing the body on a mound of legal papers, Nell pulled Judge Healey's head into her lap. Handfuls of maggots rained down from his nose and ears and slack mouth. She began tearing out the luminescent maggots from the back of his head. The wormy pellets were moist and hot. She also grabbed some of the fire-eyed flies that had trailed her inside, smashing them with the palm of her hand, pulling them apart by the wings, flinging them, one after another, across the room in empty vengeance. What was heard and seen next made her produce a roar loud enough to ring straight through New England.

Two grooms from the stable next door found Nell crawling away from the study on her hands and knees, crying insensibly.

"But what is it, Nellie, what is it? By Jesus, you ain't hurt now?"

It was later, when Nell Ranney told Ednah Healey that Judge Healey had groaned before dying in her arms, that the widow ran out and threw a vase at the chief of police. That her husband might have been conscious for those four days, even remotely aware, was too much to ask her to permit.

Mrs. Healey's professed knowledge of her husband's killer turned out to be rather imprecise. "It was Boston that killed him," she revealed later that day to Chief Kurtz, after she had stopped shaking. "This entire hideous city. It ate him alive."

She insisted Kurtz bring her to the body. It had taken the coroner's deputies three hours to slice out the quarter-inch spiraled maggots from their places inside the corpse; the tiny horny mouths had to be pried off. The pockets of devoured flesh left in their wake spanned all open areas; the terrible swelling at the back of the head still seemed to pulse with maggots even after their removal. The nostrils were now barely divided and the armpits eaten away. With the false teeth gone the face sagged low and loose like a dead accordion. Most humiliating, most pitiable, was not the broken condition, not even the fact that the body had been so maggot-ridden and layered in flies and wasps, but the simple fact of the nakedness. Sometimes a corpse, it is said, looks for all the world like a forked radish with a head fantastically carved upon it. Judge Healey had one of those bodies never meant to be seen naked by anyone except his wife.

In the stale chill of the coroner's rooms Ednah Healey took in this view, and knew in that instant what it meant to be a widow, what an ungodly jealousy it produced. With a sudden jerk of her arm, she swiped the coroner's razor-edged shears from a shelf. Kurtz, remembering the vase, stumbled backward into the confused, cursing coroner.

Ednah kneeled down and tenderly snipped a clump from the judge's wild crown of hair. Crumpling to her knees, her voluminous skirts spreading to every corner of the small room, a tiny woman unfolded across a cold, purple body, with one gauze-gloved hand clenching the blades and the other caressing the plundered tuft, thick and dry as horsehair.

• • •

"Well, I've never seen a man so cleaned out by worms," Kurtz said with a tenuous voice at the deadhouse after two of Kurtz's men escorted Ednah Healey home.

Barnicoat, the coroner, had a shapeless and small head cruelly punctured by lobster eyes. His nostrils were stuffed to double capacity with cotton balls.

"Maggots," Barnicoat said, grinning. He picked up one of the wriggling white beans that had fallen to the floor. It struggled against his meaty palm before he flung it into the incinerator, where it fizzled black and then popped into smoke. "Bodies aren't as a practice left to rot out in a field. Still, it is true that the winged mob our Judge Healey attracted is more common to sheep or goat carcasses left outdoors." The truth was that the sheer number of maggots that had bred inside Healey for the four days he was left in his yard was astounding, but Barnicoat did not possess knowledge enough to admit this. The coroner was a political appointee, and the position required no special medical or scientific expertise, only a tolerance for dead bodies.

"The chambermaid who took the body into the house," Kurtz explained. "She was trying to clear the insects from the wound and she thought she saw, I daresay I don't know how . . ."

Barnicoat coughed for Kurtz to get on with it.

"She heard Judge Healey moan before dying," Kurtz said. "That's what she says, Mr. Barnicoat."

"Oh, very like!" Barnicoat laughed lightheartedly. "Maggots of blowflies can live only on dead tissue, Chief." Which was why, he explained, the female flies looked for wounds on cattle to nest on, or spoiled meat. If they happened to find themselves in a wound of a living being who was unconscious or otherwise incapable of removing them, the maggots could ingest only the dead portions of tissue—which did little harm. "This head wound looks to have doubled or tripled from its original circumference, meaning that all the tissue was dead, meaning that the chief justice was quite finished by the time the insects had their feast."

"So the blow to the head," Kurtz said, "that caused the original wound—that's what killed him?"

"Oh, very like, Chief," said Barnicoat. "And hard enough to knock his teeth out at that. You say he was found in their yard?"

Kurtz nodded. Barnicoat speculated that the killing had not been intentional. An assault with the purpose of murder would have included something to guarantee the enterprise beyond a blow, like a pistol or ax. "Even a dagger. No, this seems more likely an ordinary breaking-in then. The rogue clubs the chief justice on the head in the bedchamber, knocks him out cold, then drops him outside to get him out of the way while he ransacks the house for valuables, probably never once thinking that Healey would have been so hurt," he said, almost sympathetic to the misguided thief.

Kurtz looked right at Barnicoat with an ominous stare. "Only, nothing was taken from the house. Not merely that. The chief justice's clothes were removed and folded up neatly, even down to his drawers." He caught his voice creaking, as if it had been stepped on. "With his wallet, gold chain, and watch all left in a stack by his clothes!"

One of Barnicoat's lobster eyes shot wide open at Kurtz. "He was stripped? And nothing at all was taken?"

"This was plain madness," Kurtz said, the fact hitting him anew for the third or fourth time.

"Think of that!" exclaimed Barnicoat, looking around as though to find more people to tell.

"You and your deputies are to keep this completely confidential, by order of the mayor. You know that, right, Mr. Barnicoat? Not a word outside these walls!"

"Oh, very like, Chief Kurtz." Then Barnicoat laughed quickly, irresponsibly, like a child. "Well, old Healey would have been an awfully fat man to haul about. At least we can trust it was not the grieving *widder.*"

Kurtz made every plea to logic and emotion when he explained, at Wide Oaks, why he needed time to look into the matter before the public could know what had happened. But Ednah Healey gave no response as her upstairs girl arranged the bedcovers around her.

"You see—well, if there's a circus about us, if the press savages our methods as they do, what can be discovered?"

Her eyes, usually darting and judgmental, were sadly immobilized. Even the maids, who feared her fierce look of reprimand, cried for her current state as much as for the loss of Judge Healey.

Kurtz shrank back, almost ready to surrender. He noticed that Mrs. Healey closed her eyes tightly when Nell Ranney came into the room with tea. "Mr. Barnicoat, the coroner, says that your chambermaid's belief that the chief justice was alive when she found him is scientifically impossible—a hallucination. For Barnicoat can tell by the number of maggots that the chief justice had already passed on."

Ednah Healey turned to Kurtz with a quizzical open look.

"Truly, Mrs. Healey," Kurtz continued with new self-assurance. "The flies' maggots by their nature only eat *dead tissue*, you see."

"Then he could not have suffered while he was out there?" Mrs. Healey pleaded with a broken voice.

Kurtz shook his head firmly. Before he left Wide Oaks, Ednah called in Nell Ranney and forbade her ever to repeat that most horrific portion of her story again.

"But, Mrs. Healey, I know I . . ." Nell trailed off, shaking her head.

"Nell Ranney! You shall heed my words!"

Next, to repay the chief, the widow agreed to conceal the circumstances of her husband's death.

"But you must do this," she said, gripping his coat sleeve. "You must vow to find his murderer."

Kurtz nodded. "Mrs. Healey, the department is beginning everything that our resources and current state . . ."

"No." Her colorless hand clung, immovable, to his coat, as though if he left the room now it would still hang there quite undaunted. "No, Chief Kurtz. Not to begin. To finish. To find. Vow to me."

She left him little choice. "I vow we will, Mrs. Healey." He did not mean to say anything more, but the pounding doubt in his chest made him speak its voice too. "Some way."

✠

J. T. Fields, publisher of poets, was squeezed into the window seat of his office at the New Corner, studying the cantos Longfellow had selected for the evening, when a junior clerk interrupted with a visitor. The slim figure of Augustus Manning materialized from the hall, imprisoned in a stiff frock coat. He drifted into the office, as though he had no idea how he had come to find himself on the second floor of the newly renovated mansion on Tremont Street that now housed Ticknor, Fields & Co.

"The space looks grand, Mr. Fields—grand. Though you shall always be to me the junior partner huddled behind your green curtain at the Old Corner, preaching to your little authorial congregation."

Fields, now the senior partner and the most successful publisher in America, smiled and moved to his desk, extending his foot swiftly down onto the third of four pedals—A, B, C, and D—that sat in a row under his chair. In a distant room of the offices, a little bell marked C gave a slight note, startling a messenger boy. Bell C signified that the publisher was to be interrupted in twenty-five; bell B, ten minutes; bell A, five. Ticknor & Fields was the exclusive publisher of official Harvard University texts, pamphlets, memoirs, and college histories. So Dr. Augustus Manning, the puller of all the institution's purse strings, on this day received a most generous C.

Manning removed his hat and passed a hand over the bare ravine between waves of frothy hair that crashed down from either side of his head. "As the treasurer of the Harvard Corporation," he said, "I must present to you word of a potential problem that has been lately brought to our attention, Mr. Fields. You understand that a publishing house engaged by Harvard University must boast nothing less than an unimpeachable reputation."

"Dr. Manning, I daresay there are no houses with reputations as unimpeached as our own."

Manning braided his crooked fingers together into a steeple and emitted a long, scratchy sigh or cough, Fields could not tell which. "We have heard of a new literary translation you plan to publish, Mr. Fields, by Mr. Longfellow. Of course, we cherished Mr. Longfellow's years of contribution at the College, and his own poems are first-rate indeed. Yet we have heard something of this project, of its subject matter, and have some concerns that this type of drivel . . ."

Fields composed a cold stare, at which Manning's steepled fingers slid apart. The publisher lowered with his heel the fourth, most urgent, knob of request. "You do know, my dear Dr. Manning, how society values the work of my poets. Longfellow. Lowell. Holmes." The triumvirate of names reinforced his position of strength.

"Mr. Fields, it is in the name of *society* that we speak. Your authors hang on to the skirts of your coat. Advise them properly. Do not mention this meeting if you like, and neither shall I. I know you wish your house to be held in esteem, and I do not doubt that you would consider all the repercussions of your publication."

"Thank you for that faith, Dr. Manning." Fields breathed into his wide spade of a beard, struggling to maintain his famous diplomacy. "I have considered the repercussions thoroughly and look forward to them. If you do not wish to proceed with the university's pending publications, I shall happily return the plates to your possession at once without cost. You know, I hope, that you shall offend me if you say aught disparaging about my authors to the public. Ah, Mr. Osgood."

Fields's senior clerk, J. R. Osgood, shuffled in and Fields ordered a tour of the new offices for Dr. Manning.

"Unnecessary." The word seeped out from Manning's stiff patrician beard, durable as the century, as he stood. "I suppose you anticipate a good many pleasant days to come in this place, Mr. Fields," he said, throwing a cold glance at the shining black walnut paneling. "There will be times, remember, when even you shall not be able to protect your authors from their ambitions." He bowed super-politely and started down the stairwell.

"Osgood," Fields said, and pushed the door closed. "I want you to place a gossip bit in the *New York Tribune* for the translation."

"Ah, is Mr. Longfellow done already?" Osgood asked brightly.

Fields pursed his full, overbearing lips. "Did you know, Mr. Osgood, that Napoleon once shot a book peddler for being too aggressive?"

Osgood considered this. "No, I hadn't heard that, Mr. Fields."

"The happy advantage of a democracy is that we are free to puff our books as hard as we can manage and be perfectly safe of any harm. I want no family of any respectability to sleep unapprised by the time we go to the binders." And anyone within a mile of his voice would believe he would make that happen. "To Mr. Greeley, New York, for immediate inclusion in the 'Literary Boston' page." Fields's fingers were plunking and strumming the air, a musician playing a remembered piano. His wrist cramped when he wrote, so Osgood was a surrogate hand for most of the publisher's writing, including his fits of poetry.

It came together in his mind in almost finished form. " 'WHAT THE LITERARY MEN ARE DOING IN BOSTON: It is rumored that a new translation is in the press of Ticknor, Fields and Co., which will attract considerable attention in many quarters. The author is said to be a gentleman of our city, whose poetry has for many years inspired public adoration on both sides of the Atlantic. We understand furthermore that this gentleman has recruited help from the finest literary minds of Boston . . .' Hold there, Osgood. Make that 'of New England.' We don't want old Greene to simper, do we?"

"Of course not, sir," Osgood managed to reply between scribblings.

" '. . . the finest minds of New England to manage the task of revising and completing his new and elaborate poetical translation. The content of the work is at this time unknown, except to say that it has never before been read in our country, and shall transform the literary landscape.' Et cetera. Have Greeley mark it 'Anonymous Source.' Have you got all that?"

"I shall send it by the first post in the morning," said Osgood.

"Wire it to New York."

"For printing next week?" Osgood thought he had misheard.

"Yes, yes!" Fields threw up his hands. The publisher was rarely flustered. "And, I tell you, we'll have another ready the week after!"

Osgood turned back cautiously as he reached the door. "What was Dr. Manning's business here this afternoon, Mr. Fields, if I might ask?"

"Nothing to think of." Fields blew a long sigh into his beard that contradicted this. He returned to the fat cushion of stacked manuscripts on his window seat. Below them was the Boston Common, where pedestrians still clung to summer linens, even a few straw hats. As Osgood started to leave again, Fields felt the desire to explain. "If we go ahead with Longfellow's Dante, Augustus Manning will see to it that all publishing contracts between Harvard and Ticknor and Fields are canceled."

"Why, that's thousands of dollars in value—tens more over the next years!" Osgood said with alarm.

Fields nodded patiently. "Hmm. Do you know, Osgood, why we did not publish Whitman when he brought us his *Leaves of Grass*?" He did not wait for a reply. "Because Bill Ticknor did not want to call down trouble on the house over the carnal passages."

"May I ask whether you regret that, Mr. Fields?"

He was pleased with the question. His tone modulated from employer's to mentor's. "No I don't, my dear Osgood. Whitman belongs to New York, as did Poe." That name he said more bitterly, for reasons that still smoldered. "And I'll let them keep what few they have. But from true literature we mustn't ever cower, not in Boston. And we shall not now."

He meant "now that Ticknor was gone." It was not that the late William D. Ticknor had no sense of literature. In fact, it might be said the Ticknors had literature running in their blood, or at least in some primary organ, as their cousin George Ticknor had once been Boston's literary authority, preceding Longfellow and Lowell as the first Smith Professor at Harvard. But William D. Ticknor had started in Boston in the field of complex financing, and he brought to publishing, which at the time was little more than bookselling, the mind of a fine banker. It was Fields who had recognized genius in half-finished manuscripts and monographs, Fields who had nurtured friendships with the great New England authors as other publishers closed their doors for lack of profits or spent too much time retailing.

Fields, while a young clerk, was even said to exhibit preternatural (or "very queer," as the other clerks put it) abilities; he could predict by the demeanor and appearance of a customer what book would be desired. At first he kept this to himself, but when the other clerks discovered his gift, it became a source of frequent wagers, and those who bet against Fields always ended the day unhappily. Fields would soon after transform the industry by convincing William Ticknor to reward authors rather than cheat them, and by realizing that publicity could turn poets into personalities. As a partner, Fields bought out *The Atlantic Monthly* and *The North American Review* as venues for his authors.

Osgood would never be a man of letters like Fields, a litterateur, and so hesitated to compare ideas of True Literature. "Why would Augustus Manning threaten such a measure? It's extortion, that's what," he said indignantly.

At this Fields smiled to himself, thinking of how much there still was to teach Osgood. "We extort everyone we know, Osgood, or nothing should get done. Dante's poetry is foreign and unknown. The Corporation lords over Harvard's reputation by controlling every word allowed past the College gates, Osgood—anything unknown, anything unknowable, stands to frighten them beyond measure." Fields picked up the pocket edition of Dante's *Divina Commedia* he had found in Rome. "Here is revolt enough between two covers to unravel it all. The mind of our country is moving with the speed of a telegraph, Osgood, and our great institutions are stagecoaching behind it."

"But why would their good name be affected in this instance? They have never sanctioned Longfellow's translation."

The publisher mocked indignation. "I rather think not. But they still have association, most fearful, for it is something that can scarce be erased."

Fields's connection to Harvard was as the university's publisher. The other scholars had stronger ties: Longfellow had been its most famous professor until retiring about ten years earlier to devote himself fully to his poetry; Oliver Wendell Holmes, James Russell Lowell, and George Washington Greene were alumni; and Holmes and Lowell were celebrated professors—Holmes holding the Parkman anatomy chair at the Medical College and Lowell being the head of modern languages and literature at Harvard College, which had been Longfellow's former post.

"This will be seen as a masterwork springing from the heart of Boston and from the soul of Harvard, my dear Osgood. Even Augustus Manning is not so blind as to miss that."

Dr. Oliver Wendell Holmes, medical professor and poet, hurried through the cropped paths of the Boston Common in the direction of his publisher's office as though he were being chased (stopping twice, however, to sign his autograph). If you passed close enough to Dr. Holmes or were one of those amblers who wielded your pen on behalf of your autograph book, you could hear him humming with purpose. In his moiré silk waistcoat pocket burned the folded rectangle of paper that drove the little doctor on toward the Corner (that is, the office of his publisher) and drove him to fear.

When encountered by admirers, he sparkled to hear them name their favorites. "Oh, *that*. They say President Lincoln recited that poem by memory. Well, truly, he told me himself . . ." The shape of Holmes's boyish face, the small mouth pushing against the loose jaw, made it appear an effort for him to keep his mouth closed for any noticeable period of time.

After the autograph hounds, he came to a stop only once, haltingly, at the Dutton & Company Bookstore, where he counted out three novels and four volumes of poetry from entirely new and (in all probability) young New York authors. Every week the literary notices announced that the most extraordinary book of the age had just been published. "Profound originality" had become so plentiful that, not knowing better, one could take it for the most common national product. Just a few years before the war, it seemed the only book in the world was his *Autocrat of the Breakfast-Table*, the serialized essay with which Holmes had surpassed all expectations by inventing a new attitude for literature, one of personal observation.

Holmes burst into the vast front showroom of Ticknor & Fields. Like the Jews of old at the Second Temple remembering the glories it replaced, Dr. Holmes could not help resisting the oiled and polished glare and smuggling in his sensory recall of the musty quarters of the Old Corner Bookstore, on Washington and School streets, into which the publishing house and its authors had squeezed for decades. Fields's authors called the new palace, at the corner of Tremont Street and Hamilton Place, the Corner or New Corner—in part from habit, but also as pointed nostalgia for their beginnings.

"Good evening, Dr. Holmes. Here for Mr. Fields?"

Miss Cecilia Emory, the pleasing blue-bonneted girl at the front desk, received Dr. Holmes in a cloud of perfume and a warming smile. Fields had taken on several women as secretaries when the Corner opened a month earlier, despite a chorus of critics, who condemned the practice for a building otherwise crowded with men. The idea almost certainly originated with Fields's wife, Annie, willful and beautiful (qualities usually allied).

"Yes, my dear." Holmes bowed. "Is he in?"

"Ah, is that the great Autocrat of the Breakfast-Table descended before us?"

Samuel Ticknor, one of the clerks, was passing an overlong good-bye with Cecilia Emory as he slipped on his gloves. Not the average publishing-house clerk, Ticknor would be welcomed home by wife and servants on one of the most desirable corners of Back Bay.

Holmes took his hand. "Grand little place the New Corner is, isn't it, my dear Mr. Ticknor?" He laughed. "I'm half surprised our Mr. Fields hasn't gotten lost in here yet."

"Hasn't he," Samuel Ticknor muttered back seriously, followed by a light snigger or grunt.

J. R. Osgood came to usher Holmes upstairs. "Pay him no mind, Dr. Holmes," Osgood sniffed, watching the him in question saunter onto Tremont Street and toss money at the peanut vendor on the corner as he would at a beggar. "I daresay young Ticknor believes he should command the same view of the Common as his father would have were he alive, on the basis of name alone. And wants everyone to know it, too."

Dr. Holmes had no time for gossip—not today, at least.

Osgood noted that Fields was in meetings, so Holmes was purgatoried in the Authors' Room, a plush chamber for the comfort and pleasure of the house's writers. On an ordinary day, Holmes might well spend his time here admiring the literary mementos and autographs hanging on the wall that included his name. Instead, his attention turned to the check that he drew flinchingly out of his pocket. In the taunting number written out in careless hand Holmes saw his failures. He saw in the stray ink spots his life as a poet, battered by the events of the last years, incapable of rising to past achievements. He sat in silence and rubbed the check roughly between his forefinger and thumb as Aladdin might his old lamp. Holmes imagined all the fearless, fresher authors Fields was courting, convincing, shaping.

He wandered from the Authors' Room twice, twice finding Fields's office shut. But before he could turn back this second time, the voice of James Russell Lowell, poet and editor, found its way out. Lowell was speaking forcefully (as always), even dramatically, and Dr. Holmes, instead of knocking or turning away, tried to decipher the conversation, for he believed it would almost certainly have something to do with him.

Narrowing his eyes as though he could transfer their share of power to his ears, Holmes was just making out an intriguing word when he hit something and tumbled.

The young man who had come to a sudden halt in front of the eavesdropper flailed his hands in stupid repentance.

"My fault entirely, dear lad," the poet said, laughing. "Dr. Holmes, and it's . . ."

"Teal, Doctor, sir," the trembler, a shop boy, managed to introduce himself before turning yellow and scurrying away.

"I see you've met Daniel Teal." Osgood, the senior clerk, appeared from the hall. "Couldn't keep a hotel, but as hard a worker as we have." Holmes chuckled with Osgood: poor lad, still green around the ears at the firm and nearly knocking heads with Oliver Wendell Holmes! This renewed self-importance made the poet smile.

"Would you like me to check on Mr. Fields?" Osgood asked.

Then the door opened from inside. James Russell Lowell, majestically untidy, his penetrating gray eyes taking one's attention from the woolliness of his hair and the beard that he smoothed with two fingers, looked out from the threshold. He was in Fields's office alone with today's newspaper.

Holmes imagined what Lowell would say if he attempted to share his anxiety: *This is a time to concentrate all energies on Longfellow, on Dante, Holmes, not our petty vanities . . .* "Come, *come,* Wendell!" Lowell started to make him a drink.

Holmes said, "Why, Lowell, I did believe I heard voices in here just now. Ghosts?"

"When Coleridge was asked whether he believed in ghosts, he replied in the negative, explaining he had seen far too many of them." He laughed gleefully and twisted out the glowing end of his cigar. "Oh, the Dante Club shall celebrate tonight. I was just reading this aloud to see how it sounded, you see." Lowell pointed to the newspaper on the side table. Fields, he explained, had stepped down to the cafeteria.

"Tell me, Lowell, do you know whether the *Atlantic* has changed its payment policies? I mean, I haven't heard whether you gave in any verses for the last number. Certainly, you're busy enough with the *Review.*" Holmes's fingers tangled with the check in his pocket.

Lowell wasn't listening. "Holmes, you must have a good eyeful of this! Fields has outdone himself. There, go on. Have a look." He nodded conspiratorially and watched carefully. The newspaper was folded back to the literary page and smelled of Lowell's cigar.

"But what I mean to ask, my dear Lowell," Holmes said insistently, putting the paper out of the way, "is whether recently—oh, many thanks." He accepted a brandy and water.

Fields returned with a broad smile, stretching his rolling beard. He was as inexplicably cheery and complacent as Lowell. "Holmes! Wasn't expecting the pleasure today. I was just about to send for you at the Medical College to see Mr. Clark. There was a blasted mistake in some of the checks for the last number of the *Atlantic.* You might receive one for seventy-five rather than a hundred for your poem." Since the rapid inflation due to the war, top poets received a hundred dollars per poem with the exception of Longfellow, who got $150. Lesser names were paid between twenty-five and fifty.

"Truly?" Holmes asked with a gasp of relief that instantly felt embarrassing. "Well, I'm always happy for more."

"This new batch of clerks, such creatures as you've never seen." Fields shook his head. "I find myself at the helm of an enormous ship, my friends, that will drive upon the rocks if I do not watch it all times."

Holmes sat back contentedly and finally glanced down at the *New York Tribune* in his hands. In stunned silence, he slipped deeply into the armchair, allowing its thick leather folds to swallow him.

James Russell Lowell had come to the Corner from Cambridge to fulfill long-neglected obligations at *The North American Review.* Lowell left the bulk of his work at the *Review,* one of Fields's two top magazines, to a team of assistant editors, whose names he confused, until his presence was required for final proofing. Fields knew Lowell would appreciate the advance publicity more than anybody, more than Longfellow himself.

"Exquisite! You have a bit of the Jew in you yet, my dear Fields!" Lowell said, swiping the newspaper back from Holmes. His friends did not particularly notice Lowell's strange gloss, for they were accustomed to his tendency toward theorizing that everyone of ability, including himself, was in some unknown way Jewish, or at least of Jewish descent.

"My booksellers will chomp at the bit," Fields boasted. "We'll build a shiny coach from the Boston profits alone!"

"My dear Fields," Lowell said, laughing briskly. He patted the newspaper as if it held a secret prize. "If you had been Dante's publisher, I daresay he would have been welcomed back to Florence with a street festival!"

Oliver Wendell Holmes laughed, but there was a little pleading too as he said, "If Fields had been Dante's publisher, Lowell, he could have never been exiled."

When Dr. Holmes excused himself to find Mr. Clark, the financial clerk, before they started for Longfellow's house, Fields could see that Lowell was troubled. The poet was not one to hide displeasure, in any event.

"Don't you think Holmes should seem more committed?" Lowell demanded. "He might have been reading an obituary," he sniped, knowing Fields's sensitivity about the reception of his puffs. "His own."

But Fields laughed this off. "He is preoccupied with his novel, that's all, and whether the critics will treat him fairly this time. Well, and he always has a hundred things on his mind. You know that, Lowell."

"That is just the thing! If Harvard tries to daunt us further—" Lowell began, then started again. "I don't want anyone to come to a notion that we're not behind this to the end, Fields. Do you not ever wonder that this might be just another club for Wendell?"

Lowell and Holmes liked to sharpen their wits against each other, Fields doing what he could to discourage them. They competed mostly for attention. After a recent banquet, Mrs. Fields reported having heard Lowell demonstrating to Harriet Beecher Stowe why *Tom Jones* was the best novel ever written, while Holmes was proving to Stowe's husband, the divinity professor, that religion was responsible for all the swearing in the world. The publisher was worried about more than the return of serious tension between two of his best poets; he was worried Lowell would stubbornly try to prove that his doubts about Holmes were correct. Fields could not afford that any more than he could afford Holmes's trepidation.

Fields made a show of his pride in Holmes, standing beside a framed daguerreotype of the little doctor that hung on the wall. He put a hand on Lowell's strong shoulder and spoke with sincerity. "Our Dante Club would be a lost spirit without him, my dear Lowell. Certainly he has his distractions, but that's what keeps his brilliance. Why, he's what Dr. Johnson would have proclaimed a *clubbable* man. But he's been there for us all along, hasn't he. And for Longfellow."

Dr. Augustus Manning, treasurer of the Harvard Corporation, remained at University Hall later into the evenings than the other Harvard fellows. He often turned his head from his desk to the darkening window that glared back with indistinct light from his lamp, and he thought of the perils that daily rose up to shake the foundations of the College. Just that afternoon, he had been out for his ten-minute constitutional and recorded the names of several offenders. Three students were talking to one another near Grays Hall. By the time they saw him approach, it was too late; phantomlike, he made no noise, even when walking over crisp leaves. They would be admonished by the faculty board for "congregating"—that is, standing stationary in the Yard in groups of two or more.

That morning, at the College's required six o'clock chapel, Manning also had called the attention of Tutor Bradlee to a student who was reading a book under his Bible. The offender, a sophomore, would be privately admonished for reading during chapel, as well as for the agitating tendency of the author—a French philosopher of immoral politics. At the next meeting of the College faculty, judgment would be entered under the young man's name, there would be a fine of several dollars imposed, and points would be removed from his class standing.

Manning now thought about how to address the Dante problem. A staunch loyalist to classical studies and languages, Manning, it was said, had once spent an entire year conducting all his personal and business affairs in Latin; some doubted this, noting that his wife did not know the language, while other acquaintances remarked that this fact confirmed the story's veracity. The living languages, as they were called by the Harvard fellows, were little more than cheap imitations, low distortions. Italian, like Spanish and German, particularly represented the loose political passions, bodily appetites, and absent morals of decadent Europe. Dr. Manning had no intention of allowing foreign poisons to be spread under the disguise of literature.

As he sat, Manning heard a surprising clicking sound from his anteroom. Any noise would be unexpected at this hour, as Manning's secretary had gone home. Manning walked to the door and pushed on the handle. But it was stuck. He looked up and saw a metal point pushing into the doorframe, then another one several inches to the right. Manning yanked the door hard, again and again, harder and harder until his arm hurt and the door cracked open unwillingly. On the other side a student, armed with a wooden board and some screws, balanced on a stool, laughing as he tried to seal Manning's door.

The offender's cohort ran at the sight of Manning.

Manning grabbed the student from the stool. "Tutor! Tutor!"

"Just a prank, I tell you! Now let me go!" The sixteen-year-old instantly looked five years younger, and, hooked by Manning's marble eyes, panicked.

He struck Manning several times and then sank his teeth into the man's hand, which released its grip. But a resident tutor arrived and caught the student by the collar in the doorway.

Manning approached with deliberate steps and a cold stare. He stared so long, looking increasingly small and feeble, that even the tutor became uncomfortable and asked loudly what he should do. Manning looked down at his hand, where two bright spots of blood bubbled up in the teeth marks between the bones.

Manning's words seemed to emerge directly from his stiff beard rather than his mouth. "Have him tell you the names of his accomplices in this endeavor, Tutor Pearce. And find out where he's been drinking spirits. Then hand him to the police."

Pearce hesitated. "Police, sir?"

The student protested, "Now, if that isn't a scrubby trick, to call the police in a college matter!"

"At once, Tutor Pearce!"

Augustus Manning locked his door behind them. He ignored the fact that his breathing was heavy with fury as he resumed his place and sat up straight, with dignity. He picked up the *New York Tribune* again to remind himself of matters that were in desperate need of his attention. As he read J. T. Fields's puff on the "Literary Boston" page, as his hand throbbed at the points where his skin was broken, the following thoughts, more or less, passed through the treasurer's mind: Fields believes himself invincible in his new fortress . . . That same arrogance worn proudly by Lowell like a new coat . . . Longfellow remains untouchable; Mr. Greene, a relic, long a mental paraplegic . . . *But Dr. Holmes* . . . the Autocrat courts controversy only out of fear, not principle . . . The panic on the little doctor's face as he watched what befell Professor Webster those many years ago—not even the murder conviction or the hanging, but the loss of his place, which had been earned in society by such a good name, by training and career as a Harvard man . . . *Yes, Holmes: Dr. Holmes shall prove our greatest ally.*

II

All over Boston, all through the night, policemen herded "suspicious persons" by the half-dozen, by order of the chief. Each officer eyed his colleagues' suspicious persons warily as they registered them at the Central Station lest his own ruffians be adjudged inferior. Detectives in plainclothes, avoiding the uniforms, stalked upstairs from the Tombs—the underground holding cells—consorting in hushed codes and half-delivered nods.

The detective bureau, derived from a European model, had been established in Boston with the aim of providing intimate knowledge of criminals' whereabouts, and therefore most of the chosen detectives were former rogues themselves. However, there were no sophisticated methods of investigation with which they were armed, so detectives reverted to old tricks (their favorites being extortion, intimidation, and fabrication) to secure their share of arrests and warrant their salaries. Chief Kurtz had done all he could to make sure that the detectives, along with the press, thought the new murder victim a John Smith. The last problem in the world he needed now would be his detectives trying to connive money from the wealthy Healeys' grief.

Some of the gathered subjects were singing obscene songs or covering their faces with their hands. Others hurled curses and threats at the officers who brought them in. A few huddled together on wooden benches lining one side of the room. Every class of criminal was here, from high-tobers—the classiest crooks—down to window smashers, sneak thieves, and the prettily bonneted bludgets who lured passersby into alleys before their accomplices would do the rest. Warm peanuts were peppered down from above by pasty Irish urchins, who were kneeling at the public balcony, holding greasy paper bags, and taking aim through the rails. They supplemented these projectiles with a round of rotten eggs.

"You heard anyone swelling about croaking a man? You listening here?"

"Where did you get that gold watch chain, boy? This silk handkerchief?"

"What're you planning to do with this billy?"

"How 'bout it? You ever try to kill a man, chum, just to see how it is?"

Red-faced officers shouted out these questions. Then Chief Kurtz began detailing Healey's demise, skating skillfully around the victim's identity, but before long he would be interrupted.

"Hey, Chiefy." A big black rogue coughed in bemusement, his bulging eyes fixed on the corner of the room. "Hey, Chiefy. What's with the new darky booly-dog? Where's his uniform? I don't think you're about to recruit nigger detectives. Or can I apply too?"

Nicholas Rey stood up straighter at the laughter that followed. He felt suddenly conscious of his lack of participation in the questioning, and of his plainclothes.

"Now, fellow, that ain't no darky," said a dapper string bean of a man as he stepped forward and surveyed Patrolman Rey with the look of an expert appraiser. "He looks to be a *half*-breed to me, and a mighty fine specimen at that. Mother a slave, father a plantation hand. That's right, ain't it, friend?"

Rey stepped closer to the line. "How about answering the chief's questions, sir? Let's help each other out if we're able."

"Handsomely said, Lily White." The string bean held an appreciative finger to his thin mustache, which circled down from his lips to bracket his mouth, seeming to signal the start of a beard but dropping off abruptly before the chin.

Chief Kurtz thrust his blackjack at the diamond stud on Langdon Peaslee's breastbone. "Don't rile me, Peaslee!"

"Careful, won't you?" Peaslee, Boston's greatest safecracker, dusted off his vest. "That little luster's worth eight hundred dollars, Chief, legitimately purchased!"

Laughter from all sides, including some detectives. Kurtz should not have let Langdon Peaslee wind him up, not on this day. "I got a sense you had something to do with the round of safes blown on Commercial Street last Sunday," Kurtz said. "I'll bag you with breaking the Sabbath laws right now, and you can sleep in the Tombs with the other twopenny pickpockets!"

Willard Burndy, a few spots down the line, guffawed.

"Well, I'll tell you something about that, my dear chief," Peaslee said, raising his voice theatrically for the benefit of the whole meeting room (including the suddenly rapt groundlings up in the high seats). "It sure weren't our friend Mr. Burndy over there, who could pull off anything like the Commercial Street run. Or did those safes belong to an old ladies' society?"

Burndy's bright pink eyes doubled in size as he shoved men out of the way, clawing toward Langdon Peaslee and nearly igniting a riot among the rowdier crooks as he went, while the ragged boys above cheered and hooted. This entertainment held its own even against the secret rat pits that operated in North End cellars, and those charged twenty-five cents a head.

As officers restrained Burndy, a confused man was pushed out of line. He stumbled wildly. Nicholas Rey caught him before he could fall.

He was slightly built, his dark eyes handsome but worn, with a waywardness of expression. The stranger displayed a chessboard of missing and rotting teeth and emitted something like a hiss, releasing a stench of Medford rum. He either didn't notice or didn't mind that his clothes were coated in rotten egg.

Kurtz marched down the reshuffled gallery of rogues and explained again. He explained about the man found naked in a field near the river, his body swarming in flies, wasps, maggots, eating into his skin, soaked in his blood. One of the present company, Kurtz informed them, had killed him with a blow to the head and carried him there to leave to nature's blights. He mentioned another odd touch: a flag, white and tattered, planted over the body.

Rey propped his disoriented ward to his feet. The man's nose and mouth were red and irregular, overwhelming his thin mustache and beard. One of his legs was lame, the casualty of a long forgotten accident or fight. His large hands shook in wild gesticulations. The stranger's trembling increased at each detail thrown out by the chief of police.

Deputy Chief Savage said, "Oh, this chap! Who brought him in, do you know, Rey? He wouldn't give a name earlier when they were photographing all the new ones for the rogues' picture gallery. Silent as an Egyptian sphinx!"

The sphinx's paper collar was all but hidden under his slovenly black scarf, wrapped loosely to one side. He stared emptily and flailed his oversize hands in the air in rough, concentric circles.

"Trying to sketch something?" Savage commented jokingly.

His hands were sketching indeed—a map of sorts, one that would have aided the police immeasurably in the weeks to come had they known what to look for. This stranger had long been an intimate of the locale of Healey's murder but not the richly paneled parlors of Beacon Hill. No, the man was sketching an image in the air not of any earthly place at all but of a murky antechamber into an otherworld. For it was *there*—there, the man understood, as the image of Artemus Healey's death seeped into his mind and grew with every particular—yes, it was there that punishment had been meted out.

"I daresay he's deaf and dumb," Deputy Chief Savage whispered to Rey after several thoughtful hand gestures failed to get through. "And at a real altitude, from the smell. I'll bring him for some bread and cheese. Keep an eye on that Burndy fellow, won't you, Rey." Savage nodded toward the show-up's incumbent troublemaker, who was now rubbing his pink eyes with his shackled hands, spellbound by Kurtz's grotesque descriptions.

The deputy chief gently separated the trembling man from Patrolman Rey's stewardship and walked him across the room. But the man shook, weeping hard, then with what seemed like accidental effort hurled the deputy chief of police away, sending him headlong into a bench.

The man then leapt up behind Rey, his left arm springing across Rey's neck, his fingers hooking underneath Rey's right armpit and his other hand knocking off Rey's hat and locking on to his eyes, twisting Rey's head toward him, so that the officer's ear was trapped in the raw dew of his lips. The man's whisper was so low, so desperate and throaty, so confessional, that only Rey could know words had been spoken at all.

Happy chaos erupted among the rogues.

The stranger suddenly released Rey and gripped a fluted column. He hurled himself hard around its circumference, catapulting ahead. The obscure hissed words ensnared Rey's mind, a meaningless code of sounds, so jarring and powerful as to suggest more meaning than Rey could imagine. *Dinanzi.* Rey struggled to remember, to hear the whisper again, just as he struggled (*etterne etterno, etterne etterno*) not to lose his balance as he lunged for the fugitive. But the stranger had launched himself with such great momentum that he could not have stopped himself had he wanted to in this, his last moment of life.

He crashed through the thick plane of a bay window. One loose shard of glass, shaped perfectly like a scythe, swiveled out in an almost graceful dance, catching the black scarf and slicing cleanly through his windpipe, flinging his limp head forward as he hit the air. He dropped hard through the shattered mass onto the yard below.

Everything fell silent. Shavings of glass, delicate as snowflakes, popped under Rey's blunt-toed shoes as he approached the window frame and stared down. The body unfurled over a thick cushion of autumn leaves, and the lens of the window's shattered glass cut the body and its bed into a kaleidoscope of yellow, black, hectic red. The ragged urchins, the first down to the courtyard, pointed and hollered, dancing around the splayed body. Rey, as he descended, couldn't escape from the blurring words the man had chosen for whatever reason to bequeath unto him as his last act of life: *Voi Ch'intrate. Voi Ch'intrate.* You Who Enter. You Who Enter.

※

James Russell Lowell felt much like Sir Launfal, the grail-seeking hero of his most popular poem, as he galloped through the iron portal of Harvard Yard. Indeed, the poet might have looked the part of gallant knight as he entered today, high on his white steed and outlined crisply by the autumn colors, had it not been for his peculiar grooming preferences: his beard trimmed into a square shape some two or three inches below his chin, but his mustache grown out far longer, leaving it to hang below. Some of his detractors, and many friends, noted privately that this was perhaps not the most becoming choice for his otherwise bold face. Lowell's opinion was that beards should be worn or God would not have given them, though he did not specify whether this particular style was theologically required.

His imagined knighthood was felt with stronger passion these days, when the Yard was an increasingly hostile citadel. A few weeks earlier, the Corporation had attempted to persuade Professor Lowell to adopt a proposal of reforms that would have eliminated many of the obstacles faced by his department (for instance, that students receive half the number of credits for enrolling in a modern foreign language that they would for a classical language) but in return would have granted the Corporation final approval over all of Lowell's classes. Lowell had loudly refused their offer. If they wanted to pass their proposal, they would have to go through the lengthy process of pushing it through the Harvard Board of Overseers, that twenty-headed Hydra.

Then one afternoon Lowell was given advice by the president that made him realize the board's demand for approval over all classes had been a lark.

"Lowell, at least cancel that Dante seminar of yours and Manning may well improve things for you." The president grabbed Lowell by the elbow confidentially.

Lowell narrowed his eyes. "That's what this is? That's all they're after!" He turned with outrage. "I shall not be humbugged into bending to them! They drove Ticknor out. By God, they made *Longfellow* resent them. I think every man who feels like a gentleman ought to speak out against them, nay, every man who hasn't passed his master's degree in *blackguardism.*"

"You think me a great churl, Professor Lowell. I don't control the Corporation any more than you do, you know, and it is like talking through a knothole to them most days. Alas, I am just the *president* of this college," he chortled. Indeed, Thomas Hill was just the president of Harvard, and a new one at that—the third in a decade, a pattern resulting in Corporation members stockpiling far more power than he possessed. "But they believe Dante an improper part of your department's development—that is plain. They will make an example of it, Lowell. Manning *will* make an example of it!" he warned, and grabbed Lowell's arm again as though at any moment the poet would have to be steered away from some danger.

Lowell said he would not suffer the fellows of the Corporation to sit in judgment of a literature of which they knew nothing. And Hill did not even try to argue this point. It was a matter of principle for the Harvard fellows that they knew nothing of the living languages.

The next time Lowell saw Hill, the president was armed with a slip of blue paper on which was a handwritten quotation from a recently deceased British poet of some standing on the subject of Dante's poem. "'What hatred against the whole human race! What exultation and merriment at eternal and immitigable sufferings! We hold our nostrils as we read; we cover up our ears. Did one ever before see brought together such striking odors, filth, excrement, blood, mutilated bodies, agonizing shrieks, mythical monsters of punishment? Seeing this, I cannot but consider it the most *immoral* and *impious* book that ever was written.'" Hill smiled with self-satisfaction, as though he had written this himself.

Lowell laughed. "Shall we have England lord over our bookshelves? Why did we not just hand Lexington over to the redcoats and spare General Washington the trouble of war?" Lowell glimpsed something in Hill's eye, something he sometimes saw in the untrained expression of a student, that made him believe the president could understand. "Till America has learned to love literature not as an amusement, not as mere doggerel to memorize in a college room, but for its humanizing and ennobling energy, my dear reverend president, she will not have succeeded in that high sense which alone makes a nation out of a people. That which raises it from a dead name to a living power."

Hill tried hard not to sway from his purpose. "This idea of traveling through the afterlife, of recording Hell's punishments—that's downright harsh, Lowell. And a work like this so inaptly titled a 'Comedy'! It's medieval, it's scholastic, and . . ."

"Catholic." This shut Hill up. "That is what you mean, Reverend President. That it's all too Italian, too Catholic for Harvard College?"

Hill raised a sly white eyebrow. "You must own that such frightful notions of God could not be sustained to our Protestant ears."

The truth was Lowell was as unfriendly as the Harvard fellows toward the crowding of Irish papists along the wharfsides and in outlying suburbs of Boston. But the idea that the poem was some kind of edict from the Vatican . . . "Yes, we rather condemn people for eternity without the courtesy of informing them. And Dante calls it a *commedia*, my dear sir, because it is written in his rustic Italian tongue instead of Latin and because it ends happily, with the poet rising to Heaven, as opposed to a *tragedia*. Instead of endeavoring to manufacture a great poem out of what was foreign and artificial, he lets the poem make itself out of him."

Lowell was pleased to see that the president was exasperated. "For pity's sake, Professor, do you not think there is something at all rancorous, something malevolent, on the part of one to inflict merciless tortures on all who practice a list of particular sins? Imagine some man in public life today declaring his enemies' places in Hell!" he argued.

"My dear reverend president, I am imagining it even as we speak. And do not misunderstand. Dante sends his friends down there, too. You may tell *that* to Augustus Manning. Pity without rigor would be cowardly egotism, mere sentimentality."

The members of the Harvard Corporation, the president and six pious men of affairs chosen from outside the College faculty, were firm in their commitment to the long-standing curriculum that had served them well—Greek, Latin, Hebrew, ancient history, mathematics, and science—and their corollary assertion that the inferior modern languages and literature would remain a novelty, something to fatten their catalogs. Longfellow had made some headway after Professor Ticknor's departure, including initiating a Dante seminar and hiring a brilliant Italian exile named Pietro Bachi as an Italian instructor. His Dante seminar, from a lack of interest in the subject and the language, was consistently his least popular. Still, the poet enjoyed the zeal of a few minds passing through that course. One of the zealous was James Russell Lowell.

Now, after ten years of his own tussles with the administration, Lowell faced an event for which he had waited, for which the time was ripe as destiny: the discovery of Dante by America. But not only was Harvard swift and thorough in its discouragement, the Dante Club also faced an obstacle from inside: Holmes and his straddling.

Lowell sometimes took walks in Cambridge with Holmes's oldest son, Oliver Wendell Holmes Junior. Twice a week, the law student would emerge from the Dane Law School building just when Lowell had finished his teaching at University Hall. Holmes could not appreciate his good fortune at having Junior, because he had made his son hate him—if only Holmes would *listen*, instead of making Junior *talk*. Lowell had asked the young man once whether Dr. Holmes ever spoke at home about the Dante Club. "Oh, certainly, Mr. Lowell," Junior, handsome and tall, said, smirking, "and the Atlantic Club and the Union Club and the Saturday Club and the Scientific Club and the Historical Association and the Medical Society . . ."

Phineas Jennison, one of Boston's wealthiest new businessmen, was sitting next to Lowell at a recent Saturday Club supper at the Parker House when all this darkened Lowell's mind. "Harvard is harassing you again," Jennison said. Lowell was stunned that his face could be read as easily as a sign board. "Do not jump so, my dear friend," Jennison said, laughing, the deep dimple in his chin jiggling. Jennison's near relations said that his gold-flaxen hair and his regal dimple had betokened his vast fortune even from the time he was a boy, though, accurately speaking, it was perhaps a *regici-*

dal dimple, inherited as it was supposed to be from an ancestor who had beheaded Charles I. "It is only that I chanced to speak with some of the Corporation fellows the other day. You know nothing happens in Boston or Cambridge without coming under my nose."

"Building another library for us, are you?" Lowell asked.

"The fellows seemed to be heated up speaking amongst themselves of your department anyway. They seemed downright determined. I do not mean to pry into your affairs, of course, only—"

"Between us, my dear Jennison, they mean to rid me of my Dante class," Lowell interrupted. "I sometimes fear they've become as set against Dante as I am for him. They even offered to increase enrollment for students in my classes if I allow them approval over my seminar topics." Jennison's expression conveyed his concern.

"I refused, of course," Lowell said.

Jennison flashed his wide smile. "Did you?"

They were interrupted by a few toasts, including the night's most cheered improvisational rhyme, which had been demanded by the revelers from Dr. Holmes. Holmes, quick as always, even managed to draw attention to the raw style of the format.

"A verse too polished will not stick at all:
The worst back-scratcher is a billiard ball."

"These after-dinner verses could kill any poet but Holmes," Lowell said with an admiring grin. He had a hazy look in his eyes. "Sometimes I feel I am not the stuff that professors are made of, Jennison. Better in some ways, worse in others. Too sensitive and not conceited enough—physically conceited, I should call it. I know it is all wearing me out." He paused. "And why shouldn't sitting in the professor's chair all these years benumb me to the world? What must someone like you, prince of industry, think of such a paltry existence?"

"Child's talk, my dear Lowell!" Jennison seemed tired with the topic but after a moment's thought was newly interested. "You have a larger duty to the world and to yourself than any mere spectator! I shan't hear a bit of your hesitancy! I wouldn't know what Dante is to save my soul. But a genius the likes of you, my dear friend, assumes a divine *responsibility* to fight for all those exiled from the world."

Lowell mumbled something inaudible but no doubt self-effacing.

"Now, now, Lowell," Jennison said. "Were you not the one to convince the Saturday Club that a mere merchant was good enough to dine with such immortals as your friends?"

"Could they have refused you after you offered to buy the Parker House?" Lowell laughed.

"They could have refused me if I had given up my fight to belong among great men. May I quote from my favorite poet: 'And what they dare to dream of, dare to do.' Oh, how good that is!"

Lowell fell into more laughter at the idea of being inspired by his own poetry, but in truth, he was. Why shouldn't he be? The proof of poetry was, in Lowell's mind, that it reduced to the essence of a single line the vague philosophy that floated in all men's minds, so as to render it portable and useful, ready to the hand.

Now, on his way to another lecture, the very thought of entering a room full of students, who still thought it was possible to learn all about something, made him yawn.

Lowell hitched his horse to the old water pump outside Hollis Hall. "Kick them like hell if they come, old boy," he said, lighting a cigar. Horses and cigars were among the catalog of prohibited items on Harvard Yard.

A man was leaning idly against an elm. He wore a bright yellow-checkered waistcoat and had a gaunt, or rather wasted, set of features. The man, who towered over the poet even at his slanting angle, too old for a student and too worn for a faculty member, stared at him with the familiar, insatiable gleam of the literary admirer.

Fame did not mean much to Lowell, who liked only to think that his friends found some good in what he wrote and that Mabel Lowell would be proud of being his daughter after he was gone. Otherwise he thought himself *teres atque rotundus:* a microcosm in himself, his own author, public, critic, and posterity. Still, the praise of men and women on the streets could not fail to warm him. Sometimes he would go for a stroll in Cambridge with his heart so full of yearning that an indifferent look, even from an entire stranger, would bring tears into his eyes. But there was something equally painful in encountering the opaque, dazed glare of recognition. That made him feel wholly transparent and separate: Poet Lowell, apparition.

This yellow-vested watcher leaning on the tree touched the brim of his black bowler as Lowell passed. The poet bowed his head confusedly, his cheeks tingling. As he rushed through the College campus to vanquish his day's obligations, Lowell did not notice how strangely intent the observer remained.

Dr. Holmes bounded into the steep amphitheater. A round of boot stomping, employed by those whose pencils and notebooks made the use of hands inconvenient, rumbled forth upon his entrance. This was followed by rapid *hurrahs* from the rowdies (Holmes called them his young barbarians) collected in that upper region of the classroom known as the Mountain (as though this were the assembly of the French Revolution). Here Holmes constructed the human body inside out each term. Here, four times a week, were fifty adoring sons waiting on his every word. Standing before his class in the belly of the amphitheater, he felt twelve feet tall rather than his actual five-five (and that in particularly substantial boots, made by the best shoemaker in Boston).

Oliver Wendell Holmes was the only member of the faculty ever able to manage the one o'clock assignment, when hunger and exhaustion combined with the narcotized air of the two-story brick box on North Grove. Some envious colleagues said his literary fame won over the students. In fact, most of the boys who chose medicine over law and theology were rustics, and if they had encountered any real literature before arriving in Boston, it would have been some poem of Longfellow's. Still, word of Holmes's literary reputation would spread like sensational gossip, someone securing a copy of *The Autocrat of the Breakfast-Table* and circulating it, remarking with an incredulous stare to a fellow, "You haven't yet read the Autocrat?" But his literary reputation among the students was more a reputation of a reputation.

"Today," said Holmes, "we shall begin with a topic with which I trust you boys are not at *all* familiar." He yanked at a clean white sheet that covered a female cadaver, then held up his palms at the foot stomping and hollering that followed.

"Respect, gentlemen! Respect for humanity and God's divinest work!"

Dr. Holmes was too lost in the ocean of attention to notice the intruder among his students.

"Yes, the female body shall begin today's subject," Holmes continued.

A timid young man, Alvah Smith, one of the half-dozen bright faces in any class to which the professor naturally directs his lecture to intermediate for the rest, blushed vibrantly in the front row, where his neighbors were happy to taunt his embarrassment.

Holmes saw this. "And here, on Smith, we find exhibited the inhibitory action of the vasomotor nerves on the arterioles suddenly relaxing and filling the surface capillaries with blood—that same pleasing phenomenon which *some* of you may witness on the cheek of that young person whom you expect to visit this evening."

Smith laughed along with the rest. But Holmes also heard an involuntary guffaw that cracked with the slowness of age. He squinted up the aisle at the Reverend Dr. Putnam, one of the lesser powers of the Harvard Corporation. The fellows of the Corporation, though they comprised the highest level of supervision, never actually attended classes in their university; tramping from Cambridge to the medical building, which was located across the river in Boston for proximity to the hospitals, would have been an unacceptable notion to most administrators.

"Now," Holmes said to his class distractedly, setting his tools to the cadavers, where his two demonstrators gathered. "Let us plunge into the depths of our subject."

After class ended and the barbarians elbowed their way through the aisles, Holmes led the Reverend Dr. Putnam to his office.

"You, my dearest Dr. Holmes, represent the gold standard for men of American letters. None have worked so hard to rise in so many fields. Your name has become a symbol of scholarship and authorship. Why, just yesterday I was speaking with a gentleman from England who was saying how you are revered in the mother country."

Holmes smiled, oblivious. "What did he say? What did he say, Reverend Putnam? You know I like to have it laid on thick."

Putnam frowned at the interruption. "Despite this, Augustus Manning has developed concern about certain of your literary activities, Dr. Holmes."

Holmes was surprised. "You mean about Mr. Longfellow's Dante work? Longfellow is the translator. I am but one of his aides-de-camp, so to speak. I suggest you wait and read the work; surely you will enjoy it."

"James Russell Lowell. J. T. Fields. George Greene. Dr. Oliver Wendell Holmes. Quite a selection of 'aides,' now, isn't it?"

Holmes was annoyed. He had not thought their club a matter of general interest and did not like speaking of it with an outsider. The Dante Club was one of his few activities not belonging to the public world. "Oh, throw a stone in Cambridge and you're bound to hit a two-volumer, my dear Putnam."

Putnam folded his arms and waited.

Holmes waved a hand in an arbitrary direction. "Mr. Fields deals with such matters."

"Pray remove yourself from this precarious association," Putnam said with dead seriousness. "Talk some sense into your friends. Professor Lowell, for instance, has only compounded—"

"If you're in search of someone to whom Lowell listens, my dear reverend," Holmes interrupted with a laugh, "you've made a wrong turn into the Medical College."

"Holmes," Putnam said kindly. "I've come chiefly to warn *you*, because I count you a friend. If Dr. Manning knew I was speaking with you like this, he would . . ." Putnam paused and lowered his tone eulogistically, "Dear Holmes, your future will be hitched to Dante. I fear what shall happen to your poetry, your name, by the time Manning is through, in your current situation."

"Manning has no call to assault me personally even if he objects to our little club's chosen interests."

Putnam replied, "We're talking of Augustus Manning. Consider this."

When Dr. Holmes turned away, he looked like he was swallowing a globe. Putnam often wondered why all men did not wear beards. He was cheerful, even on the bumpy ride back into Cambridge, for he knew that Dr. Manning would be highly pleased with his report.

Artemus Prescott Healey, b. 1804, d. 1865, was placed into a large family plot, one of the first purchased on the main hillside of Mount Auburn Cemetery years earlier.

There were still many among the Brahmins who begrudged Healey his cowardly decisions before the war. But it was agreed by all that only the most extreme former radical would offend the memory of their state's chief justice by spurning his final ceremonies.

Dr. Holmes leaned over to his wife. "Only four years' difference, 'Melia."

She requested elaboration with a brief purr.

"Justice Healey's sixty," Holmes continued in his whisper. "Or would be. Only four years older than I am, dear, almost to the day!" Really almost to the month; nonetheless, Dr. Holmes genuinely appreciated the proximity of dead persons to his own age. Amelia Holmes, by a shift in her eyes, told him to stay silent during the eulogies. Holmes settled his mouth and looked ahead over the quiet acres.

Holmes could not claim to have been an intimate of the deceased; few men could, even among the Brahmins. Chief Justice Healey had served on the Harvard Board of Overseers, so Dr. Holmes had enjoyed some routine interaction with the judge in Healey's capacity as administrator. Holmes also had known Healey through the doctor's membership in Phi Beta Kappa, for Healey had presided for a time over that proud society. Dr. Holmes kept his ΦBK key on his watch chain, an item with which his fingers now wrestled as Healey's body settled into its new bed. At least, Holmes thought with a doctor's special sympathy for dying, poor Healey never suffered.

Dr. Holmes's most prolonged contact with the judge had come at the courthouse, at a time that shook Holmes, that made him want to retreat fully into a world of poetry. The defense in the Webster trial, presided over, as all capital crimes, by a three-judge panel chaired by the chief justice, had requested Dr. Holmes's testimony as a character witness for John W. Webster. It was during the heat of the trial so many years before that Wendell Holmes witnessed the ponderous, grueling style of speech by which Artemus Healey surrendered his legal opinions.

"Harvard professors do *not* commit murder." That was what the then-president of Harvard, taking the stand shortly before Dr. Holmes, testified on behalf of Webster.

The murder of Dr. Parkman had transpired in the laboratory below Holmes's lecture room, while Holmes was lecturing. It was hard enough that Holmes had been friends with both murderer and victim—not knowing whom to lament more. At least the customary rolling laughter of Holmes's students had drowned out Professor Webster's hacking of the body into pieces.

"A devout man, and one that feared God with all his house . . ."

The preacher's shrill promises of Heaven, with his chief-mourner expression, did not sit well with Holmes. As a matter of principle, few ornaments of religious ceremony ever had sat well with Dr. Holmes, son of one of those stalwart ministers whose Calvinism had remained hard and fast in the face of the Unitarian upheaval. Oliver Wendell Holmes and his shy younger brother, John, had been reared with that awful bosh that still buzzed in the doctor's ears: "In Adam's fall, we sinned all." Fortunately, they were sheltered by the quick wit of their mother, who whispered witty asides while the Reverend Holmes and his guest ministers preached advance damnation and inborn sin. She would promise them that new ideas would come, particularly to Wendell when he was shaken by some story of the devil's control over their souls. And so did the new ideas arrive, for Boston and for Oliver Wendell Holmes. Only Unitarians could have built Mount Auburn Cemetery, a burial place that was also a garden.

While Holmes took stock of the many notables in attendance to occupy himself, many others were tilting their heads in Dr. Holmes's direction, for he was part of a pocket of celebrities known by various names—the New England Saints or the Fireside Poets. Whatever their name, they were the top literary contingent of the country. Near the Holmeses stood James Russell Lowell, poet, professor, and editor, idly twisting the long tusk of his mustache until Fanny Lowell would pull at his sleeve; to the other side, J. T. Fields, publisher of New England's greatest poets, his head and beard pointed downward in a perfect triangle of serious contemplation, a striking figure to be juxtaposed with the angelic pink cheeks and perfect poise of his young wife. Lowell and Fields were no more intimate with Chief Justice Healey than was Holmes, but they had attended the service out of respect for Healey's position and family (to whom the Lowells, in addition, happened to be cousins in some fashion or another).

Those attendees viewing this trio of litterateurs looked in vain for the most illustrious of their company. Henry Wadsworth Longfellow had, as a matter of fact, prepared to accompany his friends to Mount Auburn, which was no more than a stroll from his house, but as usual had kept to his fireside instead. There was little in the world outside Craigie House that would presume to draw out Longfellow. After so many years dedicated to this project, the reality of pending publication brought full concentration. Besides, Longfellow feared (and rightly so) that had he come to Mount Auburn, his fame would have drawn the mourners' attention away from the Healey family. Whenever Longfellow walked through the streets of Cambridge, people whispered, children threw themselves into his arms, hats were lifted in such great numbers that it seemed all of Middlesex County had simultaneously entered a chapel.

Holmes could remember one time jouncing along with Lowell in a hackney cab, years earlier, before the war. They passed the window of Craigie House that framed Fanny and Henry Longfellow at their fireside, surrounded by their five beautiful children at the piano. Back then, Longfellow's face still was open for the world to see.

"I tremble to look at Longfellow's house," Holmes had said.

Lowell, who had been complaining about a defective Thoreau essay he was editing, responded with a light laugh that detached him from Holmes's tone.

"Their happiness is so perfect," Holmes had continued, "that no change, of the changes which must come to them, could fail to be for the worse."

As the oration of Reverend Young came to a close and solemn whispering commenced on the cemetery's quiet acres, as Holmes brushed small yellow leaves from his velvet collar and let his eyes travel over the engraved faces of the mourners, he noticed that Reverend Elisha Talbot, Cambridge's most prominent minister, appeared openly irritated by the warm reception Young's oration had produced; no doubt, he was rehearsing what he would have delivered had he been Healey's minister. Holmes admired the Widow Healey's restrained expression. Easy-crying widows always took new husbands soonest. Holmes also happened to linger on the sight of Mr. Kurtz, for the chief of police had inserted himself assertively next to Widow Healey and pulled her aside, apparently attempting to persuade her of something—but in such abbreviated fashion that their exchange must have been a recapitulation of some earlier talk; Chief Kurtz was not making an argument but rather tendering a reminder to Widow Healey. The widow nodded deferentially; oh, but how very *tightly*, thought Holmes. Chief Kurtz ended with a sigh of relief that Aeolus might have envied.

Supper that night at 21 Charles Street was quieter than usual, though it was never *quiet*. Guests to the house always departed flabbergasted by the rate, not to mention the sheer volume, of the Holmeses' talk, wondering whether any of these family members ever listened to one another at all. It was a tradition started by the doctor to award an extra serving of marmalade to the best conversationalist of the evening. Today, Dr. Holmes's daughter, "little" Amelia, was chattering more than usual, telling of the latest engagement, of Miss B______ to Colonel F______, and of what her sewing circle had been making for wedding gifts.

"Why, Father," said Oliver Wendell Holmes Junior, hero, with a small grin. "I believe you'll be deprived of the marmalade this evening." Junior was out of place at the Holmes table: Not only was he six feet tall in a household of quick, little persons, but he was stoically deliberate in speech and movement.

Holmes smiled thoughtfully over his roast. "But, Wendy, I haven't heard much from you tonight."

Junior hated when his father called him that. "Oh, I won't win the helping. But neither will you, Father." He turned to his younger brother, Edward, who was home only occasionally now that he boarded at the College. "They say they are raising a subscription to name a chair after poor Healey at the law school. Do you believe it, Neddie? After he ducked the Fugitive Slave Act, too, for all those years. Dying's the only way Boston will pardon your past, for aught I know."

On his after-supper walk, Dr. Holmes stopped to give some children playing marbles a handful of pennies with which to spell a word on the sidewalk. He chose *knot* (why not?), and when they formed the copper letters correctly, he let them keep the coins. He was glad the Boston summer was winding down, and with it the parching heat, which inflamed his asthma.

Holmes sat under the tall trees behind his house thinking of "the finest literary minds of New England" from Fields's newspaper puff in the *New York Tribune*. Their Dante Club: It had importance for Lowell's mission to introduce Dante's poetry to America, for Fields's publishing plans. Yes, there were the academic and the business stakes. But for Holmes the triumph of the club was its union of interests of that group of friends whom he felt most fortunate to have. He loved more than anything the free chatter and brilliant spark that were brought out when they were unlocking the poetry. The Dante Club was a healing association—for these last years that had suddenly aged them all—uniting Holmes and Lowell after their rifts over the war, uniting Fields with his best authors in his first year without his partner William Ticknor to provide security, uniting Longfellow with the outside world, or at least with some of its more literarily inclined ambassadors.

Holmes's talent for translating was not extraordinary. He had the imagination needed but did not have that quality possessed by Longfellow, which allowed one poet to open fully to another poet's voice. Still, in a nation with little free trade in thought with foreign countries, Oliver Wendell Holmes was happy to consider himself well versed in Dante: a Dantean more than Dante scholar. When Holmes was in college, Professor George Ticknor, the aristocratic litterateur, was nearing the end of his tolerance for the Harvard

Corporation's constant obstruction of his post as the first Smith Professor. Wendell Holmes, meanwhile, having mastered Greek and Latin at the age of twelve, was strangled by boredom in the required recitation hours of rote memorizing and repeating verses of Euripides' *Hecuba* that had long ago been pummeled of meaning.

When they met in the Holmes family drawing room, Professor Ticknor's steady black eyes took in the collegian, who was shifting his weight from one foot to the other. "Never still for a moment," Oliver Wendell Holmes's father, the Reverend Holmes, sighed. Ticknor suggested that Italian could discipline him. At the time, the department's resources were too strained to formally offer the language. But Holmes soon received a loan of grammar and vocabulary instruction prepared by Ticknor, along with an edition of Dante's *Divina Commedia,* a poem divided into "canticles" called *Inferno, Purgatorio,* and *Paradiso.*

Holmes feared now that the swells at Harvard had hit on something about Dante from the insightful position of ignorance. In medical school, the sciences had allowed Oliver Wendell Holmes to discover how nature operated when freed from superstition and fear. He believed that just as astronomy had replaced astrology, so would "theonomy" rise up one day over its slow-witted twin. With this faith, Holmes prospered as a poet and a professor.

Then the war ambushed Dr. Holmes, and so did Dante Alighieri.

It began one evening in the winter of 1861. Holmes was sitting in Elmwood, Lowell's mansion, fidgeting at the news of Wendell Junior's departure with the 25th Massachusetts Regiment. Lowell was the right antidote for his nerves: brash and loudly confident that the world was at all times exactly as he said it was; derisive, if necessary, if one's concerns were too dominant.

Since that summer, society had sorely missed the soothing presence of Henry Wadsworth Longfellow. Longfellow wrote his friends notes declining all invitations that would have compelled him to leave Craigie House, explaining that he was occupied. He had begun translating Dante, he said, and did not plan to stop: *I have done this work when I can do nothing else.*

Coming from the reticent Longfellow, these notes were screaming laments. He was outwardly calm but inwardly bleeding to death.

So Lowell, planted on Longfellow's doorstep, insisted on helping. Lowell had long bemoaned the fact that Americans, ill-trained in modern languages, hadn't access even to the few regrettable British translations that existed.

"I need a *poet's* name to sell such a book to the donkey public!" Fields would say to Lowell's apocalyptic warnings about America's blindness to Dante. Whenever Fields wished to discourage his authors from a risky project, he pointed out the stupidity of the reading public.

Lowell had bothered Longfellow to translate the tripartite poem many times over the years, even once threatening to do it himself—something for which he did not have the inner strength. Now he couldn't *not* help. After all, Lowell was one of the few American scholars to know anything of Dante; indeed, he seemed to know everything.

Lowell detailed for Holmes how remarkably Longfellow was capturing Dante, from the cantos Longfellow had shown him. "He was born for the task, I rather think, Wendell." Longfellow was starting with *Paradiso* and then would turn to *Purgatorio* and finally *Inferno.*

"Moving backwards?" Holmes asked, intrigued.

Lowell nodded and grinned. "I daresay dear Longfellow wants to make sure of Heaven before committing himself to Hell."

"I never can go all the way through to Lucifer," Holmes said, commenting on *Inferno.* "Purgatory and Paradise are all music and hope, and you feel you are floating toward God. But the hideousness, the savagery, of that medieval nightmare! Alexander the Great ought to have slept with it under the pillow."

"Dante's Hell is part of our world as much as part of the underworld, and shouldn't be avoided," Lowell said, "but rather confronted. We sound the depths of Hell very often in this life."

The force of Dante's poetry resonated most in those who did not confess the Catholic faith, for believers inevitably would have quibbles with Dante's theology. But for those most distant theologically, Dante's faith was so perfect, so unyielding, that a reader found himself compelled by the poetry to take it all to heart. This is why Holmes feared the Dante Club: He feared that it would usher in a new Hell, one empowered by the poets' sheer literary genius. And, worse yet, he feared that he himself, after a life spent running away from the devil preached by his father, would be partially to blame.

In the Elmwood study that night in 1861, a messenger interrupted the poets' tea. Dr. Holmes knew quite definitively that it would be a telegram that had been elaborately redirected from his own house, informing him of poor Wendell Junior's death on some frozen battlefield, probably from exhaustion—of all the explanations on the casualty lists, Holmes found "died of exhaustion" the most frightening and vivid. But instead, it was a servant sent by Henry Longfellow, whose Craigie House estate was around the corner: a simple note requesting Lowell's help with some more translated cantos. Lowell persuaded Holmes to accompany him. "I have so many irons in the fire already that I dread a new temptation," Holmes said, laughing it off at first. "I fear I will catch your Dante mania."

Lowell convinced Fields to take up Dante, too. Though no Italianist, the publisher had a workable amount of the language at his disposal from traveling for business (this business traveling was mostly for his pleasure and Annie's, since there was little trade of books between Rome and Boston), and now he immersed himself in dictionaries and commentaries. Fields's interest, his wife liked to say, was what interested others. And old George Washington Greene, who had given Longfellow his first copy of Dante while they were touring the Italian countryside together thirty years earlier, began stopping by whenever he was in town from Rhode Island, offering wide-eyed assessments of the labor. It was Fields, most in need of schedules, who suggested Wednesday evenings for their Dante gatherings at the Craigie House study, and it was Dr. Holmes, a consummate namer, who christened the enterprise the Dante Club, though Holmes himself usually referred to them as their "séances"—insisting that if you looked hard enough, you could meet Dante face-to-face at Longfellow's fireside.

Holmes's new novel would stand his own name right side up again for the public. It would be the American Story readers awaited at every bookseller and library—the one Hawthorne had failed to find before his death; the one promising spirits, like Herman Melville, muddled out of peculiarity on the way to anonymity and isolation. Dante dared to make himself into an almost divine hero, transforming his own defective personality through the swagger of the poetry. But for this the Florentine sacrificed his home, his life with his wife and children, his place in the crooked city he loved. In impoverished solitude he defined his nation; only in his imagination could he experience peace. Dr. Holmes, in his usual fashion, would accomplish everything, all at once.

And after his novel garnered the nation's loyalty, then let Dr. Manning and the other vultures of the world try picking at his reputation! On the crest of redoubled adoration, Oliver Wendell Holmes could single-handedly shield Dante from attackers and assure Longfellow's triumph. But if the

Dante translation too hastily opened a battle that deepened the scars already cutting into his name, then his American Story could come and go unnoticed, or worse.

Holmes saw with the clarity of a courtroom verdict what had to be done. He had to slow them down just enough to finish his novel before the translation was complete. This was not just Dante business; this was Oliver Wendell Holmes business, his literary fate. Besides, Dante had plaintively bided his time for several hundred years before appearing to the New World. What could a few extra weeks bring?

In the lobby of the police station in Court Square, Nicholas Rey looked up from his notepad, squinting at the gaslight after a long engagement with a sheet of paper. A hefty bear of an indigoed uniformed man, swaying a small paper parcel as if it were an infant, waited in front of his desk.

"You're Patrolman Rey, right? Sergeant Stoneweather. Don't want to interrupt." The man advanced and extended his impressive paw. "I think it takes a man of nerve to be the first Negro policeman, whatever some of the others say. What you writing there, Rey?"

"Might I be of some help, Sergeant?" Rey asked.

"I might, just might. You're the one been asking around the stations 'bout that devilish beggar who jumped out the window, aren't you? It was me that brung him in for the show-up."

Rey made sure Kurtz's office door was still closed. Sergeant Stoneweather took out a blueberry pie from his parcel and nourished himself at intervals in their talk.

"Do you recall where you were when you took him in?" Rey asked.

"Aye—out looking for anyone who couldn't account for themselves, just how we was instructed. The grogshops, the public houses. The South Boston horsecar office, that's where I'd been at that hour, 'cause I knew a few dips who work the pockets there. That beggar a yours was slumped over on one of the benches, half sleeping, but shaking too, like, *tremulous demendous* or *delirious tremendous* or somethin' of that sort."

"You know who he was?" Rey asked.

Stoneweather spoke around his chewing. "Lots of loungers and lushingtons always coming and going by the horsecar. Didn't look familiar to me, though. Wasn't even of the mind to take him in, to say sooth. Seemed harmless enough."

Rey was surprised by this. "What made you change your mind?"

"That damned beggar, that's what!" Stoneweather blurted out, losing some piecrust in his beard. "He sees me rounding up some rogues, right, and he runs up to me, wrists held out and turned up in front of him like he wanted to be shackled and booked for bloody murder on the spot! So I thought to myself, Heaven sent him to me to take to this here show-up, I guess. The damned foolish simkin'. Everything happens for some of God's reason, I believe that. Don't you, Patrolman?"

Rey had trouble envisioning the leaper in any circumstance other than flight. "Did he say anything to you on the way? Was he doing anything? Speaking to someone else? Reading a newspaper maybe? A book?"

Stoneweather shrugged. "Didn't notice." As Stoneweather searched his coat pockets for a handkerchief to wipe his hands, Rey noticed with distracting interest the revolver peeking out from his leather belt. On the day Rey was appointed to the police by Governor Andrew, the aldermanic council had issued a resolution instituting restrictions on him. Rey could not wear a uniform, could not carry any weapon stronger than a billy club, and could not arrest a white person without the presence of another officer.

In that first month, the city stationed Nicholas Rey at the District Two ward. The captain of the station house decided Rey could only be effective on patrol in Nigger Hill. But there were enough blacks there who resented and distrusted a mulatto officer that the other patrolman in the area feared a riot. The station house was not much better. Only two or three policemen spoke with Rey at all, and the others signed a letter to Chief Kurtz recommending an end to the experiment of a colored officer.

"You really want to know what drove him to it, Patrolman?" Stoneweather asked. "Sometimes a man just can't go on how things are, in my experience."

"He died in this station house, Sergeant Stoneweather," Rey said. "But in his mind, he was somewhere else—far from us, far from safety."

This was more than Stoneweather could grasp. "I wish I knew more about the poor fellow, I do."

That afternoon, Chief Kurtz and Deputy Chief Savage visited Beacon Hill. Rey, in the driver's box, was even quieter than usual. When they stepped down, Kurtz said, "You still thinking of that damned vagrant, Patrolman?"

"I can find out who he was, Chief," Rey said.

Kurtz frowned, but his eyes and voice softened. "Well, what do you know of him?"

"Sergeant Stoneweather brought him in from a horsecar office. He could have been from that area."

"A horsecar station! He could have been coming from anywhere."

Rey did not disagree and did not argue. Deputy Chief Savage, who had been listening, said noncommittally, "We also have his likeness, Chief, from just before the show-up."

"Listen close," Kurtz said. "Both of you: The old Healey hen will have me by the ears if she's not happy. And she won't be happy, not till we give her a day as hangman. Rey, I don't want you poking around about that leaper, you hear? We've got enough trouble without calling the world down on our head for a man that died at our feet."

The windows of the Wide Oaks mansion were draped in heavy black cloth, permitting only faint stripes of daylight along the sides. Widow Healey lifted her head from a mound of lotus-leaf pillows. "You have found the murderer, Chief Kurtz," she stated rather than asked when Kurtz entered.

"My dear madam," Chief Kurtz removed his hat and placed it on a table at the foot of her bed. "We have men on every lead. The inquiry is still in its early morning stages . . ." Kurtz explained the possibilities: There were two men who owed Healey money and a notorious criminal whose sentence had been upheld five years earlier by the chief justice.

The widow held her head steadily enough to maintain a hot compress balanced on the white peaks of her brows. Since the funeral and the various memorial services for the chief justice, Ednah Healey had refused to leave her chamber and had turned away all callers outside her immediate family. From her neck hung the crystal brooch imprisoning the judge's tangled lock of hair, an ornament the widow had asked Nell Ranney to string onto a necklace.

Her two sons, as big around the shoulders and heads as Chief Justice Healey but nowhere near as massive, sat slumped on armchairs flanking the door like two granite bulldogs.

Roland Healey interrupted Kurtz: "I don't understand why you have advanced so slowly, Chief Kurtz."

"If only we'd offer a reward!" the older son, Richard, added to his brother's complaint. "We'd be sure to nab someone with enough money put up! Demonish greed, that's all that drives the public to help."

The deputy chief heard this with professional patience. "My good Mr. Healey, if we reveal the true circumstances of your father's decease, you would be flooded with false reports from those looking only to turn a dollar. You must keep the entire matter dark to the public and let us continue.

"Trust when I say, my friends," he added, "that you would not like what should come from wide knowledge of this."

The widow spoke up. "The man who died at your show-up. Have you discovered anything of his identity?"

Kurtz put up his hands. "So many of our good citizens belong to the same family when brought in to show themselves to the police," he said, and smiled wryly. "Smith or Jones."

"And this one," said Mrs. Healey. "What family was he?"

"He did not give us any name, madam," said Kurtz, penitently tucking his smile under the uncombed overhang of his mustache. "But we have no reason to believe he had any information on Judge Healey's murder. He was merely *cracked* in the head, and a bit cup-shot, as well."

"Potentially deaf and dumb," added Savage.

"Why would he be so desperate to get away, Chief Kurtz?" asked Richard Healey.

This was an excellent question, though Kurtz did not want to show it. "I cannot begin to tell you how many men we find on the street who believe themselves chased by demons and report to us their pursuers' descriptions, horns included."

Mrs. Healey leaned forward and squinted. "Chief Kurtz, your porter?"

Kurtz motioned Rey in from the hall. "Madam, may I make you acquainted with Patrolman Nicholas Rey. You requested that we bring him with us today, regarding the man who passed away at the show-up."

"A Negro police officer?" she asked with visible discomfort.

"Mulatto, in actuality, madam," Savage announced proudly. "Patrolman Rey's the Commonwealth's very first. The first in all New England, they say." He held out his hand and made Rey shake it.

Mrs. Healey managed to twist and crane her neck enough to view the mulatto to her apparent satisfaction. "You *are* the officer who had charge of the vagrant, the one who died there?"

Rey nodded.

"Tell me then, Officer. What do *you* think made him act in such a way?"

Chief Kurtz coughed nervously in Rey's direction.

"I cannot say positively, madam," replied Rey honestly. "I cannot say that he understood or considered any danger to his physical being at the time."

"Did he speak to you?" asked Roland.

"He did, Mr. Healey. At least he tried. But I fear nothing in his whisper could be comprehended," said Rey.

"Ha! You cannot even discover the identity of an idler who dies on your own floor! I trust you think my husband deserved to meet his end, Chief Kurtz!"

"I?" Kurtz looked back helplessly at his deputy chief. "Madam!"

"I am a sick woman, before God, but shan't be deceived! You think us fools and villains and wish us all go to the devil!"

"Madam!" Savage echoed the chief.

"I shan't give you the pleasure of seeing me dead in this world, Chief Kurtz! You and your ungrateful nigger police! He did everything he knew to do and we haven't shame for any of it!" The compress crashed to the floor as she raked her neck with her nails. This was a new compulsion, shown by the fresh scabs and red marks covering her skin. She tore her neck, digging into her flesh, scratching at a cluster of invisible insects that were lying in wait in the crevices of her mind.

Her sons jumped from their chairs but could only back away toward the door, where Kurtz and Savage had also helplessly receded, as though the widow might burst into flames at any second.

Rey waited another moment, then calmly took a step toward the side of her bed.

"Madam Healey." Her scratching had loosened the strings of her night-dress. Rey reached over and dimmed the flame of the lamp until she could be seen only in silhouette. "Madam, I wish you to know that your husband helped me once."

She was stilled.

Kurtz and Savage traded surprised glances in the doorway. Rey spoke too quietly for them to hear every word from the other end of the room and they were too frightened of renewing the widow's mania to move forward. But they could sense, even in the dark, how tranquil she had become, how still and silent but for her troubled breathing.

"Tell me please," she said.

"I was brought to Boston as a child by a Virginia woman traveling here on a holiday. Some abolitionists took me away from her to bring me before the chief justice. The chief justice ruled that a slave became emancipated by law once crossing into a free state. He assigned me to the care of a colored blacksmith, Rey, and his family."

"Before that wretched Fugitive Slave Act did us all in." Mrs. Healey's lids snapped shut and she sighed, her mouth curling strangely. "I know what friends of your race think, because of that Sims boy. The chief justice did not like me to attend court, but I went—there was so much talk then. Sims was like you, a handsome Negro, but dark as the blackness in some people's heads. The chief justice would have never sent him back if he didn't have to. He had no choice, you understand that. But he gave you a family. A family that made you happy?"

He nodded.

"Why must mistakes only be made up for afterwards? Can't they sometimes be mended by what came before? It is so tiring. So tiring."

Some sense returned to her, and she knew now what had to be done once the officers were gone. But she needed one more thing from Rey. "Pray, did he speak to you when you were a boy? Judge Healey always liked talking with children more than anyone." She remembered Healey with their own children.

"He asked me if I did wish to stay here, Mrs. Healey, before he wrote his orders. He said that we would always be safe in Boston but that it had to be my choice to be a Boston man, a man who stood for himself and for his city at the same time, or I would always be an outsider. He told me that when a Boston man reaches the pearly gates, an angel comes out to warn him: 'You won't like it here, for it is not Boston.' "

He heard the whisper as he listened to Widow Healey fall asleep; he heard it in the bareness of his shivering rooming house. He awoke each morning with the words on his tongue. He could taste them, could smell the potent odor that coated them, could brush against the crusted whiskers that recited them, but when he tried to speak the whisper himself, sometimes while driving, sometimes before a looking glass, it was nonsense. He sat with his pen at all hours, using up inkwells, writing it out, and the nonsense looked worse than it sounded. He could see the whisperer, reeking of rot, shocked eyes glaring at him before the body carried itself through the glass. The nameless man had been dropped from the sky from a faraway place, Rey couldn't help thinking, into Rey's arms, from where he had dropped him again. He trained himself to put it out of his mind. But how clearly he could see the plummet onto the courtyard, where the man became all blood and leaves, over and over again, as smooth and constant as pictures passed through the slide of a magic lantern. He had to stop the fall, Chief Kurtz's command be damned. He had to find some meaning for the words left hanging on the dead air.

⁂

"I wouldn't let him go with anybody else," said Amelia Holmes, her small face pleated, pulling her husband's coat collar to cover his neck cloth. "Mr. Fields, he ought not to go out tonight. I am worried what will come of it. Hear how he wheezes with the asthma. Now, Wendell, *when* will you get home?"

J. T. Fields's well-appointed carriage had driven up to 21 Charles Street. Though it was only two blocks down from his house, Fields never made Holmes walk. The doctor was breathing with difficulty on the front step, accusing the cooling weather, as he often did the heat.

"Oh, I don't know," Dr. Holmes said, slightly annoyed. "I put myself into Mr. Fields's hands."

She said somberly, "Well, Mr. Fields, how early will you get him back?"

Fields considered this with the utmost gravity. A wife's comfort was as important to him as an author's, and Amelia Holmes had been apprehensive lately.

"I wish Wendell would not publish anything more, Mr. Fields," Amelia had said at a breakfast at the Fieldses' earlier in the month, in their pretty room looking out through leaves and flowers at the well-tempered river. "He'll only call down newspaper criticism, and where is the use?"

Fields had opened his mouth to set her mind at rest, but Holmes was too quick—when he was agitated or panicked, no one could talk as fast, especially about himself. "How do you mean, 'Melia? I have written something new which the critics won't complain of. This is the 'American Story' Mr. Fields has long been pressing me to make. You'll see, dear, it'll be better than anything I have ever done."

"Oh, that's what you always say, Wendell." She shook her head sadly. "But I wish you'd let it alone."

Fields knew Amelia had endured Holmes's disappointment when his sequel serial to *The Autocrat—The Professor at the Breakfast-Table*—was dismissed as repetitive, despite Fields's promises of success. Still, Holmes planned a third in the series, which he would call *The Poet at the Breakfast-Table.* There had also been his devastation over the critical attacks and only modest success wrought by *Elsie Veneer,* his first novel, which he had written breathlessly and published shortly before the war.

The new set of Bohemian critics in New York liked to attack the Boston establishment, and Holmes represented his proud city more than anybody—he, after all, had dubbed Boston the Hub of the Universe and had named his own class the Boston Brahmins, after those in more exotic lands. Now the ruffians who called themselves Young America and dwelt in subterranean Manhattan taverns along Broadway had declared Fields's long dominant Fireside Poets irrelevant to the next age. What had the Longfellow coterie's quaint rhymes and village settings done to prevent the catastrophe of a civil war? they demanded to know. Holmes, for his part, years before the war, had spoken out for compromise and had even signed, along with Artemus Healey, a resolution to support the Fugitive Slave Act, which would send escaped slaves back to their masters, as a hopeful measure to avoid conflict.

"But don't you see, Amelia," Holmes had continued at the breakfast table. "I shall make money by it, and that won't come amiss." Suddenly he looked up at Fields. "If anything should happen to me before I get the story done, you wouldn't come down upon the widow for the money, would you now?" They'd all laughed.

Now, standing next to his carriage, Fields glanced at the checkered sky as if it could tell him the answer Amelia waited on. "About twelve," he said. "How does twelve sound, my dear Mrs. Holmes?" He looked at her with his kind brown eyes, though he knew it would be closer to two in the morning.

The poet took his publisher's arm. "That's pretty well for a Dante night. 'Melia, Mr. Fields will take care of me. Why, it's one of the greatest compliments one man ever paid another, my going out to Longfellow's tonight with all I've been doing lately, between my lectures and my novel and the fine dinners. Why, I ought not to go out at all tonight."

Fields decided not to hear this last comment, lighthearted though it was.

It was popular Cambridge legend by 1865 that Henry Wadsworth Longfellow would divine precisely when to appear outside his sun-yellow Colonial mansion to greet arrivals, whether long anticipated guests or entirely unforeseen callers. Of course, legends often disappoint, and commonly one of the poet's servants would answer the massive door to Craigie House, so named for its previous owners; in recent years there had been times when Henry Longfellow had simply been of the mind to receive no one at all.

But this afternoon, faithful enough to village lore, Longfellow was on his doorstep when Fields's horses towed their cargo up the Craigie House carriageway. Holmes, leaning on the carriage window, made out the erect figure from up the street before the white-dusted hedges parted and bowed. His pleasant view of Longfellow standing serenely under the lamplight in the downy snow, weighted by his flowing leonine beard and impeccably fitted frock coat, matched the representation of the poet embossed in the public mind. This image had crystallized in the wake of the unfathomable loss of Fanny Longfellow, when the world seemed intent on memorializing the poet (as if he, rather than his wife, had been the one who died) as some divine apparition sent to answer for the human race, when his admirers sought to sculpt his persona into a permanent allegory of genius and suffering.

The three Longfellow girls rushed in from playing in the unexpected snow, pausing just long enough at the entrance hall to kick off their overshoes before scrambling over the sharply angled stairs.

From my study I see in the lamplight,
Descending the broad hall-stair,
Grave Alice and laughing Allegra,
And Edith with golden hair.

Holmes had just passed that broad stair and now stood with Longfellow in that study, where the lamplight illumined the poet's writing desk. All the while, the three girls tumbled from sight. *Still he walks through a living poem.*

Holmes smiled to himself and took the paw of Longfellow's yappy little dog, who showed all his teeth and shook his piglike body.

Then Holmes greeted the feeble, goat-bearded scholar who sat bent in a chair by the fire, looking lost in an oversize folio. "How is the liveliest George Washington in Longfellow's collection, my dear Greene?"

"Better, better, thank you, Dr. Holmes. I'm afraid, though, I was not well enough to attend Judge Healey's funeral." George Washington Greene was generally referred to as "old" by the rest of them, but he was actually sixty—just four years older than Holmes and two years ahead of Longfellow. Chronic illnesses had aged the retired Unitarian minister and historian decades beyond his years. But he railroaded in each week from East Greenwich, Rhode Island, with as much enthusiasm for the Wednesday nights at Craigie House as for the guest sermons he offered whenever called upon—or for the Revolutionary War histories that his name had fated him to compile. "Longfellow, were you present?"

"I'm afraid not, my dear Mr. Greene," said Longfellow. Longfellow had not been to Mount Auburn Cemetery since before Fanny Longfellow's funeral, a ceremony during which he was confined to his bed. "But I trust it was well attended?"

"Oh, quite so, Longfellow." Holmes locked his fingers over his chest thoughtfully. "A beautiful and fitting tribute."

"Too well attended, perhaps," Lowell said, coming in from the library with a handful of books and ignoring the fact that Holmes had already answered the question.

"Old Healey knew the best of himself," Holmes pointed out gently. "He knew his place was the courthouse, not the barbaric arena of politics."

"Wendell! You can't mean that," said Lowell authoritatively.

"Lowell." Fields gazed pointedly at him.

"To think we became the hunters of slaves." Lowell backed away from Holmes only for a second. Lowell was a sixth or seventh cousin to the Healeys, as the Lowells were sixth or seventh cousins—at least—to all the best Brahmin families, and this only increased his resistance. "Would you ever have ruled as cowardly as Healey, Wendell? If I proposed that it had been your choice, would you have sent that Sims boy back to his plantation in chains? Tell me that. Just tell me that, Holmes."

"We must respect the family's loss," said Holmes quietly, directing his comment mainly at the half-deaf Mr. Greene, who nodded politely.

Longfellow excused himself when a bell sounded from upstairs. There could be professors or reverends, senators or kings among his guests, but at the signal, Longfellow would make his way to listen to the bedtime prayers of Alice, Edith, and Annie Allegra.

By the time he returned, Fields had deftly redirected the conversation toward lighter fare, so the poet walked into a round of laughter produced by an anecdote jointly retold by Holmes and Lowell. The host checked his Aaron Willard mahogany clock, an old timepiece he was partial to, not because of its looks or accuracy but because it seemed to tick more leisurely than others.

"Schooltime," he said softly.

The room fell hush. Longfellow closed the green shutters over the windows. Holmes turned down the flames of the moderator lamps while the others helped arrange a row of candles. This series of overlapping halos communed with the flickering glow of the fire. The five scholars and Trap—Longfellow's plump Scotch terrier—assumed their preordained posts along the circumference of the small room.

Longfellow gathered up a sheaf of papers from his drawer and passed out a few pages of Dante's Italian to each guest, along with a set of printed proof sheets with his corresponding line-by-line translation. In the delicately woven chiaroscuro of hearth, lamp, and wick, the ink seemed to lift off Longfellow's proofs, as if a page of Dante suddenly came alive under one's eyes. Dante had arranged his verse in a *terza rima,* every three lines a poetic set, the first and third rhyming and the middle projecting a rhyme with the first line of the next set, so that the verses leaned ahead in forward motion.

Holmes always relished how Longfellow opened their Dante meetings with a recitation of the first lines of the *Commedia* in unassumingly perfect Italian.

" 'Midway through the journey of our life, I found myself within a dark wood, for the right way had been lost.' "

III

As the first order of business in a Dante Club meeting, the host reviewed the proof sheets from the previous week's session.

"Good work, my dear Longfellow," Dr. Holmes said. He was satisfied whenever one of his suggested amendments was approved, and *two* from last Wednesday had found their way into Longfellow's final proofs. Holmes turned his attention to this evening's cantos. He had taken extra care to prepare, because today he would have to persuade them he had come to protect Dante.

"In the seventh circle," Longfellow said, "Dante tells us how he and Virgil come upon a black forest." In each region of Hell, Dante followed his adored guide, the Roman poet Virgil. Along the way, he learned the fate of each group of sinners, singling out one or two to address the living world.

"The lost forest that has occupied the private nightmares of all of Dante's readers at one time or another," Lowell said. "Dante writes like Rembrandt, with a brush dipped in darkness and a gleam of hellfire as his light."

Lowell, as usual, would have every inch of Dante at his tongue's end; he lived Dante's poetry, body and mind. Holmes, for one of the only instances in his life, envied another person's talent.

Longfellow read from his translation. His reading voice rang deep and true, without any harshness, like the sound of water running under a fresh cover of snow. George Washington Greene seemed particularly lulled, for the scholar, in the spacious green armchair in the corner, drifted to sleep amid the soft intonations of the poet and the mild heat from the fire. The little terrier Trap, who had rolled onto his plump stomach under Greene's chair, also dozed off, and their snores arranged themselves in tandem, like the grumbling bass in a Beethoven symphony.

In the canto at hand, Dante found himself in the Wood of Suicides, where the "shades" of sinners have been turned into trees, dripping blood where sap belonged. Then further punishment arrived: Bestial harpies, faces and necks of women and bodies of birds, feet clawed and bellies bulging, crashed through the brush, feeding and tearing at every tree in their way. But along with great pain, the rips and tears in the trees provided the only outlet for the shades to utter their pain, to tell their stories to Dante.

"The blood and words must come out together." So said Longfellow.

After two cantos of punishments witnessed by Dante, books were marked and stored, papers shuffled, and admiration exchanged. Longfellow said, "School is done, gentlemen. It is only half-past nine and we deserve some refreshment for our labors."

"You know," Holmes said, "I was thinking of our Dante work in a new light just the other day."

Longfellow's servant, Peter, knocked and conveyed a message to Lowell in a hesitant whisper.

"Someone to see me?" Lowell protested, interrupting Holmes. "Who would find me here?" When Peter stammered a vague response, Lowell thundered loud enough for the whole household to hear. "Who in the name of Heaven would come on the night of our club?"

Peter leaned closer to Lowell. "Mistah Lowell, he say he's a policeman, sah."

In the front hall, Patrolman Nicholas Rey stomped the fresh snow from his boots, then froze at Longfellow's army of George Washington sculptures and paintings. The house had headquartered Washington in the earliest days of the American Revolution.

Peter, the black servant, had cocked his head doubtfully when Rey showed him his badge. Rey was told that Mr. Longfellow's Wednesday meeting could not be disturbed and, policeman or no policeman, he would have to wait in the parlor. The room into which he was led was enshrined with an intangibly light decor—flowered wallpaper and curtains suspended from Gothic acorns. A creamy marble bust of a woman was guarded under an arch by the chimneypiece, curls of stone hair falling gently over softly carved features.

Rey stood up when two men entered the room. One had a flowing beard and a dignity that made him appear quite tall, although he was of average height; his companion was a stout, confident man, with walrus tusks swinging as though to introduce themselves first. This was James Russell Lowell, who paused for a long gaping moment, then rushed forward.

He laughed with the smugness of advance knowledge. "Longfellow, wouldn't you know I've read everything about this chap in the freemen's newspaper! He was a hero in the Negro regiment, the Fifty-fourth, and Andrew appointed him to the police department the week of President Lincoln's death. What an honor to meet you, my friend!"

"Fifty-fifth regiment, Professor Lowell, the sister regiment. Thank you," Rey said. "Professor Longfellow, I apologize for taking you away from your company."

"We have just finished the serious portion, Officer," Longfellow said, smiling, "and Mister shall do nicely." His silver hair and loose beard lent him a patriarchal manner befitting someone older than fifty-eight. The eyes were blue and ageless. Longfellow wore an impeccable dark frock coat with gilt buttons and a buff waistcoat fitted to his form. "I wore out my professor's gown years ago now, and Professor Lowell has taken it up in my stead."

"But I still cannot get used to that confounded title," muttered Lowell.

Rey turned to him. "A young lady at your house kindly directed me here. She said you would not be caught in a gunshot of anywhere else but here on a Wednesday evening."

"Ah, that would be my Mabel!" Lowell laughed. "She did not throw you out, did she?"

Rey smiled. "She is a most charming young lady, sir. I was sent to you, Professor, from University Hall."

Lowell looked stunned. "What?" he whispered. Then he exploded, his cheeks and ears baked a hot burgundy and his voice scorching his own throat: "They sent a *police officer*! With what possible justification? Are they not men who can speak their own minds without pulling the wires of some City Hall marionette! Explain yourself, sir!"

Rey remained as still as the marble statue of Longfellow's wife by the fireplace.

Longfellow draped a hand on his friend's sleeve. "You see, Officer, Professor Lowell is kind enough to assist me, along with some of our colleagues, in a literary endeavor of sorts that does not presently meet with the favor of members of the College government. But is that why . . ."

"My apologies," the policeman said, allowing his gaze to loiter on the first man who had spoken, whose redness drained from his face as abruptly as it had appeared. "I called on University Hall, not the other way around. You see, I'm in search of an expert in languages and was given your name by some students there."

"Then, Officer, *my* apologies," said Lowell. "But you are lucky you've found me. I can speak six languages like a native—of Cambridge." The poet laughed and rested the paper that Rey passed to him on Longfellow's rosewood marquetry desk. He ran his finger across the slanted, scrawled lettering.

Rey saw Lowell's high forehead furrow into creases. "A gentleman said some words to me. It was softly spoken, whatever he meant to communicate, and all rather sudden. I can only conclude it was in some strange and foreign tongue."

"When?" Lowell asked.

"A few weeks ago. It was a strange and unexpected encounter." Rey allowed his eyes to shut. He remembered the whisperer's grip stretch across his skull. He could hear the words form so distinctly, but was without the power to repeat any of them. "I fear mine is only a rough transcription, Professor."

"A choke-pear, indeed!" Lowell said as he passed the paper to Longfellow. "I'm afraid that little can be made from this hieroglyphic. Can you not ask the person what he meant? Or at least find out what language he purports to speak?"

Rey hesitated to answer.

Longfellow said, "Officer, we have a cabinet of hungry scholars locked away whose wisdom might be bribed with oysters and macaroni. Would you be kind enough to leave a copy of this paper with us?"

"I greatly appreciate it, Mr. Longfellow," said Rey. He studied the poets before adding, "I must request that you not mention to anyone outside yourselves my visit today. This deals with a delicate police matter."

Lowell raised his eyebrows skeptically.

"Of course," Longfellow said, and bowed his head in a nod, as though that trust were implicit inside Craigie House.

• • •

"*Do* keep the good godson of Cerberus away from the table tonight, my dear Longfellow!" Fields was tucking a napkin into his shirt collar. They were settled in their places around the dining room table. Trap protested with a quiet whine.

"Oh, he is quite a friend to poets, Fields," Longfellow said.

"Ah! You should have seen it last week, Mr. Greene," said Fields. "While you were holed up in your bed, that friendly fellow helped himself to a partridge from the supper table when we were in the study with the eleventh canto!"

"That was only his view of the *Divine Comedy,*" Longfellow said, smiling.

"A strange encounter," said Holmes, vaguely interested. "That is what the police officer said of it?" He was studying the policeman's note, holding it under the chandelier's warm lights and turning it over before passing it on.

Lowell nodded. "Like Nimrod, whatever our Officer Rey heard is like all the gigantic infancy of the world."

"I partly wish to say the writing is a poor attempt at Italian." George Washington Greene shrugged apologetically and yielded the note to Fields with a windy sigh.

The historian returned his concentration to his meal. He grew self-conscious when, the Dante Club having shelved its books in exchange for supper-table banter, he had to compete with the bright stars that inhabited Longfellow's social constellation. Greene's life had been cobbled together of small promise and great setbacks. His public lectures had never been strong enough to secure him a professorship, and his work as a minister never defined enough to allow him to gain his own parish (his lectures, detractors said, were too sermonizing and his sermons too historical). Longfellow watched his old friend faithfully and sent choice portions across the table that he thought Greene would prefer.

"Patrolman Rey," said Lowell admiringly. "The very image of a man, isn't he, Longfellow? A soldier in our greatest war and now the first colored member of the police. Alas, we professors just stand on the gangway, watching the few who take the voyage on the steamer."

"Oh, but we shall live much longer through our intellectual pursuits," said Holmes, "according to an article in the last number of the *Atlantic* concerning learning's salutary effects on longevity. Compliments on another fine issue, my dear Fields."

"Yes, I saw that! An excellent piece. Make much of that young author, Fields," said Lowell.

"Hmm." Fields smiled at him. "Apparently, I should consult with you before letting any writer put pen to paper. The *Review* certainly made short work of our *Life of Percival.* A stranger might well wonder that you don't show me slightly more consideration!"

"Fields, I give no puffs for mere mush," said Lowell. "You know better than to publish a book which is not only poor in itself but will stand in the way of a better work on the subject."

"I ask the table whether it is right for Lowell to publish in *The North American Review,* one of *my* periodicals, an attack on one of *my* house's books!"

"Well, I ask in return," Lowell said, "if anyone here has read the book and disputed my findings."

"I would venture a resounding no for the entire table," Fields submitted, "for I assure you that from the day Lowell's article appeared, not a single copy of the book has been sold!"

Holmes tapped his fork against his glass. "I hereby arraign Lowell as a murderer, for he completely killed the *Life.*"

They all laughed.

"Oh, it died a-borning, Judge Holmes," replied the defendant, "and I but hammered the nails into its coffin!"

"Say," Greene tried to sound casual in returning to his preferred topic. "Has anyone noted a Dantesque character to the days and dates of this year?"

"They correspond exactly with those of the Dantesque 1300," said Longfellow, nodding. "So in both years, Good Friday fell on the twenty-fifth of March."

"Glory!" said Lowell. "Five hundred and sixty-five years ago this year, Dante descended into the *città dolente,* the dolorous city. Won't this be the year of Dante! Is it a good omen for a translation," Lowell asked with a boyish smile, "or an ill one?" His comment reminded him of the persistence of the Harvard Corporation, however, and his large smile wilted.

Longfellow said, "Tomorrow, with our latest cantos of the *Inferno* in hand, I shall descend among the printer's devils—the *Malebranche* of the

Riverside Press—and we shall creep closer to completion. I have promised to send a private edition of *Inferno* to the Florentine Committee by the end of the year, to be made a part, however humbly, of Dante's six-hundredth-birthday commemoration."

"You know, my dear friends," Lowell said, frowning. "Those damned fools at Harvard are still in a white heat trying to close down my Dante course."

"And after Augustus Manning warned me about the consequences of publishing the translation," Fields put in, drumming the table in frustration.

"Why should they go to such lengths?" Greene asked with alarm.

"One way or another, they seek to gain as much distance from Dante as possible," explained Longfellow gently. "They fear its influence, that it's foreign—that it's Catholic, my dear Greene."

Holmes said, projecting offhanded sympathy, "I suppose it could be partially understood when it comes to some of Dante. How many fathers went to Mount Auburn Cemetery to visit their sons last June instead of to the meetinghouse for commencement? For many, I think we need no other Hell than what we have just come out of."

Lowell was pouring himself a third or fourth glass of red Falernian. Across the table, Fields tried unsuccessfully to calm him with a placating glance. But Lowell said, "Once they start throwing books in the fire, they shall put us all into an inferno we won't soon escape, my dear Holmes!"

"Oh, do not think I like the idea of trying to waterproof the American mind against questions that Heaven rains down upon it, my dear Lowell. But perhaps . . ." Holmes hesitated. Here was his opportunity. He turned to Longfellow. "Perhaps we should consider a less ambitious publication schedule, my dear Longfellow—a private issue of a few dozen books first, so that our friends and fellow scholars can appreciate it, can learn its strengths, before we spread it to the masses."

Lowell nearly jumped from his seat. "Did Dr. Manning talk to you? Did Manning send someone to scare you into that, Holmes?"

"Lowell, please." Fields smiled diplomatically. "Manning wouldn't approach Holmes about this."

"What?" Dr. Holmes pretended not to register this. Lowell was still waiting for an answer. "Of course not, Lowell. Manning is just one of those fungi that always grow upon older universities. But it seems to me that we do not want to court unnecessary conflict. It would only distract from what we cherish about Dante. It would become about the fight, not about the poetry. Too many doctors use medicine by cramming as much of it as possible down their patients' throats. We should be judicious in our most well-meaning cures, and cautious in our literary advancements."

"The more allies, the better," Fields said to the table.

"We cannot tiptoe around tyrants!" Lowell said.

"Nor do we wish to be an army of five against the world," Holmes added. He was thrilled that Fields was already warming to his idea of stalling: He would complete his novel before the nation even heard of Dante.

"I would be burned at the stake," Lowell cried. "Nay, I would agree to be shut up alone for an hour with the entire Harvard Corporation before I would push back the translation's publication."

"Of course, we shan't change publication plans at all," Fields said. The wind came out of Holmes's sails. "But Holmes is right about us carrying this out alone," Fields continued. "We can certainly try to recruit support. I could call on old Professor Ticknor to use whatever influence is left in him. And perhaps Mr. Emerson, who read Dante years ago. No one on earth knows whether a book will sell five thousand copies or not when published. But if five thousand copies are sold, nothing is more certain than that twenty-five thousand copies can be."

"Could they try to take away your teaching post, Mr. Lowell?" Greene interrupted, still preoccupied by the Harvard Corporation.

"Jamey is far too famous a poet for that," insisted Fields.

"I don't care a fig what they do to me, in any respect! I shall not hand Dante to the Philistines."

"Nor shall any of us!" Holmes was quick to say. To his own surprise, he was not defeated; rather, all the more determined—not only that he was right, but that he could save his friends from Dante and save Dante from the ardor of his friends. The encouraging volume of his exclamation took in the table. "Hear, hear" and "That's it! That's it!" were shouted, Lowell's voice the loudest.

Greene, seeing a remnant of tomato farcie lodged on his clinking fork, bent down to share the wealth with Trap. From under the table, Greene noticed Longfellow rise to his feet.

Though they were just five friends around Longfellow's dining room in the infinite privacy of Craigie House, the sheer rarity of Longfellow standing to speak for a toast produced a complete stillness.

"To the health of the table."

That was all he said. But they hurrahed as though it were another Emancipation Proclamation. Then there was cherry cobbler and ice cream, and cognac with flaming cubes of sugar, and unwrapped cigars lit on the candles at the center of the table.

Before the night came to an end, Longfellow was persuaded by Fields to tell the table of the cigars' history. In coaxing Longfellow to speak of himself in any capacity, one was required to cloak interest in a neutral topic, such as cigars.

"I had called on the Corner on business," Longfellow began, while Fields laughed in advance, "when Mr. Fields persuaded me to accompany him to a nearby tobacconist's to procure some gifts. The tobacconist brought over a box of a certain brand of cigars I swear I had never before heard of. And he said, with all the earnestness in the world, 'These, sir, are the kind Longfellow prefers to smoke.' "

"What was your reply?" Greene asked over the gleeful din.

"I glanced at the man, looked down at the cigars, and said, 'Well then, I must try them.' And paid him to send a box over."

"So what do you think now, my dear Longfellow?" Lowell's dessert caught in his throat from laughing.

Longfellow exhaled. "Oh, I believe the man was quite right. I *do* find them good."

⌘

" 'Therefore it is good that I should arm myself with foresight, so, if I am driven from the place most dear to me, I will . . .' " the student hummed with frustration, rubbing his finger back and forth under the Italian.

For several years now, Lowell's study in Elmwood had doubled as a classroom for his course on Dante. In his first term as Smith Professor, he had requested a room and received a bleak space in the basement of University Hall, with long wooden boards instead of desks and a pulpit for the professor that had to have descended from the Puritans. The course was not sufficiently well attended, Lowell was told, to merit one of the more desirable classrooms. It was just as well. Holding court at Elmwood provided him the comfort of a pipe and the warmth of a wood fire, and was another reason not to have to leave home.

The class met twice a week on days of Lowell's choosing—sometimes on a Sunday, for Lowell liked the idea of meeting on the same day of the week that Boccaccio, centuries before him, had held the first Dante lectures in Florence. Mabel Lowell often sat and listened to her father's lessons from the adjoining room, which was connected by two open archways.

"Remember, Mead," said Professor Lowell when the student stopped in frustration. "Remember, in this fifth sphere of Heaven, the sphere of Martyrs, Cacciaguida has prophesied to Dante that the Poet will be exiled from Florence soon after he returns to the living world, under the sentence of death by fire if he reenters the city gates. Now, Mead, translate his next phrase—'*io non perdessi li altri per i miei carmi*'—with that in mind."

Lowell's Italian was fluent and always technically correct. But Mead, a Harvard junior, liked to think that Lowell's Americanness came out in the scrupulous pronunciation of each syllable, as if each had no connection to the next.

" 'I will not lose other places for reason of my poems.' "

"Stay with the text, Mead! *Carmi* are songs—not just his poems, but the very music of his voice. In the days of minstrels, you would pay your money and have a choice whether he would give you his stories as song or sermon. A sermon which sings and a song which preaches—*that* is Dante's *Comedy*. 'So that through my *songs* I shall not lose the other places.' A fair reading, Mead," Lowell said with a gesture resembling a stretch, which communicated his general approval.

"Dante repeats himself," Pliny Mead said flatly. Edward Sheldon, the student beside him, squirmed at this. "As you say," Mead continued, "a divine prophet has already foreseen that Dante will find sanctuary and protection under Can Grande. So what 'other' places would Dante need? Nonsense for the sake of poetry."

Lowell said, "When Dante speaks of a new home in the future by virtue of his work, when he speaks of the *other* places he seeks, he speaks not of his life in 1302—the date of his exile—but of his *second* life, his life as he will live on through the poem for hundreds of years."

Mead persisted. "But the 'dearest place' is never truly taken from Dante; he takes *himself* away from it. Florence offered him a chance to return home, to his wife and family, yet he refused!"

Pliny Mead was never one to impress instructors or peers with geniality, but since the morning he had received his marks on last term's papers—and had been sorely disappointed—he had eyed Lowell with sourness. Mead attributed his low mark—and his resulting drop in the class of 1867 rank book from twelfth to fifteenth scholar—to the fact that he had disagreed with Lowell on several occasions during discussions of French literature and that the professor could not stand being thought wrong. Mead would have dropped his course work in the living languages altogether but for the Corporation's rule that once enrolled in a language course, the student had to remain three more terms in the department—one of the contrivances meant to dissuade the boys from even dipping a toe. So Mead was stuck with that great bag of wind James Russell Lowell. And with Dante Alighieri.

"What an offer they made!" Lowell laughed. "Full clemency for Dante and restoration of his rightful place in Florence: in return for the poet's request for absolution and a hefty payment of money! We marched Johnny Reb back into the Union with less degradation. Far be it for a man who cries aloud for justice to accept such a rotten compromise with his persecutors."

"Well, Dante is still a Florentine, no matter what *we* say!" Mead asserted, trying to recruit Sheldon's support with a collusive glance. "Sheldon, can't you see it? Dante writes incessantly of Florence, and of the Florentines he meets and speaks with in his visit to the afterlife, and he writes all this while in exile! Clear enough to me, friends, he longs only for return. The man's death in exile and poverty is his great final failure."

With irritation, Edward Sheldon noticed that Mead was grinning at having silenced Lowell, who had risen and thrust his hands into his rather shabby smoking jacket. But Sheldon could see in Lowell, could see in the puffing of his pipe, a heightened frame of mind. He seemed to be treading on another plane of mental cognizance, far above the Elmwood study, as he paced the rug with his heavy-laced boots. Lowell typically wouldn't allow a freshman admission to an advanced literature class, but young Sheldon had been persistent and Lowell had told him they would see whether he could manage. Sheldon remained grateful for the opportunity, and hoped for the chance to defend Lowell and Dante against Mead, the sort who had no doubt put coppers on the railroad track as a younger boy. Sheldon opened his mouth, but Mead shot him a look that made Sheldon stuff his thoughts back inside.

Lowell betrayed a look of disappointment at Sheldon, then turned to Mead. "Where is the Jew in you, my boy?" he asked.

"What?" Mead cried, offended.

"No, never mind, I didn't think so. Mead, Dante's theme is man—not *a* man," Lowell said finally with a mild patience that he reserved only for students. "The Italians forever twitch at Dante's sleeves trying to make him say he is of their politics and their way of thinking. Their way indeed! To confine it to Florence or Italy is to banish it from the sympathies of mankind. We read *Paradise Lost* as a poem but Dante's *Comedy* as a chronicle of our inner lives. Do you boys know of Isaiah 38:10?"

Sheldon thought hard; Mead sat with iron-faced stubbornness, purposefully not thinking about whether he did know it.

" '*Ego dixi: In dimidio dierum meorum vadam ad portas inferi*'!" Lowell crowed, then rushed to his crowded bookshelves, where somehow he instantly found the cited chapter and verse in a Latin Bible. "You see?" he asked, placing it open on the rug at the foot of his students, most delighted to show that he had remembered the quote exactly.

"Shall I translate?" Lowell asked. " 'I say: In the midst of my days I shall go to the gates of hell.' Is there anything our old Scripture writers didn't think of? Sometime in the middle of our lives, we all, each one of us, journey to face a Hell of our own. What is the very first line of Dante's poem?"

" 'Midway through the journey of our life,' " Edward Sheldon volunteered happily, having read that opening salvo of *Inferno* again and again in his room at Stoughton Hall, never having been so ambushed by any verse of poetry, so emboldened by another's cry. " 'I found myself in a dark wood, for the correct path had been lost.' "

" '*Nel mezzo del cammin di nostra vita.* Midway through the journey of *our* life,' " Lowell repeated with such a wide glare in the direction of his fireplace that Sheldon glanced over his shoulder, thinking pretty Mabel Lowell must have entered behind him, but her shadow showed her still sitting in the adjoining room. " '*Our* life.' From the very first line of Dante's poem, *we* are involved in the journey, we are taking the pilgrimage as much as he is, and we must face our Hell as squarely as Dante faces his. You see that the poem's great and lasting value is as the autobiography of a human soul. Yours and mine, it may be, just as much as Dante's."

Lowell thought to himself as he heard Sheldon read the next fifteen lines of Italian how good it felt to teach something real. How foolish was Socrates to think of banishing the poets from Athens! How thoroughly Lowell would enjoy watching Augustus Manning's defeat when Longfellow's translation proved itself an immense success.

The next day, Lowell was departing from University Hall after delivering a lecture on Goethe. He was not a little taken aback when he found himself facing a short Italian man rushing past, dressed in a withered but desperately pressed sackcoat.

"Bachi?" said Lowell.

Pietro Bachi had been hired as an Italian instructor by Longfellow years before. The Corporation had never liked the idea of employing foreigners, particularly an Italian papist—the fact that Bachi had been banished by the Vatican did not change their minds. By the time Lowell had assumed control of the department, the Corporation had stumbled upon very reasonable grounds to eliminate Pietro Bachi: his intemperance and insolvency. On the day he was fired, the Italian had grumbled to Professor Lowell, "I shan't be caught here again, not even dead." Lowell had, on whatever fancy, taken Bachi at his word.

"My dear professor." Bachi now offered his hand to his former department head, who pumped vigorously in his usual way.

"Well," Lowell started, not sure whether to ask how Bachi, plainly alive and breathing, came to be in Harvard Yard.

"Out for a stroll, professor," Bachi explained. Yet he seemed to be looking anxiously past Lowell, so the professor kept the pleasantries short. But Lowell noticed, as he turned back briefly in increasing wonder at Bachi's appearance, that Bachi was heading for a vaguely familiar figure. It was the fellow in the black bowler hat and checkered waistcoat, the poetry admirer whom Lowell had seen idling against an American elm some weeks before. Now, what business would he have with Bachi? Lowell planted himself to see whether Bachi would greet the unknown character, who certainly seemed to be waiting for *someone*. But then a sea of students, grateful to have been released from Greek recitations, swarmed around them, and the curious pair—if the two men were indeed to be spoken of together—were lost to Lowell's sight.

Lowell, forgetting the scene entirely, started toward the law school, where Oliver Wendell Junior stood surrounded by classmates, explaining to them their mistake on some point of law. The general appearance was not dissimiliar to Dr. Holmes—but it was as though someone had taken the little doctor and stretched him to twice his stature on a rack.

Dr. Holmes idled at the foot of the servants' stairs of his house. He stopped at a low-hung mirror and flung his thick shock of brown hair to one side with a comb. He thought his face not a very flattering likeness of himself. "More a convenience than an ornament," he liked to say to people. A complexion one shade darker, the nose shapelier on the incline, the neck more pronounced, he could have been looking at the reflection of Wendell Junior. Neddie, Holmes's youngest, had been unfortunate enough to align his looks with Dr. Holmes's, inheriting too his breathing problems. Dr. Holmes and Neddie were Wendells, the Reverend Holmes would have said; Wendell Junior, a pure Holmes. With that blood, Junior would no doubt rise above his father's name, not only Holmes Esq. but His Excellency Holmes or President Holmes. Dr. Holmes perked up at the sound of heavy boots and swiftly backed into an adjoining room. Then he started for the staircase again with a casual stride, his gaze pointed down in an old book. Oliver Wendell Holmes Junior burst into the house and seemed to make one great leap for the second floor.

"Why, Wendy," Holmes called out with a quick smile. "That you?"

Junior slowed down midway up the stairs. "Hello, Father."

"Your mother was just asking had I seen you today, and I realized I had not. Where are you coming from so late in the day, my boy?"

"A walk."

"That so? Just you?"

Junior paused grudgingly at the landing. Under his dark eyebrows, Junior glared at his father, kneading the wooden baluster at the bottom of the stairs. "I was out talking with James Lowell, as a matter of fact."

Holmes put on a show of surprise. "Lowell? Have you been spending time together of late? You and Professor Lowell?"

A broad shoulder lifted slightly.

"Well, what is it you talk about with our dear mutual friend, might I ask?" Dr. Holmes went on with an amiable smile.

"Politics, my time in the war, my law classes. We get on quite well, I'd say."

"Well, you're spending far too much time in common leisure these days. I order that you cease these trifling excursions with Mr. Lowell!" No reply. "It robs your time for studying, you know. We can't have that, can we?"

Junior laughed. "Every morning it's, 'What's the point, Wendy? A lawyer can never be a great man, Wendy.'" This was said with a light, husky voice. "Now you wish me to study the law harder?"

"Right, Junior. It costs sweat, it costs nerve-fat, it costs phosphorus to do anything worth doing. And I shall have a word with Mr. Lowell about your habits at our next Dante Club session. I'm sure he shall agree with me. He himself was a lawyer once, and knows what it requires." Holmes started for the hall, rather satisfied in his firm position.

Junior grunted.

Dr. Holmes turned back. "Something more, my boy?"

"I only wonder," Junior said. "I'd like to hear further about your Dante Club, Father."

Wendell Junior had never shown any interest in his literary or professional activities. He had never read the doctor's poems or his first novel, nor had he attended his lyceum lectures on medical advances or the history of poetry. This had been the case more pointedly after Holmes published "My Hunt After the Captain" in *The Atlantic Monthly*, retelling his journey through the South after receiving a telegram mistakenly reporting Junior's death on the battlefield.

Junior had in fact skimmed through the proof sheets, feeling his wounds throb as he took it in. He could not believe how his father could think to roll up the war into a few thousand words, which mostly told anecdotes of dying Rebels in hospital beds and hotel clerks in small towns asking if he was not the Autocrat of the Breakfast-Table.

"I mean," Junior continued with a cocked grin, "do you really bother calling yourself a member?"

"I beg your pardon, Wendy? What's the meaning of that? What do you know of it?"

"Only that Mr. Lowell says that your voice is heard mostly at the supper table, not in the study. For Mr. Longfellow, that work is life itself; for Lowell, his calling. You see, he *acts* on his beliefs, doesn't just talk of them, just as he did when he defended slaves as a lawyer. For you, it's just another place to chime glasses."

"Did Lowell say . . ." Dr. Holmes began. "Now see here, Junior!"

Junior reached the top floor, where he shut himself in his room.

"How could you know the first thing about our Dante Club!" Dr. Holmes cried.

Holmes wandered the house helplessly before retiring into his study. His voice heard mostly at table? The more he repeated the allegation to himself, the more stinging it was: Lowell was trying to preserve his place at the right hand of Longfellow by showing himself superior at the expense of Holmes.

With Junior's words in Lowell's loud baritone hanging on him, he wrote doggedly over the next weeks, with a sustained progress that did not come to him naturally. The time at which any new thought struck Holmes was his Sibylline moment, but the act of composition usually was attended with a dull, disagreeable sensation about the forehead—interrupted only from time to time by the simultaneous descent of some group of words or unexpected image, which produced a burst of the most insane enthusiasm and self-gratulation and during which he sometimes committed puerile excesses of language and action.

He could not work many hours consecutively, in any case, without deranging his whole system. His feet were apt to get cold, his head hot, his muscles restless, and he would feel as if he *must* get up. In the evening, he would stop all hard work before eleven o'clock and take a book of light reading to clear his mind of its previous contents. Too much brain work gave him a sense of disgust, like overeating. He attributed this in part to the depleting, nerve-straining qualities of the climate. Brown-Séquard, a fellow medical man from Paris, had said that animals do not *bleed* so much in America as they did in Europe. Was that not startling to think? Despite this biological shortcoming, Holmes now felt himself writing like a madman.

"You know I should be the one to speak with Professor Ticknor about helping our Dante cause," Holmes said to Fields. He had stopped by Fields's office at the Corner.

"What's that?" Fields was reading three things at once: a manuscript, a contract, and a letter. "Where are those royalty agreements?"

J. R. Osgood handed him another pile of papers.

"Your time is much occupied, Fields, and you have the next number of the *Atlantic* to think about—you need to rest your tired brain, in any case," argued Holmes. "Professor Ticknor was my teacher, after all. I may well have the most influence over the old fellow, for Longfellow's sake."

Holmes still remembered a time when Boston was known as Ticknorville by the literary set: If you were not invited to Ticknor's library salon, you were nobody. That chamber had once been known as Ticknor's Throne Room; now, more often, Ticknor's Iceberg. The former professor had fallen into disrepute with much of their society as a refined idler and an anti-abolitionist, but his position as one of the city's first literary masters would always remain. His influence could be revived to their benefit.

"My life is worn by more creatures than I can endure, my dear Holmes," Fields said, sighing. "The sight of a manuscript is like a swordfish nowadays—it cuts me in two." He looked Holmes over for a long moment, then agreed to send him in his place to Park Street. "But remember me kindly to him, won't you, Wendell."

Holmes knew that Fields was relieved to pass on the task of speaking with George Ticknor. Professor Ticknor—that title was still insisted upon, though he had taught nothing since his retirement thirty years earlier—had never thought much of his younger cousin, William D. Ticknor, and his low opinion extended to William's partner, J. T. Fields, as he made clear to Holmes after the doctor was led up the winding staircase of nearby 9 Park Street.

"The noisy shuffle of profits, viewing books as sales and losses," Professor Ticknor said with dried lips puckered in revulsion. "My cousin William suffered that malady, Dr. Holmes, and infected my nephews too, I'm afraid. Those who sweat over labors must not control the literary arts. Don't you believe so, Holmes?"

"But Mr. Fields has something of a brilliant eye, though, doesn't he? He knew your *History* would flourish, Professor. He does think Longfellow's Dante will find an audience." In fact, Ticknor's *History of Spanish Literature* found few readers outside of the contributors to the magazines, but the professor thought that an exacting measure of its success.

Ticknor ignored Holmes's loyalty and delicately pulled his hands out of a bulky machine. He had had the writing machine—a sort of miniature printing press, as he described it—built when his hands began to be too shaky to write. As a result, he had not seen his own handwriting in several years. He had been at work on a letter when Holmes arrived.

Ticknor, sitting in his purple velvet skullcap and slippers, let his critical eye take in, for the second time, the cut of Holmes's clothes and the quality of his necktie and handkerchief.

"I'm afraid, Doctor, that while Mr. Fields knows *what* people read, he shall never quite understand *why*. He grows carried away by the enthusiasm of close friends. A dangerous trait."

"You always said how important it was to spread knowledge of foreign cultures to the educated class," Holmes reminded him. With the curtains drawn, the old professor was lit faintly by the library's wood fire, which in its subdued light was merciful to his crow's-feet. Holmes dabbed his forehead. Ticknor's Iceberg was in fact rather boiling from the always stoked hearth.

"We must work to understand our foreigners, Dr. Holmes. If we do not conform newcomers to our national character and bring them in willing subjection to our institutions, the multitudes of outside people will one day conform *us*."

Holmes persisted, "But between us, Professor, what do you think the chances for Mr. Longfellow's translation to be embraced by the public?" Holmes had such a look of resolute concentration that Ticknor paused to genuinely deliberate. His old age had bought, as a defense to sadness, a tendency to offer the same dozen or so automatic replies to all questions concerning his health or the state of the world.

"There can be, I think, no doubt that Mr. Longfellow shall do something astonishing. Is that not why I selected him to succeed me at Harvard? But remember, I too once envisioned introducing Dante here, until the Corporation made my post a farce . . ." A mist clouded Ticknor's jet-black eyes. "I had not thought it possible that I would live to see an American translate Dante, and I cannot comprehend how he will accomplish the task. Whether or not the ungloved masses will accept it is a different question, one that must be settled by the popular voice, as separate from that of scholarly lovers of Dante. On that bench of judges, I can never be competent to sit," Ticknor said with unrestrained pride that brightened him. "But I grow to believe that when we hold out hope that Dante shall be read widely, we fall prey to pedantic folly. Do not misunderstand, Dr. Holmes. I have owed Dante many years of my life, as Longfellow does. Do not ask what brings Dante to man but what brings man to Dante—to personally enter his sphere, though it is forever severe and unforgiving."

IV

BENEATH THE STREETS that Sunday, among the dead, Reverend Elisha Talbot, minister of the Second Unitarian Church of Cambridge, held a lantern high as he weaved through the passageway, sidestepping the staggered coffins and heaps of broken bones. He wondered whether he required the guidance of his kerosene lantern at all by now, for he had grown quite accustomed to the elaborate darkness of the winding underground passage, his nasal contractions invincible to its unpleasant stew of decomposition. One day, he dared himself, he would conquer the way without a lamp, with only his trust in God before him.

For a moment, he thought he heard a rustle. He spun around, but the tombs and slate columns did not stir.

"Anyone alive tonight?" His famously melancholy voice struck the black air. It was perhaps an inappropriate comment coming from a minister, but the truth was he was suddenly scared. Talbot, like all men who lived most of their life alone, suffered many closeted fears. Death had always frightened him beyond the normal measure; this was his great shame. This might have provided one reason he walked the underground tombs of his church, to overcome his irreligious fear of corporeal mortality. Perhaps it also helped to explain, if one were to write his biography, how anxiously Talbot upheld the rationalistic precepts of Unitarianism over the Calvinist demons of the older generations. Talbot whistled nervously into his lantern and soon approached the stairwell at the far end of the vault, which promised a return to the warm gaslights and a shorter route to his home than the streets.

"Who's there?" he asked, swinging his lantern around, this time certain he had heard movement. But again nothing. The movement was too heavy for rodents, too quiet for street urchins. What the Moses? he thought.

Reverend Talbot steadied the humming lantern at eye level. He had heard that bands of vandals, displaced by development and war, had lately taken to congregating in abandoned burial vaults. Talbot decided he would send for a policeman to look into the matter the next morning. Although what good had it done him a day earlier, when he had reported the robbery of a thousand dollars from his home safe? He was sure the Cambridge police had done nothing about it. He was only glad that the thieves of Cambridge were equally incompetent, neglecting to take the safe's valuable remaining contents.

Reverend Talbot was virtuous, always doing right by his neighbors and his congregation. Except there were times when he was perhaps too zealous. Thirty years before, early in his stewardship of the Second Church, he had agreed to recruit men from Germany and the Netherlands to move to Boston with the promise of a place to worship in his congregation and a well-paying job. If Catholics could pour in from Ireland, why not bring some Protestants? Only the job was building the railroads, and scores of his recruits died of overwork and disease, leaving orphans and derelict widows. Talbot had quietly pulled out of the arrangement and then spent years removing any trace of his involvement. But he had accepted "consultation" payments from the railroad builders, and though he had told himself he would return the money, he didn't. Instead, he locked it out of his mind and made each decision in life with an eye toward thoroughly skewering the wrongheadedness of others.

As Reverend Talbot took drawn-out, skeptical strides in reverse, he stumbled against something hard. He thought for a moment, as he stood transfixed, that he had lost his inner compass and steered into a wall. Elisha Talbot had not been held by another person, or even touched—except for shaking hands—for many years. But there was no doubt now, even to him, that the warmth of the arms wrapping around his chest and removing the lantern belonged to another being. The grasp was alive with passion, with offense.

When Talbot came to consciousness again, he realized, in a brief moment of eternity, that a different, impenetrable blackness surrounded him. The pungent odor of the vault persisted in his lungs, but now a cold, thick moistness brushed against his cheeks and a saltiness he recognized as his own sweat crept into his mouth, and he felt tears streaming from the corners of his eyes onto his forehead. It was cold, cold as an icehouse. His body, deprived of all garments, was shivering. Yet heat ate into his numb flesh and furnished an unbearable sensation never before known. Was it some horrible nightmare? Yes, of course! It was that awful rubbish he was lately reading before bed, of demons and beasts, et cetera. Yet he could not remember climbing out of the vault, could not remember reaching his modest peach-painted clapboard house and fetching water to his washstand. He had never emerged from the world below to the sidewalks of Cambridge. Somehow, he realized, the beating of his heart had moved upward. It was suspended above him, pounding desperately, plunging the blood in his body *down* into his head. He breathed in faint ejaculations.

The minister felt himself kicking his feet in the air madly and he knew by the heat that this was no dream: He was about to die. It was strange. The emotion most distant from him at this moment was fear. Perhaps he had used it all up in life. Instead, he was filled with a deep and raging anger that this could happen—that our condition could be such that one child of God could die while all others went on unbothered and unchanged.

In his last moment, he tried to pray in a tearful voice, "God, forgive me if I'm wrong," but instead a piercing yell burst forth from his lips, lost in the merciless thundering of his heart.

V

ON SUNDAY, the twenty-second day of October 1865, the late edition of the *Boston Transcript* contained on its front page an advertisement offering a reward of ten thousand dollars. Such bewilderment, such halts of clanging carriages at newspaper peddlers' had not been known in what seemed like a lifetime since Fort Sumter had been attacked, when it was certain that a ninety-day campaign could end the South's wild rebellion.

Widow Healey had wired Chief Kurtz a simple telegram to reveal her plans. The use of the telegram made her point, for it was known that many eyes in the police station house would see it before the chief's. She was writing to five Boston newspapers, she told Kurtz, describing the true nature of her husband's death and announcing a reward for information leading to the capture of his murderer. Because of past corruption in the detective bureau, the aldermen had passed regulations prohibiting policemen from receiving rewards, but members of the public certainly could enrich themselves. Kurtz might not be happy, she admitted, but he had failed in his promise to her. The late edition of the *Transcript* was first to carry the news.

Ednah Healey now imagined specific machinations by which the villain might suffer and repent. Her favorite brought the murderer to Gallows Hill, but instead of hanging he was stripped bare of clothes and set on fire, then permitted to try (unsuccessfully, of course) to put out the flames. She was thrilled and terrified by these thoughts. They served the additional purpose of distracting her from thinking about her husband and from the rising hate she felt toward him for leaving her.

Mittens were bound to her wrists to prevent her from scratching off more skin. Her mania had become constant, and clothing could no longer cover the scars of her self-mutilation. In the fit of a nightmare one evening, she had rushed from her bedchamber and desperately found a hiding place for the brooch containing the lock of her husband's hair. In the morning, her servants and sons searched all of Wide Oaks, from under the floorboards and to the skeleton rafters, but couldn't find anything. It was for the best. With those thoughts dangling from her neck, Widow Healey might never have slept again.

Mercifully, she could not know that during those cataclysmic days, during that autumn heat spell, Chief Justice Healey had slowly mumbled "Gentlemen of the jury . . ." again and again as hungry maggots bore by the hundreds through the wound into the quivering sponge of his brain, the fertile flies each birthing hundreds more flesh-eating larvae. First, Chief Justice Artemus Prescott Healey couldn't move one arm. Then he moved his fingers when he thought he was kicking his leg out. After a while his words weren't coming out right. "Jurors under our gentlemen . . ." He could hear it was nonsense but could do nothing about it. The portion of the brain that arranged syntax was being tasted by creatures who did not even enjoy their feeding, but needed it nonetheless. When sense returned briefly during the four days, Healey's anguish made him believe he was dead, and he prayed to die again. "Butterflies and the last bed . . ." He stared at the shabby flag above him and, with the little sense left to his mind, wondered.

The sexton of the Second Unitarian Church of Cambridge had been recording the week's events in the church diary in the late afternoon after Reverend Talbot departed. Talbot had performed a riveting sermon that morning. He spent time in the church afterward, basking in glowing notices from the church deacons. But Sexton Gregg had frowned to himself when Talbot asked him to unlock the heavy stone door at the end of the wing of the church that held their offices.

It seemed as though only a few minutes had passed after that when the sexton heard a rising cry. The noise seemed to come from nowhere and yet was clearly rooted somewhere in the church. Then, almost whimsically, with thoughts of the long buried, Sexton Gregg put his ear to that slate door that led down to the underground burial vaults, the church's bleak catacombs. Remarkably, the noise, though now gone, did seem from its reverberations to originate from the hollowness behind the door! The sexton, taking his clattering ring of keys from his belt, unlocked the door as he had done for Talbot. He sucked in his breath and stepped down.

Sexton Gregg had worked there for twelve years. He had first heard Reverend Talbot speak in a series of public debates with Bishop Fenwick on the dangers of the rise of the Catholic Church in Boston.

Talbot had argued vigorously three chief points in these discourses:

1. that the superstitious rituals and lavish cathedrals of the Catholic faith constituted blasphemous idolatry;
2. that the tendency of the Irish to cluster in neighborhoods around their cathedrals and convents would give rise to secret plotting against America and signaled resistance to Americanization;
3. that popery, the great foreign menace controlling all aspects of the Catholic operation, threatened the independence of all American religions with its proselytizing and its goal of overrunning the country.

Of course, none of the anti-Catholic Unitarian ministers condoned the acts of enraged Boston laborers who burned down a Catholic convent after witnesses said that Protestant girls had been kidnapped and kept in dungeons to be made into nuns. The rioters chalked HELL TO THE POPE! on the rubble. That was less a disagreement with the Vatican than a warning to the Irish increasingly receiving their jobs.

On the strength of his debates and his anti-Catholic sermons and writings, Reverend Talbot was encouraged by some to succeed Professor Norton at the Harvard Divinity School. He declined. Talbot enjoyed too greatly the sensation of entering his crowded meetinghouse on a Sunday morning, coming in from the Sabbath quiet of Cambridge, and hearing the solemn peals of the organ as he stood over the pulpit robed grandly in his plain college gown. Although he had an awful squint and a deep, melancholy intonation with the perpetual character that one's voice assumes when a dead person is lying somewhere in the house, Talbot's presence at the pulpit was confident and his pastorate loyal. That was where his powers mattered. Since his wife had died in childbirth in 1825, Talbot had never had a family and never desired another one, because of the satisfaction brought by his congregation.

Sexton Gregg's oil lamp timidly lost its luster as he lost his courage. When the sexton had to exhale, mist encased his face and tingled his whiskers. In Cambridge it was still autumn, but in the Second Church's underground vault it was the dead of winter.

"Anyone about here? You ain't supposed to . . ." The sexton's voice seemed to have no physical bearing within the vault's blackness, and he shut his mouth quickly. Strewn along the edges of the vault he noticed small white dots. When their number increased, he stooped down to inspect the litter, but his attention was redirected by a sharp crackling from up ahead. A stench horrible enough to subdue even the air of the burial vault reached out to him.

With his hat held in front of his face, the sexton continued ahead between the coffins lining the dirt floor, through the sad slate archways. Gigantic rats scurried along the walls. A flickering glow, not from his own lamp, illuminated the way ahead of him, where the crackling was a continuous sizzling.

"Someone there?" the sexton continued cautiously, gripping the dirty bricks of the wall as he turned the corner.

"Upon the Eternal!" he cried.

From the mouth of an unevenly dug hole in the ground up ahead projected the feet of a man, the legs visible as far as the calf, with the rest of the body jammed inside the hole. The soles of both feet were on fire. The joints quivered so violently that the feet seemed to be kicking back and forth in pain. The flesh of the man's feet melted, while the raging flames began to spread to the ankles.

Sexton Gregg fell on his backside. On the cold ground beside him was a pile of clothing. He grabbed the top garment and batted it against the blazing feet until they were extinguished.

"Who are you?" he cried out, but the man, who was just a pair of feet to the sexton, was dead.

It took the sexton a moment to realize that the garment he had used to put out the fire was a minister's gown. Crawling through a trail of human bones that had risen from the earth, he returned to the tidy stack of clothing and dug through them: undergarments, a familiar cape, and the white cravat, shawl, and well-blacked shoes of the beloved Reverend Elisha Talbot.

As he closed the door to his office on the second floor of the medical college, Oliver Wendell Holmes nearly collided with a city patrolman in the corridor. It had taken Holmes longer to finish his work for the next day than he planned, having hoped to start earlier so he might have time with Wendell Junior before Junior's usual group of friends arrived. The patrolman was searching for someone with authority, explaining to Holmes that the chief of police requested the use of the school's examining room and that Professor Haywood had been sent for to assist in the inquest of an unfortunate gentleman's body that had been discovered. The coroner, Mr. Barnicoat, could not be located—he did not say that Barnicoat was known to frequent the public houses on weekends, and surely would be in no condition to conduct an inquest. Finding the dean's rooms empty, Holmes reasoned that since he was the former dean (Yes, yes, five years at the stern of the ship was enough for me, and at fifty-six, who needs so much responsibility?—Holmes carried on both sides of the conversation), he could rightfully indulge the patrolman's request.

A police carriage carrying Chief Kurtz and Deputy Chief Savage arrived and a stretcher covered by a blanket was rushed inside, accompanied by Professor Haywood and his student assistant. Haywood taught surgical practice and had developed a keen interest in autopsy. Over Barnicoat's objections, the police occasionally asked the professor to the deadhouse for an opinion, as when they found an infant walled up in a cellar or a man hanging in a closet.

Holmes noted with interest that Chief Kurtz posted two state constables at the door. Who would care to intrude at the medical college at this evening hour? Kurtz rolled up the blanket only to the body's knees. This was enough. Holmes had to stop himself from gasping at the sight of the man's bare feet, if that word could still be applied.

The feet—only the feet—had been torched by fire after a smart dousing with what smelled of kerosene. Charred to a crisp, Holmes thought, horrified. The two remaining blobs were protruding awkwardly from the ankles, displaced from the joints. The skin, hardly recognizable as such, was bloated, cracked open by the fire. Pink tissue was pushing out. Professor Haywood bent down for a better view.

Though he'd cut open hundreds of corpses, Dr. Holmes did not possess the iron stomach of his medical colleagues for such procedures and had to back away from the examination table. As a professor, Holmes had more than once left his classroom when a live rabbit was to be chloroformed, beseeching his demonstrator not to let it squeak.

Holmes's head began to spin, and it seemed to him that there was suddenly very little air in the room, with the paltry amount present encased in ether and chloroform. He did not know how long the inquest could last, but he was quite certain he would not remain long without dropping to the floor. Haywood uncovered the rest of the body, introducing the dead man's pained, scarlet face to the room and brushing away dirt from his eyes and cheeks. Holmes allowed his eyes to travel across the whole of the naked body.

He barely registered the familiar face as Haywood stooped over the body and Chief Kurtz delivered question after question to Haywood. Nobody had asked Holmes to remain quiet, and as Harvard's Parkman Professor of Anatomy and Physiology, he could have contributed to the discussion. But Holmes could only concentrate on loosening his silk neck cloth. He blinked convulsively, not knowing whether he should hold his breath to save the oxygen he had already collected or breathe in quick spurts to stockpile the last pockets of air available before the others, whose apparent obliviousness to the dense air made Holmes certain they would all drop to the floor at any moment.

One of the men present asked Dr. Holmes if he was unwell. He had a gentle, striking face and shining eyes, and he looked to be mulatto. He spoke with a touch of familiarity, and in his daze Holmes remembered: The officer who had come to see Lowell at the Dante Club meeting.

"Professor Holmes? Do you concur with the assessment of Professor Haywood?" Chief Kurtz then asked, perhaps in a polite attempt to include him in the proceeding, as Holmes had gone nowhere near enough to the body to make any but the most presumptuous medical assessment. Holmes tried to think whether he had noted Haywood's dialogue with Chief Kurtz and seemed to recall Haywood remarking that the deceased had been alive while his feet were set aflame, that he must have been in a position helpless to stop the torture, and that from the look of the face and the absence of other injuries, it was not unlikely that he had died from shock to the heart.

"Why, of course," Holmes remarked. "Yes, of course, Officer." Holmes stepped backward to the door as though in escape from a deadly peril. "Perhaps you gentlemen could carry on without me for a spell?"

Chief Kurtz continued his catechism with Professor Haywood, and with that Holmes reached the door, the hall, and soon the outside courtyard, taking in as much air as possible in every quick, desperate breath.

• • •

As the violet hour was overtaking Boston, the doctor, wandering through the rows of pushcarts, walking aimlessly past the seedcakes, the jugs of ginger beer, the white-smocked oyster- and lobstermen holding out their monstrosities, could not suffer the thought of his behavior at the side of Reverend Talbot's corpse. Out of embarrassment, he had not yet unburdened himself of the knowledge that Talbot had been killed, had not yet rushed to share the sensational tidings with Fields or Lowell. How could he, Dr. Oliver Wendell Holmes, doctor and professor of medical science, renowned lecturer and medical reformer, shiver so at the sight of a corpse as if it were a ghost in some sentimental set-novel? Wendell Junior would be particularly bemused by his father's chickenhearted stumbling. The younger Holmes made no secret of his feeling that he would have made a better doctor than the elder, as well as a better professor, husband, and father.

Though not yet twenty-five, Junior had been in the battlefield and had seen bodies shredded, whole gaps in his ranks mowed down by cannon fire, limbs dropping off like leaves and amputations, performed with ax-saws, by amateur surgeons while screamers were held down on doors used for operating tables by volunteer nurses splattered in blood. When his cousin asked why Wendell Junior could easily grow a mustache while his own attempt could not move past the earliest stages, Junior had replied curtly, "Mine was nourished in blood."

Now Dr. Holmes mustered all he had ever known about the process of baking the best quality of bread. He summoned all the tips known to him for finding the finest-quality vendors in a Boston marketplace by clothing or demeanor or nativity. He grabbed and squeezed the wares of the vendors harshly, absently, but with the commanding touch of a doctor's hand. His forehead soaked his handkerchief as he dabbed it. At the next provision stall, some horrid older women poked their fingers into the salt-meat. The distractions of the task at hand could not last.

As he reached the stall of an Irish matron, the doctor realized that his tremors at the medical college had been deeper than they had first seemed. It was not caused merely by his distaste for the distorted body and its silent tale of dread. And it was not only because Elisha Talbot, as much a fixture in Cambridge as the Washington Elm, had been done in, and so brutally. No—something in the murder had been *familiar,* so familiar.

Holmes purchased a warm brown loaf of bread and started home. He considered whether he could have dreamt about Talbot's death in some strange brush with prescience. But Holmes did not believe in such bugbears. He must have once read a description of this gruesome act, the details of which then flooded back to him without warning when he saw Talbot's body. But what text would contain such a horror? Not a medical journal. Not the *Boston Transcript*, certainly, for the murder had just happened. Holmes stopped in the middle of the street and envisioned the preacher kicking his flaming feet in the air, while the flames moved . . .

"'*Dai calcagni a le punte,*'" Holmes whispered aloud: From their heels to their toes—that's where the corrupt clerics, the Simoniacs, burn forever in their craggy ditches. His heart sank. "Dante! It's Dante!"

Amelia Holmes centered the cold game pie on the fully set dining room table. She passed some directions to the help, smoothed her dress, and leaned out on the front step to look for her husband. She was certain she had seen Wendell turning onto Charles Street from the upstairs window not five minutes ago, presumably with the bread she had asked him to bring for her supper hosting several friends, including Annie Fields. (And how could a hostess live up to the salon of Annie Fields without everything perfect?) But Charles Street was empty save for the dissolving shadows of its trees. Perhaps it was another short man in a long tailcoat she had seen through the window.

Henry Wadsworth Longfellow tested the notepaper left by Patrolman Rey. He prodded the jumble of letters, copied out the text several times on a separate sheet, anagrammatizing the words at different junctions to form new scrambles, buttressing himself from thoughts of the past. His daughters were visiting his sister's family in Portland and his two sons were traveling abroad separately, so there would be days of solitude, which he relished more in idea than in practice.

That morning, the same day on which the Reverend Talbot was killed, the poet had sat up in his bed just before dawn without the faintest consciousness of having slept at all. It was his usual routine. Longfellow's sleeplessness was not caused by frightful dreams or traumatized by tossing or turning. In fact, he would describe the haze he entered during the night as rather peaceful, something analogous to sleeping. He was grateful that even after the long insomniac watches of the night he could still feel rested at daybreak from having laid himself down for so many hours. But sometimes, in the pale nimbus of the night lamp, Longfellow thought he could see her gentle face staring at him from the corner of the bedchamber, here in the room where she died. At these times, he would jump with a start. The sinking of the heart that followed his half-formed joy was a terror worse than any nightmare Longfellow could remember or invent, for whatever phantom image he might see during the night, he would still rise in the morning alone. As Longfellow slipped into his calamanco dressing gown, the flowing silver tresses of his beard felt heavier than when he had put himself to bed.

When Longfellow made his way down the back stairway, he was wearing a dress coat, with a rose in his buttonhole. He did not like to be at all untidy, even at home. At the bottom landing was a print of Giotto's portrait of the young Dante, with one eye replaced by a blank hole. Giotto's fresco had been painted in the Bargello at Florence but over the centuries had been whitewashed and forgotten. Now only a lithograph of the damaged fresco remained. Dante had sat for Giotto before the pains of exile, his war with fate, had overtaken him; he was still the silent suitor of Beatrice, a young man of medium stature, with a dark, melancholy, thoughtful face. His eyes are large, his nose aquiline, his underlip projecting, with an almost feminine softness in the lines of the face.

The young Dante seldom spoke unless questioned, so said the legends. A particularly pleasing contemplation would preclude attention to anything outside his own thoughts. Dante once found a rare volume in an apothecary's shop in Siena and spent the whole day reading on a bench outside without ever noticing the street festival going on directly in front of him, unconscious of the musicians and the dancing women.

When he had settled in the study with a bowl of oatmeal and milk, a meal he would be content to repeat for dinner most days, Longfellow could not help thinking of Patrolman Rey's note. He imagined a million different possibilities and a dozen languages for the scribbled writing before abandoning the hieroglyphic—as Lowell had branded it—to its place in the back of the drawer. From the same drawer he brought out proof sheets of Cantos Sixteen and Seventeen of *Inferno*, annotated neatly with the suggestions from the latest Dante séance. His desk had remained empty of original poems for some time now. Fields had issued a new "Household Edition" of Longfellow's most famous poems and convinced him to complete *Tales of a Wayside Inn,* hoping to spur new poems. But it seemed to Longfellow that he would never write anything original again, nor did he care to try. Translating Dante had once been an interlude to his own poetry, his Minnehahas, his Priscillas, his Evangelines. The practice had begun twenty-five years ago. Now, over the last four years, Dante had become his morning prayer and his day's work.

As Longfellow poured his second and final cup of coffee, he thought of the report Francis Child had been rumored to have made to friends in England: "Longfellow and his coterie are so infected with the Tuscan malady that they dare classify Milton as a second-rate genius in comparison to Dante." Milton was the gold standard of religious poets for English and American scholars. But Milton wrote of Hell and Heaven from above and below, respectively, not from the inside: safer vantages. Fields, diplomatic as long as nobody was hurt, had laughed when Arthur Hugh Clough had relayed Child's comment in the Authors' Room at the Corner, but it had irked Longfellow quite a bit to hear of the exchange.

Longfellow soaked his quill pen. Of his three finely decorative inkwells, this one he prized most, having once belonged to Samuel Taylor Coleridge and then to Lord Tennyson, who had sent it to Longfellow as a gift to wish him well on the Dante translation. The reclusive Tennyson was one of too small a contingent in that country that truly understood Dante and held him in high esteem, and had known more of the *Comedy* than a few episodes of the *Inferno.* Spain had shown an early appreciation for Dante until strangled by official dogma and bludgeoned by the reign of the Inquisition. Voltaire had initiated the French animosity toward Dante's "barbarity" that continued still. Even in Italy, where Dante was most widely known, the poet had been drafted into the service of various factions fighting for control. Longfellow often thought of the two things Dante must have yearned for the most as he wrote the *Divine Comedy* while sitting in exile from his beloved Florence: The first was to win a return to his homeland, which he would never succeed in doing; the second was to see his Beatrice again, which the poet never could.

Dante wandered about homeless as he composed, almost having to borrow the ink in which he wrote. When he approached a strange city's gates, surely he could not but be reminded that he would never again enter the gates of Florence. When he beheld the towers of the feudal castles cresting the distant hills, he felt how arrogant are the strong, how much abused the weak. Every brook and river reminded him of the Arno; every voice he heard told him by its strange accent that he was an exile. Dante's poem was no less than his search for home.

Longfellow was methodical about mastering his time and set aside the early hours for his writing and the late morning for his personal business, refusing to admit any visitors until after twelve o'clock—except, of course, his children.

The poet sifted through his piles of unanswered letters, pulling close to him his box of autographs written on small squares of paper. Since the publication of *Evangeline* years earlier had broadened his popularity, Longfellow regularly received mail from strangers, most of whom requested a signature. A young woman from Virginia included her own *carte de visite* portrait, on the back of which was written: "What fault can be found with this?" with her address below it. Longfellow raised an eyebrow and sent her a standard autograph without comment. "The fault of too great youth," he considered replying. After sealing some two dozen envelopes, Longfellow wrote a gracious rebuff of another lady. He did not like to be discourteous, but this particular solicitant requested fifty autographs, explaining that she wanted to offer them as place settings for her guests at a dinner party. He was delighted, on the other hand, by a woman relating the story of her daughter running into the parlor after finding a daddy longlegs on her pillow. When asked the matter, the girl announced: "Mr. Longfellow is in my room!"

Longfellow was pleased to find in his pile of new mail a note from Mary Frere, a young lady from Auburn, New York, with whom Longfellow had recently become acquainted when summering at Nahant, where they walked many evenings, after the girls fell asleep, along the rocky shore, talking of new poetry or music. Longfellow wrote her a long letter, relating to her how the three girls ask often after her doings; the girls also beg him to find out where Miss Frere will be spending the next summer.

He was lured away from his letters by the ever-present temptation of the window in front of his writing desk. The poet always expected a revival of creative power with the onset of autumn. His fireless grate was heaped with autumnal leaves that imitated a flame. He noticed that the warm, bright day had waned more quickly than it seemed from inside the brown walls of his study. The window overlooked the open meadows, several acres of which Longfellow had recently purchased, stretching all the way to the gleaming waters of the Charles River. He found it amusing to think of the popular superstition that he made the purchase with a view to a rise in property value, while in fact all he wanted to secure was the view.

On the trees were no longer only leaves but brown fruits, on the bushes no longer blossoms but clusters of red berries. And the wind had a rough manliness in its voice—the tone not of a lover but of a husband.

Longfellow's day settled into just the right pace. Supper over, he dismissed the help and resolved to catch up on his newspaper reading. But after lighting the lamp in his study, he spent only a few minutes with the paper. The late edition of the *Transcript* carried Ednah Healey's startling announcement. The article contained details of the murder of Artemus Healey, which had until then been suppressed by the widow "on the counsel of the office of the Chief of Police and other official persons." Longfellow could read no further, though certain details from the article, he would realize in the next eventful hours, had burrowed into his mind uninvited; it was not the pain of the chief justice that ended Longfellow's tolerance for the story for now so much as that of the widow.

July 1861. The Longfellows should have been at Nahant. There was a cool sea breeze that caressed Nahant, but for reasons nobody remembered the Longfellows had not yet left the fervent sunshine and heat of Cambridge.

A tormenting scream burrowing into the study from the adjoining library. Two little girls shouting in terror. Fanny Longfellow had been sitting with little Edith, who was then eight, and Alice, eleven, sealing packages of the girls' freshly cut curls as mementos; little Annie Allegra slept soundly upstairs. Fanny had opened a window in the unlikely hope for a puff of air. The best conjecture in the days that followed—for nobody had seen precisely what happened, nobody could ever truly see something so brief and so arbitrary—was that a flake of hot sealing wax drifted onto her light summer dress. In a single moment, she was burning.

Longfellow had been at his standing desk in the study, throwing some black sand on a newly inked poem to blot it. Fanny ran in screaming from the adjoining room. Her dress was now all flames, hugging her body like tailored Oriental silk. Longfellow bundled her in a rug and laid her on the floor.

With the fire out, he carried the trembling body upstairs to the bedroom. Later that night, the doctors put her to rest with ether. In the morning, assuring Longfellow in a bold whisper that she could feel very little pain, she took some coffee and then drifted into a coma. The funeral service in the Craigie House library fell on their eighteenth wedding anniversary. Her head was the only part of her the fire had spared, and on her beautiful hair was laid a wreath of orange blossoms.

The poet was confined to his bed that day by his own burns, but he could hear the unrestrained weeping of his friends, women and men, down in the parlor, weeping for him, he knew, as well as for Fanny. He found, in his delusional but alert state of mind, that he could make out individuals by their crying. His facial burns would necessitate his growing a full and heavy beard—not only to conceal the scars, but also because he could no longer shave. The orange discoloring on the palms of his limp hands would last painfully long, reminding him of his failure, before whitening away.

Longfellow, recuperating in his bedchamber, raised his bandaged hands upward. For nearly a week, the children could hear delirious words float into the hall whenever they passed by. Little Annie, thankfully, was too young to understand.

"Why could I not save her? Why could I not save her?"

After Fanny's death had become real to him, after he could look at his little girls again without breaking down, Longfellow unlocked his notepaper drawer where he had once deposited fragments of Dante translations. Most of what he had done as class exercises in lighter times would be of no use. It was food for the fire. It was not the poetry of Dante Alighieri; it was the poetry of Henry Longfellow—the language, the style, the rhythm—the poetry of one content with his own life. As he started again, beginning with *Paradiso,* he was not chasing after a fitting style to render Dante's words this time. He was chasing after Dante. Longfellow tucked himself away at his desk, watched over by his three young daughters, the children's governess, his patient sons—now restless men—his hired help, and Dante. Longfellow found he could barely write a word of his own poetry, yet he could not stop himself from working on Dante. The pen felt like a sledgehammer in his hand. Difficult to wield nimbly, but what volatile power.

Soon Longfellow found reinforcements around his table: first Lowell, then Holmes, Fields, and Greene. Longfellow often said they had formed the Dante Club to amuse themselves during bleak New England winters. This was the diffident way he expressed its importance to him. The attention to defects and deficiencies was sometimes not the most agreeable interaction for Longfellow, but when critiques were harsh, the supper afterward made amends.

Resuming his editing of these latest *Inferno* cantos, Longfellow heard a hollow thud come from outside Craigie House. Trap let out a sharp bark.

"Master Trap? What is it, old fellow?"

But Trap, finding no source for the disturbance, yawned and burrowed back into the warm straw lining of his champagne basket. Longfellow peered outside his unlit dining room but saw nothing. Then a pair of eyes jumped out from the darkness, followed by what seemed a blinding flash of light. Longfellow's heart leapt, not so much at the sight of a face appearing but at the sight of the face, if that is what it was, suddenly vanishing after locking eyes with him, the glass misting under Longfellow's gasp. Longfellow stumbled backward, knocking into a cabinet and sending headlong onto the floor an entire set of Appleton family dishes (a wedding gift, as was Craigie House itself, from Fanny's father). The cumulative shattering that followed echoed riotously, causing Longfellow to throw forth an irrational scream of distress.

Trap pounced and yapped with his entire diminutive might. Longfellow escaped from the dining room to the parlor, and then to the lazy wood fire of the library, where he examined the windows for any further sign of the eyes. He was hoping Jamey Lowell or Wendell Holmes would appear at the door and apologize for the unintended fright and the late hour. But as Longfellow's writing hand trembled, all he could discern out his window was blackness.

As Longfellow's scream rang down Brattle Street, James Russell Lowell's ears were half submerged in his tub. He was listening to the hollow skip of the water, letting his eyelids droop shut, wondering where life had gone. The small window overhead was propped open and the night was cool. If Fanny came in, she would no doubt command him to the warm bed at once.

Lowell had risen to fame when most of the celebrated poets were significantly older than he, including Longfellow and Holmes, who were both around ten years his senior. He had grown so content with the title Young Poet that it had seemed at forty-eight he had done something wrong to lose it.

He puffed indifferently on his fourth cigar of the day, carelessly letting the ashes defile his water. He could recall times only a few years earlier when the tub had seemed much roomier for his body. He wondered at the spare razor blades, now missing, that he had hidden years earlier on the shelf above. Had Fanny or Mab, more perceptive than he allowed himself to believe, surmised the black thoughts that often tingled as he soaked? In his youth, before meeting his first wife, Lowell had carried strychnine in his waistcoat pocket. He said he inherited his drop of black blood from his poor mother. Around the same time, Lowell had put a cocked pistol to his forehead but was too afraid to pull the trigger, a fact of which he was still heartily ashamed. He had only been flattering himself that he could be responsible for so conclusive an act.

When Maria White Lowell died, her husband of nine years felt old for the first time, felt as if he suddenly had a past, something alien to his present life, from which he was now exiled. Lowell consulted Dr. Holmes in a professional capacity about his dark emotions. Holmes recommended punctual retirement by ten-thirty at night and cold water rather than coffee in the morning. It was for the best, Lowell now thought, that Wendell had turned in the stethoscope for the professor's lectern; he did not have the patience to see suffering through to the end.

Fanny Dunlap had been little Mabel's governess after Maria's death, and perhaps someone outside his life would have known it was inevitable that she would assume a position as Maria's substitute in Lowell's eyes. The transition to a new, plainer wife was not so difficult as Lowell had feared, and for this many friends blamed him. But he would not wear grief on his sleeve. Lowell abhorred sentimentality from the bottom of his soul. Besides, the truth was that Maria no longer felt real to him most of the time. She was a vision, an idea, a faint gleam in the sky like the stars fading out before sunset. "My Beatrice," Lowell had written in his journal. But even that doctrine demanded all the energy of the soul to believe in, and before long only the most vague specter of Maria occupied his thoughts.

Besides Mabel, Lowell had fathered three children with Maria, the healthiest of whom lived two years. The death of this last child, Walter, preceded Maria's by a year. Fanny had a miscarriage soon after their marriage and was left incapable of bearing children. So James Russell Lowell had one living child, a daughter, raised forthrightly by a barren second wife.

When she was young, Lowell thought it would be enough to hope Mabel would be a great, strong, vulgar, mud pudding–baking, tree-climbing little wench. He taught her to swim, to skate, and to walk twenty miles a day, as he could.

But the Lowells from time immemorial had had sons. Jamey Lowell himself had three nephews who had served and died in the Union army. That was destined. Lowell's grandfather had been the author of the original antislavery law in Massachusetts. But J. R. Lowell had borne no sons, no James Lowell Juniors to contribute to the greatest cause of their age. Walt had been such a sturdy boy for a few months; he would have been as tall and brave as Captain Oliver Wendell Holmes Junior, certainly.

Lowell let his hands indulge themselves in pulling at the corners of his walrus-tusk mustache, the wet tips curling like a sultan's. He thought of *The North American Review* and how much of his time it swallowed. Organizing manuscripts and submissions was beyond the pale of his talents, and he had formerly left these tasks to his more punctilious co-editor, Charles Eliot Norton, before the latter left for a European journey undertaken for Mrs. Norton to recover her health. Questions of style, grammar, and punctuation in other people's articles—and the pressure of personal appeals from qualified and unqualified friends alike wanting to be published—all robbed from Lowell his head for writing. And the routine of teaching, too, further dismantled poetic impulses. More than ever, he felt the Harvard Corporation was always looking over his shoulder, racking and sifting and pickaxing and hoeing and shoveling and dredging and scratching (and, he feared, also damning) his brain like so many Californian immigrants. All he needed to recover his imagination was to lie under a tree for a year, with no other industry than to watch the dapples of sunlight on the grass. He had envied Hawthorne on his last visit to his friend in Concord, for the rooftop tower he had built himself could only be entered by a secret trapdoor, upon which the novelist placed a heavy chair.

Lowell did not hear the light tread up the stairs and did not notice when the door of the bathroom opened wider. Fanny closed it behind her.

Lowell sat up guiltily. "There's hardly a breeze in here, dear."

Fanny had a troubled spark in her wide-set, nearly Oriental eyes. "Jamey, the yardman's son is here. I asked him the matter, but he says he wishes to speak with you. I've put him in the music room. Poor little thing's short of breath."

Lowell wrapped himself in his dressing gown and took the stairs two at a time. The gawky young man, wide horse's teeth protruding from under his upper lip, idled at the piano as though nervously preparing for a concert.

"Sir, beg your pardon for the bother . . . I was coming along Brattle and thought I heard a loud sound from the old Craigie House . . . I thought to call on Professor Longfellow to check if all was right—all the fellas do say he is such a kind one—but I ain't never met him so . . ."

Lowell's heart raced with panic. He grabbed the boy by his shoulders. "What was the sound you heard, lad?"

"A great impact. A crash of sorts." The young man tried unsuccessfully to demonstrate the sound with a gesture. "The little mutt—uh, Trap, is it?—barking enough to raise Pluto. And a loud shout, I believe, sir. I have never raised the hue and cry before, sir."

Lowell told the boy to wait and rushed to his dressing closet, grabbing his slippers and the plaid trousers to which, under ordinary circumstances, Fanny would state her aesthetic objections.

"Jamey, you shan't go out at this hour," insisted Fanny Lowell. "There have been a rash of garrotings of late!"

"It's Longfellow," he said. "The boy thinks something might be the matter."

She grew quiet.

Lowell promised Fanny to take along his hunting rifle and, with it slung over his shoulder, Lowell and the yardman's son made their way down to Brattle Street.

Longfellow was still rather shaken when he came to the door, and shaken further by the sight of Lowell's gun. He apologized for the commotion and described the incident without embellishment, insisting that his imagination had merely been momentarily agitated.

"Karl," Lowell said, and took the yardman's son by his shoulders again. "You hurry to the police station for a patrolman."

"Oh, that won't be needed," Longfellow said.

"There has been a wave of robberies, Longfellow. The police will check the whole neighborhood and make sure it is safe. Now, don't you be selfish."

Lowell waited for Longfellow to put up more of a fight, but he did not. Lowell nodded to Karl, who sped off to the Cambridge station with a boy's enthusiasm for emergencies. Inside the Craigie House study, Lowell slumped in the chair next to Longfellow and adjusted his dressing gown over his trousers. Longfellow apologized for drawing Lowell out for such a petty matter and insisted he return to Elmwood. But he also insisted on brewing some tea.

James Russell Lowell sensed there was nothing petty about Longfellow's fear.

"Fanny is probably grateful," he said, laughing. "She calls my habit of opening the bathroom window while in the tub 'death by bathing.'"

Even now, Lowell felt uncomfortable saying Fanny's name to Longfellow and tried unconsciously to alter his inflection. The name robbed Longfellow of something; his wounds were still fresh. He never spoke of his own Fanny. He would not write about her, not even a sonnet or an elegiac poem in her memory. His journal did not contain a single mention of Fanny Longfellow's death; on the first entry after she died, Longfellow had copied out some lines from a Tennyson poem: "Sleep sweetly, tender heart, in peace." Lowell believed he understood quite well the reason Longfellow had written so little original poetry over the last few years in his retreat into Dante. If it were his own words Longfellow was writing, the temptation to write her name would be too strong, and then she would merely be a word.

"Perhaps it was just a tourist here to see Washington's house." Longfellow laughed gently. "Did I tell you that one came by the other week to see 'General Washington's headquarters, if you please'? On his way out, planning his next stop I suppose, he asked if Shakespeare did not live in the neighborhood."

They both laughed. "Daughter of Eve! What did you tell him?"

"I said that if Shakespeare has moved nearby I had not met him."

Lowell leaned back in the easy chair. "Good answer as any. I think that the moon never sets in Cambridge, which accounts for the number of lunatics here. Working on Dante at this hour?" The proofs Longfellow had taken out were on his green table. "My dear friend. Your pen is wet at all times. You'll tire yourself out by and by."

"I do not grow at all weary. Of course, there are times I feel it drag, like wheels in deep sand. But something urges me on with this work, Lowell, and will not let me rest."

Lowell studied the proof sheet.

"Canto Sixteen," Longfellow said. "It's due to go to the printer's, but I am reluctant to part with it. When Dante meets the three Florentines, he says, '*S'i' fossi stato dal foco coperto . . .*' "

" 'Could I have been protected from the fire' "—Lowell read his friend's translation as Longfellow recited the Italian—" 'I should have thrown myself down among them, and I think my Leader would have suffered it.' Yes, we should never forget that Dante is no mere observer of Hell; he too is in physical and metaphysical danger along the way."

"I cannot quite find the right version in English. Some would say, I suppose, that in translating, the foreign author's voice should be modified to gain smoothness to the verse. On the contrary, I wish as translator, like a witness on a stand, to hold up my right hand and swear to tell the truth, the whole truth, and nothing but the truth."

Trap began barking at Longfellow and scratched his pants leg.

Longfellow smiled. "Trap has been to the printing office so often he thinks he has translated Dante all along."

But Trap was not barking at the philosophy of Longfellow's translation. The terrier shot into the front hall. A thundering knock sounded at Longfellow's door.

"Ah, the police," Lowell said, impressed with the speed of their arrival. He wrung out his soggy mustache.

Longfellow opened his front door. "Well, this is a surprise," he said in the most hospitable voice he could find at the moment.

"How so?" J. T. Fields, standing on the wide threshold, angled his eyebrows together and removed his hat. "I received a message in the middle of our whist game—on a hand where I had Bartlett beat, too!" He smiled briefly as he hung his hat. "It said to come here at once. Is everything all right, my dear Longfellow?"

"I sent no such message, Fields," Longfellow apologized. "Wasn't Holmes with you?"

"No, and we waited a half-hour for him before dealing."

A rustle of dried leaves advanced toward them. In a moment, the small figure of Oliver Wendell Holmes, his elevated boots crunching leaves by the half-dozen underfoot, swerved up Longfellow's brick footpath in a double-quick march. Fields stepped aside and Holmes sprinted past him into the hall, wheezing.

"Holmes?" Longfellow said.

The frantic doctor noticed with horror that Longfellow was cradling a sheaf of Dante cantos.

"Dear *God,* Longfellow," Dr. Holmes cried. "Put those away!"

VI

After ensuring the door was tightly shut, Holmes explained in rapid-fire speech how it had flashed over him while coming home from the market and how he had rushed back to the medical college, where he found—thank heavens!—that the police had left for the Cambridge station house. Holmes dispatched a message to his brother's whist table to fetch Fields to Craigie House at once.

The doctor grabbed Lowell's hand and shook it urgently, more thankful he was there than he would have admitted. "I was about to send to Elmwood for you, my dear Lowell," Holmes said.

"Holmes, did you say something of police?" Longfellow asked.

"Longfellow, everyone, please—into the study. You must promise to lock away all I am about to tell you in the strictest of confidence."

Nobody objected. It was unusual to see the little doctor so serious; his role of aristocratic jester had long been crystallized—much to Boston's joy and to Amelia Holmes's chagrin. "There was a murder discovered today," Holmes announced in a tenuous whisper, as if to test the house for eaves-droppers or to shield his dreadful story from the crowded shelves of folios. He turned away from the fire, genuinely afraid the talk could go up through the chimney. "I was at the medical college," he finally began, "making headway on some work, when the police arrived to commission one of our rooms for an inquest. The body they brought in was covered with dirt, you understand?"

Holmes paused, not for rhetorical effect but to catch his breath. In the commotion, he had neglected the whirring signs of his asthma.

"Holmes, what has this to do with us? Why did you have me rush over from John's game?" Fields asked.

"Hold," Holmes said with a sharp wave of his hand. He put aside Amelia's loaf and fished out his handkerchief. "The body, the dead man, his feet . . . God help us!"

Longfellow's eyes lit up bright blue. He had not said much but had paid the closest attention to Holmes's demeanor. "A drink, Holmes?" he asked gently.

"Yes. Thank you," Holmes agreed, wiping his watery brow. "My apologies. I hastened here with the speed of an arrow, too restless to ride in a hackney cab, too impatient and fearful of encountering anyone in the horsecars!"

Longfellow walked serenely to the kitchen. Holmes waited for his drink. The other two men waited for Holmes. Lowell shook his head with grave piety at his friend's jumpiness. Their host reappeared with a glass of brandy choked by ice, which was how Holmes preferred it. Holmes grabbed for it. It coated his throat.

"Though a woman tempted man to eat, my dear Longfellow," said Holmes, "you never hear of Eve having to do with his drinking, for he took to that of his own notion."

"Come on, then, Wendell," Lowell urged.

"Very well. I saw it. You understand? I saw the corpse close, as close as I am to Jamey right now." Dr. Holmes closed in on Lowell's chair. "That body had been buried alive, upside down, his feet straight up into the air. And the soles of both feet, gentlemen, were horribly burned. They were toasted to a crisp that I shan't ever . . . well, I shall remember it till nature has tucked me up well under the yearly violets!"

"My dear Holmes," Longfellow said, but Holmes would not pause yet, not even for Longfellow.

"His clothes were off. I don't know if the police had removed the clothes—no, I believe he was found that way by some things they said. I saw his face, you see." Holmes reached for another dose of his drink but found only a trace left. He clamped his teeth onto a piece of ice.

"He was a minister," said Longfellow.

Holmes turned with an incredulous stare and cracked the ice on his back teeth. "Yes. Exactly."

"Longfellow, how did you know about this?" Fields turned, suddenly very confused at a story he still felt had nothing to do with him. "This couldn't have been in any papers yet if Wendell just witnessed . . ." But then Fields realized how Longfellow had known. Lowell realized, too.

Lowell stormed up to Holmes as if to strike him. "How could you know the body had been left upside down, Holmes? Did the police tell you?"

"Well, not exactly."

"You have been searching out a reason for us to stop the translation so that you don't have to worry about Harvard bringing down trouble. It's all conjecture."

"Nobody need tell me what I saw," Dr. Holmes snapped back. "Medicine is a subject none of you have studied. I have devoted the best part of my life in Europe and America to the study of my profession. Now, if you or Longfellow should begin to talk about Cervantes, I should feel my ignorance—well, no, I am respectfully informed about Cervantes, but I should listen to you because you have given your time to the study of it!"

Fields saw how truly nervous Holmes was. "We understand, Wendell. Please."

If Holmes had not stopped for a breath, he would have fainted. "That corpse *had* been put on his head, Lowell. I saw the streaks of the tears and sweat that had rolled up his forehead—hear me: *up* his forehead. The blood was locked in his face. It was when I saw the horror fixed upon the face that I recognized the Reverend Elisha Talbot."

The name surprised them all. The old tyrant of Cambridge mounted on his head, imprisoned, blinded by dirt, helpless to move at all except perhaps to kick his flaming feet in despair, just like one of Dante's Simoniacs, the clerics who accepted money to misuse their titles . . .

"There's more if you need it." Holmes was chewing his ice with great celerity now. "A policeman at the inquest said he was found at the Second Unitarian Church burial ground—that's Talbot's church! The body was covered in dirt, from the waist up. *But there was not a speck below the waist.* He was buried naked, upside down, with his feet sticking up in the air!"

"When did they find him? Who was there?" Lowell demanded.

"For God's sake," Holmes cried. "How could I know such particulars!"

Longfellow watched the thick hand of his leisurely ticking clock slouch for eleven. "Widow Healey announced a reward in the evening paper. Judge Healey did not die a natural death. She believes it was a murder as well."

"But Talbot's isn't just a *murder,* Longfellow! Must I spell out what is as plain as print? It's Dante! Someone has used Dante to kill Talbot!" Holmes cried out, frustration painting his cheeks red.

"You've read the late edition, my dear Holmes?" Longfellow asked patiently.

"Of course! I think so." He had, in fact, glanced only briefly at the paper in the entrance hall of the medical college on his way to prepare anatomical drawings for Monday's class. "What did it say?"

Longfellow found the newspaper. Fields took it and read it aloud. " 'New revelations regarding the uncanny death of Chief Justice Artemus S. Healey,' " Fields read after opening a pair of square eyeglasses from his waistcoat pocket. "Typical printer's error. Healey's middle name was Prescott."

Longfellow said, "Fields, please pass over the first column. Read how the body was found—in the meadows behind the Healey home, not far from the river."

" 'Bloody . . . stripped fully of his suit and underclothes . . . found immoderately swarmed in . . .' "

"Go on, Fields."

"Insects?"

Flies, wasps, maggots—those were the particular insects cataloged by the newspaper. And nearby in the yard of Wide Oaks was found a flag that the Healeys could not explain. Lowell wanted to deny the thoughts that were being passed around the room with the paper, but instead he fell back into a reclining position in the easy chair, his bottom lip quivering as it did when he could not think of what to say.

They exchanged searching glances, hoping there would be one among them smarter than the next who could explain it all away as coincidence with a well-placed allusion or a clever quip, one who could banish the conclusion that the Reverend Talbot had been roasted with the Simoniacs and Chief Justice Healey thrown in among the Neutrals. Every detail further confirmed what they could not deny.

"It fits together," said Holmes. "It all fits together for Healey: the sin of neutrality, the punishment. For too long he had refused to act on the Fugitive Slave Act. But what of Talbot? I have never heard even a whisper that he abused the power of his pulpit—help me, Phoebus!" Holmes jumped when he noticed the rifle leaning against the wall. "Longfellow, why in the land is that out here?"

Lowell was shaken with the remembrance of why he had come to Craigie House in the first place. "You see, Wendell, Longfellow thought he might have seen a burglar lurking outside. We sent the yardman's boy to fetch the police."

"A burglar?" Holmes asked.

"A phantasm." Longfellow shook his head.

Fields stomped on the rug with a graceless leap to his feet. "Well, perfect timing!" He turned to Holmes. "My dear Wendell, you shall be remembered as a good citizen for this. When the policeman arrives, we explain that we have information on these crimes and instruct him to return with the chief of police." Fields had mustered his greatest tone of authority, yet he tapered off with a glance to Longfellow for endorsement.

Longfellow did not move. His stone-blue eyes stared ahead into the richly cracked spines of his books. It was not clear whether he'd remained a part of the conversation. This infrequent, remote look, when he sat silently running his hand through the locks of his beard, when his invincible tranquillity turned cool, when his maiden complexion seemed a bit dusky, put all his friends ill at ease.

"Yes," Lowell said, trying to project something like collective relief at Fields's statement. "Of course we'll inform the police of our suppositions. This shall no doubt prove vital information to the unriddling of such a mess."

"No!" Holmes gasped. "No, we mustn't tell *anyone.* Longfellow," the doctor said with desperation. "We must keep this to ourselves! Everyone in this room must keep the matter dark, as promised, though the heavens cave in!"

"Come, Wendell!" Lowell leaned over the diminutive doctor. "This is not a time to put your hands in your pockets! Two people have been killed, two men of our own set!"

"Yes, and who are we to meddle in such horrendous business?" Holmes pleaded. "The police are investigating, to be sure, and they will find whoever is responsible without our interference!"

"Who are we to meddle!" Lowell repeated mockingly. "There's no chance the police will think of *this,* Wendell! They must be chasing their tails even as we sit here!"

"Would you rather they chase our wild *tales,* Lowell? What do we know of such a matter as a murder?"

"Why did you bother coming to us with this then, Wendell?"

"So we know to protect ourselves! I've done us all a good turn," Holmes said. "This could put us in a dangerous way!"

"Jamey, Wendell, please . . ." Fields stood between them.

"If you go to the police, you can just count me out of this," Holmes added with a treble voice as he took a seat. "Do it over my principled objection and my stated refusal."

"Observe, gentlemen," Lowell said with a demonstrative flick of his hand at Holmes, "Dr. Holmes in his usual position when the world needs him—sitting on his arse."

Holmes looked around the room, hoping someone would speak up in his support, then sank deeper into his chair, meekly removing his gold chain, tangled with his Phi Beta Kappa key, and checking his watch against Longfellow's mahogany clock, half certain that any moment all the timepieces of Cambridge would tick to a dead stop.

Lowell was at his most persuasive when he spoke with soft assertiveness as he did when turning to Longfellow. "My dear Longfellow, when the officer arrives, we should have a note prepared, addressed to the chief of police, explaining what we believe to have discovered here tonight. Then we can put this behind us as our dear Dr. Holmes wishes to do."

"I'll begin." Fields reached for Longfellow's stationery drawer. Holmes and Lowell began their argument again.

Longfellow breathed a small sigh.

Fields halted with his hand in the drawer. Holmes and Lowell shut their mouths.

"Pray, do not leap in the dark. First tell me," Longfellow said. "Who in Boston and Cambridge knows about these murders?"

"Well, there's a question." Lowell was frightened enough to be impolite even to the one man, after his late father, whom he worshipped. "Everyone in the blessed city, Longfellow! One's on the front page of every paper"—he grabbed the headlining page on Healey's death—"and Talbot's will follow suit before the cock crows. A judge and a preacher! You might as well try to lock up the beef and beer as to keep that away from the public!"

"Very well. And who else in the city knows about Dante? Who else knows how *le piante erano a tutti accese intrambe*? How many are strolling down Washington and School Streets peering into the shops or stopping in at

Jordan, Marsh for the latest fashion in hats, thinking to themselves that *rigavan lor di sangue il volto, che, mischiato di lagrime* and imagining the fright of those *fastidiosi vermi*—the loathsome worms?

"Tell me, who in our city—no, who in *America* today—knows the words of Dante in his every work, in his every canto, his every tercet? Enough to even begin to think how to turn the entrails of Dante's punishments in *Inferno* into models of murder?"

Longfellow's study, holding New England's most sought after conversationalists, fell uncannily silent. Nobody in the room thought to answer the question, because the room was the answer: Henry Wadsworth Longfellow; Professor James Russell Lowell; Professor Dr. Oliver Wendell Holmes; James Thomas Fields; and a small cross-section of friends and colleagues.

"Why, dear God," Fields said. "There's only a handful of people who would be able to read Italian, not to speak of Dante's Italian, and, even of those who might make some of it out with a heap of grammar books and dictionaries, most have never beheld a copy of Dante's works!" Fields should know. The publisher made it his business to know the reading habits of every litterateur and scholar in New England and everyone who counted outside it. "That is to say," he continued, "will never behold one until there's a completed translation of Dante to be published in all corners of America . . ."

"Like the one we're working on?" Longfellow held up the proofs for Canto Sixteen. "If we do disclose to the police the precision with which these murders have been drawn from Dante and carried out, whom could they possibly single out with knowledge sufficient to commit these crimes?

"We will not only be their first suspects," Longfellow said. "We will have to be their prime suspects."

"Come now, my dear Longfellow," Fields said with a desperately serious laugh. "Let us get our heads out from under this excitement, gentlemen. Look around the room: professors, leading citizens of the Commonwealth, poets, the frequent hosts and guests of senators and dignitaries, bookmen—who would really think us involved in a *murder*? I do little to inflate our status by reminding us that we are men of great standing in Boston, men of society!"

"As was Professor Webster. The gallows tell us there's no law against stringing up a Harvard man," Longfellow replied.

Dr. Holmes grew whiter yet. Although he was relieved that Longfellow had taken his side, this last comment pierced him.

"I had just been at my post at the medical college a few years," Holmes said, staring ahead glassily. "At first, every teacher and staff hand in the school was a suspect—even a poet like me." Holmes tried to laugh, but it came up dry. "I was put on their list of possible assailants. They came to the house to question me. Wendell Junior and little Amelia were just children, Neddie not more than a baby. It was the worst fright of my life."

Longfellow said calmly, "My dear friends, pray agree, if you can, on this point: Even if the police wanted to trust us, even if they *did* trust and believe us, we would be under suspicion until the killer is caught. And then, even with the killer caught, Dante would be tainted with blood before Americans saw his words, and in a time when our country can bear no more death. Dr. Manning and the Corporation already wish to bury Dante to preserve their curriculum, and this would be an iron coffin. Dante would fall under the same curse in America he did in Florence, for a thousand years to come. Holmes is right: We tell no one."

Fields turned to Longfellow in astonishment.

"We've vowed to protect Dante, under this very roof," Lowell said quietly at the sight of his publisher's tightened face.

"Let us make certain we protect ourselves first, and our city, or there shall be nobody left standing with Dante!" said Fields.

"Protecting ourselves and Dante is one and the same now, my dear Fields," Holmes stated matter-of-factly, tempted by the vague feeling that he had been right all along that trouble would come. "One and the same. It would not be we alone who would be blamed if all this was known but the Catholics as well, the immigrants . . ."

Fields knew his poets were right. If they went to the police now, their standing would be in limbo, if not in actual jeopardy. "Heaven help us. We'd be ruined." He exhaled. It was not the law Fields was thinking about. In Boston, reputation and rumor could do in a gentleman far more efficiently than the hangman. As beloved as his poets were, the public always harbored an unhealthy pinch of jealousy against its celebrities. News of even the slightest association with such scandalous murder would spread quicker than the telegraph could carry it. Fields had been disgusted to see unblemished reputations eagerly dragged through the mire of the streets on the basis of mere gossip.

"They may be getting close already," said Longfellow. "You remember this?" He removed a slip of paper from the drawer. "Shall we take a look now? I think it shall reveal itself."

Longfellow flattened Patrolman Rey's paper with the palm of his hand. The scholars leaned in to examine the scrawled transcription. The firelight gleamed streaks of crimson across their astonished faces.

Rey's *Deenan see amno atesennone turnay eeotur nodur lasheeato nay* stared back at them from under the shadow of Longfellow's leonine beard. "It's in the middle of a tercet," Lowell whispered. "Yes! How could we have missed *that*?"

Fields snatched up the paper. The publisher was not ready to admit he could not yet see it; his head was too dizzied by all that had happened to access his Italian. The paper shook in Fields's hand. He delicately laid it back on the table and drew his fingers away.

"'*Dinanzi a me non fuor cose create se non etterne, e io etterno duro, lasciate ogne,*'" Lowell recited to Fields. "From the inscription over the gates of Hell, this is just a fragment of it! '*Lasciate ogne speranza, voi ch'intrate.*'"

Lowell snapped his eyes closed as he translated:

> "'*Before me nothing was created,*
> *If not eternal, and eternal I shall endure.*
> *All hope abandon, ye who enter.*'"

The leaper, also, had seen this sign appear before him at the Central Police Station. He had seen the Neutrals: *Ignavi.* They swatted helplessly in the air and then swatted their own bodies. Wasps and flies circled their white, naked forms. Gross maggots crawled out from rotted gaps in their teeth, gathering in heaps below, sipping up their blood mixed with salt of their tears. The souls followed a blank banner ahead of them as a symbol of their pointless paths. The leaper felt his own skin alive with flies, flapping up and down with globs of gnawed flesh, and he had to escape . . . at least to try.

Longfellow found his proof for the corrected translation of Canto Three and laid it on the table for comparison.

"Heavens above," Holmes wheezed, clinging to Longfellow's sleeve. "Why, that mulatto officer was at the inquest of the Reverend Talbot. And he came to *us* with this after Judge Healey's death! He must know something already!"

Longfellow shook his head. "Remember, Lowell is the College's Smith Professor. The patrolman wished to identify an unknown language, which we were all too blind at the time to decipher. Some students directed him to Elmwood on the night of our Dante Club session, and Mabel directed him here. There is no reason to believe he knows anything at all of the Dantesque nature of these crimes or that he knows about our translation project."

"How could we not have seen it right away?" Holmes asked. "Greene thought it might be Italian, and we ignored him."

"Thank heavens," Fields exclaimed, "or the police would have been on us right then and there!"

Holmes continued in a refreshed panic: "But who would have recited the portal's inscription to the patrolman? This cannot be an entire coincidence of timing. It must have *something* to do with these murders!"

"I suspect that's right." Longfellow nodded calmly.

"Who could have said this?" Holmes pressed, turning the piece of paper over again and again in his hand. "That inscription," Holmes continued. "The gates to Hell—it comes in Canto *Three*, the same canto where Dante and Virgil walk among the Neutrals! The model for Chief Justice Healey's murder!"

Footfalls multiplied up the Craigie House walkway and Longfellow opened the door for the yardman's son, who rushed in, his obtrusive teeth chattering. Looking out onto the front step, Longfellow found himself facing Nicholas Rey.

"He made me take him along, Mr. Longfellow sir," Karl whinnied, seeing Longfellow's surprise, then looking up at Rey with a sour grimace.

Rey said, "I was at the Cambridge station house on another matter when this boy arrived to report your trouble. A local officer is looking outside."

Rey could almost hear the heavy silence that set in from the study at the sound of his voice.

"Would you come in, Officer Rey?" Longfellow did not know what else to say. He explained the source of his scare.

Nicholas Rey was back among the George Washington troop in the front hall. With his hand in his trousers pocket, he stroked the gobs of paper that had been scattered about the underground vault, still moist from the damp burial clay. Some of the scraps of paper had one or two letters on them; others were smudged beyond recognition.

Rey stepped into the study and surveyed the three gentlemen: walrus-tusked Lowell with his overcoat wrapped around his dressing gown and plaid trousers; the other two in slackened collars and tangled neck cloths. An imposing rifle leaned against the wall; a loaf of bread waited on the table.

Rey rested his eyes on the agitated man with the boyish features, the only one not shielded by a beard. "Dr. Holmes assisted us with an examination this afternoon at the medical college," Rey explained to Longfellow. "In fact, that is the same business which now brings me to Cambridge. Thank you again, Doctor, for your help in that matter."

The doctor jumped to his feet and gave a wobbly bow from the waist. "Not at all, sir. And if you ever are in need of further assistance, please send for me without hesitation," he blurted out humbly, then handed Rey his card, forgetting for a moment that he had been of no help whatsoever. Holmes was too nervous to speak wisely. "Perhaps what sounds like a useless Latin prognosis could help in some small way to catch this killer running about our city."

Rey paused and nodded appreciatively.

The yardman's son took Longfellow's arm and pulled him aside. "I'm sorry, Mr. Longfellow," the boy said. "I didn't believe he was no policeman. He ain't got no uniform or anythin', just a regular day coat. But the other officer there told me the aldermen makes him wear regular clothes so nobody gets mad at him for being a nigger cop and licks him!"

Longfellow dismissed Karl with a promise of sweets on another day.

In the study, Holmes, shifting from one foot to the other as though standing on hot coals, blocked the center table from Rey's sight. There, a newspaper headlined the Healey murder; there, Longfellow's English translation of Canto Three, the model for that murder, was next to it; in between was the scrap of paper with Nicholas Rey's jotting: *Deenan see amno atesennone turnay eeotur nodur lasheeato nay.*

Behind Rey, Longfellow stepped into the threshold of the study. Rey could feel his quick spurts of breathing. He noticed Lowell and Fields staring oddly at the table behind Holmes.

Swiftly, in a motion almost undetectable, Dr. Holmes stretched his arm, snatching the officer's notepaper from the table. "Oh, and Officer," announced the doctor. "Might we return your note to you?"

Rey felt a sudden rush of hope. He said quietly, "Have you . . ."

"Yes, yes," Holmes said. "Part of it, anyhow. We've run the sounds through every language on the books, my dear officer, and I fear broken

English seems our most likely conclusion. Part of it reads"—Holmes took a breath and stared hard, reciting—" 'See no one tour, nay, O turn no doorlatch out today.' Rather Shakespearean, if a bit of balderdash, don't you think?"

Rey glanced at Longfellow, who seemed as surprised as him. "Well, I thank you for remembering, Dr. Holmes," said Rey. "I shall bid you gentlemen goodnight now."

They flocked to the entryway as Rey vanished down the footpath.

"Turn no doorlatch?" Lowell asked.

"It shall keep him from suspecting anything, Lowell!" cried Holmes. "You could have looked more convinced. It is a good rule for the actor who manages Punch and Judy not to let the audience see his legs!"

"It was pretty good thinking, Wendell." Fields patted Holmes's shoulder warmly.

Longfellow started to speak but could not. He went into his study and closed the door, leaving his friends awkwardly stationed in the front hall.

"Longfellow? My dear Longfellow?" Fields knocked gently.

Lowell took his publisher's arm and shook his head. Holmes realized he was holding something. He threw it down. Rey's notepaper. "Look here. Officer Rey forgot this."

They were no longer seeing Rey's notebook paper. It was the cold, carved stone of colorless iron at the summit of the open gates to Hell, where Dante had stopped reluctantly, Virgil pushing him forward.

Lowell snatched the paper angrily and thrust Dante's garbled words into the flame of the hall lamp.

VII

OLIVER WENDELL HOLMES was late arriving at the next Dante Club meeting, which he knew would be his last. He wouldn't accept a ride in Fields's carriage, though the sky over the city was hooded black. The poet-doctor barely heaved a sigh when the spine of his umbrella cracked in the downpour as he slipped on layers of leaves, the last deposit of autumn, in front of Longfellow's house. There was too much wrong in the world for him to spar with physical annoyances. In Longfellow's pristine welcoming eyes there was no comfort, no serenity to impart, no answer to the question tightening the doctor's stomach: How do we go on with this *now*?

He would tell them at supper that he was giving up his role in the Dante translation. Lowell might even be too disorientated by recent events to blame him for desertion. Holmes feared being known as a dilettante. But there was no way he could pretend to read Dante as usual with the aroma of the Reverend Talbot's scorched flesh in the air. He was choking on an indistinct sense that somehow they had been responsible, that they had gone too far, that their readings of Dante each week had released *Inferno*'s punishments into the air of Boston by virtue of their own blithe faith in poetry.

One man had stomped in a half-hour earlier like an army of thousands.

James Russell Lowell. He was drenched, though he had only walked from around the corner; he ridiculed umbrellas as senseless contraptions. The soft fire of cannel coal with hickory logs radiated from the wide chimney, the heat making the moisture on Lowell's beard gleam as though from an inner light.

Lowell had pulled Fields aside at the Corner that week and explained that he could not live in this manner. Their silence to the police was necessary—very well. Their good names had to be protected—very well. Dante had to be protected—also very well. But none of this fine rationale erased a plain fact: Lives were at stake.

Fields had said he would try to arrive at a sensible idea. Longfellow had said he did not know what Lowell imagined they could do. Holmes had successfully avoided his friend. Lowell tried his best to arrange for the four men to meet at one time, but until today they had resisted assembling as resolutely as opposing magnets.

Now that they sat in a circle, the same circle they had been sitting around for two and a half years, there was only one reason Lowell did not shake them by the shoulders one after the other. And that reason was crouched delicately in his favorite green easy chair and weighed down by Dante folios: They had all promised not to tell George Washington Greene what they had discovered.

There he was, brittle fingers unfolded out in front, warming himself at the hearth. The others knew that Greene, in fragile health, could not cope with the violent tidings they possessed. So the old historian and retired preacher, complaining lightheartedly about not having enough time to prepare his thoughts because of Longfellow's last-minute switch of canto assignments, proved the only cheery member this Wednesday evening.

Earlier in the week, Longfellow had sent word to his scholars that they would review Canto Twenty-six, where Dante meets the flaming soul of Ulysses, the Greek hero of the Trojan War. This was a favorite among the group, so there was a hope it would reinvigorate them.

"Thank you, everyone, for coming," Longfellow said.

Holmes remembered the funeral that, in retrospect, had heralded the start of the Dante translation. When news spread of Fanny's death, some Boston Brahmins had felt an involuntary touch of pleasure—something they would never acknowledge or admit even to themselves—upon waking one morning to find that misfortune had visited someone so impossibly blessed in life. Longfellow had seemed to arrive at talent and luxury without the slightest strain. If Dr. Holmes had experienced anything less respectable than complete and utter anguish for the loss of Fanny to that terrible fire, it was perhaps a feeling that might be called wonder, or selfish excitement, that he would dare to aid Henry Wadsworth Longfellow in a time when he needed healing.

The Dante Club had restored life to a friend. And now—now two murders had been committed through the guise of Dante. And, presumably, there could be a third, or a fourth, while they sat by the fire, proof sheets in hand.

"How can we ignore . . ." James Russell Lowell blurted out before swallowing his thought with a bitter glance at the oblivious Greene, who was jotting a note in the margin of his proof sheet.

Longfellow read and discussed the Ulysses canto, not stopping to acknowledge the miscarried comment. His ever-present smile was strained and faded, as though borrowed from a previous meeting.

Ulysses found himself in Hell among the Evil Counselors as a bodiless flame, waving his tip back and forth like a wagging tongue. Some in Hell were resistant to telling Dante their stories; others were unbecomingly eager. Ulysses was above both vanities.

Ulysses tells Dante how after the Trojan War, as an aged soldier, he did not sail back to Ithaca to his wife and family. He convinced the few remaining members of his crew to continue forward past the line that no mortal should cross, to flout destiny and pursue knowledge. A whirlwind rose up and the sea swallowed them.

Greene was the only one to say much on the topic. He was thinking of the Tennyson poem that was based on this Ulysses episode. He smiled sadly and commented, "I think we should consider the inspiration Dante provides for Lord Tennyson's interpretation of the scene.

" 'How dull it is to pause, to make an end,' " Greene said, daintily reciting the Tennyson poem from memory. " 'To rust unburnish'd, not to shine in use! As though to breathe were life! Life piled on life were all too little, and of one to me' "—he paused with a visible mist in his eyes—" 'little remains.' Let Tennyson be our guide, dear friends, for in his sorrow he lived a bit of Ulysses, of the desire to triumph in the final voyage of life."

After eager responses by Longfellow and Fields, old Greene's commentary gave way to high-pitched snores. Having made his contribution, he was spent. Lowell was clutching his proof sheets tightly, his lips clamped together like those of a recalcitrant schoolboy. His frustration at the genteel charade was growing, his temper open to all comers.

When he could find nobody to speak, Longfellow said pleadingly, "Lowell, have you any comments on this *tercet?*"

A white marble statuette of Dante Alighieri stood over one of the study's mirrors. The hollow eyes faced them heartlessly. Lowell mumbled, "Did not

Dante himself once write that no poetry can be translated? Yet we come together weekly and gleefully murder his words."

"Lowell, peace!" gasped Fields, who then apologized with his eyes to Longfellow. "We are doing all we must," the publisher whispered hoarsely in a volume loud enough to chide Lowell but not so loud as to wake Greene.

Lowell leaned forward eagerly. "We need to do something . . . we need to decide . . ."

Holmes widened his quick eyes at Lowell and pointed at Greene, or, more precisely, at Greene's shaggy ear canal. The old man could wake at any moment. Holmes then reeled in his finger and dragged it across his outstretched neck to signal their silence on the subject.

"What would you have us do anyway?" Holmes asked. He meant this to sound ridiculous enough to quash the muted asides. But the rhetorical question arched above the room with the enormity of a cathedral ceiling. "There's nothing *to* do, unfortunately," Holmes murmured now, pulling at his necktie, trying to retrieve his question. Unsuccessfully.

Holmes had unleashed something. This was the challenge waiting to be posed, the challenge that could be avoided only until that moment it was spoken aloud, when all four men were breathing the same air.

Lowell's face flushed red with a burning need. He stared at George Washington Greene's rhythmic respiration and his mind was filled simultaneously with all the sounds of their meeting: Longfellow desperately thanking them for coming, Greene croaking Tennyson, Holmes's wheezing sighs, the majestic words of Ulysses, first spoken from the deck of his doomed ship and then repeated in Hell. All of this rumbled together in his brain and forged something new.

Dr. Holmes watched Lowell clasp his forehead with his strong fingers. Holmes did not know what made Lowell say it at first. He was surprised. Perhaps he expected Lowell to yell and scream to rouse them; perhaps he even hoped for this as one hopes for anything familiar. But Lowell had the exquisite sensibilities of a great poet in times of crisis. He began in a speculative whisper, every tight feature in his red face gradually relaxing. "'My mariners, souls that have toiled, and wrought, and thought with me . . .'" This was a verse from Tennyson's poem, Ulysses stirring his crew to defy mortality.

Lowell leaned in and, smiling, continued with an earnestness that came as much from his iron-trimmed voice as from the words.

"'. . . you and I are old;
Old age hath yet his honor and his toil.
Death closes all; but something ere the end,
Some work of noble note, may yet be done, . . .'"

Holmes was stunned, though not at the power of the words, for he had long ago committed Tennyson's poem to memory. He was overwhelmed at their immediate meaning for him. He felt a tremor inside. This was no recitation: Lowell was talking to them. Longfellow and Fields were also staring with heightened rapture and fear, because they too clearly understood. Lowell had, with a smile as he spoke, just dared them to find the truth behind two murders.

The sheets of cold, howling rain pounded the windows, seeming to land first only on one and then shift their attack clockwise. There was a flash of light, the ancient beckoning of thunder, and a rattling of windowpanes. Before Holmes knew it, Lowell's voice was drowned out for a moment and he was no longer reciting.

Then Longfellow spoke, seamless in picking up the Tennyson poem in the same imploring whisper:

"'. . . the deep
Moans round with many voices. Come, my friends.
'T is not too late to seek a newer world. . . .'"

Then Longfellow spun his head to his publisher with a searching gaze: Your turn now, Fields.

Fields ducked his head at the invitation, his beard nestling in his parted frock coat and rubbing against the guard chain of his waistcoat. Holmes was panicked that Lowell and Longfellow had rushed into the impossible cause, but here was hope. Fields was the guardian angel of his poets and would not lead them headfirst into peril. Fields had stayed clear of trauma in his personal life, never trying to have children and thus sparing himself the sorrow of babes who did not live past their first or second birthday or mothers turned into corpses on their birthing beds. Free of domestic constraints, he devoted his protective energies to his authors. Once, Fields had spent an entire afternoon arguing with Longfellow about a poem that narrated the shipwreck of *Hesperus*. The argument made Longfellow miss his planned excursion on Cornelius Vanderbilt's luxury ship, which hours later burned and sank. Likewise, Holmes prayed to himself, this would be a time when Fields would pester and nudge until the danger passed.

The publisher had to know that these were men of letters, not of action (and getting on in years at that). This madness was what they read about, what they versified on for the nourishment of a longing audience, humanity in shirtsleeves, warriors entering into battles they could never win, the stuff of poetry.

Fields's mouth parted, but then he hesitated, like someone who tries to speak in a troubled dream but cannot. He seemed suddenly seasick. Holmes sighed sympathetically, telegraphing his approval of the demurral. But then Fields, looking with furrowed brow first to Longfellow and then to Lowell, leapt to his feet with a flourish and whispered Tennyson's poem forward. Accepting what was to come:

> "'*. . . and tho'*
> *We are not now that strength which in old days*
> *Moved earth and heaven, that which we are, we are, . . .*'"

Are we strong enough to unravel a murder? Dr. Holmes wondered. Moonshine, that's what it was! There had been two murders, horrendous stuff, but it could not be proven, thought Holmes, recruiting his scientific mind, that any more would follow. Their involvement could be uncalled-for or worse, hazardous. Half of him regretted ever having observed the inquest at the medical college, and the other half regretted having reported his discovery to his friends. Still, he could not stop himself from wondering: What would Junior do? Captain Holmes. The doctor understood life from so many vistas that he could move easily over and under and around a given situation. Junior, however, had the gift and talent of narrow determination. Only the narrow could be truly brave. Holmes clamped his eyes shut.

What would Junior do? He thought about seeing off Wendell Junior's army company in their shiny blue and gold as they left their training camp. "Good luck. Wish I were young enough to fight." And so on. But he had not wished that. He had thanked heaven that he was no longer young.

Lowell leaned toward Holmes and repeated Fields's words with a patient softness and a voice of indulgence rare and heart-wrenching in him. "That which we are, we are."

That which we are, we are: what we choose to be. This calmed Holmes a bit. The three friends waiting for him had agreed. Still, he could walk away with his hands in his pockets. He drew in a deep asthmatic breath, the sort followed by an equally pronounced exhale of release. But instead of completing the motion, Holmes chose. He did not recognize his own voice, a voice composed enough to belong to the noble flame that spoke to Dante. He only barely recognized his reason for the decision that his words, Tennyson's words, carried into existence: "'. . . that which we are, we are, / One equal temper of heroic hearts, / Made weak by time and fate, but strong in will / To strive, to seek, to find,'"—he paused—"'and not to yield.'"

"To strive," Lowell whispered meditatively, methodically, studying the face of each of his companions in turn and pausing on Holmes's. "To seek. To find . . ."

The clock chimed the hour and Greene stirred, but there was no need for further intercourse: The Dante Club had been reborn.

"Oh, a thousand apologies, my dear Longfellow." Greene snorted himself awake over the unhurried peals of the old clock. "Did I miss much of anything?"

CANTICLE TWO

VIII

IN THE LOW WORLD of Boston, much was the same on the week the Reverend Talbot's body was discovered. Unaltered was the triangle of streets where slums and public houses and brothels and cheap hotels had driven out those residents who could afford being driven out, where chalky steam gushed from pipes bending outward from glass- and ironworks, where sidewalks were littered with orange peels and filled with mirthful singing and dancing at odd hours. Hordes of black people were coming and going on the public horsecars: young ladies, laundresses and household servants, whose hair was caught up loudly in colored handkerchiefs, whose dangling jewelry made brash music; a black soldier or sailor in uniform might be seen, still a jarring sight. So too was a certain mulatto walking with notable poise along the streets, ignored by some, laughed at by others, glared at by the more wizened blacks, who in their wisdom knew that Rey was a policeman and thus unlike them in that regard as well as in his mixed race. Blacks had been safe in Boston, were even permitted schooling and public transportation alongside whites, and therefore they kept quiet. Rey, however, would stir up hatred if he made a wrong move or crossed the wrong person in his duties. The blacks had exiled him from their world for these reasons, and because these reasons were right, no explanation or regret was ever delivered to him.

Several chattering young women holding baskets on their heads paused to look sideways at him, his beautiful bronze skin seeming to absorb all the lamplight as he went and carry it away. On the other side of the street, Rey recognized a bulky man loitering at the corner, a Spanish Jew, a notorious thief sometimes brought in for questioning to the Central Station. Nicholas Rey mounted the narrow stairs of his rooming house. His door faced the second-floor landing, and although the lamp was broken, he could see from the shadows that someone was blocking the way to his room.

The week's events had been unrelenting. When Rey first drove Chief Kurtz to see the Reverend Talbot's body, the sexton had ushered Kurtz and some sergeants to the steps that led below. Kurtz had stopped and surprised Rey by turning back. "Patrolman." He had motioned Rey to follow. Inside the burial vault, Patrolman Rey had required a moment of staring at the display, the body stuffed wrong side up into an uneven hole, before even noticing the protruding feet: inflamed, blistered, and distorted. The sexton told them what he had seen.

The toes were ready to break off and fall from the pink, skinless, and misshapen extremities, making it difficult to distinguish between the ends of the feet that held the toes and the ends that, anatomically, would have to be called the heels. This detail—the burned feet, revelatory to the Danteans mere blocks away—was to the policemen merely insane.

"Only the feet were set on fire?" Patrolman Rey asked, squinting, delicately touching, with just a fingertip, the charred, crumbling flesh. He pulled back at the smoldering heat still baking the flesh, half expecting his finger to be singed. He wondered how much heat the human body could conduct before losing its physical form entirely. After two sergeants carried away the body, Sexton Gregg, in his tearful daze, remembered something.

"The paper," he said, grabbing Rey, who was the only policeman left below. "There's bits of paper along the tombs. They ain't supposed to be there. He shouldn't have been there! I shouldn't have let him in!" He wept uncontrollably. Rey lowered his lantern and saw the trail of letters like remorse left unspoken.

The newspapers would speak of both terrible murders—Healey's and Talbot's—so frequently that they became partners in the public mind—often referred to in street corner conversation as the Healey-Talbot murders. Had the public's syndrome exposed itself in Dr. Oliver Wendell Holmes's queer remark at Longfellow's house the night Talbot was discovered? Holmes had been offering his expertise to Rey as nervously as a medical student. "Perhaps what sounds like a useless Latin prognosis can help catch this killer running about our city." The word pierced Rey: *killer.* Dr. Holmes was assuming that the murders were executed by the same party. Yet there was nothing obvious to tie them into one, besides their respective brutishness. There was also the nakedness of the bodies and the neatly folded clothes stripped from them—but that had not yet been reported in the papers when Rey heard Holmes speak. Perhaps it was a slip of the tongue on the part of the conceited little doctor. Perhaps.

The papers supplemented the headlining murders with healthy doses of other senseless violence: garrotings, hold-ups, safe blowing, a prostitute found half-strangled steps away from a police station, a child discovered beaten to a living pulp in a Fort Hill boardinghouse. And there was the strange incident of a vagrant brought for questioning to the Central Station, who was permitted by the police to throw himself to his death through the window, in plain sight of the helpless Chief Kurtz. The papers clamored: "Do the Police have any responsibility for the safety of citizens?"

In the dark well of his rooming house, Rey had come to a stop mid-stair and made sure nobody was behind him. Hand on his billy club underneath his coat, he proceeded. "Only a poor beggar, good sir." The man from whom these words emerged at the top of the stairs was easily recognizable once the angle revealed a pair of stringy trousered legs growing out from iron-heeled shoes: Langdon Peaslee, safecracker, nonchalantly buffing his diamond breast-pin with the wide cuff of his shirt.

"Why, Lily White." Peaslee grinned, showing a beautiful set of teeth sharp as stalagmites. "Have a shake." He grabbed Rey's hand. "Ain't seen that prize phiz of yours since that show-up. Say, this wouldn't be your room up here?" He pointed behind him innocently.

"Hello, Mr. Peaslee. I understand you robbed the Lexington bank two nights ago." Nicholas Rey said this to demonstrate that he had just as much information as the thief.

Peaslee had left no evidence that would survive his lawyers in court and had thoroughly selected and fenced only untraceable valuables. "Why, tell me, who's crack enough these days to heave a bank all alone?"

"You, I'm certain. Have you come to turn yourself in?" Rey said with a serious face.

Peaslee laughed sneeringly. "No, no, dear boy. But I do think these restrictions they put on you—what are they? No uniform, can't arrest white men, so on—well, they are unfair, unfair indeed. But there are some conciliatory factors. You've become such close pals with Chief Kurtz, and that can go a ways to bringing someone to justice. Like the murderers of Judge Healey and

Reverend Talbot, rest their souls. I hear the deacons of Talbot's church are even now building up a subscription for a reward."

Rey started for his room with an uninterested nod. "I'm tired," he said quietly. "Unless you have someone specific who must be brought to justice at the moment, you'll excuse me."

Peaslee twirled a hand into Rey's scarf and held him still. "Policemen cannot accept rewards, but a just citizen, like myself, most certainly would. And if some finds its way to a deserving copper's door . . ." There was no reaction in the mulatto's face. Peaslee showed his irritation, turned off his charm. He pulled the scarf tight like a dropped noose. "This is how that dumb beggar at the show-up met Old Grim, now, isn't it? Listen close. There's a fool about our city who can be made very guilty for killing Talbot, my dear prigger-napper. I'll jacket him easily. Help me see to it, half the boodle will be yours," he said bluntly. "Thick enough to choke a hog, then you can go your own way as you please. The floodgates are opened: Everything's going to change in Boston. The war lined this whole place with money. These times are too dusty to walk alone."

"You'll excuse me, Mr. Peaslee," Rey repeated with stoic equanimity.

Peaslee waited a moment, then lapsed into a defeated laugh. He brushed some imaginary lint from Rey's tweed coat. "Just as well, Lily White. I should've known by looking that you wear a Joseph's coat. It's only I feel sorry for you, my friend, very sorry. The darkies hate you for being white and everyone else hates you for being black. Me, I judge a bloke by whether this is up to snuff." He pointed to the side of his head. "Once I found myself in a country town in Louisiana, Lily White, where you could see the white blood in half the Negro children. The streets were full of hybrids. I imagine you've wished you lived somewhere like that, haven't you?"

Rey ignored him and reached for the latchkey in his pocket. Peaslee said he would do the honors. He pushed Rey's door open with a single arachnid finger.

Rey looked up, alarmed for the first time in their encounter.

"Locks are my game, understand," Peaslee said, cocking his hat boastfully. Then he pretended to surrender, turning up his wrists. "You can bag me for trespass, Patrolman. Oh, no, no, you can't, can you?" A departing grin.

Nothing was missing from the apartment. That last trick had just been a show of power by the great safecracker, in case any unwise notions ever visited Nicholas Rey.

• • •

It was strange for Oliver Wendell Holmes being out with Longfellow like this, to see him pass among the common faces and sounds and wonderful, terrible scents of the streets, as though he were part of the same world as the man driving a horse team with a sprinkling machine to clean the street. Not that the poet had never left Craigie House the last few years, but his outside activities were concise, confined. Dropping off proof sheets at Riverside Press, dining with Fields at an unpopular hour at the Revere or Parker House. Holmes felt ashamed for having been the first one to stumble on something that could so inconceivably break Longfellow's peaceful suspension. It should have been Lowell. He would never think to feel guilt at forcing Longfellow into the bricked-up, soul-confusing Babylon of the world. Holmes wondered whether Longfellow resented him for it—whether he was capable of resentment or whether he was, as he was with so many unsavory human emotions, immune.

Holmes thought of Edgar Allan Poe, who had written an article entitled "Longfellow and Other Plagiarists," accusing Longfellow and all the Boston poets of copying every writer, living and dead, including Poe himself. This was at a time when Longfellow was helping keep Poe alive through loans. An infuriated Fields forever banned any of Poe's writings from appearing in Ticknor & Fields publications. Lowell barraged newspapers with letters conclusively demonstrating the New York scribbler's outrageous errors. Holmes became consumed with the idea that every word he wrote was indeed a theft from some better poet before him, and in his dreams it was not uncommon for the ghost of some old dead master to appear to demand his poetry back. Longfellow, for his part, said nothing publicly, privately attributing Poe's acts to the irritation of a sensitive nature chafed by some indefinite sense of wrong. And remarkably enough to Holmes, Longfellow genuinely mourned Poe's melancholy death.

Both men were carrying flower bouquets under their arms while they traveled into the part of Cambridge that was less a village, more a town. They walked around Elisha Talbot's church, looking with each step for the location of the terrible demise of Talbot, stooping under trees and feeling the ground between grave markers. Several passersby asked for autographs on handkerchiefs or inside hats—often from Dr. Holmes, always from Longfellow. Though the nighttime would have granted welcome anonymity,

Longfellow had decided it would be best if they appeared as mourners visiting the churchyard rather than overdressed resurrection-men looking for a body to steal.

Holmes was thankful that Longfellow had assumed leadership in the days since they had agreed to . . . What *had* they agreed to do, with Ulysses' fiery words singeing their tongues? Lowell said investigating (always with an outward-thrust chest). Holmes preferred calling it "making inquiries," and did so pointedly when speaking to Lowell.

There were of course the few Danteans besides themselves who had to be accounted for. Several were spending time in Europe, on either a temporary or permanent basis, including Longfellow's neighbor Charles Eliot Norton, another former student of the poet's, and William Dean Howells, a young acolyte of Fields's, appointed envoy to Venice. Then there was Professor Ticknor, seventy-four, holed up in his library for three decades of solitude; and Pietro Bachi, who had been an Italian tutor under both Longfellow and Lowell before being fired by Harvard; and all of the past students of Longfellow's and Lowell's Dante seminars (and a handful more from Ticknor's time). Lists would be made and private meetings scheduled. But Holmes prayed they would uncover an explanation before they made fools of themselves in front of people whom they respected and who had, at least up to the present, respected them in return.

If there had been a death scene on the outside grounds of the Second Unitarian Church of Cambridge, it was not to be found today. Then again, if their speculations were accurate and there had been a hole in the yard where Talbot was buried, the church deacons would have covered it up with fresh grass hurriedly. A dead preacher set upside down out front would not provide the best advertisement for a congregation.

"Now, let us look inside," Longfellow suggested, seemingly at peace with their complete lack of progress.

Holmes followed closely in Longfellow's steps.

In the rear vestry, where the offices and changing rooms were located, there was an oversize slate door against one wall, but it did not connect to another room, and there was no other wing of the church.

Longfellow removed his gloves and ran a hand over the cold stone. A bitter chill was behind it.

"Yes!" Holmes whispered. The chill crept inside of him when he opened his mouth to speak. "The vault, Longfellow! The vault down below . . ."

Until three years ago, many of the area's churches had maintained interments underground. There were lavish private vaults that could be purchased by families, as well as inferior public ones housing any member of the congregation for a minimal fee. For years, these burial vaults were considered a prudent use of space for crowded cities with spreading churchyards. But when Bostonians dropped dead by the hundreds from yellow fever, the Board of Public Health declared the cause the proximity of decaying flesh, and new vaults beneath church grounds were strictly prohibited. Families with enough money to do so relocated casketed loved ones to Mount Auburn and other newly fashioned bucolic resting places. But tucked away beneath the ground, the "public"—or poorer—portions of the vaults were teeming. Rows of unmarked coffins, decrepit tombs, subterranean potter's fields.

"Dante finds the Simoniacs within the *pietra livida*, the livid stone," said Longfellow.

A quivering voice interrupted. "Help you, gents?" The church sexton, who had first come upon Talbot roasting, was a tall, thin man in a long black robe, with white hair, or, more accurately, bristles, standing out in all directions like a brush. His eyes appeared to be staring wide, so that he looked permanently like the picture of a man seeing a ghost.

"Good morning, sir." Holmes approached, flipping his hat up and down in his hands. Holmes wished Lowell were there, or Fields, both natural authority mongers. "Sir, my friend and I must request leave to enter your interment vault below if we can trouble you for admittance."

The sexton made no indication of entertaining the idea.

Holmes looked back. Longfellow was standing with hands folded over walking stick, placid, as though he were an uninvited bystander.

"Now, as I was saying, my good sir, you see it is quite important that we . . . well, I'm Dr. Oliver Wendell Holmes. I have a chair in Anatomy and Physiology at the Medical College—really more a settee than a chair, for the breadth of its subjects. Probably you've read some of my poems in . . ."

"Sir!" The squeaky sting in the sexton's voice approximated a shriek of pain when raised. "Do you not know, guvnor, that our minister was of late found . . ." he stammered in horror and then recoiled. "I tended the grounds, and not a soul came in-er-out! Upon the Eternal, if it happened on my watch, I own it was a demon spirit without the need of physical convey'nce, not a man!" He stopped himself. "The feet," he said with a glazed stare, and looked as though he could not go on.

"His feet, sir," Dr. Holmes said, wanting to hear it, though he knew precisely the destined lot of Talbot's feet—knew of it firsthand. "What of them?"

The four members of the Dante Club sans Mr. Greene had collected all newspaper accounts available on Talbot's death. Whereas the true circumstances of Healey's death had been concealed for several weeks before their revelation, in the newspaper columns Elisha Talbot was slain in every conceivable manner, with a sloppiness that would have made Dante, for whom every punishment was ordained by divine love, wince. Sexton Gregg, for his part, did not need to know Dante. He was a witness to and a carrier of the truth. In this way, he had the strength and simplicity of an old prophet.

"The feet," the sexton continued after a long pause, "were aflame, guvnor; they were chariots of fire in the dark vaults. Please, gents." His head hung in dejection, and he gestured for them to leave.

"Good sir," Longfellow said softly. "It is the Reverend Talbot's passing which brings us here."

The sexton's eyes relaxed at once. It was not clear to Holmes whether the man recognized the silver-bearded visage of the beloved poet or whether he was calmed like the wild beast by the stirring quiet of Longfellow's organ voice. Holmes realized that if the Dante Club were to make any progress with this endeavor, it would be because Longfellow had the same celestial ease over people through his presence that he had over the English language through his pen.

Longfellow went on: "Though we possess only our words of promise to prove ourselves to you, dear sir, we ask for assistance. I pray you have faith without further evidence on our part, for I fear we may be the only ones who can truly make sense from what has occurred. More than that we must not reveal."

The vast, blank chasm stewed with mist. Dr. Holmes was fanning away the fetid air that stung his eyes and ears like pepper dust as they marched with small, cautious steps down to the narrow vault. Longfellow breathed more or less freely. His sense of smell was, advantageously, limited: It allowed him the pleasure of spring flowers and other agreeable aromas but screened out anything noxious.

Sexton Gregg explained that the public vault extended underneath the streets for several city blocks in both directions.

Longfellow shone a lantern against the slate columns, then lowered the light to examine the plain stone coffins.

The sexton started to make a remark about the Reverend Talbot but hesitated. "You mustn't think poorly of him, guvnors, if I tell you, but our dear reverend would walk along this vault passage for, well, not for church business, to be candid."

"Why would he come *here?*" Holmes asked.

"A shorter route to get to home. Didn't like it so much, m'self, say sooth."

One of the scattered paper bits, with the letters *a* and *h,* missed by Rey, was trampled under Holmes's boot and sank into the thick soil.

Longfellow asked whether someone else could have entered the vault from above the street, the place where the minister would have exited.

"No," said the sexton definitively. "That door can only be opened from the inside. The police checked all the same, found no tamperin'. And there was no sign that the Reverend Talbot ever reached the door leading to the streets on that last evening he came through here."

Holmes pulled Longfellow back, out of earshot of the sexton. He talked in hushed tones. "Do you not think it significant that Talbot would use this as a shortcut? We must question the sexton some more. We still do not know Talbot's simony, and this could be an indication!" They had found nothing to suggest Talbot was anything but the good shepherd to his flock.

Longfellow said, "I think it is safe to say that walking through a burial vault does not qualify as a sin, inadvisable as it may be, don't you? Besides, we know that simony must do with money—taking it or paying it. The sexton is as enamored of Talbot as the congregation, and too many questions about the minister's habits would only dry up any information he has to volunteer. Remember, Sexton Gregg like all Boston, believes Talbot's death to have been exclusively a product of someone else's sin, not of his own."

"So how did our Lucifer gain his entry here? If the vault exit to the street only opens from the inside . . . and the sexton says he was in the church and saw nobody come through the vestry . . ."

"Perhaps our rogue waited for Talbot to climb the stairs and exit the vault and then pushed him back underground from above the street," Longfellow speculated.

"But to dig a hole deep enough in the ground for a man to fit in so quickly? It seems more likely that our villain ambushed Talbot—dug the hole, waited, and then grabbed him, pushed him in the hole, doused the kerosene on his feet . . ."

Ahead of them, the sexton came to a sudden stop. Half his muscles locked up and the other half shook violently. He tried to speak, but only a dry, mournful whimper emerged. By the extension of his chin he managed to indicate a thick slab sitting on the dirt carpeting the vault floor. The sexton ran back for the sanctuary of the church.

The place was at hand. It could be sensed and smelled.

Longfellow and Holmes together heaved with all their strength, to remove the slab. In the dirt was a round hole, big enough for a body of medium build. Stored by the slab and released by its removal, the smell of burning flesh attacked the air like the stench of rotted meat and fried onions. Holmes smothered his face with his neck cloth.

Longfellow knelt and cupped a handful of dirt from around the hole. "Yes, you are right, Holmes. This hole is deep and well formed. It must have been dug in advance. The killer must have been waiting when Talbot entered. He gains entry, somehow eluding our jittery friend the sexton, and knocks Talbot cold," Longfellow theorized, "positions him headfirst in the hole, and then performs his horrible act."

"Imagine the sheer torment! Talbot must have been conscious of what was happening before his heart gave in. The feeling of your flesh burning alive . . ." Holmes nearly swallowed his tongue. "I don't mean, Longfellow . . ." He cursed his mouth for speaking so much and then for not taking a mistake quietly. "You know, I only meant . . ."

Longfellow did not seem to hear. He let the dirt slide through his fingers. He gingerly lowered the bright flower bouquet to a spot near the hole. " 'Stay here, for thou art justly punished,' " Longfellow said, quoting a verse from Canto Nineteen as though he were reading it from the air in front of him. "That is what Dante cries to the Simoniac he speaks to in Hell, Nicholas the Third, my dear Holmes."

Dr. Holmes was ready to leave. The thick air was nourishing a revolt in his lungs, and his misspoken words had broken his own heart.

Longfellow, however, directed the halo of his gas lantern above the hole, which had been left undisturbed. He was not through. "We must dig deeper, below what we can see of the hole. The police would never think of it."

Holmes stared incredulously at him. "Nor would I! Talbot was put *in* the hole, not *below* it, my dear Longfellow!"

Longfellow said, "Recall what Dante says to Nicholas as the sinner thrashes around in the wretched hole of his punishment."

Holmes whispered some verses to himself. " 'Stay here, for thou art justly punished . . . and keep safe guard over your ill-gotten loot—' " He stopped short. "Keep safe guard over your *loot.* But isn't Dante just displaying some of his not uncommon sarcasm, taunting the poor sinner for his money-grubbing actions in life?"

"Indeed, that is how I happen to read the line," said Longfellow. "But Dante might be read to mean the statement literally. It could be argued that Dante's phrase actually reveals that part of the *contrapasso* of the Simoniacs is that they are buried upside down with the money they immorally accumulated in life below their heads. Surely Dante could have been thinking of Peter's words to Simon Magus in Acts: 'May thy money go to destruction with thee.' In this interpretation, the hole which holds Dante's sinner becomes his eternal purse."

Holmes offered a medley of guttural sounds at the interpretation.

"If we dig," said Longfellow with a slight smile, "your doubts might be proven unnecessary." He extended his walking stick to reach the bottom of the hole, but the pit was too deep. "I cannot fit, I suppose." Longfellow gauged the size of the hole. Then he looked at the little doctor, who was wriggling with asthma.

Holmes stood stock-still. "Oh but, Longfellow . . ." He looked down the hole. "Why did nature not ask me my advice about my features?" There was no point in arguing. Longfellow could not be argued with properly; he was too invincibly tranquil. If Lowell were here, he would have been digging in the hole like a rabbit.

"Ten to one I crack a fingernail."

Longfellow nodded appreciatively. The doctor pinched his eyes closed and slid feet first down the hole. "It is too narrow. I cannot bend down. I do not think I can squeeze myself in to dig."

Longfellow helped Holmes climb out of the hole. The doctor reentered the narrow opening, this time headfirst, with Longfellow holding on to his gray trousers at the ankles. The poet had the easy grasp of a puppet master.

"Careful, Longfellow! Careful!"

"You can see well enough?" asked Longfellow.

Holmes barely heard him. He raked at the earth with his hands, the moist dirt rising under his fingernails, at once sickeningly warm and cold and hard as ice. The worst was the odor, the festering stench of burning flesh that had been preserved in the tight abyss. Holmes tried holding his breath, but this tactic, coupled with his heaving asthma, made his head feel light, as if it might drift off like a balloon.

He was where the Reverend Talbot had been; upside down, like him. But instead of punishing fire at his feet he felt the unflinching hands of Mr. Longfellow.

Longfellow's muffled voice floated down, a concerned question. The doctor could not hear inside his vague sensation of faintness and wondered idly whether a loss of consciousness would cause Longfellow to release his ankles and if he, in the meantime, might send himself tumbling through the core of the earth. He suddenly felt the danger they had put themselves in by trying to fight a book. The floating pageant of thoughts seemed to go on endlessly before the doctor hit something with his hands.

With the feel of a material object, hard clarity returned. A piece of clothing of some sort. No: a bag. A glazed cloth bag.

Holmes shuddered. He tried to speak, but the stench and the dirt were terrible obstacles. For a moment he was frozen in panic, then sanity returned and he kicked his legs frantically.

Longfellow, understanding this was a signal, lifted his friend's body from the cavity. Holmes gasped for air, spitting and sputtering as Longfellow tended to him solicitously.

Holmes wriggled to his knees. "See what it is, for God's sake, Longfellow!" Holmes pulled the drawstring wrapped around the discovery and tore open the dirt-encrusted pouch.

Longfellow watched as Dr. Holmes released a thousand dollars of legal-tender notes over the hard burial-vault ground.

And keep safe guard over your ill-gotten loot . . .

At grand Wide Oaks, the estate of the Healey family for three generations, Nell Ranney led two callers through the long entrance hall. They were strangely withdrawn, their bodies forcibly businesslike but their eyes rapid and mobile. Making them stand out even more in the maid's mind were their fashions, for two such outlandishly conflicting styles were rarely seen.

James Russell Lowell, with a short beard and drooping mustache, wore a rather shabby double-breasted sack coat, an unbrushed silk hat made into a mockery by the casual suit, and in his necktie, done up in a sailor-knot, a type of pin that was no longer fashionable in Boston. The other man, whose massive russet beard cascaded in thick wiry rolls, removed his gloves, which were of a violent color, and pocketed them in his impeccably tailored Scottish tweed frock coat, below which was tightly strung, around his green-vested belly, like a Christmas ornament, a sparkling gold watch chain.

Nell was slow to leave the room even while Richard Sullivan Healey, the eldest son of the chief justice, greeted his two literary guests.

"Forgive my chambermaid's behavior," Healey said after ordering Nell Ranney away. "She was the one who found Father's body and took him inside the house, and since then, I'm afraid she examines every person as though he could be responsible. We worry that she imagines almost as many demonish things as Mother does these days."

"We were hoping to see dear Mrs. Healey this morning if you please, Richard," said Lowell very politely. "Mr. Fields thought we might discuss with her a book of memorial tributes to the chief justice that could be made up by Ticknor and Fields." It was customary for relatives, even distant cousins, to make personal calls to the family of the recently deceased, but the publisher required a pretense.

Richard Healey bunched his bulky mouth into an amiable curve. "I fear a visit with her won't be possible, cousin Lowell. Today is one of her bad days. She is confined to bed."

"Why, do not say she is ill." Lowell leaned forward with a trace of morbid curiosity.

Richard Healey hesitated with a series of heavy blinks. "Not physically, or so according to the doctors. But she has developed a mania that I fear has worsened over the last weeks, so it may as well be physical. She feels a constant presence on her. Pardon me to speak vulgarly, gentlemen, but a crawling across her very flesh for which she insists she must scratch and dig into her skin, no matter how many diagnose imagination as the culprit."

"Is there anything we might do to assist her, my dear Healey?" asked Fields.

"Find Father's murderer." Healey chuckled sadly. He noticed with some unease that the two men responded to this with steely looks.

Lowell wished to see where the body of Artemus Healey had been discovered. Richard Healey balked at this strange request, but attributing Lowell's eccentricities to his poetic sensibilities, he escorted the two visitors outside. They went out the back doors of the mansion, past the flower gardens and into the meadows that led down to the riverbank. Healey noticed that James Russell Lowell walked with a surprisingly quick, athletic stride for a poet.

A strong wind blew particles of fine-grain sand into Lowell's beard and mouth. With the rough taste on his tongue, a catch in his throat, and the image of Healey's death in his mind, Lowell was transported by a vivid idea.

The Neutrals of Dante's third canto choose neither good nor evil and thus are despised by Heaven and Hell alike. So they are placed in an antechamber, not even Hell proper, and here these cowardly shades float naked following a blank banner, for they had refused to follow a course of action in life. They are stung incessantly by gadflies and wasps, their blood mingles with the salt of their tears, and all this is mopped up at their feet by loathsome worms. This putrid flesh gives rise to more flies and worms. Flies, wasps, and maggots were the three types of insects found on Artemus Healey's body.

To Lowell, it showed something about their killer that made him real.

"Our Lucifer knew how to transport these insects," Lowell had said.

It had been a gathering at Craigie House the first morning of their investigation, the small study inundated with newspapers and their fingers spotted with ink and blood from turning too many pages. Fields, reviewing the notes Longfellow had been compiling in a journal, wanted to know why Lucifer, as Lowell had named their adversary, would choose Healey for the Neutrals.

Lowell pulled thoughtfully on one of his walrus tusks. He was in full pedagogical mode when his friends became his audience. "Well, Fields, the only shade Dante singles out in this group of the Lukewarm, or 'Neutrals,' is the one who made the great refusal, he says. This must be Pontius Pilate, for he made the greatest refusal—the most terrible act of neutrality in Christian history—when he neither authorized nor stopped the crucifixion of the Savior. Judge Healey, likewise, was asked to deal a grave blow to the Fugitive Slave Act but instead did nothing at all. He sent the escaped slave Thomas Sims, barely a boy, back to Savannah, where he was whipped until he bled and then paraded with his wounds before the town. And old Healey growled all the while that it was not his place to overturn Congress's law. No! In the name of God, it was the place of us all."

"There is no known solution to the puzzle of this *gran rifuto*, the great refusal. Dante does not give a name," Longfellow chimed in, brushing away the thick smoke tail from Lowell's cigar.

"Dante cannot give a name to the sinner," insisted Lowell passionately. "These shades who ignored life, 'who never were alive,' as Virgil says, must be ignored in death, pestered without end by the most insignificant vile creatures. That is their *contrapasso*, their eternal punishment."

"A Dutch scholar has suggested this figure is not Pontius Pilate, my dear Lowell, but rather the young man in Matthew 19:22 who is offered eternal life and refuses it," said Longfellow. "Mr. Greene and I both favor reading the great refusal as having been made by Pope Celestine the Fifth, another man who took a neutral path by turning down the papal throne, giving way to the rise of the corrupt Pope Boniface, who led ultimately to Dante's exile."

"That is too much confining Dante's poem to the borders of Italy!" protested Lowell. "Typical of our dear Greene. This is Pilate. I can almost see him before us scowling as Dante must have."

Fields and Holmes had remained silent during this exchange. Now Fields said kindly but reproachfully that their work must not become a club session. They had to find a better way to understand these murders, and for that they would have to not merely read the cantos that gave rise to the deaths but cross *into* them.

At that moment, Lowell was scared for the first time of what might come of all this. "Well, what do you suggest?"

"We must see firsthand," Fields said, "where Dante's visions came to life."

Now, making his way through the Healey estate, Lowell grabbed his publisher's arm. " '*Come la rena quando turbo spira*,' " he whispered.

Fields did not understand. "Say again, Lowell?"

Lowell sped ahead and stopped where the dark dirt lining gave way to a circle of smooth, light sand. He bent down. "Here!" he said triumphantly.

Richard Healey, trailing slightly behind, said, "Why, yes." When his mind caught up, he looked flabbergasted. "How did you know that, cousin? How did you know this is where my father's body was found?"

"Oh," Lowell said disingenuously. "It was a question. You seemed to be slowing your walk, so I asked, 'Is it here?' Was he not slowing?" He turned to Fields for help.

"I believe so, Mr. Healey." Fields, puffing for breath, nodded eagerly.

Richard Healey did not think he had been slowing. "Ah well, the answer then is yes," he said, making a point not to hide the fact that he was impressed with, and wary of, Lowell's intuition. "This is precisely where it happened, cousin. At the most demonish ugly portion of our yard, too," he said bitterly. It was the one patch in the meadow where nothing at all could grow.

Lowell traced his finger in the sand. "It was here," he said as though caught in a trance. For the first time, Lowell began to feel real and quickening sympathy for Healey. Here he had been sprawled naked and left to be devoured. The worst part was that he had met an end he would never understand, even in the ever after, nor would his wife or his sons.

Richard Healey thought Lowell was on the verge of tears. "He always kept a soft place in his heart for you, cousin," he said, and knelt beside Lowell.

"What?" Lowell demanded, his sympathy quickly broken.

Healey recoiled at the brusque response. "The chief justice. You were one of his favorite relations. Oh, he read your poetry with great praise and admiration. And whenever the new number of *The North American Review* would come, he would fill his pipe and read it from beginning to end. He said he felt you had a higher sense for things of truth."

"He did?" Lowell asked with some bewilderment.

Lowell avoided his publisher's smiling eyes and muttered a strained compliment about the chief justice's fine judgment.

When they returned to the house, a hired man appeared with a bundle from the post office. Richard Healey excused himself.

Fields pulled Lowell aside quickly. "How the devil did you know where Healey was killed, Lowell? We had not discussed that in our meetings."

"Well, any decent Dantean would savor the proximity of the Charles River to the Healeys' yard. Remember, the Neutrals are found only a few rods from Acheron, the first river of Hell."

"Yes. But the newspaper reports were not at all specific as to *where* in the yard he was found."

"The newspapers were not fit to light a cigar on." Lowell balked, delaying his answer to enjoy Fields's anticipation. "It was the *sand* that led me."

"The sand?"

"Yes, yes. '*Come la rena quando turbo spira.*' Remember your Dante," he rebuked Fields. "Imagine entering the circle of Neutrals. What do we see as we look upon the mass of sinners?"

Fields was a material reader and tended to recall quotes by page numbers, the weight of paper, the layout of the type, the smell of the calf leather. He could feel the gilded corners of his edition of Dante graze his fingers. " 'Accents of anger,' "—Fields sounded out the poetry carefully as he translated in his mind—" 'words of agony, and voices high and hoarse . . .' " He could not remember. What he would give to remember what was next, to understand whatever it was Lowell now knew that made the situation less uncontrollable. He had brought along a pocket edition of Dante in Italian and began thumbing through.

Lowell pulled this away. "Further along, Fields! '*Facevano un tumulto, il qual s'aggira sempre in quell' aura sanza tempo tinta, come la rena quando turbo spira*': 'Made up a tumult that goes whirling on / Forever in that dark and timeless air, / Even as the sand doth, when the whirlwind breathes.' "

"So . . ." Fields digested this.

Lowell exhaled impatiently. "The meadows behind the house are largely billowing grass, or of dirt and rock. But a very different, fine grain of loose sand was blowing in our faces, so I followed it. The punishment of the Neutrals occurs in Dante's Hell accompanied by a tumult *like sand when a whirlwind blows.* That metaphor of loose sand is not idle language, Fields! It is the emblem of the shifting and unstable minds of these sinners, who chose to do nothing when they had the power to act and so in Hell lose that power!"

"Hang it, Jamey!" Fields said a little too loudly. The chambermaid was running a feather duster along an adjacent wall. Fields didn't notice this. "Hang it all! Sand like a whirlwind! The three types of insects, the flag, the nearby river, that's quite enough. But the sand? If our fiend can stage even such a minute metaphor of Dante's into his acts . . ."

Lowell nodded somberly. "He truly is a Dantean," he said with a tinge of admiration.

"Sirs?" Nell Ranney appeared next to the poets, and they both jumped back.

Lowell demanded ferociously to know whether she had been listening.

She shook her sturdy head in protest. "No, good sir, I vow it. But I wonder if . . ." She looked over one shoulder nervously, then the other. "You gentlemen are different than the others who come to pay their respects. The way you've looked over the house . . . and the yard where . . . Won't you come back another time? I must . . ."

Richard Healey returned and, in mid-sentence, the chambermaid crossed over to the other side of the massive entrance hall, master of the household art of disappearance.

He sighed heavily, deflating half the bulk of his large barrel chest. "Since the posting of our reward, each morning I am taken in by the foolish revival of hope, leaping headfirst into the letters, truly thinking somewhere the truth waits to be shared." He moved to the fireplace and tossed in the latest pile. "I can't say whether people are cruel or merely crazy."

"Pray, my dear cousin," said Lowell. "Do not the police have any information that can assist you?"

"The venerated Boston police. Might I tell you, cousin Lowell. They brought in every demonish criminal they could find to the station house, and do you know what came of it?"

Richard was actually waiting for an answer. Lowell replied, hoarse with suspense, that he did not.

"Well, I'll tell you then. One of them jumped out a window to his death. Can you imagine? The mulatto officer who supposedly tried to save him said something of him whispering words that could not be understood."

Lowell sprang forward and grabbed Healey as though to shake more from him. Fields yanked Lowell's coat. "A mulatto officer, you say?" Lowell demanded.

"The venerated Boston police," Richard repeated with restrained bitterness. "We would hire a private detective," Healey said, frowning, "but they are nearly as demonish corrupt as the city's."

Moans came from a room above, and Roland Healey ran halfway down the stairs. He told Richard that their mother was having another fit.

Richard broke away. Nell Ranney started toward Lowell and Fields, but Richard Healey noticed this on his way up. He leaned over the wide banister and commanded her. "Nell, finish the work in the basement, won't you." He waited until she had descended before continuing upstairs.

"So Patrolman Rey was investigating Healey's murder when he heard the whisper," Fields said when he and Lowell were alone.

"And now we know who it was that whispered—whoever died that day at the station house." Lowell thought for a moment. "We must see what has frightened that chambermaid so."

"Mind, Lowell. You'll have her in hot water if the Healey boy sees you." Fields's concern held Lowell in place. "He said she's been imagining things, in any case."

Just then, there was a loud bang from the nearby kitchen. Lowell made sure they were still alone and then headed for the kitchen door. He knocked lightly. No answer. He pushed in the door and could hear a residual noise to the side of the stove: the vibration of the dumbwaiter. It had just bounced up from the basement. He opened the wood-paneled door to the dumbwaiter car. It was empty but for a piece of paper.

He hurried past Fields.

"What is it? What's the matter?" Fields asked.

"We cannot call that a dumb waiter. I need to find the study. You stay and watch, make certain the Healey boy doesn't return yet," Lowell said.

"But, Lowell!" Fields said. "What shall I do if he comes?"

Lowell did not answer. He handed the publisher the note.

The poet rushed through the halls, peering into open doors until he saw one blocked by a settee. Pushing it out of the way, he stepped lightly inside. The room had been cleaned, but just barely, as though in the middle of the process it had become too painful a prospect for Nell Ranney, or one of the younger servants, to stay. And not just because this was where Healey had died but because of the memories of Judge Healey that lived on, sustained in the fragrance of old book leather.

From above, Lowell could hear Ednah Healey's moaning climb to a terrible crescendo, and he tried to ignore that they were in a deadhouse all around.

Left standing in the hall, Fields read the note written by Nell Ranney: *They tell me I must keep this to myself, but I cannot, and know not who to tell. When I took Judge Healey into his study, he groaned in my arms before dying. Won't someone help?*

"Oh good Lord!" Fields involuntarily crumbled the note. "He was still alive!"

In the study, Lowell knelt down and put his head close to the floor. "You were still alive," he whispered. "The great refuser. That's why you were done in." He broke it to Artemus Healey gently. "What did Lucifer say to you? You were trying to tell your maid something when she found you. Or were you trying to ask something?" He saw specks of blood still on the floor. He saw something else along the edges of the rug: squashed wormlike maggots, strange insect parts Lowell did not recognize, the wings and trunks of a few of the fire-eyed insects Nell Ranney had torn to pieces over the body of Judge Healey. He rummaged through Healey's overflowing desk until he found a pocket lens and passed it over the insects. They, too, were traced with his blood.

Suddenly, from underneath piles of paper behind the desk, four or five fire-eyed flies shot out and bolted in a line toward Lowell.

He gasped foolishly and stumbled over a heavy chair, banged his leg hard against a cast-iron umbrella stand and fell over.

Lowell, with a thirst for revenge, brought down a ponderous law book methodically against each of the flies. "Do not think you can scare off a Lowell." Then he felt a slight tingle above his ankle. A fly had slipped inside, and when Lowell lifted his pants leg, the fly, disoriented, twisted out and tried to get away. Lowell smashed it into the rug with his boot heel with childish pleasure. That was when he noticed a red abrasion just above his ankle where he had hit the umbrella stand.

"Damn you," he said to the dead infantry of flies. He stopped cold, noticing how the heads of the flies seemed to have the expressions of dead men.

Fields murmured from outside to hurry. Lowell, breathing in irregular spurts, ignored the warnings until footsteps and voices could be heard from above.

Lowell took out his handkerchief, embroidered with JRL by Fanny Lowell, and scooped up the insects he had just killed, as well as the other insect parts he could find. Stuffing the cargo into his coat, he ran out of the study. Fields helped him wheel the settee back into place as the voices of his beleaguered cousins grew closer.

The publisher was parched for knowledge. "Well? Well, Lowell? Did you find anything?"

Lowell patted the handkerchief in his pocket. "Witnesses, my dear Fields."

IX

THE WEEK AFTER Elisha Talbot's funeral, every minister in New England had preached an impassioned eulogy to his fallen peer. The following Sunday, the sermons focused on the commandment not to murder. When neither Talbot's nor Healey's murder seemed any closer to being resolved, Boston's clergymen preached on every sin committed since before the war—culminating with the force of the Last Judgment in tirades against the police department's futile work, with a mesmerizing spirit that would have made Talbot, the old tyrant of the Cambridge pulpit, tear up with pride.

Newspapermen asked how the murders of two leading citizens could happen without consequence. Where had the money gone that the aldermanic council had voted to improve police efficiency? To flashy silver numbers on the officers' uniforms, said one newspaper sardonically. Why had the city approved Kurtz's petition for policemen to be permitted to carry firearms if they could not find criminals on which to use them?

Nicholas Rey read with interest these and other critiques from his desk at the Central Station. In fact, the police department was making some real improvements. Fire-alarm bells were arranged so as to call the entire police force, or some part, to any section of the city. The chief had also ordered sentinels and scouts to deliver constant reports back to the Central Station, with all policemen ready for duty at the smallest sign of a potential problem.

Kurtz privately asked Patrolman Rey for his assessment of the murders. Rey considered the situation. He had the rare gift in a man of allowing himself to be silent before speaking, so that he said just what he meant. "When a soldier was caught trying to desert in the army, the whole division was ordered into a field, where there was an open grave and a coffin beside it. The deserter would be marched before us with a chaplain at his side and ordered to sit on the coffin, where he was blindfolded and his hands and feet bound. A firing squad of his own men would line up and wait for the command. Ready, aim . . . With *fire,* he would fall dead into the coffin and be buried on the spot, with no marker left in the ground. We would shoulder arms back to camp."

"Healey and Talbot were done in as examples of some kind?" Kurtz seemed skeptical.

"The deserter could as easily have been shot in the brigadier general's tent or in the woods, or been sent to a court-martial. The public performance was to show us that the deserter would be abandoned, just as he abandoned our ranks. Slave masters used similar tactics to make an example of slaves who tried to escape. The fact that Healey and Talbot were murdered might be secondary. First and foremost, we are dealing with punishments of these men. We are meant to fall in line and observe."

Kurtz was fascinated but not won over. "Just so. Punishments by whom, Patrolman? And for what errors? If someone did want us to learn from these acts, wouldn't it make sense they would do it in a way we could understand? The naked body left under a flag. The feet on fire. No sense in it at all!"

They must make sense to someone though, Rey thought. He and Kurtz might not be the ones being spoken to.

"What do you know of Oliver Wendell Holmes?" Rey asked Kurtz during another conversation as he was escorting the police chief down the steps of the State House to the waiting carriage.

"Holmes." Kurtz shrugged, indifferent. "Poet and doctor. Social gadfly. He was a friend of old Professor Webster's before Webster was hung. One of the last to accept Webster's guilt. Wasn't much help at the inquest of Talbot, though."

"No, he wasn't," Rey said, thinking about Holmes's nervousness at the sight of Talbot's feet. "I believe he was not well, that he suffers from asthma."

"Yes—asthma of the mind," Kurtz said.

After Talbot's body was discovered, Rey had shown Chief Kurtz the two dozen bits of paper he had picked up from the ground near Talbot's vertical grave. They were tiny squares, each one no bigger than a carpet tack and each containing at least one typeset printed letter, with some showing barely discernible print on the reverse side. Some were smudged beyond recognition by the constant moisture in the vault. Kurtz wondered at Rey's interest in the litter. This formed a general dent in his confidence in his mulatto patrolman.

But Rey laid them out carefully on a table. These scraps glowed with importance, and he was certain they signified something, as certain as he had been of the leaper's whisper. He could identify the contents of twelve of the bits: *e, di, ca, t, I, vic, B, as, im, n, y,* and another *e.* One of the smudged bits contained the letter *g,* although, in truth, it could just as easily have been *q.*

When Rey was not transporting Chief Kurtz to interviews with acquaintances of the deceased or to meetings with station captains, he would steal some free minutes to remove the bits from his trouser pocket and sprinkle the letters over a table. Sometimes he could make words, and he kept track in a memorandum book of the phrases that arose. He closed his gold-tinted eyes tight, opening them to double size with the unconscious expectation that the letters would string together on their own to explain what had happened or what should be done, like the dial-plates of the spiritualists, which, it was claimed, spelled out the words of the dead when operated by a sufficiently talented medium. One afternoon, Rey placed the station-house leaper's final words, at least as the patrolman had transcribed them, amid the new jumble of letters, hoping that the two lost voices would in some way commune.

He had a favorite grouping for the loose bits of letters: *I cant die as im . . .* Rey always stalled at that point, but wasn't there something to it? He tried one of the others: *Be vice as I . . .* What to do with that torn piece with *g* or *q?*

Central Station was flooded daily with letters of such spirited conviction that they might have been thought to clear up all questions had they shown the smallest trace of credibility. Chief Kurtz assigned Rey the task of reviewing this correspondence, in part to get him away from the "litter."

Five people claimed to have seen Chief Justice Healey at the Music Hall a week after the discovery of his wasted body. Rey tracked down the thunderstruck fellow in question by his season-ticket seat number: He was a Roxbury carriage painter with a mass of untamable curls somewhat similar to the judge's. An anonymous letter informed the police that Reverend Talbot's murderer, an acquaintance and distant relative of the letter writer, had boarded a ship to Liverpool in a surtout borrowed without permission and, there, had been dealt with foully, never to be heard from again (with the coat, presumably, never to be reunited with the rightful wearer). Another note claimed that a woman had spontaneously confessed at a tailor's shop to having committed the murder of Judge Healey in a jealous rage and had then escaped by train to New York, where she might be found in one of four listed hotels.

When Rey tore open an anonymous note comprised of two sentences, however, he felt the quickening sensation of discovery: It was a fine-grade stationery and the message was written in a blocky, broken penmanship—a mild disguise for the writer's true hand:

Dig deeper under the Reverend's hole. Something missed beneath his head.

The note was signed "Respectfully yours, a citizen of our city."

"Something missed?" Kurtz responded mockingly.

"There's nothing to prove here, no story to invent," said Rey with uncharacteristic enthusiasm. "The writer simply has something to tell. And, remember: The newspaper accounts have varied widely as to what happened to Talbot. Now we must use that to our advantage. This person knows the true circumstances, or at least that Talbot was buried in a hole, and that he was upside down. Look here, Chief." Rey read aloud and pointed: " 'Beneath his head.' "

"Rey, the number of problems I have! The *Transcript*'s found someone at City Hall to confirm that Talbot was found with his clothes in a pile, just like Healey. They're printing it tomorrow and the whole blasted city will know we're dealing with a single killer. Then people won't blame 'crime'—they'll want someone's name." Kurtz turned back to the letter. "Well, why would the letter not say what 'something' we might find in Talbot's hole then? And why wouldn't your citizen walk up to our station house and tell me to my face what he knows?"

Rey did not answer. "Do let me have a look in the vault, Chief Kurtz."

Kurtz shook his head. "You've heard the heat we've taken from every cursed pulpit in the Commonwealth, Rey. We can't go digging up the Second Church's vault to pull out imagined mementos!"

"We left the hole intact in the event there was further observation required," Rey argued.

"Just so. I don't want to hear another word about it, Patrolman."

Rey nodded, but his expression of certainty did not diminish. Chief Kurtz's stubborn refusals could not compete with Rey's unwavering silent disapproval. Later in the afternoon, Kurtz snatched his greatcoat. He walked by Rey's desk and ordered, "Patrolman: Second Unitarian Church, in Cambridge."

A new sexton, a merchantlike gentleman with red whiskers, ushered them inside. He explained that his predecessor, Sexton Gregg, had become increasingly distraught since his discovery of Talbot's body and had resigned to look after his health. The sexton searched clumsily for the keys to the underground vaults.

"There'd better be something to this," Kurtz warned Rey when the stench of the vault reached out to them.

There was.

After only a few strokes with a long-handled shovel, Rey unearthed the pouch of money exactly where Longfellow and Holmes had reburied it.

"One thousand. Exactly one thousand, Chief Kurtz." Rey counted out the money under the glow of a gas lantern. "Chief," Rey said, having realized something remarkable. "Chief Kurtz, the Cambridge station house—the night we found Talbot's body. Do you remember what they told us? The reverend had reported his safe robbed the very day before the murder."

"How much had been taken from his safe?"

Rey nodded to the money.

"One thousand." Kurtz gasped in disbelief. "Well, I don't know whether this helps us or confounds the matter even more. I'll be damned if even Langdon W. Peaslee or Willard Burndy would blow a minister's safe one night and butcher him the next and, if they did, leave the money behind for Talbot to enjoy from the grave!"

It was then that Rey almost stepped on a bouquet of flowers, the token left there by Longfellow. He picked them up and showed them to Kurtz.

"No, no, I haven't let anyone else in these vaults," the new sexton assured them back in the vestry. "Been closed off since the . . . occurrence."

"Then maybe your predecessor did. Do you know where we can find Mr. Gregg?" Chief Kurtz asked.

"Right here. Every Sunday, faithful as could be," the sexton replied.

"Well, when he's here next, I want that you ask him to call on us immediately. Here's my card. If he permitted someone inside there, we shall have to know."

Back at the station house, there was much to be done. The Cambridge patrolman to whom Reverend Talbot had reported the robbery had to be interviewed again; they had to trace the legal-tender notes through the banks to confirm they originated from Talbot's safe; Talbot's Cambridge neighborhood would be scoured to find any information regarding the night his safe was broken into, and an expert in handwriting would analyze the note that provided the information.

Rey could see that Kurtz was feeling genuine optimism, probably for the first time since he'd been told of Healey's death. He was almost giddy. "That's what it takes to be a good policeman, Rey—a touch of instinct. It's all we have sometimes. It fades with each disappointment in life and career, I'm afraid. I would have thrown that note out with the other rubbish, but not you. So tell me. What should we do that we haven't?"

Rey smiled gratefully.

"There must be something. Come, come."

"You won't like what I say, Chief," Rey responded.

Kurtz shrugged. "As long as it's not more of your damned scraps of paper."

Rey generally refused favors, but there was something for which he longed. He walked to the window framing the trees outside the station and looked out. "There's a danger we can't see out there, Chief, that someone who was brought into our station house felt more strongly than his own life. I want to know who died on our courtyard."

※

Oliver Wendell Holmes was happy to have a task suited to him. He was neither entomologist nor naturalist and was interested in the scientific study of animals only insofar as it revealed more about humans' inner workings, and more specifically his own. But within two days of Lowell's dropping off the hodgepodge of crushed insects and maggots, Dr. Holmes had assembled every book on insects he could find from Boston's best scientific libraries and began extensive studies.

In the meantime, Lowell arranged a meeting with the Healeys' maid, Nell, at her sister's home on the outskirts of Cambridge. She told him what it had been like to find Chief Justice Healey, how he had seemed to want to talk and could only gurgle before he died. She had fallen to her knees at the sound of Healey's voice, as though touched by some divine power, and crawled away.

As for the discovery at Talbot's church, the Dante Club had decided that the police must uncover for themselves the money buried in the vault. Holmes and Lowell were both against this: Holmes from fear and Lowell from a sense of possessiveness. Longfellow urged his friends not to view the police as rivals, even though knowledge of their activities by the police would be perilous. They were all working toward one end: stopping the murders. Only, the Dante Club was working primarily with what they could find literarily and the police with what they could find physically. So after reburying the pouch with its invaluable one thousand dollars, Longfellow had composed a simple note addressed to the office of the chief of police: *Dig deeper . . .* They hoped someone at the police station with a keen eye would see it and understand just enough, and perhaps discover something more of the murder.

When Holmes had finished his study of the insects, Longfellow, Fields, and Lowell met at his house. Though Holmes could see all guests to 21 Charles Street arrive through the window of his study, he liked the formality of having his Irish maid settle visitors in the little reception room and then carry up a name to him. Holmes would then scamper down the stairs.

"Longfellow? Fields? Lowell? Are you here? Come up, come up! Let me show you what I have been at work on."

The exquisite study was more orderly than most authors' rooms, with books stretching from floor to ceiling, many—considering Holmes's height—accessible only by the sliding ladder he had built. Holmes showed them his latest contrivance—a reaching bookcase at the corner of his desk so that one did not have to stand to retrieve something.

"Very good, Holmes," said Lowell, who was looking toward the microscopes.

Holmes prepared a slide. "Up to the time of the living generation, nature had kept over all her inner workshops the forbidding inscription NO ADMITTANCE. If any prying observer ventured to spy into the mysteries of her glands and canals and fluids, she covered up her work in blinding mists and bewildering halos, like the deities of old."

He explained that the specimens were maggot-producing blowflies, just as Barnicoat, the city coroner, had pronounced the day the body was discovered. This type of fly lays its eggs on dead tissue. The eggs then became maggots that eat the decomposing flesh, nourishing themselves into flies and beginning the cycle again.

Fields, rocking in one of Holmes's chairs, said, "But Healey cried out before he died, according to that maid. That means he was still alive! Though I suppose only barely hanging to a thread of life. Four days after he was attacked . . . and he was filled with maggots in every crevice of his body."

Holmes would have been revolted at the thought of such suffering had the idea not been so fantastic. He shook his head. "Fortunately for Judge Healey and humanity, it can't be. Either there were only a handful of maggots, four or five perhaps, on the surface of the head wound, where there would have been some dead tissue, *or* he was not alive. With the maggots feeding inside him in such mass quantities as has been reported, all the tissue would be dead. *He* would be dead."

"Perhaps the maid is given to phantasms," Longfellow suggested, seeing Lowell's defeated expression.

"If you could see her, Longfellow," Lowell said. "If you could see the flash in her eyes, Holmes. Fields, you were there!"

Fields nodded, though he was now less sure. "She saw something terrible, or thought she did."

Lowell crossed his arms disapprovingly, "She is the only one who knows, for God's sake. I believe her. *We* must believe her."

Holmes spoke with authority. His findings at least provided some order—some reason—to their activities. "I'm sorry, Lowell. She certainly saw *something* horrible: Healey's condition. But this—*this* is science."

Later, Lowell took the horsecars back to Cambridge. He was strolling under a scarlet canopy of maples, frustrated with his inability to prevent the dismissal of the chambermaid's story, when Phineas Jennison, Boston's great merchant prince, glided by in his plush brougham coach. Lowell frowned. He was not in the frame of mind for company, though part of him craved the distraction.

"Hullo! Give me your hand!" Jennison extended his well-tailored sleeve out the window as his sleek bay horses slowed to a leisurely gait.

"My dear Jennison," Lowell said.

"Oh, how good it feels! The hand of an old friend," Jennison said with elaborate sincerity. Though not possessing Lowell's viselike grip, Jennison shook hands in the rather avid way of the Boston businessman, something akin to shaking up a bottle. He stepped down and knocked on the green door of the silver-mounted chaise for his driver to stay put.

Jennison's shining white overcoat was loosely buttoned, revealing a dark crimson frock coat over a green velvet waistcoat. He looped his arm through Lowell's. "On your way to Elmwood?"

"Guilty, my lord," replied Lowell.

"Tell me, has the accursed Corporation let you be already about that Dante class of yours?" Jennison asked, with serious concern slashing his strong brow.

"I suppose they have tapered off a bit, thankfully," Lowell said, sighing. "I only hope they do not mistake the fact that I have suspended my Dante class as a victory for their side."

Jennison stopped in the middle of the street, his face paling. He spoke in a small voice, holding his dimpled chin in the palm of his hand. "Lowell? Is this the Jemmy Lowell who was banished to Concord for disobedience when he was at Harvard? What of standing up to Manning and the Corporation, on behalf of the future geniuses of America? You must, or they shall . . ."

"It has nothing to do with the confounded fellows," Lowell assured him. "I have something I must sort out at the moment that demands my complete attention, and I cannot be bothered with seminar classes. I am lecturing only."

"A domestic cat will not answer when one wants a Bengal tiger!" Jennison made a fist. He was satisfied with the rather poetic image.

" 'Tis not my line, Jennison. I know not how you manage men like the fellows. You deal with idlers and dunces at every turn."

"Is there any other kind in business?" Jennison flashed his enormous smile. "Here is the secret, Lowell. You call up a row until you get what you're after—that's the ticket. You know what's important, what must be done, and everything else may go to the devil!" he added with zeal. "Now, if I could be of any help in your fight, any help at all . . ."

Lowell was tempted for a brief second to tell Jennison everything and plead for help, though he did not know why exactly. The poet was terrible with finances, always shuffling his money between unwise investments, so to him, successful businessmen seemed to possess supernal powers.

"No, no, I have recruited more help for my fights than good conscience should allow, but I thank you all the same." Lowell patted the rich London broadcloth of the millionaire's shoulder. "Besides, young Mead shall be grateful for the holiday from his Dante."

"Every good battle needs a strong ally," Jennison said, disappointed. Then it seemed as if he wanted to reveal something he could not. "I have observed Dr. Manning. He will not stop his campaign, and so you must never stop. Do not trust what they tell you. Remember that I said that."

Lowell felt a black cloud of irony after speaking about the class he had fought to preserve for so many years. He felt the same awkward confusion later that day when he was passing through the white wooden gates of Elmwood, on his way to Longfellow's.

"Professor!"

Lowell turned to see a young man, in the collegian's standard black frock coat, running, fists up, elbows to his side, mouth stern. "Mr. Sheldon? What are you doing here?"

"I must speak with you at once." The college freshman was panting from exertion.

Longfellow and Lowell had spent the last week compiling lists of all their former Dante students. They could not use the official Harvard records, since that would risk attracting attention. This was a particularly taxing development for Lowell, who kept loose records and remembered only a handful of names at any given time. Even a student from a few years earlier might receive the warmest greeting upon meeting Lowell on the streets. "My dear boy!" and then, "Your name again?"

Fortunately, his two current students, Edward Sheldon and Pliny Mead, were immediately removed from any possibility of suspicion, as Lowell had been teaching them in his Dante seminar at Elmwood at the very time (by their best calculations) of Reverend Talbot's murder.

"Professor Lowell. I received this notice in my box!" Sheldon shoved a slip of paper into Lowell's hand. "A mistake?"

Lowell glanced at it indifferently. "No mistake. I have some things to tend to which necessitate freeing my time, only for a week or so, I hope. I have no doubt you are occupied enough to put Dante out of your mind for a spell."

Sheldon shook his head in dismay. "But what of all you always say to us? What of a new circle of admirers finally widening to relieve Dante's wandering? You have not yielded to the Corporation? You have not tired of the study of Dante, Professor?" the student pressed.

Lowell felt himself shiver at the question. "I know not the thinking man who can tire of Dante, my young Sheldon! Few men have meaning enough in themselves to penetrate a life and work of such depth. I prize him more as man, poet, and teacher every day. He gives hope, in our darkest hour, of a second chance. And until I meet Dante himself in the first purgatorial terrace above, upon my honor I shall never give an inch to the blasted tyrants of the Corporation!"

Sheldon swallowed hard. "So you will keep in mind my eagerness to continue through the *Comedy*?"

Lowell put his arm on Sheldon's shoulder and walked with him. "You know, my lad, there is a story that Boccaccio tells of a woman passing by a door in Verona, where Dante was staying during his exile. She saw Dante across the street and pointed him out to another woman, saying, 'That is Alighieri, the man who goes to Hell whenever he pleases and brings back news of the dead.' And the other replied, 'Very likely. Don't you see what a curly beard he has, and what a dark face? Owing, I daresay, to the heat and smoke!' "

The student laughed loudly.

"This exchange, it is said," Lowell continued, "made Dante smile. Do you know why I doubt the story's veracity, my dear boy?"

Sheldon contemplated the question with the same serious expression he wore during their Dante classes. "Perhaps, Professor, because this woman of Verona would in all actuality not know of the contents of Dante's poem," he postulated, "as only a select number of people of his day, his protectors prime among them, would have seen the manuscript before the end of his life, and even then only in small installments."

"I do not for a second believe that Dante smiled," Lowell answered with relish.

Sheldon started to respond, but Lowell lifted his hat and continued on his way toward Craigie House.

"Remember my eagerness, do!" Sheldon shouted after him.

Dr. Holmes, sitting in Longfellow's library, had noticed a striking engraving printed in the newspaper by the arrangement of Nicholas Rey. The illustration showed the man who had died in the courtyard of the Central Station. The notice in the newspaper referenced nothing of that incident. But it showed the straggly, sunken face of the leaper as he appeared shortly before the show-up, and asked that any information on the man's family be reported to the office of the chief of police.

"When do you hope to find a man's family rather than the man himself?" Holmes asked the others. "When he's dead," he answered himself.

Lowell examined the likeness. "A sadder-looking man I don't believe I've ever seen. And this matter is important enough to involve the chief of police. Wendell, I believe you're right. The Healey boy said the police have not yet identified the man who whispered to Patrolman Rey before throwing himself out the window. It makes perfect sense they would submit a notice to the newspapers."

The newspaper publisher owed Fields a favor. So Fields stopped by its office downtown. He was told that a mulatto police officer had placed the notice.

"Nicholas Rey." Fields found this strange. "With all that's going on between Healey and Talbot, it seems a bit queer that any policeman would expend any energy on a dead loafer." They were eating their supper at Longfellow's. "Could they know there is some connection with the murders? Could that patrolman have some idea what it was the man whispered?"

"It's doubtful," Lowell said. "Once he does, he could well be led to us."

Holmes was unnerved by this. "Then we must find this man's identity before Patrolman Rey!"

"Well, six cheers for Richard Healey then. We now know how it came to pass that Rey came to us with that hieroglyphic," Fields said. "This leaper was brought in to show himself to the police with a horde of other beggars and thieves. The officers would have questioned them about Healey's murder. We can conclude that this poor fellow recognized Dante, grew fearful, poured into Rey's ear some verses in Italian from the very canto that inspired the murder, and ran off—a chase that ended in his fall from the window."

"What could he have been so afraid of?" Holmes wondered.

"We can be confident he was not the murderer himself, since he was dead two weeks before the Reverend Talbot's murder," Fields said.

Lowell tugged on his mustache thoughtfully. "Yes, but he could have known the murderer and feared their association. Probably knew him very well, if that was the case."

"He was frightened of his knowledge, just as we were. So how do we find out before the police who he was?" Holmes asked.

Longfellow had been mostly silent through this exchange. Now he remarked, "We possess two natural advantages over the police in finding the man's identity, my friends. We know the man recognized Dante's inspiration in the terrible details of the murder and that, in his time of crisis, Dante's verses came straightaway to his tongue. And so we can surmise that he was very likely an Italian beggar, well read in literature. And a Catholic."

A man with a harsh three-days' growth over his face and a hat pulled down over his eyes and ears was lying at the foot of Holy Cross, one of Boston's oldest Catholic churches, posed as inertly as a sacred statue. He was stretched in the most leisurely posture human bones allow on a sidewalk and eating his dinner from an earthen pot. A pedestrian passing asked a question. He did not turn his head or respond.

"Sir." Nicholas Rey knelt beside him, holding closer the newspaper likeness of the leaper. "Do you recognize this man, sir?"

Now the loafer rolled his eyes just enough to look.

Rey removed his badge from inside his coat. "Sir, my name is Nicholas Rey, I am a city police officer. It is important that I know this man's name. He has passed on. He is in no trouble. Please, do you know him or someone who might?"

The man stuck his fingers into his pot and plucked a morsel between his thumb and forefinger, then released it to his mouth. Afterward, he rolled his head in a short, untroubled negation.

Patrolman Rey started down the street, where a row of noisy grocery and butcher carts lined the route.

Only ten minutes later, a horsecar expelled passengers at a nearby platform and two other men approached the immovable loafer. One of them held up the same newspaper folded to the same illustration.

"Good fellow, can you tell us whether you know this man?" asked Oliver Wendell Holmes affably.

The recurrence was almost enough to break the reverie of the loafer, though not quite.

Lowell bent forward. "Sir?"

Holmes pushed the newspaper at him again. "Pray, tell us whether he looks at all familiar and we'll be happily on our way, dear fellow."

Nothing.

Lowell shouted, "Do you require an ear trumpet?"

This did not get them very far. The man picked out a bit of unrecognizable food from his pot and slipped it down his throat, without, apparently, bothering to swallow.

"Wouldn't you know," Lowell said to Holmes, who stood to the side. "Three days of this, and nothing. This man did not have many friends."

"We have already gone beyond the Pillar of Hercules of the fashionable quarter. Let us not yield here yet." Holmes had seen something in the loafer's eye when they held up the newspaper. He had also noticed a medal dangling from his neck: San Paolino, the patron saint of Lucca, Tuscany. Lowell followed Holmes's stare.

"Where are you from, signore?" Lowell asked in Italian.

The interrogated party still stared implacably ahead, but his mouth dropped open. "*Da Lucca, signore.*"

Lowell complimented the beauties of the named land. The Italian showed no surprise at the language. This man, like all proud Italians, had been born with the full expectation that everyone should speak his tongue; he who did not was little worthy of conversation. Lowell then renewed the questions regarding the man in the newspaper engraving. It was important, explained the poet, to know his name so that they might find his family and arrange a proper burial. "We believe this poor fellow was from Lucca too," he said sorrowfully in Italian. "He deserves burial in a Catholic churchyard—with his own people."

The Luccan took some time to ponder this before painstakingly turning his elbow into a different position so he could point his morsel-plucking finger at the massive door to the church right behind him.

The Catholic prelate who listened to their questions was a dignified though portly figure.

"Lonza," he said, handing back the newspaper. "Yes, he has been here. I believe Lonza was his name. Yes—Grifone Lonza."

"You knew him personally then?" Lowell asked hopefully.

"He knew the church, Mr. Lowell," the prelate responded with a benign air. "We have a fund entrusted to us from the Vatican for immigrants. We provide loans and some passage money for those who need to return to their homeland. Of course, we can only help a small number." He had more to say but stymied himself. "What is your business in looking for him, gentlemen? Why has his likeness been printed in the newspaper?"

"I'm afraid he has passed on, Father. We believe the police have been trying to identify him," said Dr. Holmes.

"Ah. I fear you won't find the congregants of my church or those around these neighborhoods very eager to speak with the police on any matter. It was the police, recall, who did nothing to seek justice when the Ursuline convent burned to the ground. And when there is a crime, it is the poor, the Irish Catholics who are harassed," he said with the firm-jawed anger of a clergyman. "The Irish were sent to war to die for Negroes who now steal their jobs, while the rich stayed home for a small fee."

Holmes wanted to say: Not my Wendell Junior, my good Father. But, in fact, Holmes had tried to convince Junior to do just that.

"Did Mr. Lonza wish to return to Italy?" Lowell asked.

"What anyone *wishes* in his heart, I cannot say. This man came for food, which we give on a regular basis, and a few small loans to keep afloat if I recall correctly. If *I* were Italian, I might well wish to return to my people. Most of our members are Irish. I fear the Italians do not feel so welcome among them. In all Boston and its surrounding areas, there are fewer than three hundred Italians, by our approximation. They are a very ragged lot, and require our sympathy and charity. But the more immigrants from other countries, the fewer jobs for the ones already here—you understand the potential trouble."

"Father, do you know if Mr. Lonza had family?" asked Holmes.

The prelate shook his head contemplatively, then said, "Say, there was one gentleman who was sometimes a companion to him. Lonza was something of a drunkard, I'm afraid, and needed watching. Yes, what was his name? A peculiarly Italian name it was." The prelate moved to his desk. "We should have some papers on him, as he too received some loans. Ah, this is it—a language tutor. He received some fifty dollars from us over the last year and a half. I remember he claimed to have once worked at Harvard College, though I would tend to doubt that. Here." He sounded out the name on the paper. "Pietro Bak-ee."

Nicholas Rey, questioning some ragged children splashing at a horse trough, saw two high hats exit buoyantly from the Holy Cross Cathedral and disappear around the corner. Even from a distance, they looked out of place in the crowded dinginess of the area. Rey walked to the church and called for the prelate. The prelate, hearing that Rey was a police officer searching for an unidentified man, studied the newspaper illustration, looking over and then through his heavy gold-bowed spectacles before placidly apologizing.

"I've never seen this poor fellow in my life, I'm afraid, Officer."

Rey, thinking of the two high-hatted figures, asked whether anyone else had been in the area to ask about the unidentified man. The prelate, replacing the file of Bachi in his drawer, smiled blandly and said no.

Next, Patrolman Rey went to Cambridge. A wire had been received at the Central Station detailing an attempt, in the middle of the night, to steal Artemus Healey's remains from his coffin.

"I told them what would come from public knowledge," Chief Kurtz said of the Healey family with unbecoming vindication. Mount Auburn Cemetery had now put the body into a steel coffin and hired another nighttime caretaker, this one armed with a shotgun. On a hillside not far from Healey's gravestone was the portrait statue erected over the Reverend Talbot's site, paid for by his congregation. The statue had a look of pure grace that improved on the minister's actual face. In one hand the marble preacher held the Holy Book and in the other a pair of eyeglasses; this was a tribute to one of his pulpit mannerisms, a strange habit of removing his large eyeglasses when reading text from the lectern and replacing them when preaching freely, instructively suggesting that one needed sharper vision to read from the spirit of God.

On his way to look over Mount Auburn for Chief Kurtz, Rey was stopped by a small commotion. He was told that an old man, who roomed on the second floor of a nearby building, had been absent for more than a week, not an unexpected period of time, as he sometimes traveled. But the residents demanded something be done about an offensive smell emanating from his room. Rey knocked and considered breaking through the fastened door, then borrowed a ladder and placed it outside. Climbing up, he raised the window to the room, but the horrible smell from inside almost sent him tumbling down.

When the air had traveled out sufficiently to allow him inside, Rey had to hold himself against a wall. It took several seconds for him to accept that there was nothing to be done. A man stood erect, his feet dangling near the floor, with a rope around his neck that was hooked overhead. His features were stiffened and decayed beyond normal recognition, but Rey knew the man, from his clothes, and from the still bulging, panicked eyes, to be the former sexton of the nearby Unitarian church. A card was later found on the chair. It was the calling card Chief Kurtz had left at the church to be given to Gregg. On the back of this, the sexton had written a message to the police, insisting he would have seen any man who might have entered the vaults to kill Reverend Talbot. Somewhere in Boston, he warned, had arrived a demon soul, and he could not continue fearing its return for the rest of them.

Pietro Bachi, Italian gentleman and graduate of the University of Padua, grouchily nurtured all opportunities open to him in Boston as a private tutor, though they were scarce and disagreeable. He had tried to obtain another university position after his dismissal from Harvard. "There may be room for a plain teacher of French or German," the dean of one new college in Philadelphia said, laughing, "but Italian! My friend, we do not expect our boys to turn out opera singers." Colleges up and down the Atlantic anticipated as few opera singers. And governing academic boards were quite occupied enough (thank you, Mr. Bakey) managing Greek and Latin to consider instruction in an unnecessary, unseemly, papist, vulgar living language.

Fortunately, a moderate demand materialized in certain quarters of Boston by the end of the war. A few Yankee merchants were anxious to open ports with as many language skills as they could purchase. Also, a new class of prominent families, enriched by wartime profits and profiteering, desired above all else that their daughters be cultured. Some thought it wise that young ladies obtain basic Italian in addition to French in the event that it might seem worthwhile to send them to Rome when their time came to travel (a recent fashion among blossoming Boston beauties). So Pietro Bachi, his Harvard post unceremoniously stripped from him, remained on the lookout for enterprising merchants and pampered damsels. The latter required frequent replenishment, for the singing, drawing, and dancing masters held far too much appeal to them for Bachi to lay permanent claim to the young ladies' hour-and-a-quarter pouches of time.

This life appalled Pietro Bachi.

It was not the lessons that tormented him so much as having to ask for his fees. The *americani* of Boston had built themselves a Carthage, a land stuffed with money but void of culture, destined to vanish without a trace of its existence. What had Plato said of the citizens of Agrigentum? These people build as if they were immortal and eat as if they were to die instantly.

Some twenty-five years earlier, in the beautiful countryside of Sicily, Pietro Batalo, like many Italians before him, had fallen in love with a perilous woman. Her family was of opposite political entrenchment from the Batalos, who fought vigorously against papal control of the state. When the woman felt Pietro had wronged her, her family was only too happy to arrange for his excommunication and banishment. After a series of adventures with various armies, Pietro and his brother, a merchant, who desired freedom from the destructive political and religious landscape, changed their name to Bachi and fled across the ocean. In 1843, Pietro found a Boston that was a quaint town of friendly faces, different from what would emerge by 1865, when nativists were seeing their fear of foreigners' rapid multiplication realized, and windows filled with the reminder FOREIGNERS NEED NOT APPLY. Bachi had been welcomed into Harvard College, and for a time he, like young Professor Henry Longfellow, had even boarded in a lovely section of Brattle Street. Then Pietro Bachi found passion unlike any he had known in the love of an Irish maiden. And she became his wife. But she found supplementary passions shortly after marrying the instructor. She left him, as Bachi's students said, with only his shirtsleeves in his trunk and her hearty keenness for drink in his throat. There began the steep and steady decline in the heart of Pietro Bachi . . .

"I understand she is, well, shall we say . . ." His interlocutor dug for a delicate word as he hurried after Bachi: ". . . *difficult.*"

"She is difficult?" Bachi did not stop descending the stairs. "Ha! She does not believe I am Italian," Bachi said. "She says I do not look like an Italian!"

The young girl appeared at the top of the stairs and sulkily watched her father wobble after the diminutive instructor.

"Oh, I'm sure the child does not mean what she says," he was declaiming as gravely as possible.

"I did so mean it!" the little girl screeched from her mezzanine stage at the stair landing, leaning so far against the walnut banister that it looked as if she might fall onto Pietro Bachi's knitted hat. "He does not look at all like one, Father! He is far too short!"

"Arabella!" the man shouted, then turned back with an earnest yellow-stained smile—as though he washed his mouth with gold—to the shimmering candlelit vestibule. "I say, wait a moment more, dear sir! Let us take this occasion to review your fee, shall we, Signor Bachi?" he suggested, eyebrow pulled back tight as a trembling arrow waiting on its bow.

Bachi turned to him for a moment, his face burning, his grip tightening on his satchel as he tried to subdue his temper. The webbed lines had multiplied across his face over the last few years, and each small setback made him doubt the worth of his existence. "*Amari Cani!*" was all Bachi said. Arabella stared down confusedly. He had not taught her enough to understand that his pun on *americani*—Italian for "Americans"—would translate into English as "bitter dogs."

The horsecar at this hour, bound inward, packed people in like cattle headed for the abattoir. Serving Boston and its suburbs, the horsecars were enclosed two-ton compartments lined with enough places to hold around fifteen passengers. They were set with iron wheels on flat tracks and pulled by a pair of horses. Those who had managed to secure seats watched with detached interest as three dozen others, Bachi among them, struggled to fold into themselves, knuckling and bumping into one another as they reached for the leather straps hanging from the roof. By the time the conductor had pushed through to collect the fares, the platform outside was already filled with people waiting for the next car. Two drunkards in the middle of the overheated, unventilated compartment gave off a smell like an ash heap, and struggled to sing in harmony a song with words they did not know. Bachi curved his hand to his mouth and, seeing that nobody was watching, breathed into it and momentarily widened his nostrils.

After arriving at his street, Bachi plunged down from the sidewalk into a basement complex of shadows in a tenement called Half Moon Place, happily expectant of the solitude that awaited him. But sitting on the last step down were, out of place without armchairs, James Russell Lowell and Dr. Oliver Wendell Holmes.

"A penny for your thoughts, signore." Lowell wore a charming smile as he grabbed Bachi's hand.

"That would be filching a copper from you, *Professore,*" Bachi said, his hand hanging limp as a wet rag in Lowell's clutch. "Lost your way to Cambridge?"

He eyed Holmes suspiciously, but he sounded more surprised at their visit than he looked.

"Not at all," said Lowell as he took off his hat, showing his high white forehead. "And aren't you acquainted with Dr. Holmes? We'd both like to have a few words, if you would."

Bachi frowned and pushed open his apartment door to the clanking welcome of pots hung on pegs directly behind the door. It was a subterranean room with a square of daylight dripping down from one half-window that found its way above the street. A musty odor rose up from clothes hanging at all corners that never quite dried in the dampness, imprinting Bachi's suits with defeated wrinkles. As Lowell rearranged the pots on the door in order to hang his hat, Bachi casually slipped a pile of papers from his desk into his satchel. Holmes did his best to compliment the cracked decor.

Bachi then put up a kettle of water on the hob of the chimney grate. "Your business, gentlemen?" he asked curtly.

"We've come to request your help, Signor Bachi," said Lowell.

Wry amusement crept across Bachi's face as he poured out the tea, and he grew cheerier. "What will you take with this?" He motioned to his sideboard. There were a half-dozen dirty tumblers and three decanters. They were labeled RUM, GIN, and WHISKEY.

"Plain tea, thank you," Holmes said. Lowell agreed.

"Oh, come now!" Bachi insisted, bringing Holmes one of the decanters. To placate the host, Holmes poured as few drops of whiskey into the teacup as possible, but Bachi lifted the doctor's elbow. "I think the bitter New England climate would be the death of us all, Doctor," he said, "were it not for a drop of something warm inside every now and then."

Bachi pretended to consider tea for himself, then opted instead for a full glass of rum. The guests pulled up chairs, realizing simultaneously that they had sat in them before.

"From University Hall!" said Lowell.

"The College owed me at least that much, don't you think?" Bachi said with stiff geniality. "Besides, where else could I find a seat so singularly uncomfortable, eh? Harvard men can talk as Unitarian as they wish, but they shall always be Calvinists up to the neck—they enjoy their own suffering, and that of others. Tell me, how is it you gentlemen found me here at Half Moon Place? I believe I am the only non-Dubliner for several square miles."

Lowell unrolled a copy of the *Daily Courier* and opened it to a page with a row of advertisements. One was circled.

> An Italian gentleman, a graduate of University of Padua, highly qualified by his manifold accomplishments, and by a long practice of tuition in Spanish and Italian, attends private pupils and classes at boys' schools, ladies' academies, etc. References: Hon. John Andrew, Henry Wadsworth Longfellow, and James Russell Lowell, Professor in Harvard University. Address: 2 Half Moon Place, Broad Street.

Bachi laughed to himself. "Merit, with us Italians, likes to hide its candle under a bushel. At home our proverb is 'A good wine needs no bush.' But in America it must be '*In bocca chiusa non entran mosche*': In a closed mouth, no flies enter. How can I expect people to come and buy if they do not know I have something to sell? So I open my mouth and blow my trumpet."

Holmes flinched from a sip of the strong tea. "John Andrew is one of your references, signore?" he asked.

"Tell me, Dr. Holmes, what pupil looking for Italian lessons will call on the governor to ask after me? I suspect nobody has ever sent for Professor Lowell, in any case."

Lowell conceded the point. He leaned in closer to the overlapping piles of Dante texts and commentaries blanketing Bachi's desk, promiscuously open at all angles. Above the writing desk dangled a small portrait of Bachi's estranged wife, a considerate softness from the painter's brush obscuring her tough eyes.

"Now, how is it I could help you, even as I once needed your help, *Professore*?" Bachi asked.

Lowell brought out another newspaper from his coat, this one opened to the likeness of Lonza. "Do you know this man, Signor Bachi? Or should I say *did* you know him?"

Taking in the cadaverous face on the colorless page, Bachi sank into sadness. But when he looked up, he was angry. "Do you presume I would know every such ragged oaf of a man?"

"The bishop at Holy Cross Cathedral presumed," Lowell said knowingly.

Bachi seemed startled and turned to Holmes as though surrounded.

"You've borrowed some not insignificant amounts of money there, I believe, signore," Lowell said.

This shamed Bachi into candidness. He looked down with a sheepish smirk. "These are American priests—not like the ones in Italy. They have longer purses than the pope himself. If you were in my place, even priests' money would not stink in your nostrils." He drained his rum, threw his head back, and whistled. He looked again at the newspaper. "So you want to know something about Grifone Lonza."

He paused and then pointed a thumb at the pile of Dante texts on his desk. "Like you literary gentlemen, I have always found my pleasantest companions among the dead rather than the living. There is this advantage, that when an author becomes flat or obscure or simply ceases to amuse, one can always bid him 'Shut up.'" He belabored these last words pointedly.

Bachi rose to his feet and poured a gin. He took a large gulp, half gargling his words in the wash of liquor. "It is a lonely business in America. Most of my brethren who have been forced to come here can barely read a newspaper, much less *La Commedia di Dante,* which penetrates the very soul of man equally in all its despair and all its joy. There were a few of us here in Boston, years ago, men of letters, men of minds: Antonio Gallenga, Grifone Lonza, Pietro D'Alessandro." He could not help but share a reminiscing smile, as though his current callers had been among them. "We would sit in our rooms and read Dante together aloud, first one and then the other, in this way progressing through the whole poem that records all secrets. Lonza and I were the last of the group who had not moved away or died. Now I am the only one."

"Come now, don't despise Boston," Holmes said.

"Few are worthy to stay their whole lives in Boston," Bachi said with a sardonic sincerity.

"Did you know, Signor Bachi, that Lonza died at the police station house?" Holmes asked gently.

Bachi nodded. "I've heard vaguely about it."

Lowell said, eyeing the Dante books on the desk, "Signor Bachi, how would you respond if I were to tell you that Lonza spoke a line from the third canto of *Inferno* to a police officer before falling to his death?"

Bachi did not seem at all surprised. Instead, he laughed carelessly. Most political exiles from Italy grew more virulent in their rectitude and turned even their own sins into signs of sainthood; in their minds, on the other hand, the pope was a wretched dog. But Grifone Lonza had convinced himself he had somehow betrayed his faith and had to find a way to repent his sins in the eyes of God. Once settled in Boston, Lonza had helped expand a

Catholic mission connected with the Ursuline convent, certain his faith would be reported to the pope and would win him return. Then rioters had burned the convent to the ground.

"Lonza, typically, rather than growing indignant, was shattered, certain he had done something deeply wrong sometime in his life to deserve these worst punishments from God. His place in America, in exile, became confused. He all but stopped speaking in English. It is my belief that part of him forgot how to speak it and knew only the true Italian language."

"But why would Signor Lonza recite a verse from Dante before jumping from the window, signore?" Holmes asked.

"I had a friend back home, Dr. Holmes, a jovial fellow who operated a restaurant, who answered all questions about his food with quotes from Dante. Well, that was amusing. Lonza went mad. Dante became a way for him to live out the sins he imagined he had. He felt he was guilty of everything and anything proposed to him by the end. He never actually read Dante for the last few years, had no need. Every line and every word was fixed permanently in his mind, and to his terror. He had never memorized it intentionally, but it came to him as God's warnings came to the prophets. The slightest image or word could make him slip into Dante's poem—it could take days to pull him out sometimes, to hear him speak anything else."

"It does not surprise you that he would commit suicide," Lowell remarked.

"I do not know that that's what it was, *Professore,*" Bachi snapped. "But it matters not what you call it. His life was a suicide. He gave up his soul for fear, little by little, until there was nowhere left in the universe but Hell. He stood on the precipice of eternal torment in his mind. It does not surprise me that he fell over." He paused. "Is it so different from your friend Longfellow?"

Lowell shot to his feet. Holmes quietly tried to mother him back down.

Bachi persisted: "From what I understand, Professor Longfellow has drowned his suffering in Dante for—what is it?—three or four years now."

"What can you know of a man like Henry Longfellow, Bachi?" Lowell demanded. "To judge from your desk, Dante seems to have consumed you of late as well, signore. What exactly are *you* looking for in here? Dante was searching for peace in his writing. I venture to say you are after something not so noble!" He flipped through the pages roughly.

Bachi swatted the book out of Lowell's hand.

"Do not touch my Dante! I may be in a tenement, but I need not justify my reading to any man, rich or poor, *Professore*!"

Lowell flushed in embarrassment. "That is not . . . if you require a loan, Signor Bachi . . ."

Bachi cackled. "Oh, you *amari cani*! Do you think I should take charity from you, a man who stood idly by while Harvard fed me to the wolves?"

Lowell was aghast. "Now see here, Bachi! I fought hand over fist for your job!"

"You sent a note to Harvard requesting they pay me severance. Where were you when I had nowhere to turn? Where was the great Longfellow? You have never fought for anything in your life. You write poems and articles about slavery and the murder of Indians and hope something will change. You fight what does not come near your door, *Professore.*" He broadened his invective by turning to the flustered Dr. Holmes, as though it were the polite thing to do to include him. "You've inherited everything in your lives and do not know what it is to cry for your bread! Well, with what other expectations did I come to this country? What should I complain of? The greatest bard had no home but exile. One day to come, perhaps, I shall walk on my own shores again, once more with true friends, before I leave this earth."

In another thirty seconds, Bachi drank two full glasses of whiskey and sank into his desk chair, trembling hard.

"It was the intervention of a foreigner, Charles of Valois, that caused Dante's exile. He is our last property, the last ashes of the soul of Italy. I shall not applaud as you and your worshipped Mr. Longfellow rip Dante from his rightful place and make him an American! Just remember, he shall always return to *us*! Dante is too powerful in his spirit of survival to succumb to any man!"

Holmes tried to ask about Bachi's tutoring. Lowell inquired about the bowler-hatted, checkered-waistcoated man whom he had seen Bachi approach anxiously in Harvard Yard. But they had extracted all they could from Pietro Bachi for now. When they emerged from the cellar apartment, it had grown viciously cold. They ducked under the rickety outer staircase, known by the tenants as Jacob's Ladder, because it led to the somewhat better appointed Humphrey's Place tenement above.

A red-faced Bachi thrust his head from his half-window, so he seemed to be growing out from the ground. He wriggled out up to his neck and called out drunkenly.

"You want to talk of Dante, *Professori*? Keep an eye on your Dante class!"

Lowell shouted back, demanding to know his meaning.

But the sash of the window was immoderately slammed closed by two quivering hands.

X

MR. HENRY OSCAR HOUGHTON, a tall and pious man with a Quaker-style half-beard, reviewed his accounts in the orderly congestion of his counting-room desk, which glowed under a dim moderator lamp. Through his tireless devotion to small details, his enterprise, the Riverside Press, located on the Cambridge side of the Charles River, had become the leading printing firm for many prominent publishing companies, including the most prominent, Ticknor & Fields. One of Houghton's messenger boys knocked on the open door.

Houghton did not budge until he finished inking and blotting a number into his cost book. He was worthy of his hardworking Puritan ancestors.

"Come in, boy," Houghton finally said, looking up from his work.

The boy delivered a card into Oscar Houghton's hand. Even before reading it, the printer was impressed by the heavy, inflexible paper. Reading the handwriting under the lamp, Houghton stiffened. His tightly guarded peace was now thoroughly interrupted.

Deputy Chief Savage's police carriage rolled up and expelled Chief Kurtz. Rey met him on the steps of the Central Station.

"Well?" asked Kurtz.

"I've discovered that the leaper's first name was Grifone, according to another vagrant, who claims to have seen him by the railroad sometimes," said Rey.

"There's one step," said Kurtz. "You know, I've been thinking about what you said, Rey. About these murders as forms of *punishment*." Rey expected this to be followed by something dismissive, but instead Kurtz let out a sigh. "I've been thinking of Chief Justice Healey."

Rey nodded.

"Well, we all do things we live to regret, Rey. Our own police force battled back mobs with billy clubs during the Sims trial from the courthouse steps. *We* hunted down Tom Sims like a dog and after the trial transported him to the harbor to be sent back to his slave master. You follow me? This was one of our darkest moments, all from Judge Healey's decision, or lack thereof, not to declare Congress's law invalid."

"Yes, Chief Kurtz."

Kurtz seemed saddened by his thoughts. "Find the most respectable men in Boston society, Patrolman, and I should say you have a good chance they have not been saints, not in our times. They have wavered, have thrown their weight into the wrong war chest, have let caution overstep courage, and worse."

Kurtz opened the door to his office, ready to continue. But three men in black greatcoats were standing over his desk.

"What goes on here?" Kurtz called to them, then looked around for his secretary.

The men parted, revealing Frederick Walker Lincoln sitting behind Kurtz's desk.

Kurtz uncovered his head and bowed forward slightly. "Your Honor."

Mayor Lincoln was completing a lazy, final stroke on a cigar behind the broad wings of John Kurtz's mahogany desk. "Hope you don't mind we made use of your rooms while waiting, Chief." A cough mangled Lincoln's words. Next to him sat Alderman Jonas Fitch. A sanctimonious grin seemed to have been carved on his face for some hours, at least. The alderman dismissed two of the greatcoats, members of the bureau of detectives. One remained.

"Stay in the anteroom please, Patrolman Rey," Kurtz said.

Kurtz cautiously took a seat across from his desk. He waited for the door to close. "What is this about, then? Why have you congregated those scoundrels here?"

The one remaining scoundrel, Detective Henshaw, showed no particular offense.

Mayor Lincoln said, "I'm certain you have other police matters that have been neglected during these times, Chief Kurtz. We've decided that these murders shall be turned over to your detectives for resolution."

"I won't allow that!" Kurtz said.

"Welcome the detectives to do their jobs, Chief. They are equipped to solve such matters as this with speed and vigor," Lincoln said.

"Particularly with such rewards on the table," said Alderman Fitch.

Lincoln frowned at the alderman.

Kurtz squinted. "Rewards? Detectives can't accept rewards, by your own law. What rewards, Mayor?"

The mayor snubbed out his cigar, pretending to think over Kurtz's comment. "The aldermanic council of Boston, as we speak, will be passing a resolution authored by Alderman Fitch, eliminating the restriction on receiving rewards for members of the bureau of detectives. There will also be a slight increase in the rewards."

"An increase of how much?" Kurtz asked.

"Chief Kurtz . . ." the mayor started.

"How much?"

Kurtz thought he saw Alderman Fitch smile before answering. "The reward will now be set at *thirty-five* thousand for the arrest of the murderer."

"God save the mark!" Kurtz cried. "Men would commit murder themselves to get their hands on that! Especially our blasted Bureau of Detectives!"

"We do the job someone must, Chief Kurtz," Detective Henshaw noted, "when nobody else will act."

Mayor Lincoln exhaled, and his whole face deflated. Although the mayor didn't exactly resemble his second cousin the late President Lincoln, he carried the same skeletal look of indefatigable frailness. "I want to retire after another term, John," the mayor said softly. "And I want to know that my city will look back at me with honor. We need to string up this killer now or all hell will break loose, can't you see that? Between the war and the assassination, goodness knows the papers have lived off the taste of blood for four years, and I swear they're thirstier than ever. Healey was in my college class, Chief. I do believe I am half expected to go into the streets and find this madman myself or, if not, to be hanged in the Boston Common! I beg you, let the detectives solve this and leave the Negro out of this business. We can't suffer another embarrassment."

"I beg your pardon, Mayor." Kurtz sat up straighter in his chair. "What does Patrolman Rey have to do with all this?"

"The near riot at your show-up for Justice Healey." Alderman Fitch was pleased to elaborate. "That beggar who threw himself out your precinct window. Stop me when this sounds familiar, Chief."

"Rey had nothing to do with that," Kurtz said, balking.

Lincoln shook his head sympathetically. "The aldermen have commissioned an investigation to look into his role. We have received complaints from several police officers that it was your driver's presence that provoked the commotion to begin with. We have been told the mulatto had custody of the beggar when it happened, Chief, and some think, well, speculate, he might have forced him out the window. Probably accidentally . . ."

"Blasted lies!" Kurtz reddened. "He was trying to calm things down, as we all were! That leaper was just some maniac! The detectives are trying to stop our investigation so they can get to your rewards! Henshaw, what do you know of this?"

"I know that Negro can't save Boston from what's at hand, Chief."

"Perhaps when the governor hears that his *prize* appointment has disrupted the entire police department, he shall do what's right and reconsider its wisdom," the alderman said.

"Patrolman Rey is one of the finest policemen I have ever known."

"Which brings up another matter while we're here. We have also been made to understand that you are seen all over the city with him, Chief." The mayor extended his frown. "Including the site of Talbot's death. Not just as your driver but as an equal partner in your activities."

"It's a certified miracle that darky doesn't have a lynch mob follow him with paving stones every time he walks out on the street!" Alderman Fitch laughed.

"We put in place every restriction on Nick Rey that the aldermanic council suggested and . . . I can't see how his position has anything to do with this!"

"We have a crime of terror upon us," Mayor Lincoln said, aiming a stern finger at Kurtz. "And the police department is falling apart—*that's* why it has to do with it. I shan't allow Nicholas Rey to remain involved in this matter in any capacity. One more mistake and he shall face his discharge. Some state senators came to me today, John. They're appointing another committee to propose abolishing all city police departments statewide and replacing them with a state-run metropolitan police force if we can't finish this. They're dead set. I shan't see that happen under my watch—understand that! I *won't* see my city's police department pulled apart."

Alderman Jonas Fitch could see that Kurtz was too stunned to speak. The alderman leaned in and leveled his stare. "If you had enforced our temperance and anti-vice laws, Chief Kurtz, perhaps the thieves and scoundrels would have all fled to New York City by now!"

In the early morning, the offices of Ticknor & Fields pulsed with anonymous shop boys—some just barely boys and others with gray heads—as well as with junior clerks. Dr. Holmes was the first member of the Dante Club to arrive. Pacing the hall to whittle away his earliness, Holmes decided to sit in J. T. Fields's private office.

"Oh sorry, my good sir," he said as he detected someone in there, and began to close the door.

An angular, shadowed face was turned toward the window. It took Holmes a second to make him out.

"Why, my dear Emerson!" Holmes smiled widely.

Ralph Waldo Emerson, his profile aquiline and his body long in blue cloak and black shawls, broke from his reverie and greeted Holmes. It was a rarity to find Emerson, poet and lecturer, away from Concord, a small village that had for a time rivaled Boston in its collection of literary talents, especially after Harvard had banned him from speaking on campus for declaring the Unitarian Church dead during a divinity-school address. Emerson was the only writer in America who approached the renown of Longfellow, and even Holmes, a man at the center of all literary doings, was tickled when he was in the author's company. "I've just returned from my annual Lyceum Express, arranged by our Maecenas of modern poets." Emerson raised a hand over Fields's desk as though giving a blessing, a vestigial gesture from his days as a reverend. "The guardian and protector of us all. I've just some papers to leave for him."

"Well, it is about time you should come back to Boston. We have missed you at the Saturday Club. An indignation meeting was nearly convened to call for your company!" Holmes said.

"Thankfully, I shall never be so well liked." Emerson smiled. "You know, we never make time to write to gods or friends, only to attorneys, who wish to collect debt, and the man who will slate our house." Emerson then asked after Holmes.

He answered with long, winding anecdotes. "And I have been thinking of writing another novel." He made his task prospective, because he was intimidated by the force and swiftness of Emerson's opinions, which often made everyone else's seem all wrong.

"Oh I wish you would, dear Holmes," Emerson said sincerely. "Your voice cannot fail to please. And tell me about the dashing captain. Still a lawyer-to-be?"

Holmes laughed nervously at the mention of Junior, as if the subject of his son were inherently comical; this was not quite true, as Junior lacked any sense of humor altogether. "I tried my hand at the law once but found it was much like eating sawdust without butter. Junior wrote good verses, too—not as good as mine, but good verses. Now that he lives at home again, he is like a white Othello, sitting in our library rocker impressing the young lady Desdemonas about him with stories of his wounds. Sometimes, though, I believe he despises me. Do you ever feel this from your boy, Emerson?"

Emerson paused for a solid few seconds. "There is no peace for the sons of men, Holmes."

Watching Emerson's facial gestures while he spoke was like watching a grown man cross a brook on stepping-stones, and the cautious selfishness in this image distracted Holmes from his anxieties. He wanted the conversation to keep going but knew that meetings with Emerson could end without much warning.

"My dear Waldo, might I ask you a question?" Holmes really wanted to ask advice, but Emerson never gave any. "What did you think of us, Fields and Lowell and I, I mean, assisting Longfellow with his translation of Dante?"

Emerson raised a frosted eyebrow. "If Socrates were here, Holmes, we could go talk with him out in the streets. But our dear Longfellow, we cannot go and talk with. There is a palace and servants and a row of bottles of different-colored wines and wineglasses and fine coats." Emerson bent his head in thought. "I think sometimes of the days I read Dante under Professor Ticknor's direction, as you did, yet I cannot help but feel Dante is a curiosity, like a mastodon—a relic to put in a museum, not in one's house."

"But you once said to me that Dante's introduction to America would be one of the most significant achievements of our century!" Holmes insisted.

"Yes." Emerson considered this. He liked to take all sides of an issue whenever possible. "And that also is true. Still, you know, Wendell, I prefer the society of one faithful person to an association of rapid talkers, who more than anything else seek admiration from one another."

"But what would literature be without associations?" Holmes smiled. He had the integrity of the Dante Club under his guard. "Who can tell what we owe to the mutual admiration society of Shakespeare and Ben Jonson with Beaumont and Fletcher? Or to that where Johnson and Goldsmith and Burke and Reynolds and Beauclerc and Boswell, most admiring of all admirers, met by the fireside of a parlor?"

Emerson straightened the papers he had brought to Fields in order to show that the purpose of his visit was completed. "Remember that only when past genius is transmitted into a present power shall we meet the first truly American poet. And somewhere, born to the streets rather than the athenaeum, we will come upon the first true reader. The spirit of the American is suspected to be timid, imitative, tame—the scholar decent, indolent, complaisant. The mind of our country, taught to aim at low objects, eats upon itself. Without action, the scholar is not yet man. Ideas must work through the bones and arms of good men or they are no better than dreams. When I read Longfellow, I feel utterly at ease—I am safe. This shall not yield us our future."

When Emerson left, Holmes felt he had been entrusted with a sphinx's riddle to which only he could provide an answer. He felt decidedly possessive about the conversation; he did not want to share it with the others when they arrived.

"Is it really possible?" Fields asked his friends after they had discussed Bachi. "Could this beggar Lonza have been so overcome that he would see the poem strung over all life?"

"It would not be the first or last time that literature mastered a weakened mind. Think of John Wilkes Booth," Holmes said. "As he shot Lincoln, he cried out in Latin, 'Thus always to tyrants.' That's what Brutus says while murdering Julius Caesar. Lincoln *was* the Roman emperor in Booth's mind. Booth, recall, was a Shakespearean. Just as our Lucifer is a master Dantean. The reading, the comprehending, the analyzing that we do every day did what we secretly hope for in ourselves—worked through the bones and muscles of this man."

Longfellow raised his eyebrows at this. "Only, it seemed to have done so involuntarily with Booth and Lonza."

"Bachi must be hiding something he knows about Lonza!" Lowell said with frustration. "You saw how reluctant he was, Holmes. What do you say?"

"It was like stroking a hedgehog," Holmes admitted. "After a man begins to attack Boston, when he gets bitter about the Frog Pond or the State House, you may be sure there is not much left of him. Poor Edgar Poe died in the hospital soon after he got into this way of talking, so sure as you find a fellow reduced to this, you had better stop lending him money—for he is on his last legs."

"The jingle man," Lowell muttered at the mention of Poe.

"There was always a dark spot in Bachi," Longfellow said. "Poor Bachi. The loss of his job only made him more wretched, and no doubt he views our part in his desperation unkindly."

Lowell did not meet Longfellow's eyes. He had deliberately not related the specifics of Bachi's tirade against Longfellow. "I think good gratitude a scarcer thing in this world than good verses, Longfellow. Bachi has no more feelings than a horseradish. It could be that Lonza was so afraid at the police station because he *knew* who killed Healey. He knew Bachi was the culprit—or perhaps he even helped Bachi kill Healey."

"The mention of Longfellow's work on Dante did touch him off like a lucifer match," Holmes said, but he was skeptical. "The murderer must be a man of great strength to have carried Healey from the bedroom to the yard. Bachi can barely stumble straight with his regiment of liquors. Besides, we have come across no connection between Bachi and either of the victims."

"We have no need of one!" Lowell said. "Remember, Dante places plenty of people in Hell whom he never met. Ser Bachi has two ingredients stronger than a personal connection with Healey or Talbot. First: a sterling knowledge of Dante. He is the only one outside our club, besides I suppose old Ticknor, with a level of understanding that rivals our own."

"Granted," said Holmes.

"Secondly, motivation," Lowell continued. "He's as poor as a rat. He finds himself abandoned by our city and finds solace only in drink. His occasional jobs as private tutor are all that keep him afloat. He resents us because he believes Longfellow and I sat on our hands when he was fired. And Bachi would rather see Dante ruined than rescued by treacherous Americans."

"Why, my dear Lowell, would Bachi choose Healey and Talbot?" Fields asked.

"He could have chosen anyone he pleases, so long as they fit the sins he decides to punish and Dante could eventually be exposed as the source. So he could ruin the name of Dante in America before the poetry takes hold."

"Could Bachi be our Lucifer?" Fields asked.

"Must he be our Lucifer?" Lowell said, wincing as he grabbed his ankle.

Longfellow said, "Lowell?" He looked down at Lowell's leg.

"Oh, no worries, I thank you. I might have smashed myself against an iron stand the other day at Wide Oaks, now that I remember it."

Dr. Holmes leaned forward, motioning for Lowell to roll up his trouser leg. "Has this grown in size, Lowell?" The red abrasion had gone from the size of a penny to the size of a dollar coin.

"How should I know?" He never took his own injuries seriously.

"Perhaps you should pay as much attention to yourself as to Bachi," Holmes scolded. "It doesn't look like it's a healing wound. Quite the contrary. You simply banged it, you say? It does not seem infected. Has it been bothering you at all, Lowell?"

Suddenly, his ankle felt much worse. "Now and again." Then he thought of something. "It is *possible* that while I was at Healey's, one of those blowflies made its way into my pants leg. Could that be it?"

Holmes said, "Not that I could imagine. I've never heard of a blowfly of that kind being able to *sting*. Perhaps it was some other kind of insect?"

"No, I should know. I flattened it like an oyster out of season." Lowell grinned. "It was one of those I brought you, Holmes."

Holmes considered this. "Longfellow, has Professor Agassiz returned from Brazil?"

Longfellow said, "Just this week, I believe."

"I suggest that we send the insect samples you recovered to Agassiz's museum," Holmes said to Lowell. "There is nothing he doesn't know about nature's beasts."

Lowell had had more than enough on the topic of his own well-being. "If you must. Now, I propose to follow Bachi for a few days—assuming he hasn't already dropped dead from drinking. See if he leads us somewhere revealing. Two of us shall wait outside his apartment with a carriage while the others wait here. If there are no objections, I shall lead the team to watch Bachi. Who shall come with me?"

Nobody volunteered. Fields nonchalantly pulled out his watch chain.

"Oh, come now!" Lowell said. He clapped his publisher on the shoulder. "Fields, you'll come."

"I'm sorry, Lowell. I had to promise Oscar Houghton an afternoon dinner with Longfellow and myself for today. He received a note from Augustus Manning last evening warning him to cease printing Longfellow's translation or risk the loss of Harvard's business. We must do something quickly or Houghton shall bend."

"And I have a speaking engagement at the Odeon on the latest developments in homeopathy and allopathy that could not be canceled without severe financial loss to the organizers," Dr. Holmes said preemptively. "All are welcome to come, of course!"

"But we may have just turned a corner here!" Lowell said.

"Lowell," said Fields. "If we allow Dr. Manning to overtake Dante while we are busy with this, then all our translation work, all that we have hoped for, shall be for naught. It shall only take an hour to assuage Houghton, and then we can do as you say."

That afternoon, the deep smell of steaks and the muffled content sound of midday meals came to Longfellow as he stood in front of the stone Greek façade of the Revere House. A meal with Oscar Houghton would be an hour's grace at least from talk of murder and insects. Fields, leaning on the driver's box of his carriage, was instructing his driver to return to Charles Street—Annie Fields had to get to her Ladies' Club in Cambridge. Fields was the only member of Longfellow's circle to own a private carriage, not only because the publisher had the greatest abundance of wealth but also because he valued the luxury above the headaches caused by moody drivers and sickly horses.

Longfellow noticed a pensive lady veiled in black crossing Bowdoin Square. She held a book in her hand and ambled along slowly, deliberately, eyes downcast. He thought of the days when he would encounter Fanny Appleton on Beacon Street, how she would nod politely, never stopping to speak with him. He had met her in Europe while immersing himself in languages to prepare for his professorship, and she was pleasant enough to the professorial friend of her brother's. But back in Boston, it was as if Virgil were whispering in her ear the advice he tendered to the pilgrim in the round of the Neutrals: "Let us not speak, but look, and pass." Denied conversation with the beautiful young woman, Longfellow found himself crafting a character of a beautiful maiden in his book *Hyperion* that was modeled after her.

But months passed without the young woman replying to the gesture of the man she called Professor or Prof, though surely if she had read it she had seen herself in the character. When he finally did meet Fanny again, she made it quite clear that she did not enjoy being enslaved into the professor's book for everyone to glare upon. He did not think to apologize, but over the next months did open his emotions to her in ways he had never done, not even with Mary Potter, the young bride who had died during a miscarriage only a few years after she and Longfellow married. Miss Appleton and Professor Longfellow began to come together regularly. In May 1843, Longfellow wrote a note, proposing marriage. The same day, he received her acceptance. *Oh, Day forever blessed, that ushered in this* Vita Nuova, *this New Life of happiness!* He repeated the words over and over again until they took on shape, had weight, could be embraced and sheltered like children.

"Where can Houghton be?" Fields asked as his carriage was driven away. "He had better not have forgotten our dinner."

"Perhaps he was held up at Riverside. Madam." Longfellow raised his hat to a corpulent woman passing them on the sidewalk, who smiled bashfully in return. Whenever Longfellow addressed a woman, however briefly, it was as if he were offering a bouquet of flowers.

"Who was that?" Fields crunched his eyebrows.

"That," Longfellow answered, "is the lady who waited on us at supper at Copeland's two winters ago."

"Oh well, yes. At any rate, if he is held up at Riverside, he had better be at work on your plates for the *Inferno* that we have to send to Florence."

"Fields," Longfellow said with lips tightly pursed.

"I'm sorry, Longfellow," Fields said. "Next time I see her, I promise I shall lift my hat."

Longfellow shook his head. "No. Over there." Fields followed the direction of Longfellow's stare to an oddly bent man with a shiny oilskin satchel, who was walking a little too briskly along the sidewalk opposite.

"That's Bachi."

"*He* was once a Harvard instructor?" replied the publisher. "He's as bloodshot as an autumn sunset." They watched the Italian instructor's walk crescendo into a trot and end with a sharp skip into a corner storefront with a low-shingled roof and shoddy window card that read WADE AND SON & CO.

"Do you know that store?" Longfellow asked.

Fields did not. "He seems to be in an important rush, doesn't he."

"Mr. Houghton shall not mind waiting a few moments." Longfellow took Fields's arm. "Come, we might learn something more from him by catching him unprepared."

As they started toward the corner to cross the street, they both watched George Washington Greene gingerly step out of Metcalf's Apothecary with an armful of goods; the man of many ills treated himself to new medicines as one would treat himself to ice cream. Longfellow's friends often lamented that Metcalf's potions against neuralgia, dysentery, and the like—sold under a sign depicting a wise figure with an exaggerated nose—contributed heavily to Greene's frequent Rip Van Winkle spells at their translation sessions.

"Good Lord, it's Greene," Longfellow said to his publisher. "It is imperative, Fields, that we keep him from speaking with Bachi."

"Why?" Fields asked.

But Greene's approach proscribed further discussion. "My dear Fields. And Longfellow! What brings you gentlemen out today?"

"My dear friend," Longfellow said, anxiously eyeing the canopy-shaded door of Wade and Son across the street for any sign of Bachi. "We have just come for dinner at the Revere House. But are you not meant to be in East Greenwich this time of week?"

Greene nodded and sighed at the same time. "Shelly wishes me under her care until my health takes an upturn. But I shan't stay in bed all day, though her doctor insists! Pain never killed anyone, but it is a most uncomfortable bedfellow." He went into great detail about his newest symptoms. Longfellow and Fields fixed their eyes across the street as Greene prattled on. "But I oughtn't bore everyone with the doldrums of my ailments. All would be worth the frustration for another Dante session—and still I have received no word of one for weeks! I have begun to worry the project has been abandoned. Pray tell me, dear Longfellow, that this is not the case."

"We have taken but a slight pause," Longfellow said, craning his neck to look across the street, where Bachi could be seen through the store window. He was gesturing energetically.

"We shall resume shortly, though, no doubt," Fields added. A carriage pulled up at the corner across the street, blocking their view of the storefront and of Bachi. "I'm afraid we must take our leave now, Mr. Greene," Fields said urgently, squeezing Longfellow's elbow and steering him ahead.

"But you are confused, gentlemen! You've passed the Revere House in the other direction!" Greene laughed.

"Yes, well . . ." Fields searched for a passable excuse as they waited for a pair of oncoming coaches to cross the busy intersection.

"Greene," Longfellow interrupted. "We must make a brief stop first. Pray start for the restaurant and dine with us and Mr. Houghton?"

"I'm afraid my daughter shall be cross as a terrier if I am not back," Greene worried. "Oh, look who comes now!" Greene stepped back and wobbled off the narrow sidewalk. "Mr. Houghton!"

"My most grave apologies, gentlemen." An ungainly man in undertaker's black appeared beside them and lowered his improbably long arm to the first taker, which happened to be George Washington Greene. "I was about to go into Revere House when I saw you three from the corner of my eye. I hope your wait was not long. Mr. Greene, dear sir, are you joining us? How have you been then, my good man?"

"Quite malnourished," Greene answered, now clothed fully in pathos, "in a life when our Wednesday-evening Dante circles were my first and last sustenance."

Longfellow and Fields alternated their surveillance in fifteen-second shifts. The entrance of Wade and Son was still blocked by the intrusive carriage, whose driver sat patiently as though his special commission were to frustrate the view of Messrs. Longfellow and Fields.

"Did you say *were?*" Houghton said to Greene in surprise. "Fields, has this something to do with Dr. Manning? But what of the celebration in Florence waiting for a special printing of the first volume? I must know if the publication dates have been pushed back. I shan't be kept dark!"

"Of course not, Houghton," Fields said. "We have just slackened the reins a bit."

"And what is a man accustomed to the pleasures of that weekly bit of paradise to do with himself in their stead, I ask?" lamented Greene dramatically.

"I know not," Houghton replied. "I worry, though, with the inflated prices printing a book such as this . . . I must ask, can your Dante overcome whatever Manning and Harvard plan to put in his way?"

Greene's hands shook as he raised them in the air. "If it were possible to convey an accurate idea of Dante in a single word, Mr. Houghton, that word would be *power.* That landscape of his world ever after takes its place in your memory by the side of your real world. Even the sounds which he has described linger in the ear as the types of harshness, or loudness, or sweetness, instantly coming back to you whenever you listen to the roaring of the sea or the howling of the wind, or the carol of the birds."

Bachi exited the store, and they could now see him perusing the contents of his satchel with an air of great excitement.

Greene stopped himself. "Fields? Why, whatever is the matter? You seem to be waiting for something to happen across the way."

Longfellow signaled Fields with a flick of a wrist to occupy their interlocutor. As partners in a crisis in some way manage to communicate complex strategy with the slightest gesture, Fields enacted a diversion for their old friend, draping his arm loosely around his shoulders. "You see, Greene, there are several developments in the field of publishing since the end of the war . . ."

Longfellow pulled Houghton aside and spoke under his breath. "I'm afraid we shall have to postpone our dinner for another time. A horsecar should be leaving for Back Bay in ten minutes. I beg you to walk Mr. Greene there. Put him aboard, and don't leave till the car starts. Watch that he doesn't get off," Longfellow said with a slight lifting of the eyebrows that adequately conveyed his urgency.

Houghton returned a soldierly nod without appeal for further explanation. Had Henry Longfellow ever asked a personal favor from him, or from anyone that he knew? The Riverside Press owner slipped his arm through Greene's. "Mr. Greene, shall I accompany you to the horsecars? I believe the next one is leaving shortly, and one should not be standing so long in this November chill."

With hasty farewells, Longfellow and Fields waited as two massive omnibuses rumbled down the street, ringing their bells as warning. The two men started across the street only to notice in unison that the Italian instructor was no longer on the corner. They looked one block ahead and one block behind, but he was nowhere in sight.

"Where in the devil . . . ?" Fields asked.

Longfellow pointed and Fields looked in time to see Bachi seated comfortably in the backseat of that very carriage that had been blocking their surveillance. The cab's horses clopped away, not seeming to share the impatience of their passenger.

"And not a cab in sight to be hired!" Longfellow said.

"We may be able to catch him," said Fields. "Pike the cabman's livery is a few blocks from here. The rascal asks a quarter for a seat in his carriage, a half-dollar when he feels particularly extortionate. Nobody on the block can suffer him but Holmes, and he suffers no one else but the doctor."

Fields and Longfellow, walking briskly, found Pike not at his livery but stationed stubbornly in front of the brick mansion at 21 Charles Street. The duo made a plea for Pike's services. Fields held up handfuls of cash.

"I cannot help you gents for all the money in the Commonwealth," Pike said gruffly. "I'm engaged to drive Dr. Holmes."

"Listen to us carefully, Pike." Fields exaggerated the natural command of his voice. "We are very close associates of Dr. Holmes. He would tell you himself to take us."

"You're friends of the doctor's?" Pike asked.

"Yes!" Fields cried with relief.

"Then as friends you ain't likely to take his cab away. I'm engaged to Dr. Holmes," Pike repeated blandly, and sat back to whittle the remains of an ivory toothpick with his teeth.

"Well!" Oliver Wendell Holmes beamed, strutting out onto his front step holding a handbag and dressed in a dark worsted suit with a white silk neck cloth done up nicely in a cravat, finished with a beautiful white rose in his buttonhole. "Fields. Longfellow. So you've come to hear about allopathy after all!"

Pike's horses whirled down Charles Street into the knotted streets of downtown, grazing lampposts and cutting ahead of irate horsecar drivers. Pike's was a dilapidated rockaway carriage, with a berth wide enough for four passengers to sit without smashing their knees together. Dr. Holmes had instructed the driver to arrive promptly at a quarter to one in order to drive to the Odeon, but now the destination had been changed, seemingly against the doctor's will from the perspective of the driver, and the number of passengers had tripled. Pike had a good mind to drive them to the Odeon anyway.

"What of my lecture?" Holmes asked Fields in the back of the carriage. "It's sold-out, you know!"

"Pike can have you there in no time as soon as we find Bachi and ask him a question or two," Fields said. "And I'll make certain the papers don't report that you were late. If only I had not sent my carriage away for Annie, we would not have fallen behind!"

"But whatever do you imagine you'll accomplish if we *do* find him?" Holmes asked.

Longfellow explained. "Clearly, Bachi is anxious today. If we speak to him away from his home—and his drink—he may be less resistant. If Greene had not happened upon us, we likely would have caught Ser Bachi without such haste. I half wish we could simply tell poor Greene all that has happened, but the truth would be a shock to such a weak constitution. He has had all calamities and believes the world is against him. Nothing remains for him but to be struck by lightning."

"There it is!" Fields cried. He pointed to a carriage some fifty rods ahead of them. "Longfellow, isn't that it?"

Longfellow extended his neck out the side, feeling the wind catch his beard, and signaled his assent.

"Cabby, steer right on!" Fields called out.

Pike snapped the reins, careening down the street at a pace far beyond the speed limit—which the Boston Board of Safety had recently set at a "moderate trot." "We're going quite far east!" Pike shouted over the cobbled hoof-falls. "Quite a ways from the Odeon, you know, Dr. Holmes!"

Fields asked Longfellow, "Why did we have to hide Bachi from Greene? I didn't think they'd be acquainted."

"Long ago." Longfellow nodded. "Mr. Greene met Bachi in Rome, before the worst of his maladies showed themselves. I was afraid that if we had approached Bachi with Greene present, Greene would have spoken too much of our Dante project—as he is wont to do with any who will suffer it!—and that would interfere with Bachi's willingness to talk, making him feel only more wretched in his position."

Pike lost sight of their object several times, but through quick turns, remarkably timed gallops, and patient slowdowns, he regained an advantage. The other cabdriver seemed in a hurry, too, but fully oblivious of the chase. Near the narrowing roads of the harbor area, their prey slipped away again. Then it reappeared, causing Pike to curse God's name, then apologize for it, then stop short, sending Holmes flying across the carriage onto Longfellow's lap.

"There she goes!" Pike called out as his counterpart drove his coach toward them, away from the harbor. But its passenger seat had been vacated.

"He must have gone to the harbor!" Fields said.

Pike picked up the pace once more and ousted his passengers. The trio pushed against the grain of cheerers and wavers, who were watching various ships disappear into the fog while Godspeeding with waving handkerchiefs.

"Most of the ships this time of day are toward Long Wharf," said Longfellow. In earlier years, he had frequently walked to the wharves to see the grand vessels coming in from Germany or Spain and to hear the men and women speak their native tongues. There was in Boston no greater Babylon of languages and skin tones than the wharves.

Fields had trouble keeping up. "Wendell?"

"Up here, Fields!" Holmes cried from inside a throng of people.

Holmes found Longfellow describing Bachi to a black stevedore who was loading barrels.

Fields decided to question passengers in the other direction, but soon stopped to rest on the edge of a pier.

"You there in the fancy suit." A bulky pier master with a greasy beard grabbed Fields's arm roughly and pushed him away. "Stand aside from these comin' on board if you hain't got a ticket."

"Good sir," Fields said. "I am in need of immediate assistance. A small man in a rumpled blue frock coat, with bloodshot eyes—have you seen him?"

The pier master ignored him, occupied with organizing the line of passengers by class and compartment. Fields watched as the man removed his cap (too small for his mammoth head) and twirled a sharp hand through his tangled hair.

Fields closed his eyes as though entranced, listening to the man's strange, excitable commands. Into his mind came a dim room with a little taper of restless energy burning on a mantel. "*Hawthorne,*" Fields gasped, almost involuntarily.

The pier master paused and turned to Fields. "What?"

"Hawthorne." Fields smiled, knowing he was right. "You are an avid admirer of Mr. Hawthorne's novels."

"Well, I say . . ." The pier master prayed or swore under his breath. "How did you know that? Tell me at once!"

The passengers he was organizing into categories stopped to listen, too.

"No matter." Fields felt a rush of elation that he had retained his skills of reading people that had profited him so many years earlier as a young bookseller's clerk. "Write your address on this slip of paper and I shall send you the new Blue and Gold collection of all Hawthorne's great works, authorized by his widow." Fields held out the paper, then withdrew it into his palm. "If you assist me today, sir."

The man, suddenly superstitious of Fields's powers, complied.

Fields propped himself on his toes and spotted Longfellow and Holmes coming in his direction. He called out. "Check that pier!"

Holmes and Longfellow flagged down a harbormaster. They described Bachi.

"And who might you be?"

"We're good friends of his," Holmes cried. "Pray tell us, where has he gone to?" Fields now caught up with them.

"Well, I seen him coming into the harbor," the man answered with a frustratingly meandering tempo. "I believe he ran aboard *there*, as anxious as could be," he said, pointing to a small boat at sea that could not have held more than five passengers.

"Good, that little bark can't be going very far. Where is it headed?" Fields asked.

"That? That's just a water transport, sir. The *Anonimo* is too big to fit in this pier. So it's waiting all the way out downstream. You see?"

Its outline was barely visible in the fog, disappearing and then reappearing, but it was as gigantic a steamer as they had ever seen.

"Oh, your friend was quite eager to get on, I guess. That little boat he's on is just taking the last shipment of passengers who were late coming. Then it's off."

"Off to where?" Fields asked, his heart sinking.

"Why, across the Atlantic, sir." The harbormaster glanced at his slate. "A stop at Marseilles, and, ah, here we are, then on to *Italy*!"

Dr. Holmes made it to the Odeon with more than enough time to deliver a roundly well-received lecture. His audience thought him all the more important a speaker for having been delayed. Longfellow and Fields sat attentively in the second row next to Dr. Holmes's younger son, Neddie, the two Amelias, and Holmes's brother, John. For the second of a three-part sold-out lecture series arranged by Fields, Holmes examined medical methods in relation to the war.

Healing is a living process, Holmes told his audience, greatly under the influence of mental conditions. He told them how it was often found that the same wound received in battle would heal well in the soldiers that have prevailed but would prove fatal in those who were just defeated. "Thus emerges that middle region between science and poetry that sensible men, as they are called, are very shy of meddling with."

Holmes looked out at the row of family and friends and at the empty seat reserved in case Wendell Junior had shown up.

"My oldest boy received more than one of these wounds during the war, being sent home by Uncle Sam with a few new buttonholes in his congenital waistcoat." Laughter. "There were a good many hearts pierced in this war, too, that have no bullet mark to show."

After the lecture, and the necessary amount of praise bestowed on Dr. Holmes, Longfellow and Holmes accompanied their publisher back to the Authors' Room at the Corner to wait for Lowell. There, it was decided that a meeting of their translation club should be arranged at Longfellow's house for the following Wednesday.

The planned session would serve a dual purpose. First, it would allay any concerns of Greene's as to the state of the translation and the odd behavior he and Houghton had witnessed, and so would minimize the risk of further interference of the kind that had cost them whatever information Bachi might have possessed. Second, and perhaps more important, it would allow further progress on Longfellow's translation. Longfellow intended to keep his promise to have *Inferno* ready to send to the year's final Dante Festival in Florence for the six-hundredth anniversary of the poet's birth in 1265.

Longfellow had not wanted to admit that he was unlikely to finish before the close of 1865 unless their investigations came upon some miraculous advance. Still, he had begun to work on his translations at night, alone, entreating Dante privately for wisdom in seeing through the baffling ends of Healey and Talbot.

"Is Mr. Lowell about?" said a small voice, accompanied by a knock at the Authors' Room door.

The poets were exhausted. "I'm afraid not," Fields called back with undisguised annoyance to the invisible questioner.

"Excellent!"

Boston's merchant prince, Phineas Jennison, dapper as always in white suit and hat, slid inside and slammed the door behind him without ruffling a feather. "One of your clerks said you could be found here, Mr. Fields. I wish to speak freely about Lowell and would just as soon the old boy not be present." He tossed his long silk hat onto Fields's iron rack, his shiny hair going off to the left in a superb sweep, like the handrail of a banister. "Mr. Lowell's in trouble."

The visitor gasped upon noticing the two poets. He nearly stooped down on one knee as he clasped the hands of Holmes and Longfellow, handling them like bottles of the rarest and most sensitive vintages.

Jennison enjoyed spreading his vast wealth by patronizing artists and by refining his appreciation of belles lettres; and had never ceased to be overwhelmed by the geniuses he knew only because of his riches. Jennison helped himself to a seat. "Mr. Fields. Mr. Longfellow. Dr. Holmes," he said, naming them with exaggerated ceremony. "You are all dear friends of Lowell's, dearer than is my own privilege of acquaintance, for only through genius is genius truly known."

Holmes cut him off nervously. "Mr. Jennison, has something happened with Jamey?"

"I *know*, Doctor." Jennison sighed heavily at having to elaborate. "I know of these accursed Dante happenings, and I'm here because I wish to assist you in doing what is required to reverse them."

"Dante happenings?" Fields echoed in a broken voice.

Jennison nodded solemnly.

"The accursed Corporation and their hopes to rid themselves of that Dante course of Lowell's. And their attempt to stop your translation, my dear gentlemen! Lowell told me all about it, though he's too proud to ask for help."

Three muffled sighs escaped from under the respective waistcoats at Jennison's elaboration.

"Now, as surely you know, Lowell has temporarily canceled his class," Jennison said, showing his frustration at their apparent obliviousness of their own business. "Well, it won't do, I say. It does not befit a genius of James Russell Lowell's caliber and must not be permitted without a fight. I fear Lowell is at imminent hazard of going to pieces if he starts down roads of conciliation! And over at the College, I hear Manning is gleeful." He said this with grim concern.

"What do you wish us to do, my dear Mr. Jennison?" asked Fields with a play at deference.

"Urge him to screw up his courage." Jennison demonstrated his point with a fist in his palm. "Save him from cowardice, or our city shall lose one of its strongest hearts. I have had another idea as well. Create a permanent organization devoted to the study of Dante—I myself would take up Italian to assist you!" Jennison's flashy smile broke through, as did his leather money belt, from which he now counted out large bills. "A Dante association of some sort dedicated to protecting this literature so dear to you gentlemen. What say you? No one shall have to know of my involvement, and you shall give the fellows a run for it."

Before anyone could reply, the door to the Authors' Room burst open. Lowell stood before them with a bleak look on his face.

"Why, Lowell, what's wrong?" Fields asked.

Lowell began to speak but then saw him. "Phinny? What are you doing here?"

Jennison looked to Fields for help. "Mr. Jennison and I had some business to conclude," said Fields, stuffing the money belt into the businessman's hands and pushing him out the door. "But he was just on his way out."

"I hope nothing's wrong, Lowell. I shall call on you soon, my friend!"

Fields found Teal, the evening shop boy, down the hall and asked for Jennison to be escorted downstairs. Then he barred the Authors' Room door.

Lowell poured a drink at the counter. "Oh, you won't believe the luck, my friends. I almost twisted my head off looking for Bachi at Half Moon Place, and wouldn't you know I come up with as little as I started! He was nowhere to be seen and nobody around knew where he could be found—I don't think the local Dubliners would talk to an Italian if put in a sinking raft next to one and the Italian had a plug. I might as well have been off at leisure like all of you this afternoon."

Fields, Holmes, and Longfellow were silent.

"What? What is it?" Lowell asked.

Longfellow suggested that they have supper at Craigie House, and on the way they explained to Lowell what had happened with Bachi. Over the meal, Fields told him how he had returned to the harbormaster and persuaded him, with the help of an American eagle gold piece, to check the register for information on Bachi's trip. The entry for Bachi indicated that he had purchased a discounted round-trip ticket that would not allow a return prior to January 1867.

Back in Longfellow's parlor, Lowell flopped into a chair, stunned. "He knew we had found him. Well of course—we let him find out that we knew about Lonza! Our Lucifer has slipped through our fingers like so much sand!"

"Then we should celebrate," Holmes said with a laugh. "Don't you see what this means, if you *were* right? Come, you have the small end of your opera glass pointed toward everything that looks encouraging."

Fields leaned in. "Jamey, if Bachi was the murderer . . ."

Holmes completed the thought with a bright smile: "Then we are safe. And the city's safe. And Dante! If we have driven him out by our knowledge, then we *have* defeated him, Lowell."

Fields stood up, beaming. "Oh, gentlemen, I shall throw a Dante supper to put the Saturday Club to shame. May the mutton be as tender as Longfellow's verse! And may the Moët sparkle like Holmes's wit, and the carving knives be as sharp as Lowell's satire!"

Three cheers were given to Fields.

All of this eased Lowell somewhat, as did the news of a Dante-translation session—the start of normal times again, a return to a pure enjoyment of their scholarship. He hoped they had not forfeited this pleasure by applying their knowledge of Dante to such repugnant affairs.

Longfellow seemed to know what troubled Lowell. "In Washington's day," he said, "they melted the pipes of the church organs for bullets, my dear Lowell. They hadn't any choice. Now, Lowell, Holmes, would you accompany me down to the wine cellar while Fields sees how work goes along in the kitchen?" he asked as he lifted a candle from the table.

"Ah, the true foundation of any house!" Lowell jumped from the armchair. "Do you have a good vintage, Longfellow?"

"You know my rule of thumb, Mr. Lowell:

'When you ask one friend to dine,
give him your best wine.
When you ask two,
the second best will do.'"

The company let out a collective peal of laughter, inflated by a consciousness of relief.

"But we have four thirsts to quench!" Holmes objected.

"Then let us not expect much, my dear doctor," advised Longfellow. Holmes and Lowell followed him down to the basement by the light of the taper's silver gleam. Lowell used the laughter and conversation to divert himself from the shooting pain radiating in his leg, pounding and traveling upward from the red disk covering his ankle.

Phineas Jennison, in white coat, yellow waistcoat, and insistent wide-brimmed white hat, came down the steps of his Back Bay mansion. He walked and whistled. He twirled his gold-trimmed walking staff. He laughed heartily, as if he just heard a fine joke in his head. Phineas Jennison often laughed to himself in this way while rambling through Boston, the city he had conquered, every evening. There was one world remaining to obtain, one where money had severe limits, where blood determined much of one's status, and this conquest he was about to fulfill, in spite of recent hindrances.

From the other side of the street he was watched, watched step after step from the moment he left behind his mansion. The next shade needing punishment. Look how he walks and whistles and laughs, as though he knows no wrong and has known none. Step after step. The shame of a city that could no longer direct the course of the future. A city that had lost its soul. He who sacrified the one who could reunify them all. The watcher called out.

Jennison stopped, rubbing his famously indented chin. He squinted into the night. "Someone say my name there?"

No reply.

Jennison crossed the street and glanced ahead with faint recognition and ease at the person standing motionlessly beside the church. "Ah, you. I remember you. What is it you wanted?"

Jennison felt the man twist behind him, and then something pierced the merchant prince's back.

"Take my money, sir, take it all! Please! You can have it and be on your way! How much do you want? Name it! What say you?"

"Through me the way is among the people lost. Through me."

The last thing J. T. Fields expected to find when he set off the next morning in his carriage was a dead body.

"Just up ahead," Fields said to his driver. Fields and Lowell stepped down and walked up the sidewalk to Wade and Son. "This is where Bachi went in before rushing to the harbor." Fields showed Lowell.

They had found no listing of the store in any of the city directories.

"I'll be hanged if Bachi wasn't doing something shady here," Lowell said.

They knocked quietly without producing a response. Then, after a while, the door swung open and a man in a long blue coat with bright buttons brushed past. He was holding an overfilled box of assorted cargo.

"Beg pardon," Fields said. Two other policemen were approaching now, and they opened the doors to Wade and Son wider, pushing Lowell and Fields in. Inside was a lantern-jawed older man slumped on the counter, a pen still in his hand, as though he had been in mid-sentence. The walls and shelves were bare. Lowell inched closer. A telegraph wire was still wrapped around the dead man's neck. The poet stared with fascination at how lifelike the man seemed.

Fields rushed to his side and pulled his arm toward the door. "He's dead, Lowell!"

"Dead as one of Holmes's carcasses at the medical college," Lowell agreed. "No murder so mundane could be done by our Dantean, I'm afraid."

"Lowell, come!" Fields panicked at the growing number of police busying themselves studying the room, not yet taking notice of the two intruders.

"Fields, there's a suitcase beside him. He was getting ready to flee, just as Bachi did." He looked again at the pen in the deceased's hand. "He was trying to get done his unfinished business, I would rather think."

"Lowell, please!" Fields cried.

"Very well, Fields." But Lowell circled toward the corpse and stopped at the mail tray on the desk, slipping the top envelope into his coat pocket. "Come on then." Lowell started to the door. Fields rushed ahead but stopped to look back when he did not feel Lowell's presence behind him. Lowell had paused in the middle of the room with a frightening, pained expression on his face.

"What is it, Lowell?"

"My blasted ankle."

When Fields turned back to the door, a policeman was waiting with a curious expression. "We'd just been looking for our friend, Mr. Officer, whom we last saw enter this store yesterday."

After listening to their story, the policeman decided to write it down in his memorandum book. "That friend's name was again, sir? The Eyetalian?"

"Bachi. B-a-c-h-i."

When Lowell and Fields were permitted to leave, Detective Henshaw and two other men from the detective bureau had arrived with the coroner, Mr. Barnicoat, and dismissed most of the policemen. "Bury him in the paupers' cemetery with the rest of the filth," said Henshaw when he saw the body. "Ichabod Ross. Waste of my good time. Could still be having my breakfast." Fields lingered until Henshaw met his eyes with a watchful glare.

The evening paper contained a small piece on the killing of Ichabod Ross, a minor merchant, during a robbery.

On the envelope that Lowell had pilfered was written VANE'S TIMEPIECES. It was a pawnshop on one of the less desirable streets of East Boston.

When Lowell and Fields entered the windowless storefront the next morning, they came upon a huge man, no less than three hundred pounds, with a face as red as the most seasonal tomato and a greenish beard filling out his chin. An enormous set of keys dangled from a rope around his neck and clanked whenever he moved. "Mr. Vane?"

"Dead to rights," he replied, then his smile froze as he looked up and down the questioners' clothing. "I've already told those New York detectives I didn't pass those queer bills!"

"We're not detectives," said Lowell. "We believe this belongs to you." He placed the envelope on the counter. "It's from Ichabod Ross."

An enormous smile slithered into place. "Well, ain't that nice. Oh cow! Thought the old man would be jammed without settling with me!"

"Mr. Vane, we're sorry for the loss of your friend. Do you know why Mr. Ross would be dealt with in such a manner?" Fields asked.

"Oh? Curiosity seekers, are you? Well, you have not brought your pigs to the wrong market. What can you pay?"

"We just brought you your payment from Mr. Ross," Fields reminded him.

"Rightfully mine!" said Vane. "Do you deny it?"

"Must everything be done for the sake of money?" balked Lowell.

"Lowell, please," Fields whispered.

Vane's smile froze again as he stared ahead. His eyes doubled in size. "Lowell? Lowell the poet!"

"Why, yes . . ." Lowell confessed, a bit thrown off.

" 'And what is so rare as a day in June?' " the man said, then lapsed into laughter before continuing.

"'And what is so rare as a day in June?
Then, if ever, come perfect days;
Then Heaven tries earth if it be in tune,
And over it gently her warm ear lays;
Whether we look, or whether we listen,
We hear life murmur, or see it glisten.'"

"The word in that fourth line is *softly,*" Lowell corrected him with some indignation. "You see, '*softly* her warm ear lays . . .'"

"Never tell me there is not a great American poet! Oh, the God and the Devil, I have your house, too!" Vane announced, producing from below his counter a leather-bound *Homes and Haunts of Our Poets* and digging through it to the chapter on Elmwood. "Oh, I even keep your autograph in my catalog. Next to Longfellow, Emerson, and Whittier, you are my top-priced seller. That rascal Oliver Holmes is right up there, too, and would be higher still if he didn't put his name to so *many* things."

The man, who had flushed a Bardolphian hue from the excitement, unlocked a drawer with one of the dangling keys and fished out a strip of paper on which was signed the name of James Russell Lowell.

"Why, that is not my signature at all!" Lowell said. "Whoever wrote this can't put pen to paper! I demand you hand over all fraudulent autographs of all the authors in your possession at once, sir, or you shall hear from Mr. Hillard, my attorney, by the end of today!"

"*Lowell!*" Fields pulled him away from the counter.

"How well I shall sleep tonight knowing such a fine citizen has illustrations enough in that book to map out my home!" Lowell cried.

"We need this man's help!"

"Yes." Lowell straightened his sack coat. "In church with saints, in the tavern with sinners."

"If you please, Mr. Vane." Fields turned back to the proprietor and snapped open his wallet. "We want to know about Mr. Ross and then shall leave you be. How much will you accept to convey your knowledge?"

"I shall not part with it for one red cent!" Vane laughed heartily, his eyes seeming to go quite far back into his brain. "Must everything be done for the sake of money?"

Vane proposed forty of Lowell's autographs as sufficient payment. Fields raised an advisory eyebrow at Lowell, who sourly agreed. As Lowell signed his name down two columns of a notepaper—"A superior piece of goods," Vane declared with approval of Lowell's writing—Vane told Fields that Ross was a former newspaper printer who had moved to pressing counterfeit money. Ross had made the mistake of passing the money to a gambling ring that used the queer bills to cheat the local gambling hells, and had even used some pawnshops as unwilling fences for goods purchased with the money won from that operation (the word *unwilling* was pronounced with the utmost twist in the gentleman's mouth, the tongue reaching up and over his lips, almost wetting his nose). It was only a matter of time before the schemes caught up with him.

Back at the Corner, Fields and Lowell repeated all this to Longfellow and Holmes. "I suppose we can guess what was in Bachi's satchel when he left Ross's store," said Fields. "A bag of queer bills as some sort of desperate arrangement. But what would he be doing mixed up in counterfeiting?"

"If you can't earn money, I suppose you must *make* it," said Holmes.

"Whatever brought him in," said Longfellow, "it seems Signor Bachi found his way out just in time."

When Wednesday evening came, Longfellow welcomed his guests from the Craigie House doorstep in the old manner. As they entered, they received a secondary welcome in the form of a yelp from Trap. George Washington Greene confessed how much heartier his health had been after receiving word of a meeting and that he hoped they would now resume their regular schedule. He was as diligently prepared for their assigned cantos as ever.

Longfellow called for the meeting to begin, and the scholars settled down into their places. The host passed out Dante's canto in Italian and the corresponding proofs of his English translation. Trap watched the proceedings with keen interest. Satisfied with the accustomed orderly seating arrangements and his master's comfort, the canine sentry settled down in the hollow under Greene's cavernous armchair. Trap knew the old man harbored special affection for him that manifested itself in food from the supper table and, besides, Greene's velveteen chair was positioned closest to the deep warmth of the study's hearth.

"A devil is behind here, who doth cleave us."

• • •

After taking his leave from the Central Station, Nicholas Rey tried to fight drifting off to sleep in the horsecar. It was only now that he felt how little rest he had been getting each night, though he had practically been chained to his desk by Mayor Lincoln's orders with little to fill his day. Kurtz had found a new driver, a green patrolman from Watertown. In Rey's brief dream set to the rough motions of the car, a bestial man approached him and whispered, "I can't die as I'm here," but even while dreaming, Rey knew that *here* was not a part of the puzzle left for him to solve on the grounds of Elisha Talbot's demise. *I can't die as I'm.* He was awakened by two men, hanging from the car's straps, arguing about the merits of women's suffrage, and then came drowsy decision—and a realization: that the beastly figure in his dream had the face of the leaper, though amplified in size three or four times. Soon the bell tinkled and the conductor shouted, "Mount Auburn! Mount Auburn!"

Having waited for Father to depart for his Dante Club meeting, Mabel Lowell, who had recently turned eighteen, stood over his French mahogany writing desk, which had been demoted to paper storage by Father, who preferred to write on an old pasteboard pad in his corner armchair.

She missed Father's good spirits around Elmwood. Mabel Lowell had no interest in chasing after Harvard boys or sitting with little Amelia Holmes's sewing circle and talking of whom they would accept or reject (except for foreign girls, whose rejection required no discussion) as if the whole civilized world were waiting to get into the sewing club. Mabel wanted to read and to travel the world to see in life what she had read about in books, her father's and those of other visionary writers.

Father's papers were in a customary disarray that, while decreasing the risk of future detection, necessitated special delicacy, as the unwieldy piles could tip over all at once. She found quills worn down to stumps and many half-completed poems, with frustrating blots of ink trailing off where she wished to read more. Her father often warned her never to write verses, as most turned out bad and the good ones were as unfinishable as a beautiful person.

There was a strange sketch—a pencil sketch on lined paper. It was drawn with the stilted care one devoted, she imagined, to diagramming a map when lost in the woods or, she also imagined, when tracing hieroglyphics—drawn solemnly in an attempt to decode some meaning or guidance. When she was a child and Father traveled, he had always illustrated the margins of letters home with crudely drawn figures of lyceum organizers or foreign dignitaries with whom he had supped. Now, thinking of how those humorous illustrations made her laugh, she at first concluded that the sketch depicted a man's legs, oversize ice skates on his feet and a flat board of some kind where his waist would otherwise start. Unsatisfied with the interpretation, Mabel turned the paper sideways and then upside down. She noticed that the jagged lines on the feet might represent curls of fire rather than skates.

Longfellow read from his translation of Canto Twenty-eight, where they had left off at their last session. He would be glad to drop off the final proofs of this canto with Houghton and check it off the list kept at Riverside Press. It was physically the most unpleasant section of all *Inferno.* Here, Virgil has guided Dante into the ninth ditch of a wide section of Hell known as Malebolge, the Evil Pouch. Here were the Schismatics, those who had divided nations, religions, and families in life and now find themselves divided in Hell—bodily—maimed and cut asunder.

" 'I saw one,' " Longfellow read his version of Dante's words, " 'rent from his chin to where one breaketh wind.' "

Longfellow took a long breath before moving on.

> *" 'Between his legs were hanging down his entrails;*
> *His heart was visible, as was the dismal sack*
> *That maketh excrement of what is eaten.' "*

Dante had shown restraint before this. This canto demonstrated Dante's true belief in God. Only one with the strongest faith in the immortal soul could conceive of such gross torment to the mortal body.

"The filthiness of some of these passages," said Fields, "would disgrace the drunkenest horse dealer."

> *" 'Another one, who had his throat pierced through,*
> *And nose cut off close underneath the brows,*
> *And had no longer but a single ear,*
> *Staying to look in wonder with the others,*

Before the others did his gullet open,
Which outwardly was red in every part'"

And these were men whom Dante had known! This shade with nose and ear cut off, Pier da Medicina of Bologna, had not harmed Dante personally, though he had fed dissension among the citizens of Dante's Florence. Dante had never been able to remove his thoughts from Florence as he wrote his journey into the afterworld. He needed to see his heroes redeemed in Purgatory and rewarded in Paradise; he longed to meet the wicked in the infernal circles below. The poet did not merely imagine Hell as a possibility, he felt its reality. Dante even saw an Alighieri relative there among the ones cut apart, pointing at him, demanding revenge for his death.

In the Craigie House basement kitchen, little Annie Allegra crept in from the hall, trying to rub the sleepiness from her eyes.

Peter was feeding a bucket of coal into the kitchen stove. "Miss Annie, didn't Mistah Longfellow see you to sleep already?"

She struggled to keep her eyes open. "I wish to have a cup of milk, Peter."

"I'll bring you one shortly, Miss Annie," one of the cooks said in a singsong voice as she peeked in on the bread baking. "Happily, dear, happily."

A faint knock drifted in from the front of the house. Annie excitedly claimed the privilege of answering it, always warming to tasks meant for the help, especially greeting callers. The little girl scrambled up to the front hall and pulled open the massive door.

"Shhhhhh!" Annie Allegra Longfellow whispered before she could even see the handsome face of the caller. He bent down. "Today is *Wednesday,*" she explained confidentially, cupping her hands. "If you are here to see Papa, you must wait until he is through with Mr. Lowell and the others. Those are the rules, you know. You may stay out here or in the parlor if you like," she added, pointing out his options.

"I do apologize for the intrusion, Miss Longfellow," Nicholas Rey said.

Annie Allegra nodded prettily and, fighting back the renewed weight of her eyelids, slouched up the angled stairs, forgetting why she had made the long trip down.

Nicholas Rey stood in the front hall of Craigie House among Washington's portraits. He removed the bits of paper from his pocket. He would plead their help once more, this time showing them the scraps he had picked up from the ground around Talbot's death site in hopes that there was some connection they might see that he could not. He had found several foreigners around the wharves who had recognized the likeness of the leaper; this reinforced Rey's conviction that the leaper was foreign, that it was some other language that had been whispered in his ear. And this conviction could not help but remind Rey that Dr. Holmes and the others knew something more than they could tell him.

Rey started toward the parlor but stopped before he made it out of the front hall. He turned in astonishment. Something had snagged him. What had he just heard? He retraced his steps, then moved nearer to the study door.

"*'Che le ferrite son richiuse prima ch'altri dinanzi li rivada . . .'*"

Rey shuddered. He counted out three more soundless steps to the door of the study. "*'Dinanzi li rivada.'*" He tore out a notepaper from his vest and found the word: *Deenanzee*. The word had taunted him since the beggar crashed through the station house window, spelling itself out in his dreams and the pumping of his heart. Rey leaned against the study door and pressed his ear flush with the cool white wood.

"Here Betrand de Born, who severed a son's ties with a father by instigating war between them, holds aloft his own dissevered head in his hand like a lantern, speaking to the Florentine pilgrim from his detached head and mouth." That was the soothing voice of Longfellow.

"Like Irving's Headless Horseman." The unmistakable baritone laugh of Lowell.

Rey flipped over the paper and wrote what he heard.

> *Because I parted persons so united,*
> *I now bear my brain parted—Alas!—*
> *From its beginning, which is in this body.*
> *Thus observe in me the* contrapasso.

Contrapasso? A soft nasal drone. Snoring. Rey became self-conscious and quieted his own breathing. He heard a scratchy symphony of scribbling nibs.

"Dante's most perfect punishment," said Lowell.

"Dante himself might agree," replied another.

Rey's thoughts were too snowed under for him to continue trying to distinguish the speakers, and the dialogue fell together into a chorus.

". . . It is the one time Dante calls such explicit attention to the idea of *contrapasso*—a word for which we have no exact translation, no precise definition in English, because the word in itself is its definition. . . . Well, my dear Longfellow, I would say *countersuffering* . . . the notion that each sinner must be punished by continuing the damage of his own sin against him . . . just as these Schismatics are cut apart . . ."

Rey stepped backward all the way to the front door.

"School is done, gentlemen."

Books were snapped shut and papers rustled, and Trap began barking, unnoticed, out the window.

"And we have earned some supper for our labors . . ."

※

"What a very fat pheasant this is!" James Russell Lowell, with agitated zeal, was prodding a strange skeleton's wide body and oversize flat head.

"There is no beast whose insides he hasn't taken apart and put together again," Dr. Holmes remarked laughingly, and, Lowell thought, a bit snidely.

It was early the morning after their Dante Club meeting, and Lowell and Holmes were in the laboratory of Professor Louis Agassiz at the Harvard Museum of Comparative Zoology. Agassiz had greeted them and glanced at Lowell's wound before returning to his private office to finish some business.

"Agassiz's note sounded interested in the insect samples, at least." Lowell tried to appear nonchalant. He was certain now that the insect from Healey's study had in fact bitten him, and he was deeply worried about what Agassiz would say of its terrible effects: "Ah, there's no hope, poor Lowell, what a peety." Lowell did not trust Holmes's contention that this sort of insect could not sting. What kind of insect worth a dime does not sting? Lowell waited for the fatal prognosis; it would be almost a relief to hear it spoken. He had not told Holmes how much the wound had grown in size over the last few days, how often he felt it throb violently inside his leg, and how he could trace the pain hour by hour permeating all his nerves. He would not be so weak in front of Holmes.

"Ah, do you like that, Lowell?" Louis Agassiz came in with the insect samples in his meaty hands, which always smelled of oil, fish, and alcohol, even after extensive washing. Lowell had forgotten that he was standing next to the skeleton display, which looked like a hyperbolic hen.

Agassiz said proudly, "The consul at Mauritius brought me two skeletons of the dodo while I was traveling! Isn't it a treasure?"

"Do you think it was good to eat, Agassiz?" Holmes asked.

"Oh yes. What a peety we could not have the dodo at our Saturday Club! A good dinner has always been humanity's greatest blessing. What a peety. All right then, are we ready?"

Lowell and Holmes followed him to a table and sat down. Agassiz carefully removed the insects from vials of alcohol solution. "First business, tell me. Where you did find these special leetle critters, Dr. Holmes?"

"Lowell did, actually," Holmes answered cautiously. "Near Beacon Hill."

"Beacon Hill," Agassiz echoed, though they sounded like entirely different words in his thick Swiss-German accent. "Tell me, Dr. Holmes, what do *you* think of these?"

Holmes did not like the practice of asking questions intended to produce wrong answers. " 'Tis not my line. But they are blowflies, right, Agassiz?"

"Ah yes. Genus?" Agassiz asked.

"*Cochliomyia,*" Holmes said.

"Species?"

"*Macellaria.*"

"Ah-ha!" Agassiz laughed. "They do look like that if you listen to books, don't they, dear Holmes?"

"So they're not . . . that?" Lowell asked. It looked as though all blood had drained from his face. If Holmes was wrong, then the flies might not be harmless.

"The two flies are physically almost identical," Agassiz said, then gasped in a way that cut off any response. "Almost." Agassiz made his way over to his bookshelves. His broad features and plenteous figure made him seem more successful politician than biologist and botanist. The new Museum of Comparative Zoology was the culmination of his entire career, for finally he would have the resources to complete his classification of the world's myriad unnamed species of animals and plants. "Let me show you something. There are about twenty-five hundred species of North American flies we know how to name. Yet from my estimation there are now ten thousand fly species living among us."

He laid out some drawings. They were crude, rather grotesque depictions of men's faces, their noses replaced by bizarre, darkly scribbled holes.

Agassiz explained. "A few years ago, a surgeon in the French Imperial Navy, Dr. Coquerel, was called to the colony on Devil's Island in French Guiana, South America, just north of Brazil. Five colonists were in the hospital with severe and unidentifiable symptoms. One of the men died soon after Dr. Coquerel arrived. When he flushed the body's sinuses with water, three hundred blowfly larvae were found inside."

Holmes was baffled. "The maggots were inside a man—a *living man*?"

"Don't interrupt, Holmes!" Lowell cried.

Agassiz assented to Holmes's question with a heavy silence.

"But the *Cochliomyia macellaria* can only digest dead tissue," Holmes protested. "There are no maggots capable of parasitism."

"Remember the eight thousand undiscovered flies I've just spoken of, Holmes!" Agassiz rebuked him. "This was *not* the *Cochliomyia macellaria.* This was a different species altogether, my friends. One we had never seen before—or didn't want to believe existed. A female fly of this species had laid eggs in the patient's nostrils, where the eggs hatched and the larvae developed into maggots, eating right into his head. Two more of the men on Devil's Island died of the same infestation. The doctor saved the others only by cutting out the maggots from the noses. *Macellaria* maggots can only live on dead tissue—they like corpses best. But the larvae of *this* species of fly, Holmes, survives only on *living* tissue."

Agassiz waited for reactions to show on their faces. Then he went on.

"The female fly mates only once but can lay a massive number of eggs every three days, ten or eleven times in their monthlong life cycle. A single female fly can lay up to *four hundred* eggs in one sitting. They find warm wounds on animals or humans to nest in. The eggs hatch into maggots and crawl into the wound, tearing through the body. The more infested is the flesh with maggots, the more other adult flies are attracted. The maggots feed on the living tissue until they drop out and, some days later, become flies. My friend Coquerel named this species *Cochliomyia hominivorax.*"

"*Homini . . . vorax,*" Lowell repeated. He translated hoarsely, looking at Holmes: "Man-eater."

"Exactly," said Agassiz with the reluctant enthusiasm of a scientist with a terrible discovery to announce. "Coquerel reported this to the scientific journals, though few believed his evidence."

"But you did?" Holmes asked.

"Most certainly," Agassiz said sternly. "Since Coquerel sent me these drawings, I have studied medical histories and records of the last thirty years for mentions of similar experiences by people who did not know these details. Isidore Sainte-Hilaire recorded a case of a larva found inside the skin of an infant. Dr. Livingston, according to Cobbold, found several *diptera* larvae in the shoulder of an injured Negro. In Brazil, I have discovered on my travels that these flies are called the *Warega,* known as pest of both man and animals. And in the Mexican war, it was recorded that what people called 'meat flies' would leave their eggs in the wounds of soldiers left on the field overnight. Sometimes the maggots would cause no harm, feeding only on dead tissue. These were common blowflies, common *macellaria* maggots such as you are familiar with, Dr. Holmes. But other times the body would be ravished with swellings and there would be no saving what was left of the soldiers' lives. They'd be hollowed out from the inside. You see? These were the *hominivorax.* These flies must prey on the helpless, people and animals: That is the only means of their offspring surviving. Their life requires ingestion of the living. Research is only now beginning, my friends, and it is very exciting. Why, I collected my first specimens of the *hominivorax* on my tour of Brazil. Superficially, the two types of blowflies are very much the same. You must look at the deep coloring; you must measure with the most sensitive instruments. That is how I was able to recognize your samples yesterday."

Agassiz dragged over another stool. "Now, Lowell, let us see your poor leg again, will you?"

Lowell tried to speak, but his lips were shaking too violently.

"Oh, don't you worry now, Lowell!" Agassiz broke into a laugh. "So, Lowell, you felt the leetle insect on your leg, then you brushed it away?"

"And I killed it!" Lowell reminded him.

Agassiz retrieved a scalpel from a drawer. "Good. Dr. Holmes, I want you to slip that into the center of the wound, and then pull it out."

"Are you sure, Agassiz?" Lowell asked nervously.

Holmes swallowed and knelt down. He positioned the scalpel at Lowell's ankle, then looked up into his friend's face. Lowell was staring, his jaw open. "You won't even feel this, Jamey," Holmes promised quietly, comfort just between them. Agassiz, though only inches away, kindly pretended not to hear.

Lowell nodded and gripped the sides of his stool. Holmes did as Agassiz said, inserting the point of the scalpel into the center of the swelling on Lowell's ankle. When he removed the scalpel, there was a hard white maggot, four millimeters at most, wriggling on the tip: alive.

"There, that's it! The beautiful *hominivorax*!" Agassiz laughed triumphantly. He checked Lowell's wound for more and then wrapped the ankle. He took the maggot lovingly on his hand. "You see, Lowell, the poor leetle blowfly you saw had only a few seconds before you killed it so it had time to lay only one egg. Your wound is not deep and shall heal fully, and you shall be perfectly fine. But notice how the lesion in your leg grew with one maggot crawling inside of you, how much you felt it as it tore through some tissue. Imagine hundreds. Now imagine hundreds of thousands—expanding inside of you every few minutes."

Lowell smiled wide enough to send his mustache tusks to opposite ends of his face. "You hear that, Holmes? I'll be fine!" He laughed and embraced Agassiz and then Holmes. Then he began to take in what it all meant—for Artemus Healey, for the Dante Club.

Agassiz grew serious, too, as he toweled off his hands. "There's one other thing, dear fellows. The strangest thing, really. These leetle creatures—they don't belong here, don't belong in New England nor anywhere in our vicinity. They are native to this hemisphere, that seems certain. But only in hot, swampier climates. I have just seen swarms of them in Brazil, but never would we see them in Boston. Never have they been recorded, by their correct name or any other. How they got here, I cannot speculate. Perhaps accidentally on a shipment of cattle or . . ." Agassiz lapsed into detached humor about the situation. "No matter. It is our good fortune that these critters *cannot* live in a northern climate such as ours, not in this weather and surroundings. They are not good neighbors, these *Waregas*. Luckily, the ones that did come here have surely died out from the cold already."

In the way that fear readily transfers itself, Lowell had entirely forgotten the certainty of his own doom, and his ordeal was now a source of pleasure that he had survived. But he could only think of one thing as he walked silently away from the museum alongside Holmes.

Holmes spoke first. "I was blind to listen to Barnicoat's conclusions in the newspapers. Healey did not die from a blow to his head! The insects were not just a Dantesque *tableau vivant,* some decorative show, so that Dante's punishment could be recognized by us. They were released in order to cause pain," Holmes said in rapid fire. "The insects were not ornament, they were his weapon!"

"Our Lucifer wants his victims not merely to die but to suffer, as the shades do in *Inferno.* A state between life and death which contains both and is neither." Lowell turned to Holmes and took his arm.

"To witness your own suffering. Wendell, I *felt* that creature eating away inside of me. Ingesting me. Even though it might have only snacked on a small amount of tissue, I felt it as though it was running straight through my blood into my very soul. The chambermaid was telling the truth."

"By God, she was," Holmes said, horrified. "Which means Healey . . ." Neither man could speak of the suffering they now knew Healey to have endured. The chief justice had been meant to leave for his country house on a Saturday morning and his body was not found until Tuesday. He had been alive for four days under the care of tens of thousands of *hominivorax* devouring his insides . . . his brains . . . inch after inch, hour after hour.

Holmes looked into the glass jar of insect samples they had taken back from Agassiz. "Lowell, there is something I must say. But I do not wish to call up a row with you."

"Pietro Bachi."

Holmes nodded tentatively.

"This does not seem to fit with what we know of him, does it?" Lowell asked. "This knocks all our theories into a cocked hat!"

"Think of it: Bachi was bitter; Bachi was hot-tempered; Bachi was drunk. But such methodical, profound cruelty. Could you see this in him? Honestly? Bachi might have tried to stage something to show the mistake of bringing him to America. But to re-create Dante's punishments so utterly and completely? Our mistakes must be thick throughout, Lowell, like salamanders after the rain. And a new one creeps out from under every leaf we turn over." Holmes waved his arms frantically.

"What are you doing?" Lowell asked. Longfellow's house was only a short walk and they were due back.

"I see a free coach up ahead. I want a look at some of these samples again under my microscope. I wish Agassiz had not killed this maggot—nature will tell the truth all the better for its not being put to death. I do not believe his conclusion that these insects will have already died out. We may learn something more about the murder from these creatures. Agassiz will not listen to the Darwinian theory, and this obstructs his view."

"Wendell, this is the man's vocation."

Holmes ignored Lowell's lack of faith. "Great scientists can sometimes be an impediment in the path of science, Lowell. Revolutions are not made by men in spectacles, and the first whispers of a new truth are not caught by those in need of ear trumpets. Just last month, I was reading in a book on the Sandwich Islands about an old Fejee man who had been carried away among foreigners but who prayed he might be brought home so that his brains might be beaten out in peace by his son, according to the custom of those lands. Did not Dante's son Pietro tell everyone after Dante's death that the poet did not *mean* to say he really went to Hell and Heaven? Our sons beat out their fathers' brains very regularly."

Some fathers more than others, Lowell said to himself, thinking of Oliver Wendell Holmes Junior as he watched Holmes climb into the hackney cab.

Lowell started hurriedly for Craigie House, wishing he had his horse. Crossing a street, he staggered backward with sudden vigilance at what he saw.

The tall man with the worn face and bowler hat and checkered waistcoat—the same man Lowell had seen watching him intently while leaning against an elm tree on Harvard Yard, the very man he had witnessed approaching Bachi on campus—this man stood out at the busy marketplace. That might not have been enough to hold Lowell's interest in the aftermath of Agassiz's revelations, but the man was conversing with Edward Sheldon, Lowell's student. In fact, Sheldon was not merely speaking but barking up at the man, as though he were ordering a recalcitrant domestic to perform some neglected chore.

Sheldon then took his leave in a huff, wrapping himself tightly in his black cloak. Lowell could not at first decide whom to follow. Sheldon? He could always be found at the College. Lowell decided he had to pursue the unknown man, who was making his way into a knot of pedestrians and carriage traffic along the roundabout.

Lowell ran through some market stands. A marketman pushed a lobster in Lowell's face. Lowell swatted it away. A girl passing out handbills stuffed one into the pocket of Lowell's coat skirt. "Flyer, sir?"

"Not now!" cried Lowell. In another moment, the poet spotted the phantom across the way. He was stepping into a crammed horsecar and waiting for change from the conductor.

Lowell ran for the back platform as the conductor rang his bell and as the vehicle started down the tracks toward the bridge. Lowell had no trouble catching up with the lumbering car by jogging along the tracks. He had just secured his hand on the stair railing of the rear platform when the conductor turned around.

"Leany Miller?"

"Sir, my name is Lowell. I must speak to one of your passengers." Lowell edged one foot onto the raised back stairs as the horse team accelerated.

"Leany Miller? Are you back to your tricks already?" The conductor produced a walking stick and started to hammer at Lowell's gloved hand. "You shan't blot our fair cars again, Leany! Not under my watch!"

"No! Sir, my name is not Leany!" But the thrashing of the conductor made Lowell release his grip. This sent the poet feet first onto the tracks.

Lowell shouted over the hoof falls and ringing bells to persuade the irate conductor of his innocence. But then it dawned on him that the ringing bell was coming from behind, where another horsecar was approaching. As he turned to see, Lowell's pace was slowed and the horsecar ahead of him gained distance. With no alternative but to find his heels trampled by the oncoming horses, Lowell jumped off the tracks.

At Craigie House at that moment, Longfellow led into his parlor one Robert Todd Lincoln, son of the late president and one of the three Dante students from Lowell's 1864 term. Lowell had promised to meet them at the house after seeing Agassiz, but he was late, so Longfellow would start Lincoln's interview himself.

"Oh dear Pa*pa*!" Annie Allegra said as she skipped in, interrupting. "We are almost finished with the latest number of *The Secret*, Papa! Wouldn't you like to see it in advance?"

"Yes, darling, but I'm afraid I'm occupied at the moment."

"Please, Mr. Longfellow," said the young man. "I'm in no hurry."

Longfellow took up the handwritten periodical "published" in installments by his three girls. "Oh, it seems one of the best you've ever done. Very fine, Panzie. I'll read it from beginning to end this evening. Is this the page you drew up?"

"Yes!" Annie Allegra answered. "This column, and this one. And this riddle too. Can you guess what it is?"

"The lake in America as big as three states." Longfellow smiled and ran down the rest of the page. A rebus and a featured article reviewing "My Eventful Yesterday (from breakfast to nighttime)," by A. A. Longfellow.

"Oh, it's lovely, dear heart." Longfellow paused doubtfully over one of the last items on the list. "Panzie, it says here that you let a caller in just before sleep last night."

"Oh yes. I had come down for some milk, didn't I. Did he say I made a good hostess, Papa?"

"When was that, Panzie?"

"During your club meeting, of course. You say you must not be disturbed during your club meeting."

"Annie Allegra!" Edith called down from the stairwell. "Alice wishes to revise the table of contents. You must bring your copy back up right away!"

"She's always the editor," Annie Allegra complained, reclaiming the periodical from Longfellow. He trailed Annie into the hall and called up the staircase before she could reach the private office of *The Secret*—the bedroom of one of their older brothers. "Panzie dear, who was the caller last night that you mention?"

"What, Papa? I've never seen him before yesterday."

"Could you remember what he looked like? Perhaps *that* should be added to *The Secret.* Perhaps you can interview him yourself to ask of his experience."

"How pretty that would be! A tall Negro man, very splendid-looking, in a cloth cloak. I told him to wait for you, Papa—I did. Did he not do as I said? He must have gotten bored just *standing* there and left to go home. Do you know his name, Papa?"

Longfellow nodded.

"Do tell me, Papa! I shall be able to interview him as you say."

"Patrolman Nicholas Rey, of the Boston police."

Lowell burst through the front door. "Longfellow, I have much to tell . . ." he stopped when he saw the pall on his neighbor's face. "Longfellow, what's happened?"

※

Patrolman Rey had been shown into a severe sitting room earlier that day, left to stare out at groves of weather-beaten elms shading the Yard.

A congregation of hoary men began to file into the hall, their knee-length black dress-coats and tall hats as uniform as monasterial habits.

Rey entered the Corporation Room, from which the men were departing. When Rey introduced himself to President Reverend Thomas Hill, the president was in mid-conversation with a lingering member of the College government. This other man stopped cold at Rey's mention of police.

"Does this concern one of our students, sir?" Dr. Manning dropped his conversation with Hill. He revolved so his marble-white beard faced the mulatto officer.

"I have a few questions for President Hill. Regarding Professor James Russell Lowell, actually."

Manning's yellow eyes widened, and he insisted on remaining. He closed the double doors and sat down beside President Hill at the round mahogany table across from the police officer. Rey could see at once that Hill reluctantly allowed the other man to dominate.

"I wonder how much you know about the project Mr. Lowell has been at work on, President Hill," Rey began.

"Mr. Lowell? He's one of the finest poets and satirists in all New England, of course," Hill replied with a lightening laugh. " 'The Biglow Papers.' 'The Vision of Sir Launfal.' 'A Fable for the Critics'—my favorite, I confess. Besides his *North American Review* duties. You know he was the first editor of the *Atlantic*? Why, I'm sure our troubadour is at work on any *number* of undertakings."

Nicholas Rey removed a slip of notepaper from his waistcoat pocket and rolled it between his fingers. "I am referring in particular to a poem I believe he has been helping to translate from a foreign language."

Manning steepled his crooked fingers together and stared, his eyes dropping to the folded paper in the patrolman's hand. "My dear officer," Manning said. "Has there been any sort of problem?" He looked remarkably as if he wanted the answer to be yes.

Dinanzi. Rey studied Manning's face, the way the elastic ends of the old scholar's mouth seemed to twitch with anticipation.

Manning passed a hand across the polished top of his scalp. *Dinanzi a me.*

"What I mean to ask . . ." Manning began, trying another tack—he was less anxious now. "Has there been some trouble? Some complaint of a sort?"

President Hill pinched the padding of his chin, wishing Manning had departed with the rest of the Corporation fellows. "I wonder if we should not send for Professor Lowell himself to talk this over."

Dinanzi a me non fuor cose create
Se non etterne, e io etterno duro.

What did it mean? If Longfellow and his poets had recognized the words, why would they go to lengths to keep it from him?

"Nonsense, Reverend President," Manning snapped. "Professor Lowell cannot be bothered over every trifle. Officer, I must insist that if there has been some trouble, you point it out to us *at once*, and we shall resolve it with all due speed and discretion. Understand, Patrolman," Manning said, leaning forward genially. "There have begun attempts by Professor Lowell and several literary colleagues to bring certain literature into our city that does not belong. Its teachings will endanger the peace of millions of gentle souls. As a member of the Corporation, I am bound by duty to defend the good reputation of the university against any such blemishes. The motto of the College is '*Christo et ecclesiae*,' sir, and we are beholden to live up to the Christian spirit of that ideal."

"The motto used to be '*veritas*,' though," President Hill said quietly. "Truth."

Manning shot him a sharp look.

Patrolman Rey hesitated another moment, then returned the notepaper to his pocket. "I expressed some interest in the poetry Mr. Lowell has been translating. He thought you gentlemen might be able to direct me to a proper place for its study."

Dr. Manning's cheeks streaked with color. "Do you mean to say this is a purely *literary* call?" he asked with disgust. When Rey did not respond, Manning assured the officer that Lowell wanted to make a fool of him—and the College—for sport. If Rey wished to study the Devil's poetry, he could do so at the Devil's feet.

Rey passed through Harvard Yard, where cold winds were whistling around the old brick buildings. He felt foggy and confused about his purpose. Then a fire bell began to ring, ringing, it seemed, from every corner of the universe. And Rey ran.

XI

OLIVER WENDELL HOLMES, poet and doctor, lit his slides of the insects with a candle positioned near one of his microscopes.

He bent down and peered through the lens at a blowfly, adjusting the position of the subject. The insect was jumping and squirming as though filled with great anger at his watcher.

No. It was not the insect.

The microscope slide itself was trembling. Horse hooves thundered outside, exploding in an urgent stop. Holmes rushed to the window and pushed the drapes open. Amelia came in from the hall. With frightening gravity, Holmes ordered her to remain in place, but she followed him to the front door. The dark-blue figure of a burly policeman stood out against the sky as he pulled with all his strength to idle the stormy gray-flecked mares harnessed to a carriage.

"Dr. Holmes?" he called from the driver's box. "You are to come with me at once."

Amelia stepped forward. "Wendell? What's this about?"

Holmes was wheezing already. " 'Melia, send a note to Craigie House. Tell them something has arisen, and to meet me at the Corner in an hour. I'm sorry to leave like this—can't be helped."

Before she could protest, Holmes climbed into the police carriage and the horses broke into a stormy gallop, leaving a gust of dead leaves and dust. Oliver Wendell Holmes Junior peered down through the curtains of the third-floor sitting room and wondered what new nonsense his father was at now.

A gray chill seized the air. The skies were opening. A second carriage galloped to a stop right at the spot the other had just relinquished. It was

Fields's brougham. James Russell Lowell flung open the door and asked Mrs. Holmes in an eruption of words to retrieve Dr. Holmes. She leaned forward just enough to make out the profiles of Henry Longfellow and J. T. Fields. "I don't know where he has gone, I am sure, Mr. Lowell. But he was taken by the *police.* He directed me to send a note to Craigie House for you to meet at the Corner. James Lowell, I wish to know what business this is about!"

Lowell looked around the carriage helplessly. On the corner of Charles Street, two boys were passing out handbills, crying out, "Missing! Missing! Take a flyer please. Sir. Ma'am."

Lowell thrust his hand into his sack-coat pocket, a hollow dread drying out his throat. His hand emerged with the crumpled handbill that had been stuffed into his pocket at the marketplace in Cambridge after he had seen the phantom with Edward Sheldon. He smoothed it against his sleeve. "Oh good Lord." Lowell's mouth quivered.

⁂

"We've had patrolmen and sentinels all across the city since Reverend Talbot's murder. But nothing was seen at all!" Sergeant Stoneweather cried out from the driver's box as the twin flea-bitten horses careened away from Charles Street, muscles dancing. Every few minutes, he would hold out his rattle and twirl it.

Holmes's mind was swimming upstream under the sounds of the solid trot and crashing gravel under their wheels. The only comprehensible fact the driver had told him, or at least the only one that the frightened passenger had digested, was that Patrolman Rey had sent him to retrieve Holmes. At the harbor, the carriage halted abruptly. From there a police boat took Holmes out to one of the sleepy harbor islands, where stood unused, in blocky Quincy granite, a windowless castle now ruled by rats; there were empty ramparts and prone guns alongside drooping Stars and Stripes. Into Fort Warren they went, the doctor trailing the officer past a row of ghost-white policemen already on the scene: through a maze of rooms; down into a cold, pitch-dark stone tunnel; and finally into a hollowed-out storage chamber.

The little doctor stumbled and nearly fell down. His mind jumped through time. When studying at the École de Médecine in Paris, young

Holmes had seen the *combats des animaux*, a barbaric exhibition of bulldogs fighting each other, then being turned loose on a wolf, a bear, a wild boar, a bull, and a jackass tied to a post. Holmes knew even during the audacity of youth that he could never quite get the iron of Calvinism out of his soul, no matter how much poetry he wrote. There was still the temptation to believe the world was a mere trap for human sin. But sin, the way he saw it, was only the failure of an imperfectly made being to keep a perfect law. For his forefathers, the great mystery of life was this sin; for Dr. Holmes, it was suffering. He would have never expected to find so much of it. The dark memory, the inhuman cheers and laughter, stampeded into Holmes's dazed mind now as he looked ahead.

From the center of the room, hanging on a hook meant for storing bags of salt or some similarly pouched supplies, a face stared at him. Or, more accurately, it had been a face. The nose was sliced away cleanly, all the way from the bridge to the mustached lip, causing the skin to fold over. One of the man's ears dangled deciduously from the side of the face, low enough, indeed, to brush against the rigidly arched shoulder. Both cheeks were sliced in such a manner that the jaw dropped to a permanent position of openness, as if speech might come at any moment; but instead, blood poured black from his mouth. A straight line of blood was drawn between the heavily indented chin and the reproductive organ of the man—and this organ, the only remaining confirmation of the monstrosity's gender, was itself split horribly in half, a dissection inconceivable even to the doctor. Muscles, nerves, and blood vessels unfolded themselves in unvarying anatomical harmony and baffling disorder. The body's arms hung helplessly at his sides, ending in dark pulps wrapped in flooded tourniquets. There were no hands.

It was a moment before Holmes realized he had seen the decimated face before and another moment still until he recognized the mangled victim, from the pronounced dimple doggedly remaining on his chin. *Oh no.* The interval between the two conscious moments was an annihilation.

Holmes took a step back, his shoe gliding through the vomit that had been deposited by the first discoverer of the scene, a vagrant looking for shelter. Holmes twisted himself into a nearby chair, positioned as though for the purpose of observing all this. He wheezed uncontrollably and did not notice that to the side of his feet was a vest of a distractingly bright color neatly folded atop hand-tailored white pants and, on the floor, scattered scraps of paper.

He heard his name spoken. Patrolman Rey stood nearby. Even the air in the room seemed to tremble, to push the whole arrangement upside down.

Holmes tumbled to his feet and shook his head dizzily at Rey.

A plainclothes detective, broad-shouldered and with a strong beard, marched over to Rey and began yelling that he did not belong there. Then Chief Kurtz intervened and pulled the detective away.

The doctor's nauseated wheezing spell left him standing in a place closer to the twisted carnage than he would have wished, but before he could think to move away, he felt his arm brushed by something wet. It felt like a hand, but in fact it was a bloody, tourniqueted stump. Yet Holmes had not moved an inch—he was sure of that. He was too shocked to move. He felt as if he were in that type of nightmare where one can only pray to himself that he is dreaming.

"Heaven help us, it's alive!" screamed the detective, running off, his voice strangled by his tight hold on a rising flood from his stomach. Chief Kurtz, too, disappeared, shouting.

As Holmes spun around, he looked directly into the blankly bulging eyes of the maimed, naked body of Phineas Jennison and watched the wretched limbs flail and jerk through the air. It was only a moment, really—only a fraction of a tithe of a hundredth of a second—until the body stopped cold, never to move again, yet Holmes never doubted what he had just witnessed. The doctor stood corpselike, his little mouth dry and twitching, his eyes blinking uncontrollably with unwanted moisture, and his fingers wriggling desperately. Dr. Oliver Wendell Holmes knew that Phineas Jennison's movement had not been the voluntary motions of a living being, the willed actions of a sentient man. They were the delayed, mindless convulsions of unspeakable death. But this knowledge made it no better.

The dead touch having left his blood cold, Holmes was hardly conscious of drifting back over the harbor water or of the police carriage, called Black Maria, in which they rode alongside the body of Jennison to the medical college, where it was explained to him that Barnicoat, the medical examiner, had taken to bed with a terrible pneumonia in a fight for a higher salary and Professor Haywood could not at present be located. Holmes nodded as though he were listening. Haywood's student assistant volunteered to assist Dr. Holmes in an autopsy. Holmes barely registered these urgent exchanges, he could barely feel his hands cut into the already impossibly shredded body in a dark upper chamber of the medical college.

"Observe in me the *contrapasso.*"

Holmes's head snapped up as if a child had just cried for help. Reynolds, the student assistant, looked back, as did Rey and Kurtz and two other officers who had entered the room unnoticed by Holmes. Holmes looked again at Phineas Jennison, his mouth hanging open by the cut jaw.

"Dr. Holmes?" the student assistant said. "All right, are you?"

Just a burst of imagination, the voice he had heard, the whisper, the command. But Holmes's hands trembled too much even to carve a turkey, and he had to leave the remainder of the operation to Haywood's assistant as he excused himself. Holmes wandered into an alleyway off Grove Street, gathering his breath in bits and spurts. He heard someone approach him. Rey backed the doctor farther into the alleyway.

"Please, I can't speak at the moment," Holmes said, his eyes fixed down.

"Who butchered Phineas Jennison?"

"How should I know!" Holmes cried. He lost his balance, inebriated with the mangled visions in his head.

"Translate this for me, Dr. Holmes." Rey pried open Holmes's hand and placed a notepaper there.

"Please, Patrolman Rey. We've already . . ." Holmes's hands shook violently as he fumbled with the paper.

" 'Because I parted persons so united,' " Rey recited from what he had heard the night before, " 'I now bear my brain parted. Thus observe in me the *contrapasso.*' That is what we just saw, isn't it? How do you translate *contrapasso,* Dr. Holmes? A countersuffering?"

"There's no exact . . . how did you . . ." Holmes pulled off his silk cravat and tried to breathe into the neck cloth. "I don't know anything."

Rey continued: "You read of this murder in a poem. You saw it before it happened and did nothing to prevent it."

"No! We did all we could. We tried. Please, Patrolman Rey, I can't . . ."

"Do you know this man?" Rey removed the newspaper engraving of Grifone Lonza from his pocket and handed it to the doctor. "He jumped from the window at the police station."

"Please!" Holmes was suffocating. "No more! Go away now!"

"Hey there!" Three medical college students, the rustic type Holmes referred to as his young barbarians, were passing the alleyway relishing cheap cigars. "You, moke! Get away from Professor Holmes!"

Holmes tried to call out to them, but nothing made it out of the clutter in his throat.

The swiftest barbarian collided into Rey with a fist aimed at the officer's stomach. Rey grabbed the boy's other arm and threw him down as softly as possible. The other two pounced on Rey just as Holmes's voice returned. "No! No, boys! Be still! Get away from here at once! This is a friend! Scat!" They slid away meekly.

Holmes helped Rey up. He needed to make amends. He took the newspaper and held up the page with the likeness. "Grifone Lonza," he revealed.

The glint in Rey's eyes showed he was impressed and relieved. "Translate the note for me now, Dr. Holmes, please. Lonza spoke those words before he died. Tell me what they were."

"Italian. The Tuscan dialect. Mind you, you're missing some words, but for someone with no training in the language, it is a remarkable enough transcription. *Deenan see am . . . 'Dinanzi a me . . . Dinanzi a me non fuor cose create se non etterne, e io etterno duro':* Before me nothing was made if not eternal, and I will last eternally. *'Lasciate ogne speranza, voi ch'intrate':* O ye who enter, abandon all hope."

"Abandon all hope. He was warning me," Rey said.

"No . . . I don't think so. He probably believed he was reading it over the gates to Hell, from what we know of his mental state."

"You should have told the police you knew something," Rey cried.

"It would have been a greater mess if we had!" Holmes shouted. "You don't understand—you can't, Patrolman. We're the only ones who could ever find him! We thought we had—we thought he fled. Everything the police know is coal dust! This shall never stop without us!" Holmes tasted snow as he spoke. He dabbed his brow and neck, which were bathed in hot sweat from every pore. Holmes asked if Rey wouldn't mind moving inside. He had a story to tell that Rey might not believe.

Oliver Wendell Holmes and Nicholas Rey sat in his empty lecture room.

"The year was 1300. Midway through the journey of his life, a poet named Dante awoke in a dark wood, finding that his life had taken a wrong path. James Russell Lowell likes to say, Patrolman, that we all enter the dark wood twice—sometime in the middle of our lives and again when we look back upon it . . ."

• • •

The heavy paneled door to the Authors' Room opened an inch and the three men inside jumped from their seats. A black boot edged in probatively. Holmes could no longer think what he might find to shatter his safety behind closed doors. Gaunt and ashen, he shared the sofa with Longfellow, across from Lowell and Fields, hoping that a single nod would suffice to respond to each of their greetings.

"I stopped home first before coming here. 'Melia nearly did not let me back out of the house, the way I look." Holmes laughed nervously as a drop of moisture shimmied into the corner of his eye. "Did you gentlemen know that the muscles with which we laugh and cry lie side by side? My young barbarians are always so taken with that."

They waited for Holmes to begin. Lowell handed him the crumpled handbill announcing that Phineas Jennison was missing, offering many thousands in reward for his return. "Then you know already," Holmes said. "Jennison's dead."

He began an erratic, staccato narrative commencing with the police carriage's surprise arrival at 21 Charles.

Lowell, pouring his third glass of port, said, "Fort Warren."

"An ingenious choice on the part of our Lucifer," said Longfellow. "I'm afraid the canto of the Schismatics could not be fresher to our minds. It hardly seems possible that it was only yesterday we translated it among our cantos. Malebolge is a wide field of stone—and described by Dante as a *fortress.*"

Lowell said, "Once again we see that we face a uniquely brilliant scholar's mind, strikingly equipped to transmit choice atmospheric details of Dante. Our Lucifer appreciates the exactness of Dante's poetry. All is wild in Milton's Hell, but Dante's is separated into circles, drawn with well-pointed compasses. As real as our own world."

"*Now* it is," Holmes said shakily.

Fields did not want to hear a literary argument at the moment. "Wendell, you say that the police were stationed all around the city when the murder occurred? How could Lucifer not be seen?"

"You would need the giant hands of Briareus and the hundred eyes of Argus to touch or see him," Longfellow said quietly.

Holmes gave them more. "Jennison was found by a drunkard who sometimes sleeps in the fort since it has been out of use. The vagrant was there on Monday, and all was normal. Then he returned on Wednesday, and there was the horrible display. He was too frightened to report it until the next day—I mean until today. Jennison was last seen on Tuesday afternoon, and his bed was not slept in that night. The police interviewed everyone they could find. A prostitute who was at the harbor says she saw someone come out from the fog at the harbor Tuesday evening. She tried to follow him, I suppose as obliged by her profession, but got only so far as the church, and she did not see which direction he took."

"So Jennison was killed on Tuesday night. But the body was not discovered by the police until Thursday," Fields said. "But, Holmes, you said that Jennison was still . . . is it *possible* that for such a time . . . ?"

"For it . . . him . . . to have been killed on Tuesday yet be alive when I arrived this morning? For the body to be thrown into such convulsions that were I to drink every drop of Lethe I shall never be able to forget the sight of it?" Holmes asked despairingly. "Poor Jennison had been mutilated without hope of survival—that is to be sure—but cut and bound just enough to slowly lose blood, and with it his life. It was a good deal like inspecting what remains of fireworks on the fifth of July, but I could see that no vital organs had been punctured. There was careful craftsmanship amid such wild massacre, done by one very familiar with internal wounds, perhaps a doctor," he said thickly, "with a sharp and large knife. With Jennison, our Lucifer perfects his damnation through suffering, his most perfect *contrapasso.* The movements I witnessed were not life, my dear Fields, but simply the nerves dying out in a final spasm. It was a moment as grotesque as any Dante could have envisioned. Death would have been a gift."

"But to survive for two days after the attack," Fields insisted. "What I mean to say is . . . medically speaking . . . mercy, it's not possible!"

" 'Survival' here means simply an incomplete death, not a partial life—to be trapped in the gap between the living and the dead. If I had a thousand tongues, I would not try to begin to describe the agony!"

"Why punish Phineas as a Schismatic?" Lowell tried his best to sound detached, scientific. "Whom does Dante find punished in that infernal circle? Muhammad, Bertrand de Born—the malicious adviser who split apart king and prince, father and son, as once was done to Absalom and David—those who created internal rifts within religions, families. Why *Phineas Jennison?*"

"After all our efforts, we haven't answered that question for Elisha Talbot, my dear Lowell," said Longfellow. "His thousand-dollar simony—for what?

Two *contrapasso*s, with two invisible sins. Dante has the benefit of asking the sinners themselves what has brought them to Hell."

"Were you not close with Jennison?" Fields asked Lowell. "And yet you can think of nothing?"

"He was a friend; I did not look for his misdeeds! He was an ear for me to complain about losses in stocks, about lecturing, about Dr. Manning and the blasted Corporation. He was a steam engine in trousers, and I admit sometimes he cocked his hat a bit too much—he had a hand in every flashy business enterprise over the years that I suppose had an underbelly of brine. Railroads, factories, steelworks—such business matters are hardly comprehensible to me, you know, Fields." Lowell dropped his head.

Holmes sighed heavily. "Patrolman Rey is as sharp as a blade, and likely has suspected our knowledge all along. He recognized the manner of Jennison's death from what he had overheard at our Dante Club session. The logic of the *contrapasso,* the Schismatics, he connected to Jennison, and when I explained more, he immediately understood Dante in the deaths of Chief Justice Healey and Reverend Talbot, too."

"As did Grifone Lonza when he killed himself at the station house," said Lowell. "The poor soul saw Dante in everything. This time he happened to be right. I have often thought, in like manner, of Dante's own transformation. The mind of the poet, left homeless on earth by his enemies, making its home more and more in that awful otherworld. Is it not natural that exiled from all he loved in this life, he would brood exclusively on the *next?* We praise him lavishly for his skills, but Dante Alighieri had no choice but to write the poem he did, and to write in his heart's blood. It is no wonder he died so soon after he finished."

"What shall Officer Rey do with his knowledge of our involvement?" Longfellow asked.

Holmes shrugged. "We withheld information. We obstructed an investigation into the two most horrendous murders Boston has ever seen, which now have become three! Rey may very well be turning us *and* Dante in as we speak! What loyalty does he have to a book of poetry? How much should we have?"

Holmes pushed himself to his feet and, pulling at the waist of his baggy pantaloons, paced nervously. Fields raised his head from his hands when he realized Holmes was gathering his hat and coat.

"I wanted to share what I have learned," Holmes said in a soft, dead voice. "I cannot continue."

"You'll rest now," Fields began.

Holmes shook his head. "No, my dear Fields, not just tonight."

"What?" Lowell cried.

"Holmes," Longfellow said. "I know this seems unanswerable, but it behooves us to fight."

"You can't just walk away from this anyhow!" Lowell shouted. With his voice filling their space, he felt powerful again. "We've gone too far, Holmes!"

"We had gone too far from the beginning, too far from where we belong—yes, Jamey. I'm sorry," Holmes said calmly. "I know not what Patrolman Rey shall decide, but I shall cooperate in any fashion he wishes and I expect the same from you. I only pray we are not taken in for obstruction—or worse—accessory. Isn't that what we have been? Each one of us had a role in allowing the deaths to continue."

"Then you shouldn't have given us away to Rey!" Lowell jumped to his feet.

"What would you have done in my place, Professor?" Holmes demanded.

"Walking away is not an option here, Wendell! The milk is spilt. You swore to protect Dante, as did we all, right under Longfellow's roof, though the heavens cave in!" But Holmes fitted his hat and buttoned his overcoat. " '*Qui a bu boira,*' " Lowell said. " 'He who has once been a drinker will drink again.' "

"You didn't see it!" Every emotion pent up inside Holmes erupted as he turned on Lowell. "Why has it been *I* who has seen two horribly shredded bodies instead of you brave scholars! It was *I* who went down into Talbot's fiery hold with the scent of death in my nostrils! It is *I* who have had to go through it all while *you* can analyze from the comfort of your fireside, filtering it all through alphabets!"

"The *comfort?* I was assailed by rare man-eating insects within an inch of my life, you oughtn't forget!" Lowell shouted.

Holmes laughed mockingly. "I'd take ten thousand blowflies for what I've seen!"

"Holmes," Longfellow entreated. "Remember: Virgil tells the pilgrim that fear is the main impediment to his journey."

"I do not give a copper for that! Not any longer, Longfellow! I yield my place! We are not the first to try to liberate Dante's poetry and perhaps ours shall always be the losing end! Did you never once think that Voltaire was right—Dante was but a madman and his work a *monster.* Dante lost his life in Florence, so he avenged himself by creating a literature with which he dared make himself into God. And now we have unleashed it on the city we say we love, and we shall live to pay!"

"That's enough for now, Wendell! *Enough!*" Lowell yelled, standing in front of Longfellow as though he could shield him from the words.

"Dante's own son thought him delusional to believe that he had traveled through Hell, and spent a lifetime trying to disown his father's words!" Holmes went on. "Why should *we* sacrifice our safety to save him? The *Commedia* was no love letter. Dante did not care about Beatrice, about Florence! He was venting the spleen of his exile, imagining his enemies writhe and beg for salvation! Do you ever hear him mention his wife, just once? This is how he got even for his disappointments! I only wish to protect us from losing everything we hold dear! That's all I've wanted from the beginning!"

"You don't want to find out that anyone is guilty," Lowell said, "just as you didn't ever want to think Bachi was culpable, just as you imagined Professor Webster blameless even as he dangled from the end of a rope!"

"Not so!" Holmes cried.

"Oh, this is a fine thing you're doing for us, Holmes. A fine thing!" Lowell shouted. "You've stayed as steady as your most rambling lyrics! Perhaps we should've drafted Wendell Junior into our club all along instead of you. At least we'd have a chance of victory!" He was ready to say more, but Longfellow restrained him by the arm with a tender hand, unbreakable as an iron gauntlet.

"We could not have come this far along without you, my dear friend. Pray do get some rest and give our affection to Mrs. Holmes," Longfellow said softly.

Holmes made his way out of the Authors' Room. When Longfellow released his hold, Lowell stalked the doctor to the door. Holmes hurried into the hall, looking over his shoulder as his friend trailed behind with a cold stare. Reaching the corner, Holmes smashed into a cart of papers being pushed by Teal, the night shop boy assigned to Fields's offices, whose mouth always worked in a grinding or chewing motion. Holmes went flying to the floor, the cart tipping over and spilling papers across the hall and on the toppled doctor. Teal kicked away some papers and with a look of great sympathy tried to help Oliver Wendell Holmes to his feet. Lowell rushed to

Holmes's side too, but stopped himself, renewed in anger because he was ashamed at his moment of softness.

"There, you're happy, Holmes. Longfellow needed us! You've betrayed him finally! You've betrayed the Dante Club!"

Teal, staring with fright as Lowell repeated his charge, lifted Holmes to his feet. "Many apologies," he whispered into Holmes's ear. Though it was entirely the doctor's fault, Holmes could barely reciprocate an apology. He was not experiencing his heaving, wheezing asthma any longer. It was the tight, cramping kind. Whereas the other felt like he needed more and more air to fill himself, this made all air poison.

Lowell burst back into the Authors' Room, slamming the door behind him. He found himself facing an unreadable expression on Longfellow's face. At the first sign of a thunderstorm, Longfellow would close all shutters in his house, explaining that he did not like such discordance. Now he wore the same look of retreat. Apparently Longfellow had said something to Fields, because the publisher was standing expectantly, leaning forward for more.

"Well," Lowell pleaded, "tell me how he could do that to us, Longfellow. How could Holmes do that *now*?"

Fields shook his head. "Lowell, Longfellow thinks he has realized something," he said, translating the poet's expression. "You remember how we took on the canto of the Schismatics just last night?"

"Yes. What of it, Longfellow?" Lowell asked.

Longfellow had begun to collect his coat, and was staring out the window. "Fields, would Mr. Houghton still be at Riverside?"

"Houghton's always at Riverside, at least when he's not at church. What can he do for us, Longfellow?"

"We must leave for there at once," said Longfellow.

"You've realized something that will help us, my dear Longfellow?" Lowell filled with hope.

He thought Longfellow was considering the question, but the poet made no answer on the ride over the river into Cambridge.

At the giant brick building housing the Riverside Press, Longfellow requested that H. O. Houghton provide the full printing records for the translation of Dante's *Inferno.* Despite its untested subject matter, the translation, breaking years of virtual silence by the most beloved poet in their country's history, was anxiously awaited by the literary world. With the bells and trumpets Fields had in store for it, its first printing of five thousand would sell out within a month. Anticipating this, Oscar Houghton had been preparing plates from Longfellow's proofs as the poet brought them in, maintaining a detailed, unimpeachably accurate log of dates.

The three scholars commandeered the printer's private counting room.

"I'm at a loss," Lowell said, not one to remain focused on the finer points of his own publishing projects, much less someone else's.

Fields showed him the schedule. "Longfellow submits his proofs with revisions the week after our translation sessions. So whatever date we find here recording Houghton's receipt of the proofs, the Wednesday of the week *before* that would be the meeting of our Dante circle."

The translation of Canto Three, the Neutrals, had taken place three or four days after the murder of Justice Healey. Reverend Talbot's murder had occurred three days before the Wednesday set aside for the translation of Cantos Seventeen, Eighteen, and Nineteen—the latter containing the punishment of the Simoniacs.

"But then we found out about the murder!" Lowell said.

"Yes, and I set our schedule ahead to the Ulysses canto at the last minute so that we might reinvigorate ourselves, and worked on the intermediate cantos myself. Now, the latest, the massacre of Phineas Jennison, has by all accounts occurred on this Tuesday—one day *before* yesterday's translation of the very same verses which give rise to that gross deed."

Lowell turned white and then steamy red.

"I see, Longfellow!" Fields cried.

"Each one—each crime—happens directly before our Dante Club translates the canto on which the murder has been based," Longfellow said.

"How could we have not seen that before?" cried Fields.

"Somebody has been playing with us!" Lowell boomed. Then quickly he lowered his voice to a whisper. "Someone has been watching us all along, Longfellow! It has to be someone who knows our Dante Club! Whoever it is has timed each murder with our translation!"

"Wait a minute. This could be just a dreadful coincidence." Fields looked at the chart again. "Look here. We have translated nearly two dozen *Inferno* cantos, yet there have been but three murders."

"Three deadly coincidences," said Longfellow.

"There's no coincidence," Lowell insisted. "Our Lucifer has been racing us to see what will come first—Dante translated into ink or into blood! We have been losing the race by two or three lengths each time!"

Fields protested. "But who could possibly know our schedule in advance? With enough time to plan such elaborate crimes? We write up no timetable. Sometimes we miss a week. Sometimes Longfellow skips a canto or two that he does not feel we are prepared for and goes out of order."

"My own Fanny would not know which cantos we sit down with, much less would she care to know," Lowell admitted.

"Who would possibly possess such particulars, Longfellow?" asked Fields.

"If this were all true," Lowell interrupted, "it means *we* are somehow implicated firsthand with the murders having begun at all!"

They were silent. Fields looked at Longfellow protectively. "Humbug!" he said. "Humbug, Lowell!" That was all he could think to argue.

"I do not profess to understand this strange pattern," Longfellow said as he rose from Houghton's desk. "But we cannot escape its implication. Whatever course of action Patrolman Rey decides, we can no longer consider our involvement merely as our prerogative. Thirty years have passed since the day I first sat at my desk in happier times to translate the *Commedia.* I have laid my hands upon it with such great reverence that it has sometimes amounted to unwillingness. But the time has come to make haste, to complete this work, or risk more loss."

After Fields started in his carriage for Boston, Lowell and Longfellow walked through the falling snow to their homes. Word of Phineas Jennison's murder had burned through their society. The elmy quiet of the Cambridge street was deafening. Wreaths of ascending snow-white chimney smoke vanished like ghosts. The windows not covered by shutters were blocked from the inside with clothing, shirts and blouses hanging loosely, for it was too cold to dry them outside. The latch strings were lowered on all the doors. Houses that had newly installed iron locks and metal chains, on the advice of local patrolmen, were kept tightly shut; some residents had even concocted a type of alarm for their doors, using a system of currents sold by door-to-door Jeremy Didlers from the West. No children were playing in the plush snowbanks. With these three murders, there was no hiding the certainty that there was one hand at work. Newspaper stories soon included the information that each victim had had his suit of clothing folded neatly at the scene of death and suddenly the whole city felt naked. The terror that started with the demise of Artemus Healey had now descended over Beacon Hill, along Charles Street, across Back Bay, and over the bridge to Cambridge. All at once, there seemed irrational but palpable reasons to believe in a scourge, in apocalypse.

Longfellow paused a block from Craigie House. "Could *we* be responsible?" His voice sounded frighteningly weak to his own ears.

"Don't let that maggot get into your brain. I wasn't thinking when I said that, Longfellow."

"You must be honest with me, Lowell. Do you think—"

Longfellow's words were splintered. A little girl's shout rose up from the air and shook the very foundations of Brattle Street.

Longfellow's knees buckled as his mind traced the sound back to his own house. He knew he would have to make a mad dash down Brattle Street through the virgin blanket of snow. But for a moment his thoughts trapped him in place, snared him with the trembling of possibility as one who wakes from a terrible nightmare searches for signs of bloody calamities in the peaceful room around him. Memories flooded the air ahead. *Why could I not save you, my love?*

"Should I go for my rifle?" Lowell cried frantically.

Longfellow sprinted ahead.

The two men reached the front step of Craigie House at about the same time, a remarkable feat for Longfellow, who, unlike his neighbor, was not practiced in physical exertion. They rushed side by side into the front hall. In the parlor, they found Charley Longfellow kneeling down trying to calm the excited little Annie Allegra, who was shouting and squealing joyfully at the gifts her brother had brought for them. Trap was growling in delight and wagging his pudgy tail in circles, showing all his teeth in an expression comparable to a human smile. Alice Mary came into the hall to greet them.

"Oh, Papa," she cried. "Charley has just come home for Thanksgiving! And he has brought us French jackets, striped red-and-black!" Alice posed in her jacket for Longfellow and Lowell.

"What a dasher!" Charley applauded. He embraced his father. "Why, Papa, you're whiter than a sheet, aren't you? Are you feeling unwell? I meant only to give you a small surprise! Perhaps you've gotten too old for us." He laughed.

The color had returned to Longfellow's fair skin by the time he pulled Lowell aside. "My Charley has come home," he said confidentially, as if Lowell could not see for himself.

Later that evening, after the children were asleep upstairs and Lowell had departed, Longfellow felt profoundly calm. He leaned at his standing desk and passed his hand over the smooth wood on which most of his translation was written. When he had first read Dante's poem, he had to confess to himself, he did not have faith in the great poet. He feared how it might end, beginning so gloriously. But throughout, Dante bore himself so valiantly that Longfellow could but wonder more and more, not only at his great but at his continuous power. The style rose with the theme, and swelled like tidewaters, and at length its flood lifted the reader, freighted with doubts and fears. Most often it had seemed that Longfellow was serving the Florentine, but sometimes Dante taunted, his meaning eluding all words, all language. Longfellow felt at these times as a sculptor who, unable to represent in cold marble the living beauty of the human eye, had recourse to such devices as sinking the eye deeper and making the brow above more prominent than it is in the living model.

But Dante resisted mechanical intrusions, and withheld himself, demanding patience. Whenever translator and poet came to this impasse, Longfellow would pause and think: Here Dante laid down his pen—all that follows was still a blank. How shall it be filled up? What new figures shall be brought in? What new names written? Then the poet resumed his pen—and, with an expression of joy or indignation upon his face, wrote further in his book—and Longfellow now followed without timidity.

A small scratching sound, like fingers on a chalkboard, caught the attention of Trap's triangle ears while he was wound in a ball by Longfellow's feet. It sounded like ice scraping against a window in the wind.

Longfellow was still translating at two o'clock in the morning. With furnace and fire in full blast, he could not make the mercury climb its little ladder higher than the sixtieth round, when it would go down, discouraged. He placed a candle at one window and looked out through another at the lovely trees, all feathered and plumed with snow. The air was motionless, and in their illumination they looked like one great aerial Christmas tree. As he was closing up shutters, he noticed some unusual marks in one window.

He pulled the shutters open again. The sound of scraping ice had been something else: a knife slicing into the glass. And he had been just a few feet from their rival. At first the words cut into the window were unintelligible: ƎИOIZUDAЯT AIM A⅃. Longfellow could decipher it almost immediately, but still he put on his hat, shawl, and coat and went outside, where the threat could be read clearly as he traced the sharp edges of the words with his fingers.

ƎИOIZUDAЯT AIM A⅃: "MY TRANSLATION."

XII

CHIEF KURTZ announced on the Central slate that he was leaving by train in a few hours on a lyceum tour of all New England, to address city committees and lyceum groups on new methods of policing. Kurtz explained to Rey. "'To salvage our city's reputation, quoth the aldermen. Liars."

"Then why?"

"To get me far away, far away from the detectives. By resolution I'm the only officer of the department with authority over the detective bureau. Those rogues shall have free rein. This investigation falls completely to them now. There will be no one here with the power to stop them."

"But, Chief Kurtz, they are looking in the wrong place. They only want an arrest for show."

Kurtz stared up at him. "And *you*, Patrolman, you must stay here as ordered. You know that. Until this is completely cleared up. That could be in many moons."

Rey blinked. "But I have much to tell, Chief . . ."

"You know I must instruct you to share with Detective Henshaw and his men anything you know or think you know."

"Chief Kurtz . . ."

"Anything, Rey! Should I take you to Henshaw myself?"

Rey hesitated, then shook his head.

Kurtz extended his hand to Rey's arm. "Sometimes the only satisfaction is to know there's nothing more you can do, Rey."

When Rey walked home that evening, a cloaked figure stepped next to him. She brought her hood down, breathing fast, the vapor of her breath crashing through her dark veil. Mabel Lowell cast off her veil and glared at Patrolman Rey.

"Patrolman. You remember me from when you came looking for Professor Lowell? I have something I think you should look at," she said, pulling out a thick package from under her cloak.

"How did you find me, Miss Lowell?"

"Mabel. Do you think it is so difficult to find the one mulatto police officer in Boston?" She closed her statement with a curled smirk.

Rey paused and looked at the package. He removed some sheets of paper. "I don't think I'll take this. Does it belong to your father?"

"Yes," she said. These were the proofs of Longfellow's Dante translation, which were overrun with Lowell's marginal notes. "I think that Father has discovered some aspects of Dante's poetry in those strange murders. I do not know the details that you must, and could never speak to him about this without him growing terribly warm, so please don't say you've seen me. It took much work, Officer, sneaking around Father's study hoping he would not notice."

"Please, Miss Lowell." Rey sighed.

"Mabel." Faced with the honest glow in Rey's eyes, she could not bring herself to show her desperation. "Please, Officer. Father tells Mrs. Lowell little, and me even less. But I know this: His Dante books are scattered at all times. When I hear him with his friends these days, it is all they speak about—and with such a tone of duress and anguish inappropriate to men in a translating society. Then I found a sketch of a man's feet burning, with some newspaper clippings about Reverend Talbot: *His* feet, some say, were charred when he was found. Haven't I heard Father review that canto of the nefarious clerics with Mead and Sheldon only a few months ago?"

Rey led her into the courtyard of a nearby building, where they found a vacant bench. "Mabel, you must tell nobody else that you know this," the patrolman told her. "It shall only confuse the situation and cast a dangerous shadow on your father and his friends—and, I fear, on yourself. There are interests involved that would take advantage of this information."

"You knew about this already, didn't you? Well, you must be planning to do something to stop this madness."

"I don't know, to be honest."

"You can't stand by and watch, not while Father . . . please." She placed the package of proof sheets in his hands again. Her eyes filled up, in spite of herself. "Take these. Read through them before he misses this. Your visit to

Craigie House that day must have had something to do with all this, and I know you can help."

Rey examined the package. He had not read a book since before the war. He had once consumed literature with alarming avidity, especially after the deaths of his adoptive parents and sisters: He had read histories and biographies and even romances. But now the very idea of a book struck him as offensively contained and arrogant. He preferred newspapers and broadsides, which had no chance to dominate this thoughts.

"Father is a hard man sometimes—I'm aware how he can seem," Mabel continued. "But he has been through much strain in his life, inside and out. He lives in fear of losing his ability to write, but I never thought of him as a poet at all, only as my father."

"You don't have to worry about Mr. Lowell."

"Then you are going to help him?" she asked, placing a hand on his arm. "Is there anything I can do to assist? Anything to make certain Father is safe, Patrolman?"

Rey remained silent. Passersby glared at the two of them, and he looked away.

Mabel smiled sadly and withdrew to the far side of the bench. "I understand. You are just like Father then. I must not be trusted with real matters, I suppose. On some fancy, I thought you'd feel differently."

For a moment Rey felt too much empathy to answer. "Miss Lowell, this is a matter not to get involved in, if one can choose."

"But I can't choose," she said, and returned her veil to its place as she headed toward the horsecar station.

Professor George Ticknor, an old man in decline, instructed his wife to send up his caller. His instructions were accompanied by an odd smile on his large and peculiar face. Ticknor's once-black hair was grizzled down the back of his neck and along his muttonchops, and pitifully thin below his skullcap. Hawthorne had once called Ticknor's nose the reverse of aquiline, not quite pug or snub.

The professor had never had much imagination and was thankful for the fact—it protected him from the vagaries that had beset fellow Bostonians, fellow writers especially, in times of reform thinking things would change.

Still, Ticknor could not help imagining now that the servant lifting him, helping him out of his chair, was a perfect grown image of George Junior, who had died at the age of five. Ticknor was still sad at George Junior's death thirty years later, very sad, because he could no longer see his bright smile or hear his glad voice even in his mind; because he turned his head at some familiar sound and the boy was not there; because he listened for his son's light step, which did not come.

Longfellow entered the library, bashfully bearing a gift. It was a clasped sack with gold fringe. "Please, stay seated, Professor Ticknor," he urged.

Ticknor offered cigars, which from their cracked wrappers, seemed to have been offered and rejected through many years by infrequent guests. "My dear Mr. Longfellow, what have you here?"

Longfellow placed the sack on Ticknor's desk. "Something I thought you, more than anyone, would like to see."

Ticknor looked at him in anticipation. His black eyes were impassable.

"I received it this morning from Italy. Read the letter that came with it." Longfellow handed it to Ticknor. It was from George Marsh, of the Dante Centennial Committee in Florence. Marsh was writing to assure Longfellow that there should be no concern over the acceptance of his translation of *Inferno* by the Florentine Committee.

Ticknor began to read: " 'The Duke of Caietani and the Committee shall gratefully receive the first American reproduction of the great poem as a contribution most fitting the solemnity of the Centenary, and at the same time as a worthy homage from the New World to one of the chief glories of the country of its discoverer, Columbus.'

"Why would you not feel assured?" Ticknor asked bemusedly.

Longfellow smiled. "I suppose that in his kind way, Mr. Marsh is asking me to hurry. But is it not said Columbus was far from punctual?"

" 'Please accept from our Committee,' " Ticknor continued reading, " 'in appreciation of your upcoming contribution, one of the seven sacks containing Dante Alighieri's ashes, taken lately from his tomb in Ravenna.' "

This sent a faint crimson delight into Ticknor's cheeks, and his eyes drifted toward the sack. His cheeks were no longer that hot red shade that, in collusion with dark hair, had led people to think him Spanish in his youth. Ticknor unfastened the clasp, opened the sack, and stared at what could have been coal dust. But Ticknor let some run through his fingers, like the tired pilgrim coming at last to holy water.

"For how many years did it seem I searched the wide earth for fellow scholars of Dante, with little success," Ticknor said. He swallowed hard, thinking, *For how many years?* "I tried to teach so many members of my family how Dante made me a better man, with little understanding. Did you notice, Longfellow, that last year there was not a club or society in Boston that did not hold a celebration to honor the three-hundredth anniversary of Shakespeare's birthday? Yet how many outside Italy think this year, the six-hundredth anniversary of Dante's birth, worthy of note? Shakespeare brings us to know ourselves. Dante, with his dissection of all others, bids us know one another. Tell me of the fortunes of your translation."

Longfellow took a deep breath. Then he narrated a story of murder; about Judge Healey punished as a Neutral, Elisha Talbot as a Simoniac, Phineas Jennison as a Schismatic. He explained how the Dante Club had traced Lucifer's path through the city and had come to understand that he paced himself by the progress of their translation.

"You can help us," Longfellow said. "Today begins a new phase for our fight."

"Help." Ticknor seemed to taste the word as he might a new wine and then dribble it back in disgust. "Help to do what, Longfellow?"

Longfellow leaned back, surprised.

"Foolish to try to stop something like this," Ticknor said without sympathy. "Did you know, Longfellow, that I have begun to give away my books?" He pointed with his ebony cane at the bookshelves all around the room. "I've given nearly *three thousand* volumes already to the new public library, piece by piece."

"A wonderful gesture, Professor," Longfellow said sincerely.

"Piece by piece until I fear I shall have nothing left of myself." He pushed down into his plush rug with his shiny black scepter. A wry part-smile, part-scowl stirred his tired mouth. "My very first memory of my life is the death of Washington. My father when he came home that day could not speak, so overcome was he with the news; I was terrified that he could be so stricken and I begged Mother to send for a doctor. For some weeks everyone, even the smallest children, wore black crepe on their sleeve. Did you ever pause to consider why it is that if you kill one person you are a murderer but if you kill a thousand you are a hero, as was Washington? I once thought to ensure the future of our literary arenas by study and instruction, by deference to tradition. Dante pleaded that his poetry carry on beyond him in a new home, and for forty years I toiled for him. The fate of literature prophesied by Mr. Emerson has come to life by the events you describe—literature that breathes life and death, that can punish, and can absolve."

"I know you cannot sanction what has happened, Professor Ticknor," Longfellow said thoughtfully. "Dante disfigured as a tool for murder and personal vengeance."

Ticknor's hands shook. "Here at last is a text of old, Longfellow, converted into a present power, a power of judgment before our eyes! No, if what you've discovered is true, when the world learns of what has happened in Boston—even if that is ten centuries from now—Dante shall not be *disfigured,* shall not be tainted or ruined. He will be revered as the first true creation of the American genius, the first poet to unleash the majestic power of all literature upon the unbelievers!"

"Dante wrote to remove us from times when death was incomprehensible. He wrote to give us hope for life, Professor, when we have none left, to know that our lives, our prayers, make a difference to God."

Ticknor sighed helplessly and pushed the gold-fringed sack forward. "Remember your gift, Mr. Longfellow."

Longfellow smiled. "You were the first to believe it all possible." Longfellow placed the sack of ashes in Ticknor's old hands, which grasped it greedily.

"I am too old to help anyone, Longfellow," Ticknor apologized. "But shall I give you this advice? You are not after a Lucifer—that is not the culprit you describe. Lucifer is pure dumbness when Dante finally meets him in frozen Cocytus, sobbing and mute. You see, that is how Dante triumphs over Milton—we long for Lucifer to be astounding and clever so we may defeat him, but Dante makes it more difficult. No. You are after Dante—it is Dante who decides who should be punished and where they go, what torments they suffer. It is the poet who takes those measures, yet by making himself the journeyer, he tries to make us forget: We think he too is another innocent witness to God's work."

Meanwhile in Cambridge, James Russell Lowell saw ghosts.

When he was in his easy chair with winter light streaming through, he had a distinct vision of the face of Maria, his first love, and was drawn to her by the resemblance. "By and by," he kept repeating. "By and by." She was sitting with Walter on her knee, and she said reassuringly to Lowell, "See what a fine, strong boy he is grown into."

Fanny Lowell told him that he seemed to be entranced, and she insisted that Lowell take to bed. She would fetch a doctor, or Dr. Holmes if he liked. But Lowell ignored her, because he felt so happy; he left Elmwood by the back way. He thought of how his poor mother, in the asylum, used to promise him that she was most content during her fits. Dante had said that the greatest sorrow was remembering past happiness, but Dante was wrong on that formulation—*dead wrong,* thought Lowell. There are no happinesses like our sad, regretful ones. Joy and sorrow were sisters, and very like each other too, as Holmes had said, or else both would not bring tears as they equally did. Lowell's poor baby son, Walter, Maria's last dead child, his rightful heir, seemed palpable to him as he walked the streets trying to think of anything, anything but sweet Maria, anything. But Walter's ghostly presence was not so much an image now as a babbling feeling that shadowed him, that was in him, as a pregnant woman feels life pressing within her stomach. He also thought he saw Pietro Bachi passing him on the street, saluting, taunting as if to say, "I shall always be here to remind you of failure." *You've never fought for anything, Lowell.*

"You're not here!" Lowell muttered, and a thought rang in his head: If he had not initially been so certain of Bachi's guilt, if he possessed a measure of Holmes's nervous skepticism, they might have found the murderer and Phineas Jennison might be alive. And then, before he could ask for a glass of water from one of the street's storekeepers, he saw ahead of him a shining white coat and tall white silk hat gliding joyfully away on the strength of a gold-trimmed walking stick.

Phineas Jennison.

Lowell rubbed his eyes, conscious enough of his state of mind to distrust his eyes, but he could see Jennison bumping shoulders with some passersby while others avoided him with strange looks. He was corporeal. Flesh and blood.

He was alive . . .

Jennison! Lowell tried to cry out but was too parched. The sight told him to run and at the same time tied his legs. "Oh, Jennison!" At the same time as he found his strong voice, his eyes began to pump tears. "Phinny, Phinny, I'm here, I'm here! Jemmy Lowell, you see? I haven't lost you yet!"

Lowell rushed through pedestrians and spun Jennison around by the shoulder. But the hybrid that faced him was cruel. It was Phineas Jennison's tailor-made hat and coat, his brilliant walking stick, but stuck inside them was an old man in tattered vests, face smeared with dirt, unshaven and misshapen. He was shaking in Lowell's grasp.

"Jennison," Lowell said.

"Don't turn me in, sir. I needed to stay warm . . ." The man explained: He was the vagrant who had discovered Jennison's body after swimming to the abandoned fort from a nearby island occupied by an almshouse. He had found some beautiful clothes folded neatly in a pile on the floor of the storage room where Jennison's body hung and had helped himself to a few items.

Lowell remembered and felt sharply the solitary maggot now removed from him, alone on its steep, savage path, eating into his insides. He felt a hole had been left, releasing everything that was caught up in his gut.

Harvard Yard was gagged with snow. Fruitlessly, Lowell searched the campus for Edward Sheldon. Lowell had sent him a letter on Thursday evening, after seeing Sheldon with the phantom, demanding the student's immediate presence at Elmwood. But Sheldon had not responded. Several students who knew Sheldon said they had not seen him in a few days. Some students passing Lowell reminded him of his lecture, for which he was late. When he entered his lecture room in University Hall, a spacious room formerly housing the College chapel, he gave his usual greeting. "Gentlemen and fellow students . . ." This was followed by the usual practiced laugh of students. *Fellow sinners*—that's how the Congregationalist ministers from his childhood used to begin. His father, to a child the voice of God. Holmes's father, too. *Fellow sinners.* Nothing could shake Lowell's father's sincere piety, his trust in a God who shared his strength.

"Am I the right sort of man to guide ingenuous youth? Not a bit of it!" Lowell heard himself speak these words a third of the way through a lecture on *Don Quixote.* "And then, on the other hand," he speculated, "my being a professor isn't good for me—dampens my gunpowder, as it were, so my mind, when it takes fire at all, crawls off in an unwilling fuse instead of leaping to meet the first spark."

Two concerned students tried to take him by the arm when he almost fell over. Lowell wobbled to the window and extended his head outside, eyes closed. Instead of feeling the cool brush of air he hoped for, there was an unexpected stroke of heat, as though Hell were tickling his nose and cheeks. He rubbed his mustache tusks, and they felt warm and moist too. Opening his eyes, he saw a triangle of flames down below. Lowell scrambled out of the classroom and down the stone stairs of University Hall. Down in Harvard Yard, a bonfire crackled voraciously.

Surrounding it, a semicircle of august men stared down at the flames with great attention. They were feeding books from a large pile to the fire. There were local Unitarian and Congregationalist ministers, fellows from the Harvard Corporation, and a few representatives of the Harvard Board of Overseers. One picked up a pamphlet, crushed it, and flung it like a ball. Everyone cheered as it hit the flames. Rushing forward, Lowell got down on one knee and pulled it out. The cover was too charred to read, so he opened the seared title page: *In Defense of Charles Darwin and His Evolutionary Theory.*

Lowell couldn't hold it any longer. Professor Louis Agassiz stood across from him on the other side of the fire, his face blurred and bent by fumes. The scientist waved amiably with both hands. "How fares your leg, Mr. Lowell? Ah, this—*this* is a must, Mr. Lowell, though a peety to waste good paper."

From a steam-filled window of the grotesquely Gothic granite Gore Hall, the College library, Dr. Augustus Manning, treasurer of the Corporation, looked down over the scene. Lowell rushed toward the massive entrance and through the nave, thankful for the composure and reason that came with each giant tread. No candles or gaslights were permitted in Gore Hall because of the danger of fire, so the library alcoves and the books were dim as the winter.

"Manning!" Lowell bellowed, educing a reprimand from the librarian.

Manning lurked on the platform above the reading room, gathering several books. "You have a lecture now, Professor Lowell. Leaving the students unsupervised shan't be deemed acceptable conduct by the Harvard Corporation."

Lowell had to wipe his face with a handkerchief before climbing to the platform. "You dare burn books in an institution of learning!" The copper tubes of Gore Hall's pioneering heating system always leaked steam, filling the library with billowing vapor that condensed into hot droplets on the windows, the books, and the students.

"The religious world owes us, and owes especially your friend Professor Agassiz, a debt of gratitude for triumphantly combating the monstrous teaching that we are descended from monkeys, Professor. Your father certainly would have agreed."

"Agassiz is too smart," Lowell said as he reached the top of the platform, breaking through the vapor. "He shall abandon you yet—count on it! Nothing that keeps thought out will ever be safe from thought!"

Manning smiled, and his smile seemed to cut inward into his head. "Do you know, I raised a hundred thousand dollars for Agassiz's museum through the Corporation. I daresay Agassiz will go exactly where I tell him."

"What is it, Manning? What makes you hate other men's ideas?"

Manning looked at Lowell sideways. As he answered, he lost the tight control of his voice. "We have been a noble country, with a simplicity of morals and justice, the last orphan child of the great Roman republic. Our world is strangled and demolished by infiltrators, newfangled notions of immorality coming in with every foreigner and every new idea against all the principles America was built upon. You see it yourself, Professor. Do you think we could have warred against ourselves twenty years ago? We have been poisoned. The war, our war, is far from over. It is just beginning. We have released demons into the very air we breathe. Revolutions, murders, thievery begin in our souls and move into the streets and our houses." This was the closest to being emotional that Lowell had ever seen Manning. "Chief Justice Healey was in my graduating class, Lowell—he was one of our finest overseers—and now he has been done in by some mere beast whose only knowledge is the knowledge of death! The minds in Boston are under constant assault. Harvard is the last fortress for the protection of our sublimity. And that is under *my* charge!"

Manning capped his sentiment: "You, Professor, have the luxury of rebellion only in absence of responsibility. You are truly a poet."

Lowell felt himself standing erect for the first time since Phineas Jennison's death. This gave him a rush of new strength. "We put a race of men in chains a hundred years ago, and *there* began the war. America will continue to grow no matter how many minds you chain up now, Manning. I know you threatened Oscar Houghton that if he published Longfellow's Dante translation there would be consequences."

Manning returned to the window and watched the orange fire. "And so there shall be, Professor Lowell. Italy is a world of the worst passions and loosest morals. And I welcome you to donate some copies of their Dante to Gore Hall, as some foolcap scientist did those Darwin books. That fire is where it will be swallowed up—an example to all who try to turn our institution into a shelter for ideas of filthy violence."

"Never shall I allow you," Lowell responded. "Dante is the first Christian poet, the first one whose whole system of thought is colored by a purely Christian theology. But the poem comes nearer to us than this. It is the real history of a brother man, of a tempted, purified, and at last triumphant human soul; it teaches the benign ministry of sorrow. His is the first keel that ever ventured into the silent sea of human consciousness to find a new world of poetry. He held heartbreak at bay for twenty years, and would not let himself die until he had done his task. Neither shall Longfellow. Neither shall I."

Lowell turned and started to descend.

"Three cheers, Professor." From the platform, Manning glared impassively. "But perhaps not everyone shares the same views. I received a peculiar visit from a policeman, a Patrolman Rey. He inquired after your work on Dante. Did not explain why, and he left abruptly. Can you tell me why your work attracts the police to our revered 'institution of learning'?"

Lowell stopped and looked back toward Manning.

Manning steepled his long fingers above his breastbone. "Some sensible men will rise up from your circle to betray you, Lowell—I promise that. No congregation of insurgents can stand together for long. If Mr. Houghton shall not cooperate to stop you, someone else will. Dr. Holmes, for instance."

Lowell wanted to leave, but he waited for more.

"I warned him many months ago to disassociate himself from your translation project or suffer severe damage to his reputation. What do you think he did?"

Lowell shook his head.

"He called on me at home and confided in me that he agreed with my assessment."

"You lie, Manning!"

"Oh, so Dr. Holmes has remained dedicated to the cause?" he asked as though he knew much more than Lowell could imagine.

Lowell bit his quivering lip.

Manning shook his head and smiled. "The miserable little manikin is your Benedict Arnold awaiting instructions, Professor Lowell."

"Believe that when I am once a man's friend I am always so—nor is it so very hard to bring me to it. And though a man may enjoy himself in being my enemy, he cannot make me *his* for longer than I wish. Good afternoon." Lowell had a way of leaving a conversation with the other person needing more from him.

Manning shadowed Lowell down to the reading room and caught him by the arm. "I do not understand how you can put your good name, everything you've worked for your whole life, on the line for something like *this*, Professor."

Lowell jerked away. "But don't you wish to heaven you could, Manning?" He returned to his class in time to dismiss his students.

If the murderer had somehow been monitoring Longfellow's translation and was racing them to completion, the Dante Club had little choice but to complete the thirteen remaining *Inferno* cantos with the utmost speed. They agreed to divide into two smaller camps: a company of investigators and a company of translators.

Lowell and Fields would labor in reviewing their evidence while Longfellow and George Washington Greene toiled over the translation in the study. Fields had informed Greene, to the old minister's great delight, that the translation had been placed on a strict schedule, in view of its immediate completion: There were nine previously unreviewed cantos, one partially translated, and two with which Longfellow was not fully satisfied. Longfellow's servant, Peter, would deliver the proofs to Riverside as Longfellow finished and take Trap for his constitutionals while doing so.

"It makes no sense!"

"Then move on from it, Lowell," said Fields from his place in the library's deep armchair, which had once belonged to Longfellow's grandfather, a great Revolutionary War general. He watched Lowell carefully. "Sit down. Your face is bright red. Have you slept at all lately?"

Lowell ignored him. "What would qualify Jennison as a Schismatic? Particularly in that pouch of Hell, each of the shades Dante chooses to single out is unequivocally emblematic of the sin."

"Until we find out why Lucifer would have chosen Jennison, we must cull what we can from the details of the murder," said Fields.

"Well, it confirms Lucifer's strength. Jennison had climbed with the Adirondack Club. He was a sportsman and a hunter, yet our Lucifer grabs him and chops him up with ease."

"No doubt he took him at the point of a weapon," said Fields. "The strongest man alive may fall to fear of a gun, Lowell. We know also that our killer is elusive. Patrolmen were stationed on every street in the area, at all hours, since the night Talbot was killed. And Lucifer's great attention to the details of Dante's canto—this too is certain."

"Any moment as we speak," said Lowell absently, "any moment as Longfellow translates a new verse in the next room, there could be another murder and we will have been powerless to stop it."

"Three murders and not a single witness. Precisely timed with our translations. What shall we do, roam the streets and wait? If I were a less educated man, I might begin to think it's a genuine evil spirit thrust upon us."

"We must narrow our focus to the murders' relationship with our club," Lowell said. "Let us concentrate on tracking all those who might somehow know of the translation schedule." As Lowell flipped through their investigative notebook, he absently stroked one of the library's collectibles, a cannonball fired by the British onto Boston against General Washington's troops.

They heard another knock at the front door but ignored it.

"I have sent a note to Houghton asking that he ensure that no proofs from Longfellow's translation have been removed from Riverside," Fields told Lowell. "We know all the killings were taken from cantos that at the time were not yet translated by our club. Longfellow must continue to hand in the proofs to the presses as if all were normal. In the meantime, what of young Sheldon?"

Lowell frowned. "He has not yet replied and has been seen nowhere on campus. He is the only one who can tell us about that phantom I saw him talking with, with Bachi gone."

Fields stood up and leaned down next to Lowell. "You are very certain you saw this 'phantom' yesterday, Jamey?" he asked.

Lowell was surprised. "What do you mean, Fields? I told you already—I saw him watching me in Harvard Yard, and then another time waiting for Bachi. And then again in a heated exchange with Edward Sheldon."

Fields couldn't help but cringe. "It is only that we are all under much apprehension, much anxiety of the mind, my dear Lowell. My nights are passed in uneasy snatches of sleep as well."

Lowell slammed down the notebook he was reviewing. "Are you saying I've imagined him?"

"You told me yourself that you thought you saw Jennison today, and Bachi, and your first wife, and then your dead son. For Heaven's sake!" Fields shouted.

Lowell's lips quivered. "Now look here, Fields. That is the last turn of the thumbscrew—"

"Pray calm yourself, Lowell. I didn't mean to raise my voice. I didn't mean that."

"I suppose you should know better than us what we should be doing. *We* are merely poets after all! I suppose you should know precisely how someone has traced our translation schedule!"

"Now what could *that* imply, Mr. Lowell?"

"Simply this: Who besides us is intimately aware of the activities of our Dante Club? The printer's devils, the plate makers, the binders—all of them aligned with Ticknor and Fields?"

"I say!" Fields was flabbergasted. "Don't turn the tables on me!"

The door connecting the library to the study opened.

"Gentlemen, I'm afraid I must interrupt," Longfellow said as he brought in Nicholas Rey.

A look of horror ran across the faces of Lowell and Fields. Lowell blurted out a litany of reasons why Rey could not turn them in.

Longfellow merely smiled.

"Professor Lowell," Rey said. "Please, I'm here to ask you gentlemen for leave to assist you now."

Immediately, Lowell and Fields forgot their argument and greeted Rey excitedly.

"Now, understand, I am doing this to stop the killing," Rey made clear. "Nothing else."

"That is not our only goal," said Lowell after a long pause. "But we cannot complete this without some assistance, and neither can you. This scoundrel has left the sign of Dante on everything he touches, and it is downright deadly for you to take a step in his direction without a translator by your side."

Leaving them in the library, Longfellow returned to the study. He and Greene were on their third canto of the day, having started at six in the morning and worked through the high hump of noontime. Longfellow had written Holmes a note asking that he aid in the translating, but received no response from 21 Charles. Longfellow had asked Fields whether Lowell could be convinced to reconcile with Holmes, but Fields recommended giving both time to calm themselves.

Throughout the day, Longfellow had to turn away an inordinate number of odd requests from the usual assortment of people who came to call. A Westerner brought an "order" for a poem that he wished Longfellow to write about birds, for which he would pay roundly. One woman, a regular caller, brought baggage to the door, explaining that she was Longfellow's wife, who had returned home. A purportedly wounded soldier came to beg money; Longfellow felt sorry and gave him a small amount.

"Why, Longfellow, that man's 'stump' was merely his arm tucked into his shirt!" Greene said after Longfellow had closed the door.

"Yes, I know," Longfellow replied as he returned to his chair. "But, my dear Greene, who will be kind to him if I am not?"

Longfellow reopened his materials to *Inferno,* Canto Five, of which he had postponed completion for many months. This was the circle of the Lustful. There, unceasing winds toss the sinners aimlessly, just as their unrestrained wantonness tossed them about aimlessly in life. The pilgrim asks to speak with Francesca, a beautiful young woman who had been killed when her husband found her embracing his brother, Paolo. She, with the silent spirit of her illicit lover beside her, floats to Dante's side.

"Francesca is not content to suggest that she and Paolo simply yielded themselves to their passions as she tells her story weeping to Dante," Greene remarked.

"Right," Longfellow said. "She tells Dante that they were reading of Guinevere and Lancelot's kiss when their eyes met over the book, and she says coyly, 'That day we read no further.' Paolo takes her in his arms and kisses her, yet Francesca places the blame for their transgression not on him but on the book that drew them together. The writer of the romance is their betrayer."

Greene closed his eyes, but not because he was asleep, as he so often was during their meetings. Greene believed a translator should forget himself in the author, and this is what he did in trying to help Longfellow. "And so they receive their perfect punishment—to be together forever but never to kiss again or to feel the excitement of courtship, only to feel torment side by side."

As they talked, Longfellow saw the golden locks and serious face of Edith leaning into the study. After her father's glance, the girl stole into the hall.

Longfellow suggested to Greene that they pause. The men in the library had also stopped their discussions so that Rey could examine the investigative journal Longfellow had been keeping. Greene stretched his legs in the garden.

As Longfellow put some books away, his thoughts traveled to other times in the house, times before his own. In this study, General Nathanael Greene, grandfather of their own Greene, had discussed strategy with General

George Washington when news came of the British arrival, sending all the generals in the room rushing to find their wigs. In this study, too, according to one of Greene's histories, Benedict Arnold had lowered himself to one knee and sworn his allegiance. Putting this last episode of the history of his house out of his mind, Longfellow went into the parlor, where he found his daughter Edith curled up in a Louis XVI armchair. Her chair was pulled close to the marble bust of her mother, Fanny's creamy countenance always there when the girl needed her. Longfellow could never look at a likeness of his wife without the thrill of pleasure that had come over him from the earliest days of their awkward courtship. Fanny had never left a room without leaving him with the feeling that something of the light went with her.

Edith's neck curved like a swan's to hide her face. "Well, dear heart." Longfellow smiled gently. "How is my little darling this afternoon?"

"I'm sorry for spying, Papa. I wished to ask you something and could not help but listen. That poem," she said, timid but probing, "speaks of the saddest things."

"Yes. Sometimes the Muse calls for that. It is the poet's duty to tell of our most difficult times with equal honesty as we tell of the gay times, Edie, for only in coming through the darkest moments, sometimes, is light found. Thus does Dante."

"That man and woman in the poem, why must you punish them so for loving each other?" A tear blotted her sky-blue eyes.

Longfellow sat down on the chair, rested her on his knees, and made her a throne of his arms. "The poet of that work was a gentleman christened Durante but changed in childish playfulness to Dante. He lived some six hundred years ago. He was struck by love himself—that is why he writes so. You have noticed the marble statuette above my study mirror?"

Edith nodded.

"Well, *that's* Signor Dante."

"That man? He looks to have the whole world's weight on his mind."

"Yes." Longfellow smiled. "And deeply in love with a girl he met long ago, when she was, oh, not much younger than you, my darling—about little Panzie's age—Beatrice Portinari. She was nine when he first saw her, at a festival in Florence."

"Beatrice," Edith said, imagining the spelling of the word and considering the dolls for whom she had not yet found a name.

"Bice—that is what her friends called her. But never Dante. He only called her by her full name, Beatrice. When she came near, such modesty took possession of his heart that he could not raise his eyes or return her salutation. Other times, he would ready himself to speak and she would simply walk by, barely noticing him. He would hear the townspeople whisper of her, 'This is no mortal. She is one of God's blessed.' "

"They said that of her?"

Longfellow laughed lightly. "Well, that is what Dante heard, for he was deeply in love, and when you are in love, you hear townspeople praising the one you praise."

"Did Dante ask for her hand?" Edith inquired hopefully.

"No. She only spoke to him once, to say hello. Beatrice married another Florentine. Then she became sick with a fever and died. Dante married another woman and they started a family. But he never forgot his love. He even named his daughter Beatrice."

"Wasn't his wife angry?" the little girl asked indignantly.

Longfellow reached for one of Fanny's soft brushes and ran it through Edith's hair. "We don't know much about Donna Gemma. But we do know that when the poet met with some troubles in the middle of his life, he had a vision that Beatrice, from her home in Heaven, sent a guide to help him pass through a very dark place to reach her again. When Dante trembles at the idea of this trial, his guide reminds him: 'When you see her beauteous eyes again, you will know your life's journey once more.' You understand, dear?"

"But why did he love Beatrice so much if he never spoke with her?"

Longfellow continued brushing, surprised by the difficulty of the question. "He once said, dear, that she excited such feelings in him that he could not find any words to describe them. For Dante, the poet that he was, what could capture him more than a feeling that defied his rhymes?"

Then, he recited softly, caressing her hair with the brush, " 'You, my little girl, Are better than all the ballads / That ever were sung or said; / For ye are a living poem, /And all the rest are dead.' "

The poem produced its usual smile from the recipient, who then left her father to his thoughts. Following the sound of Edith's footsteps up the stairs, Longfellow remained in the warm shadow of the creamy marble bust, suffused with his daughter's sadness.

"Ah, there you are." Greene appeared in the parlor, his arms out wide either side. "I believe I dozed off on your garden bench. No matter, I'm quite ready to return to our cantos! Say, where have Lowell and Fields disappeared?"

"Out for a ramble, I believe." Lowell had apologized to Fields for growing warm, and they had set off to get some air.

Longfellow realized how long he had been sitting. His joints clicked audibly when he stirred from his chair.

"As a matter of fact," he said, looking at the watch he removed from his waistcoat, "they've been gone for some time."

Fields tried keeping up with Lowell's long strides on their way down Brattle Street.

"Perhaps we should return now, Lowell."

Fields was thankful when Lowell came to an abrupt stop. But the poet was staring ahead with a frightful look. Without warning, he yanked Fields behind the trunk of an elm. He whispered to look ahead. Fields watched across the way as a tall figure in a bowler hat and checkered waistcoat turned a corner.

"Lowell, calm down! Who is he?" asked Fields.

"Merely the man I saw watching me in Harvard Yard! And then meeting Bachi! And then again in heated talk with Edward Sheldon!"

"Your phantom?"

Lowell nodded triumphantly.

They followed surreptitiously, Lowell directing his publisher to keep a distance from the stranger, who was turning onto a side street.

"Daughter of Eve! He's heading for your house!" said Fields. The stranger started through the white fence of Elmwood. "Lowell, we must go speak with him."

"And let him have the upper hand? I have a much better plan for this blackguard," said Lowell, leading Fields around the carriage house and barn and through the back entrance into Elmwood. Lowell ordered his chambermaid to welcome the visitor who was about to ring at the front door. She was to bring him to a specified room on the third floor of the mansion, then to close the door. Lowell snatched his hunting rifle from the library, checked it, and brought Fields up the narrow servants' stairs in the back.

"Jamey! What in God's name do you think you're going to do?"

"I'm going to see to it that this phantom does not slip away this time—not until I am satisfied with what we know," said Lowell.

"Has your knot come loose? We'll send for Rey instead."

Lowell's bright brown eyes flared gray. "Jennison was my friend. He supped in this very house—there, in my dining room, where he took my napkins to his lips and drank from my wineglasses. Now he's cut to pieces! I refuse to float timidly around the truth any longer, Fields!"

The room at the top of the stairs, Lowell's childhood bedroom, was unused and unheated. From the window of his boyhood garret, the view in winter was a wide one, taking in even a part of Boston. Now, Lowell looked out and could see the familiar long curve of the Charles and the wide fields between Elmwood and Cambridge, the flat marshes beyond the river smooth and silent with glittering snow.

"Lowell, you'll kill someone with that! As your publisher, I order you to put that gun away at once!"

Lowell put his hand over Fields's mouth and gestured at the closed door to watch for any movement. Several minutes of silence passed before the two scholars, squatting behind a sofa, heard the tread of the maid leading the guest up the front stairs. She did as instructed, showing the caller into the chamber and immediately closing the door behind him.

"Hullo?" said the man to the empty, morbidly cold room. "What kind of parlor is this? What's the meaning of this?"

Lowell rose up from his place behind the sofa, aiming his rifle squarely at the man's checkered waistcoat.

The stranger gasped. He thrust his hand into his frock coat and drew out a revolver, pointing it at the barrel of Lowell's rifle.

The poet did not flinch.

The stranger's right hand shook violently, the excess leather of his gloved finger rubbing the trigger of his revolver.

Lowell, across the room, raised the rifle above his walrus-tusk mustache, which showed itself a dark black in the insufficient light, and closed one eye, looking with the other straight down the nose of the rifle. He spoke through clenched teeth. "Try me, and whatever happens, you shall lose. Either you send us to Heaven," he added as he cocked his gun, "or we shall send you to Hell."

XIII

THE STRANGER held out his revolver for another moment and then flung it down to the rug. "This job ain't worth such bosh!"

"Collect his pistol please, Mr. Fields," Lowell said to his publisher, as if this were their daily occupation. "Now, you rascal, you'll tell us who you are and what you have come for. Tell us what you have to do with Pietro Bachi and why Mr. Sheldon was giving you orders on the street. And tell me why you're in my house!"

Fields lifted the gun from the floor.

"Put up your weapon, Professor, or I say nothing," the man said.

"Do listen to him, Lowell," Fields whispered, to the satisfaction of the third party.

Lowell lowered his gun. "Very well, but I pray for your own sake that you are straight with us." He carried over a chair for their hostage, who repeatedly pronounced the whole scene to be "bosh."

"I don't believe we had the chance to be presented before you put a rifle to my head," the visitor said. "I'm Simon Camp, a detective from the Pinkerton Agency. I was hired by Dr. Augustus Manning of Harvard College."

"Dr. Manning!" Lowell cried. "For what purpose?"

"He wished me to look into these courses taught on this Dante character, to see whether it could be demonstrated as likely to produce a 'pernicious effect' on the students. I am to look into the matter and report back my findings."

"And what have you found?"

"Pinkerton assigns me the whole Boston area. This trifling case wasn't my highest priority, Professor, but I've done my fair share of work. I did call on one of the old teachers, a Mr. Bak-*ee*, to meet me on campus," said Camp. "I interviewed several students, too. That insolent young man Mr. Sheldon was not giving orders to me, Professor. He was telling me what to do with my questions, and his language was a sight too smart to repeat in the company of such fine velvet-collared coats."

"What did the others say?" Lowell demanded.

Camp scoffed. "My work is confidential, Professor. But I did think it was time I speak to you face-to-face, ask your own opinion on this Dante. *That* is why I've come here today to your house. And what a welcome!"

Fields squinted in confusion. "Did Manning send you to speak to Lowell directly?"

"I am not under his *wing*, sir. This is *my* case. I make my own judgments," Camp answered haughtily. "You're just fortunate I've slowed up on my trigger finger, Professor Lowell."

"Oh, what a row I shall call down on Manning!" Lowell jumped up and leaned over Simon Camp. "You came here to see what I say, did you, sir? You shall cease with this witch-hunt at once! That's what I say!"

"I don't care a brass farthing, Professor!" Camp laughed in his face. "This is the case I have been given, and I shall not stand down for anyone—not for that Harvard swell and not for an old cuss like you! You may shoot me down if you like, but I take my cases to the end!" He paused, then added, "I am a professional."

With Camp's careless inflection on this last word, Fields seemed to know at once what he had come for. "Perhaps we can work something else out," the publisher said, removing some gold pieces from his wallet. "What say you enter an indefinite respite from this case, Mr. Camp?"

Fields dropped several coins into Camp's open hand. The detective waited patiently, and Fields dropped two more, prompting a stiff smile. "And my gun?"

Fields returned the revolver.

"I daresay, gentlemen, now and then a case works out for everyone involved." Simon Camp bowed and made his way down the front stairs.

"To have to pay off a man such as that!" Lowell said. "Now, how did you know he would take that, Fields?"

"Bill Ticknor always said people like the feel of gold in their hands," Fields remarked.

His face pressed against his garret window, Lowell watched with steady anger as Simon Camp crossed the brick footpath to the gates, happy-go-lucky as could be, jiggling the gold pieces, staining Elmwood with his snow prints.

That night, Lowell, overcome with exhaustion, sat still as a statue in his music room. Before entering it, he had hesitated in the doorway, as though he would find the real owner of the room sitting in his chair before the fire.

Mabel peered in from the archway. "Father? Something is the matter. I wish you would speak about it with me."

Bess, the Newfoundland pup, galloped in and licked Lowell's hand. He smiled, but it saddened him beyond measure to recall the lethargic greetings of Argus, their old Newfoundland, who had ingested a fatal amount of poison from a neighboring farm.

Mabel pulled Bess away to try to maintain some seriousness. "Father," she said. "We've spent so little time together recently. I know . . ." She restrained herself from completing her thought.

"What's that?" Lowell asked. "You know what, Mab?"

"I know something's troubling you and gives you no peace."

He grabbed her hand lovingly. "I am tired, my dear Hopkins." That had always been Lowell's name for her. "I shall go to bed and feel better. You're a very good girl, my dear. Now, salute your progenitor."

She complied by giving him a mechanical kiss on his cheek.

Upstairs in his bedchamber, Lowell plowed his face into his lotus-leaf pillow, not looking at his wife. But soon he tucked his head in Fanny Lowell's lap and cried without pause for nearly a half-hour, every emotion he had ever known coursing through and spilling out into his brain; and he could see projected on the closed lids of his eyes Holmes, devastated, sprawled on the floor of the Corner and the carved-up Phineas Jennison crying out for Lowell to save him, to deliver him from Dante.

Fanny knew her husband would not talk about what was upsetting him, so she just ran a hand through his warm auburn hair and waited for him to rock himself to sleep amidst his sobs.

"*Lowell. Lowell. Please, Lowell. Wake up. Wake up.*"

As Lowell's eyes creaked open, he was stunned by the sunlight. "What, what is it? Fields?"

Fields sat at the edge of the bed, a folded newspaper gripped close to his chest.

"All right, Fields?"

"All wrong. It's noon, Jamey. Fanny says you've been sleeping like a top all day—turning round and round. Are you unwell?"

"I feel much better." Lowell focused immediately on the object that Fields's hands seemed to want to hide from his view. "Something's happened, hasn't it?"

Fields said bleakly, "I used to think I knew just how to deal with any situation. Now I'm as rusty as an old nail, Lowell. Why, look at me, won't you? I've grown so terribly fat that my oldest creditors would hardly know me."

"Fields, please . . ."

"I need you to be stronger than I am, Lowell. For Longfellow, we must . . ."

"Another murder?"

Fields passed him the newspaper. "Not yet. Lucifer has been arrested."

✻

The sweat box in the Central Station was three and a half feet wide and seven feet long. The inside door was iron. On the outside was another door, of solid oak. When this second door was closed, the cell became a dungeon, without the slightest trace of or hope for light. A prisoner could be kept inside for days at a time, until he could no longer endure the darkness and would do whatever he was asked.

Willard Burndy, Boston's second-best safecracker behind Langdon W. Peaslee, heard a key turning in the oak door and a blinding plane of gaslight stunned him. "Keep me here ten year an' a day, grunter! I ain't pleadin' to no murders I didn't pull!"

"Cheese it, Burndy," the guard snapped.

"I swear, 'pon my honor . . ."

"Upon your *what?*" The guard laughed.

"Upon the honor of a gentleman!"

Willard Burndy was led in shackles through the hall. The watching eyes of those in the other cells knew Burndy by name if not by his appearance. A Southerner who had moved to New York to reap the wartime affluence in the North, Burndy had migrated to Boston after a long stretch in the New York Tombs. Burndy gradually learned that among the ranks of the underworld, he had earned a reputation for targeting the widows of wealthy Brahmins, a pattern that he himself had not even noticed. He had little desire to be known as an assailant of old fossocks. He had never considered himself a louse. Burndy had been quite cooperative whenever a reward was offered for stolen heirlooms and jewelry, returning a portion of the goods to a fair-minded detective in return for some of the cash.

Now, a guard twisted and pulled Burndy into a room and then pushed him down into a chair. He was a red-faced, wild-haired man with so many lines crisscrossing his face that he resembled a Thomas Nast caricature.

"What's *your* game?" Burndy drawled to the man sitting across from him. "I would extend a hand, but you see I'm barnacled. Hold . . . I read about you. The first Negro policeman. An army hero in the war. You was at the show-up when that vag jumped out the window!" Burndy laughed at the memory of the broken leaper.

"The district attorney wants you to hang," Rey said quietly, tearing the smile off Burndy's face. "The die is cast. If you know why you're here, tell me."

"My game is safe-blowing. The best in Boston, I say, better than that dog nipper Langdon Peaslee on any day! But I didn't kill no beak, and I didn't jam no brother of the cloth neither! I've got Squire Howe coming in from New York and, you'll see, I'll beat this in the courts!"

"Why are you here, Burndy?" Rey asked.

"Those fakers, the detectives, they're planting evidence at every stop!"

Rey knew this was likely. "Two witnesses saw you the night Talbot's house was robbed, the day before he was murdered, looking into the reverend's house. They're legitimate, aren't they? That's why Detective Henshaw chose you. You have just enough sin in you to take the blame."

Burndy was about to refute this, but hesitated. "Why should I trust a moke?"

"I want you to look at something," Rey said, watching carefully. "It may help you, if you can understand." He passed a sealed envelope across the table.

Despite his shackles, Burndy managed to tear open the envelope with his teeth and unfold the thrice-folded fine-quality stationery. He examined it for a few seconds before ripping it in two in wild frustration, kicking wildly and banging his head against the wall and table in a pendulum motion.

Oliver Wendell Holmes watched the newsprint curl up at the corners, slowly yielding its edges before caving into the flames.

. . . ustice of the Massachusetts Supreme Court found stripped with insects and m . . .

The doctor fed in another article. The flames rose in appreciation.

He thought about the outburst from Lowell, who was not precisely right about Holmes's blind belief in Professor Webster fifteen years ago. True, Boston had gradually lost its faith in the disgraced medical professor, but Holmes had reason not to. He had seen Webster the day after George Parkman's disappearance and had spoken to him about the mystery. There wasn't the least sign of deceit in Webster's amiable face. And Webster's story as it later emerged was entirely consistent with the facts: Parkman had come to collect on his outstanding debt, Webster paid him, Parkman canceled the note, and Parkman departed. Holmes sent contributions to help pay for Webster's defense team, enfolding the money in reassuring letters addressed to Mrs. Webster. Holmes testified to Webster's sterling character and the absolute implausibility of his involvement in such a crime. He also explained to the jury that there was no method to positively say that the human remains found in Webster's rooms belonged to Dr. Parkman—they could belong to him, yes, but they could as easily *not.*

It was not that Holmes lacked sympathy for the Parkmans. After all, George had been the Medical College's greatest patron, funding its facilities on North Grove Street and even endowing the Parkman Professorship of Anatomy and Physiology, the very chair that Dr. Holmes held. Holmes had even performed a eulogy at Parkman's memorial service. But Parkman could well have gone mad, wandering away in a fit of confusion. The man could still be alive, and here they were ready to hang one of their own on the most fantastic circumstantial evidence! Could not the janitor, fearful of losing his job after poor Webster caught him gambling, have secured bone fragments from the Medical College's large supply and positioned them throughout Webster's rooms to appear hidden?

Like Holmes, Webster had grown up in comfortable surroundings before attending Harvard College. The two medical men had never been particularly close. Yet from the day of Webster's arrest, when the poor man tried to swallow poison in distress over the disgrace to his family, there was no one with whom Dr. Holmes felt a closer bond. Could it not as easily have been he who had found himself in the middle of damaging circumstances? With their short statures, full sideburns, and clean-shaven faces, the two professors were physically similar. Holmes had been certain that he would yet play some small but noteworthy role in the inevitable exoneration of his fellow lecturer.

But then they had all found themselves at the gallows. That day had seemed so remote, so impossible, so alterable during months of testimony and appeals. Most of polite Boston had remained at home, ashamed for their neighbor. Teamsters and stevedores and factory workers and launderers: They were most publicly enthused by the Brahmin's demise and humiliation.

A heavily perspiring J. T. Fields slipped through a ring of these bystanders to reach Holmes.

"I have a driver waiting, Wendell," said Fields. "Come home to Amelia, sit with the children."

"Fields, don't you see what this has come to?"

"Wendell," Fields said, putting his hands on his author's shoulders. "The evidence."

The police tried closing off the area but hadn't brought long enough ropes. Every roof and every window in the buildings crowding the Leverett Street Jail yard showed the single-minded overflow. Holmes had at that moment felt the most paralyzing urge to do more than watch. He would address the mob. Yes, he would improvise a poem proclaiming the city's great folly. After all, was not Wendell Holmes the most celebrated toastmaster in Boston? Verses extolling Dr. Webster's virtues began to meet piecemeal in his head. At the same time, Holmes pushed up on his toes to keep an eye on the carriage path behind Fields so that he might be the first to see the clemency papers arrive or George Parkman, the supposed murder victim, stroll into view.

"If Webster must die today," Holmes said to his publisher, "he shan't die without praise." He pressed forward toward the scaffold. But as he took in the hangman's noose, he stopped cold and emitted a choking wheeze. This was the first time he had been in sight of that unearthly loop since boyhood, when Holmes had snuck his younger brother John to Gallows Hill in Cambridge just as a condemned man was writhing in his final suffering. It was this sight, Holmes always believed, that had made him both doctor and poet.

A hush swept the crowd. Holmes locked eyes with Webster, who was ascending the platform with a wobbly step, his arm held tightly by a jailer.

As Holmes took a step backward, one of the Webster daughters appeared before him clutching an envelope to her chest.

"Oh, Marianne!" Holmes said, and hugged the little angel tight. "From the governor?"

Marianne Webster held out her delivery at arm's length. "Father wished you to have this before he's gone, Dr. Holmes."

Holmes turned back to the gallows. A black hood was being fitted over Webster's head. Holmes opened the flap of the envelope.

> My dearest Wendell,
>
> How dare I strive to express my gratitude with mere sentences for all you have done? You have believed in me without a shadow of doubt on your mind, and I shall always have that feeling to support me. You alone have remained true to my character since the police snatched me from my home, when others have one by one fallen away from my side. Imagine how it feels when those of your own society, with whom you have banqueted at table and prayed at chapel, stare at you with awful dread. When even the eyes of my own sweet daughters unwillingly reveal second thoughts about their poor Papa's honor.
>
> Yet for all this I am beholden to tell you, dear Holmes, that I did it. I killed Parkman and hacked up his body, then incinerated it in my laboratory furnace. Understand, I was an only child, much indulged, and I have never secured the control over my passions that I ought to have acquired early; and the consequence is—all this! All the proceedings in my case have been just, as it is just that I should die upon the scaffold in accordance with that sentence. Everybody is right and I am wrong, and I have this morning sent full and true accounts of the murder to the several newspapers and to the brave janitor whom I so shamefully accused. If the yielding up of my life to the injured law will atone, even in part, that is a consolation.
>
> Tear this up directly without another look. You have come to watch my time pass in peace, so do not dwell on what I write so tremblingly, for I have lived with a lie in my mouth.

As the note floated down from Holmes's hands, the metallic platform supporting the black-hooded man dropped away, hitting the scaffold with a clang. It was not so much that Holmes had no longer believed in Webster's innocence at that moment, but rather that he knew they could have all been guilty if put in the same circumstance of desperation. As a doctor, Holmes had never stopped appreciating how roundly defective was the design of humankind.

Besides, could not there be a crime that was not a sin?

Amelia stepped into the room, smoothing her dress. She called her husband. "Wendell Holmes! I'm talking to you. I can't understand what's come over you lately."

"Do you know the things put in my mind as a boy, 'Melia?" Holmes said as he flung into the fire a set of proof sheets he had saved from Longfellow's Dante Club meetings.

He had kept a box of all documents related to the club: Longfellow's proofs, his own annotations, Longfellow's reminders for him to be there on Wednesday evenings. Holmes had thought that one day he might write a memoir of their meetings. He had mentioned this in passing once to Fields, who immediately began planning who might write a puff for Holmes's work. Once a publisher, always a publisher. Holmes now threw another batch into the fire. "Our country-bred kitchen servants would tell me that our shed was full of demons and black devils. Another bucolic lad informed me that if I wrote my name in my own blood, the prowling agent of Satan, if not the Evil One himself, would pocket it, and from that day forth I'd become his servant." Holmes chuckled humorlessly. "However much you educate a man out of his superstitions, he will always think as the Frenchwoman did about ghosts: *Je n'y crois pas, mais je les crains*—I don't believe in them, but I fear them, nevertheless."

"You have said that men are tattooed with their special beliefs, like a South Sea Islander."

"Did I say that, 'Melia?" Holmes asked, then repeated it to himself. "Graphic kind of phrase. I must have said it. Not at all the kind of phrase a woman would invent."

"Wendell." Amelia stamped a foot on the rug in front of her husband, who was roughly her height when stripped of his hat and boots. "If you would only explain what's upset you, I could help you. Let me hear, dear Wendell."

Holmes fidgeted. He did not respond.

"Have you written any new verses then? I'm waiting for more of yours to read at night, you know."

"With all the books on our library shelves," Holmes replied, "with Milton and Donne and Keats in all their fullness, why wait for me to do anything, my dear 'Melia?"

She leaned forward and smiled. "I like my poets better alive than dead, Wendell." She took his hand in hers. "Now will you tell me your troubles? Please."

"Pardon the interruption, ma'am." Holmes's redheaded maid stepped to the door. She announced Dr. Holmes's visitor. Holmes nodded hesitantly. The maid departed and brought up the new arrival.

"He's been in his old den all day. Well, he's in your hands now, sir!" Amelia Holmes threw up her own hands and closed the study door behind her.

"Professor Lowell."

"Dr. Holmes." James Russell Lowell removed his hat. "I cannot stop for very long. I just wanted to thank you for all the help you've given us. My apologies, Holmes, for growing warm with you. And for not helping you up when you fell on the floor. And for saying what I did . . ."

"No need, no need." The doctor tossed another batch of proofs into the fire.

Lowell watched the Dante papers fight and dance against the flames, spitting out sparks as they incinerated verses.

Holmes waited halfheartedly for Lowell to shout at the spectacle, but he did not. "If I know anything, Wendell," Lowell said, and bowed his head at the pyre, "I know it was the *Comedy* that lured me into whatever little learning I possess. Dante was the first poet who ever thought to make a poem wholly out of the fabric of himself—to think that not only might the story of some heroic person be epical but also that of *any* man, and that the way to Heaven was not outside the world but *through* it. Wendell, there is something I've always meant to say since we've been helping Longfellow."

Holmes arched his unruly eyebrows.

"When I came to know you, so many years ago, perhaps my very first thought was how much you reminded me of Dante."

"*I?*" Holmes asked, mocking humility. "I and Dante?" But he saw that Lowell was very serious.

"Yes, Wendell. Dante was schooled in every field of science of his day, a master of astronomy, philosophy, law, theology, and poetry. Some, you know, have even said he went through medical school and that is how he could think so much of how the human body suffers. Like you, he did everything well. Too well, as far as other people were concerned."

"I've always thought I had drawn a prize, a five-dollar one at least, in the intellectual sweepstakes of life." Holmes turned his back on the hearthstone and placed some translation proofs on his bookcase, feeling the weight of Lowell's errand. "I may be lazy, Jamey, or indifferent or timid, but I am by no means one of those men . . . it is just that I believe at present we cannot prevent anything."

"The lively pop of the cork has so much power over the imagination at first." Lowell said, and laughed with subdued pensiveness. "I suppose for a few blessed hours in all this I forgot that I was a professor and felt as if I were something *real.* I confess that 'do right though the heavens fall' is an admirable precept until the heavens take you at your word. I know what it is to doubt, my dearest friend. But for you to give up on Dante is for all of us to do so."

"If you could only know how Phineas Jennison remains planted in my mind's eye . . . shredded and broken and. . . . The consequences of failing this . . ."

"It could be the greatest calamity but one, Wendell. And that is being afraid of it," Lowell said, and headed solemnly for the study door. "Well, I chiefly wanted to send my apologies, and Fields, of course, insisted I should. It is my happiest thought that with all the drawbacks of my temperament, I have yet to lose a real friend." Lowell paused as he reached for the door and turned back. "And I like your lyrics. You know that, my dear Holmes."

"Yes? Well, I thank you, but perhaps there is something too hopping about them. I suppose my nature is to snatch at all the fruits of knowledge and take a good bite out of the sunny side—and after that, let in the pigs. I am a pendulum with a very short range of oscillation." Holmes's gaze met his friend's large and open eyes. "How have you been these days, Lowell?"

Lowell gave a half shrug in response.

Holmes did not let his question pass. "I won't say to you, 'Be of good courage,' because men of ideas are not put down by accidents of a day or a year."

"We all revolve around God with larger or lesser orbits, I suppose, Wendell, sometimes one half of us in the light, sometimes the other. Some people seem always in the shadow. You are one of the few people I can unbutton my heart to. . . . Well." The poet cleared his throat gruffly and lowered his voice. "I am due at an important conference at Castle Craigie."

"Oh? And the arrest of Willard Burndy?" Holmes asked cautiously, with feigned disinterest, just before Lowell could exit.

"Patrolman Rey has rushed to look into it as we speak. Do you think it a farce?"

"Pure moonshine, no question!" declared Holmes. "Yet the papers say the prosecuting attorney shall seek to hang him."

Lowell crowded his unruly waves of hair into his silk hat. "Then we have one more sinner to save."

Holmes sat with his Dante box long after Lowell's footsteps faded from the stairs. He continued to toss proof sheets into the fire, determined to finish the painful task, yet he could not stop reading Dante's words as he went. At first he read with the indifference of manner one employs when reading proofs, noting details but not arrested by the emotions. Then he read them quickly and greedily, absorbing passages even as they blackened into nonexistence. His sense of discovery recalled the times he first heard Professor Ticknor asserting with such earnest prescience the impact Dante's journey would one day have on America.

Dante and Virgil are approached by the *Malebranche* demons . . . Dante remembers, "And thus beheld I once the fearful soldiers who issued under safeguard from Caprona, seeing themselves among so many foes."

Dante was remembering the battle of Caprona against the Pisans, in which he fought. Holmes thought of something Lowell had omitted from his list of Dante's talents: Dante was a soldier. *Like you, he did everything well.* And unlike me too, thought Holmes. A soldier had to assert guilt at every step, silently and thoughtlessly. He wondered whether it had made Dante a better poet to see his friends die beside him for the soul of Florence, for some meaningless Guelf banner. Wendell Junior had been the class poet at his Harvard commencement—many said only because of the name he shared with his father—but now Holmes wondered whether Junior could still know poetry after the war. In battle, Junior had seen something that Dante had not, and it had kicked the poetry—and the poet—right out of him, leaving it only to Dr. Holmes.

Holmes flipped through the proof sheets and read for an hour. He craved the second canto of *Inferno,* where Virgil convinces Dante to commence his pilgrimage, but Dante's fears for his own safety resurface. Supreme moment of courage: to face the torment of the death of others and think with clarity how each one would feel. But Holmes had already burned Longfellow's proof sheet for that canto. He found his Italian edition of the *Commedia* and read: "*Lo giorno se n'andava*"—"Day was departing . . ." Dante slows his deliberation as he prepares to enter the infernal realms for the first time: ". . . *e io sol uno*"—"and only I alone . . ."—how lonely he felt! He has to say it three times! *io, sol, uno* . . . "*m'apparecchiava a sostener la guerra, sì del cammino e sì de la pietate.*" Holmes couldn't remember how Longfellow had translated this verse, so leaning on his mantelpiece, he did it himself, hearing the deliberative commentary of Lowell, Greene, Fields, and Longfellow in the humming fire. Encouraging him.

"And I alone, only me"—Holmes found that he had to speak aloud to translate—"made myself ready to sustain the battle . . ." No, *guerra.* ". . . to sustain the *war* . . . both of the way and likewise of the pity."

Holmes shot up from his easy chair and raced upstairs to the third floor. "I alone, only me," he repeated as he climbed.

Wendell Junior was debating the usefulness of metaphysics with William James, John Gray, and Minny Temple over gin toddies and cigars. It was while listening to one of James's meandering discourses that Junior heard, faintly at first, the clip-clop of his father struggling up the stairs. Junior cringed. Father had actually seemed preoccupied with something other than himself these days—potentially something serious. James Lowell had not been around the Law School much, probably, Junior had thought, because he was involved with whatever distracted Father. At first, Junior imagined Father had ordered Lowell to keep clear of Junior, but Junior knew Lowell would not listen to his father. Nor would Father have the fire in his belly to order Lowell.

Junior shouldn't have told Father anything of his companionship with Lowell. Of course, he had kept to himself the sudden and disruptive praise Lowell would often break into about Dr. Holmes. "He not only named the *Atlantic,* Junior," Lowell said, relating the time Father suggested the name of the *Atlantic Monthly,* "he *made* it with the *Autocrat.*" Father's gift for christening was not surprising—he was expert at categorizing the surface of things. How many times had Junior been compelled to listen in the presence of guests to the story of how Father had named *anesthesia* for the dentist who invented it? Despite all this, Junior wondered why Dr. Holmes could not have done better than Wendell Junior's own name.

Dr. Holmes knocked as a formality, then threw himself inside with a wild glow in his eyes.

"Father. We're a bit occupied."

Junior remained plain-faced at the too respectful greetings of his friends.

Holmes cried, "Wendy, I must know something at once! I must know whether you understand anything of maggots." He spoke so fast that he sounded like a buzzing bee.

Junior puffed on his cigar. Would he never grow used to his father? After thinking about it, Junior laughed loudly and his friends joined in. "Did you say *maggots*, Father?"

"What if it *is* our Lucifer sitting in that cell, playing dumb?" Fields asked anxiously.

"He didn't understand the Italian—I saw that in his eyes," assured Nicholas Rey. "And it infuriated him." They were gathered in the Craigie House study. Greene, who had assisted with translating all afternoon, had been returned to his daughter's home in Boston for the evening.

The short message on the note Rey had passed along to Willard Burndy—"*a te convien tenere altro viaggio se vuo' campar d'esto loco selvaggio*"—could be translated as "it behooves you to go by another way, if you want to escape from this savage place." They were Virgil's words to Dante, who was lost and threatened by beasts in the dark wilderness.

"The message was merely a last precaution. His history chimes with nothing we had come upon in our profile of the killer," said Lowell, tapping his cigar out Longfellow's window. "Burndy had no education. And we've found no other connections in any of our inquiries to any of the victims."

"The papers made it sound like they are amassing evidence," said Fields.

Rey nodded. "They have witnesses who saw Burndy lurking around Reverend Talbot's house the night before he was killed, the night Talbot's safe was robbed of the thousand dollars. These witnesses were interviewed by good patrolmen. Burndy wouldn't talk to me very much. But this fits the detectives' practice: They find a circumstantial fact to build their false case around. I have no doubt Langdon Peaslee is leading them by their beaks. He rids himself of his prime rival for Boston's safes, and the detectives slip him a large part of the reward money. He tried to suggest such an arrangement with me when rewards were announced."

"But what if we are missing something?" Fields lamented.

"Do you believe this Mr. Burndy could be responsible for the murders?" Longfellow inquired.

Fields pushed out his handsome lips and shook his head. "I suppose I only want some answers so we may return to our lives."

Longfellow's servant announced a Mr. Edward Sheldon of Cambridge at the door, looking for Professor Lowell.

Lowell scrambled into the front hall and led Sheldon into Longfellow's library.

Sheldon had his hat pulled tight over his head. "I beg your pardon for bothering you here, Professor. But your note sounded urgent and at Elmwood they said you might be found here. Tell me, are we ready to start the Dante class again?" he asked with an artless smile.

"I sent that note almost a week ago now!" Lowell shouted.

"Ah well, you see . . . I did not get your note until today." He looked to the floor.

"Very likely! And you'll take off your hat when you're in a gentleman's house, Sheldon!" Lowell knocked away Sheldon's hat. A purple swelling could be seen around one of his eyes, and he had a puffed jaw.

Lowell was immediately repentant. "Why, Sheldon. What has happened to you?"

"A frightful heap, sir. I was about to explain that my father sent me to recuperate with near relations in Salem. Perhaps a punishment, too, to *think well of my actions,*" Sheldon said with a demure smile. "That is why I did not receive your note." Sheldon stepped into the light to collect his hat, then noticed the horror-struck look on Lowell's face. "Oh, it's gone down very much, Professor. My eye hardly hurts in the least."

Lowell sat. "Tell me how this came to be, Sheldon."

Sheldon looked down to the floor. "I couldn't help it! You must know of this horrid fellow Simon Camp roaming around. If not, I shall tell you. He stopped me in the street. Said he was doing a survey on behalf of the Harvard faculty on whether your Dante course might produce negative repercussions on the character of its students. I almost punched him in the face, don't you know, for such an insinuation."

"Did Camp do this to you?" Lowell asked with a fierce tremor of paternalism.

"No, no, he slithered away as fits his type. You see, the next morning I happened upon Pliny Mead. A traitor if I've ever known one!"

"How so?"

"He said with pleasure how he sat down with Camp and told him of the 'horrors' of Dante's spleen. I worry, Professor Lowell, that any hint of scandal would be perilous for your class. Clearly enough, the Corporation has not relented in its fight. I told Mead he'd best call on Camp and take back his awful comments, but he refused and shouted a bloody oath at me, and, well, he cursed your name, Professor, and wasn't I mad! So we had a row right there on the old burial yard."

Lowell smiled proudly. "You started a fight with him, Mr. Sheldon?"

"I started it, sir," said Sheldon. He frowned, soothing his jaw with his hand. "But he finished."

After escorting Sheldon out with abundant promises that they would begin their Dante hours again soon, Lowell rushed back toward the study, but there was another quick knock on the door.

"Blast it, Sheldon, I've told you we'll meet for class any day now!" Lowell threw open the door.

In his excitement, Dr. Holmes was standing on his toes.

"Holmes?" Lowell's laughter had such unrestrained jubilance that it brought Longfellow running into the hall. "You've come back to the club, Wendell! We've missed you like thunder!" Lowell shouted to the others in the study. "Holmes has come back!"

"Not only that, my friends," Holmes said, stepping inside, "but I think I know where we shall find our killer."

XIV

THE RECTANGULAR SHAPE of Longfellow's library had made an ideal officers' mess for General Washington's staff and in later years provided a banquet hall for Mrs. Craigie. Now, Longfellow, Lowell, Fields, and Nicholas Rey sat at the well-polished table while Holmes circled them and explained.

"My thoughts come too quickly to govern. Only listen to all my reasons before agreeing or dissenting helter-skelter"—he said this mostly to Lowell, and everyone but Lowell understood it was meant for him—"for I believe that Dante has been telling us the truth all the while. He describes his feeling as he prepares for his first steps into Hell, trembling and insecure. '*E io sol,*' and so on. My dear Longfellow, how did you translate?"

" 'And I the only one made myself ready to sustain the war. / Both of the way and likewise of the woe, / Which unerring memory shall now retrace.' "

"Yes!" Holmes said proudly, remembering his own similar translation. This was not the time to pause on his talents, but he wondered what Longfellow would think of his rendition. "It is a war—a *guerra*—for the poet on two fronts. First, the hardships of the physical descent through Hell, and also the challenge to the poet to tap into his memory to turn experience into poetry. The images of Dante's world run loose in my mind, without a halter."

Nicholas Rey listened carefully and opened his memorandum book.

"Dante was no stranger to physical engagements of war, my dear officer," Lowell said. "At five and twenty, the same age as many of our boys in blue, he fought at Campaldino with the Guelfs, and that same year in Caprona. Dante draws on these experiences throughout *Inferno* to describe the frightful torments of Hell. In the end, Dante was exiled not by his rival Ghibellines but due to an internal split among the Guelfs."

"The aftermath of Florence's civil wars inspires his vision of Hell and his search for redemption," Holmes said. "Think, too, how Lucifer takes up arms against God and how in his fall from the heavens the once-brightest angel becomes the fountain of all evil from Adam down. It is Lucifer's physical fall to earth after he is expelled from above that hollows an abyss in the ground, the cellar of earth that Dante discovers is Hell. So war *created* Satan. War *created* Hell: *guerra.* Dante's choice of words is never happenstance. I shall suggest that the events of our own circumstances point overwhelmingly to a single hypothesis: Our murderer is a veteran of the war."

"A soldier! The chief justice of our state supreme court, a prominent Unitarian preacher, a rich merchant," Lowell said. "A defeated Reb soldier's revenge on the instruments of our Yankee system! Of course! We're damned fools!"

"Dante has no mechanical loyalty to one or another political label," said Longfellow. "He is perhaps most indignant against those who shared his views but failed their obligations, the traitors—just as a Union veteran might be. Remember that each murder has shown our Lucifer's great and natural familiarity with the layout of Boston."

"Yes," Holmes said impatiently. "That is precisely why my thought is not simply of a soldier but a Billy Yank. Think of our soldiers who still wear their army uniforms in the street and mart. I am often puzzled when seeing these great specimens: Has he come home again, yet still wears the vestments of the soldier? For whose war has he been commissioned now?"

"But does this fit with what we know of the murders, Wendell?" urged Fields.

"Quite neatly, I think. Start with Jennison's murder. It occurs to me in this new light precisely the weapon that could have been used."

Rey nodded. "A military saber."

"Right!" Holmes said. "Just the sort of blade consistent with the injuries. Now, who is trained at such usage? A soldier. And Fort Warren, the choice of locale for that killing—a soldier who trained there or had been stationed there would know it well enough! There's more: The deadly *hominivorax* maggots that feasted on Judge Healey—from somewhere outside Massachusetts, somewhere hot and swampy, Professor Agassiz insists. Perhaps brought back by a soldier as souvenirs from the deepest marshes of the

South. Wendell Junior says flies and maggots were a constant presence on the battlefield and among the thousands of wounded left for a day or night."

"Sometimes maggots would have no effect on the wounded," Rey said. "At other times, they would seem to destroy a man, leaving the surgeons helpless."

"Those were the *hominivorax*, though the war surgeons wouldn't know them from a family of beetles. Somebody familiar with their effects on injured men brought them from the South and used them on Healey," Holmes went on. "Now, we have again and again marveled at Lucifer's great physical strength in carrying the bulky Judge Healey down to the riverside. But how many comrades must a soldier have carried in his arms from battle without thinking twice of it! We have also witnessed Lucifer's easy strength in subduing Reverend Talbot, and in shredding with apparent ease the robust Jennison."

Lowell exclaimed, "You may have found our open-sesame, Holmes!"

Holmes continued, "All the murders are acts committed by one familiar with the trappings of the siege and the kill—the wounds and suffering of battle."

"But why should a Northern boy target his own people? Why should he target Boston?" Fields asked, feeling there was a need for someone to serve as doubter. "We were the victors. And victors for the side of right."

"This war was like no other since the Revolution in the confusion of feelings," Nicholas Rey said.

Longfellow added, "It was not like our country's battle with the Indians or the Mexicans, which stand as little more than conquests. Soldiers who cared to think of why they were fighting were provided the notion of the honor of the Union, the freedom of a race of enslaved people, the restoration of proper order to the universe. Yet what do the soldiers return home to? Profiteers, who once sold shoddy rifles and uniforms, now riding in broughams down our streets and prospering in oak-fronted Beacon Hill mansions."

"Dante," said Lowell, "who was banished from his home, populated Hell with people of his own city, even his own family. We have left many soldiers hanging on to nothing but our stirring lyrics of morality, and bloodstained uniforms. They are exiles from their former lives—like Dante, they become parties unto themselves. And consider how close on the heels of the end of the war these murders began. Just months! Yes, it seems to fall into place, gentlemen. The war sought an abstract moral—freedom—yet the soldiers fought their battles on very specific fields and fronts, organized into regiments and companies and battalions. The very movements in Dante's poetry have something swift, decisive, almost military in their nature." He stood up and embraced Holmes. "This vision, my dear Wendell, is from Heaven."

There was a collective sense of accomplishment rising in the room, and everyone waited for Longfellow's nod, which came with a quiet smile.

"Three cheers for Holmes!" Lowell cried out.

"Why don't you give me three times three?" Holmes asked with a whimsical pose. "I can stand it!"

Augustus Manning positioned himself over his secretary's desk tapping his fingers on the edge. "Still, that Simon Camp has not responded to my request for an interview?"

Manning's secretary shook his head, "No, sir. And the Marlboro Hotel says he is no longer staying with them. No forwarding address was left behind."

Manning was livid. He had not entirely trusted the Pinkerton detective, but he had not thought he was an outright crook, either. "Do you not think it queer that first a police officer comes to ask about Lowell's class and then the Pinkerton man I paid to find more on Dante stops responding to my calls for him?"

The secretary did not respond, but then, seeing it was expected, assented anxiously.

Manning turned and faced the window framing Harvard Hall. "Lowell has been up to something in all this, I daresay. Tell me again, Mr. Cripps. Who is enrolled in Lowell's Dante class? Edward Sheldon and . . . Pliny Mead, isn't it?"

The secretary found the answer in a sheaf of papers. "Edward Sheldon and Pliny Mead, exactly right."

"Pliny Mead. A high scholar," Manning said, smoothing his stiff beard.

"Well, he was, sir. But he has had a fall in the last rankings."

Manning turned to him with great interest.

"Yes, he has dropped some twenty spots in the class," the secretary explained, finding documentation and proudly proving the fact. "Oh yes, dropped quite precipitously, Dr. Manning! Chiefly, it seems, from Professor Lowell's mark from last term's course in French."

Manning took the papers from his secretary and read them. "What a shame for our Mr. Mead," Manning said, smiling to himself. "A terrible, terrible shame."

Late evening in Boston, J. T. Fields called on the law offices of John Codman Ropes, a hunchbacked lawyer who had made the war of the rebellion an area of expertise after his brother perished in battle. It was said he knew more about the battles than the generals who fought them. As befitted a genuine expert, he unostentatiously answered Fields's questions. Ropes listed many soldiers'-aid homes—charitable organizations that had been established, some at churches, others in abandoned buildings and warehouses, to feed and clothe veterans who were poor or struggling to return to civilian life. If one sought troubled soldiers, these homes would be the place to look.

"There's nothing like a directory of their names, of course, and I'd say these poor souls cannot be discovered unless they wish to be, Mr. Fields," Ropes said at the end of their meeting.

Fields walked briskly up Tremont Street toward the Corner. He had for weeks devoted only the fraction of his usual time to business, and worried that his ship would run aground if he were absent much longer from its tiller.

"Mr. Fields."

"Who's that?" Fields stopped and retraced his steps to an alleyway. "Addressing me, sir?"

He could not see the speaker in the dimming light. Fields advanced slowly between the buildings, into the smell of sewage.

"That's right, Mr. Fields." The tall man stepped out of the shadows and removed his hat from his gaunt head. Simon Camp, Pinkerton detective, grinned at him. "You don't have your professor friend to wave his rifle at me this time, do you?"

"Camp! What gall you have. I've paid you more than I should have to go away—now, shoo."

"You did pay me, didn't you. To tell you the truth, I had looked at this case as an annoyance, a fly in my teacup, mere bosh. But you and your friend got me thinking. What would have swells like you so excited that you'd be willing to shell out gold so I don't look into Professor Lowell's little literature course? And that would cause Professor Lowell to interrogate me as though I might have shot Lincoln?"

"A man like you would never understand what literary men prize, I'm afraid," Fields said nervously. "This is our business."

"Oh, but I *do* understand. Now I understand. I remembered something about that pismire Dr. Manning. He had mentioned a policeman visiting him to ask about Professor Lowell's Dante course. The old man was in a frenzy about it. Then I started considering: What are the Boston police busy doing of late? Well, there is the small matter of these murders going around."

Fields tried not to show his panic. "I have appointments to attend to, Mr. Camp."

Camp smiled blissfully. "Then I thought of that Pliny Mead boy, spilling everything on his tongue's end about the uncivilized, gruesome punishments against humanity in that Dante poem. It started coming together for me. I called on your Mr. Mead again and asked him some specific questions. Mr. Fields," he said, leaning forward with relish. "I know your secret."

"Stuff and nonsense. I haven't a clue what you're talking about, Camp," Fields cried.

"I know the secret of the Dante Club, Fields. I know you know the truth about these murders, and that's why you paid me to vamoose."

"That is wanton and malevolent libel!" Fields started out of the alley.

"Then I shall just go to the police," Camp said coolly. "And then to the newspapermen. And on my way, I will stop in to see Dr. Manning at Harvard too—he's been sending for me frequently anyhow. I'll see what they make of all this 'stuff and nonsense.'"

Fields turned back and gave Camp a hardened stare. "If you know what you say you know, then what makes you certain we're not the ones doing the killing, and will kill you too, Camp?"

Camp smiled. "You're a good bluff, Fields. But you're bookmen, and that's all you'll be till they change the natural order of the world."

Fields stopped and swallowed. He looked around to make certain there were no witnesses. "What will make you leave us alone, Camp?"

"Three thousand dollars, to start—in exactly a fortnight," Camp said.

"Never!"

"The real rewards offered for information are much larger, Mr. Fields. Maybe Burndy had nothing to do with all this. I don't know who killed those men, and I don't care to know. But how guilty you will look when a jury discovers you already paid me to go away when I came to ask about Dante—and lured me in to pull a gun on me!"

Fields realized all at once that Camp was doing this to avenge his cowardice in the face of Lowell's rifle. "You are a small and unclean insect," Fields could not help saying.

Camp didn't seem to mind. "But a trustworthy one, as long as you abide by our bargain. Even insects have debts to meet, Mr. Fields."

Fields agreed to rendezvous with Camp at the same location in two weeks' time.

He told the news to his friends. After their initial shock, the Dante Club members decided they were helpless to influence the outcome of Camp's scheme.

"What's the use?" said Holmes. "You already gave him ten gold coins, and that did no good. He'll just keep coming with his hand out for more."

"What Fields gave him was an appetite," Lowell said. They could not trust that any amount of money would secure their secret. Besides, Longfellow would not hear of handing out bribes to protect Dante or themselves. Dante could have paid his way out of exile and had refused, in a letter that was still fierce after all these centuries. They promised to forget about Camp. They had to continue to vigorously pursue their military exposition of the case. That night, they pored over records from the army pension office that Rey had borrowed, and visited several soldiers'-aid homes.

Fields did not return home until nearly one in the morning, much to Annie Fields's exasperation. Fields noticed as he entered the front hall that the flowers he sent home each day were piling up on the foyer table, pointedly un-vased. He took up the freshest of the bouquets and found Annie in the reception room. She was sitting on the blue velvet sofa, writing in her *Journal of Literary Events and Glimpses of Interesting People.*

"Could I honestly see you less, dear?" She did not look up, her beautiful mouth striking a pout. Her jacinth-colored hair was drawn over her ears on both sides.

"I promise things will improve. This summer—why, I shall do hardly any work in the least, and we shall spend every day in Manchester. Osgood is nearly ready to be partner. Won't we dance on that day!"

She turned away and fixed her eyes on the gray rug. "I know your obligations. Yet I waste my substance on housekeeping, without even time with you as reward. I have hardly had an hour for study or reading except when too tired. Catherine is sick again, and so the laundress must sleep three in a bed with the upstairs maid . . ."

"I'm home now, my love," he pointed out.

"No you're not." She gathered his coat and hat from the downstairs girl and handed them back to him.

"Dear?" Fields's face fell.

She pulled her dressing gown tight and started upstairs. "A messenger boy from the Corner came frantically looking for you some hours ago."

"At such a witching hour of the night?"

"He said you must go there now or it is feared the police will come first."

Fields wanted to follow Annie upstairs but rushed to his offices on Tremont Street and found his senior clerk, J. R. Osgood, in the back room. Cecilia Emory, the front receptionist, was in a comfortable armchair, sobbing and hiding her face. Dan Teal, the night shop boy, was sitting quietly in the room, holding a cloth to his bloodied lip.

"What's wrong? Why, what's happened to Miss Emory?" Fields asked.

Osgood guided Fields away from the hysterical girl. "It's Samuel Ticknor." Osgood paused to choose his words. "Ticknor was kissing Miss Emory behind the counter after hours. She resisted, shouted to him to stop, and Mr. Teal intervened. I'm afraid Teal had to physically subdue Mr. Ticknor."

Fields pulled a chair up and questioned Cecilia Emory in a kind voice. "You can speak freely, my dear," he promised.

Miss Emory labored to stop crying. "I'm so sorry, Mr. Fields. I need this job, and he said that if I didn't do as he asked . . . well, he's the son of William Ticknor, and they say you shall have to make him a junior partner soon because of his name . . ." She covered her mouth with her hand, as though to catch the dreaded words.

"You . . . pushed him away?" Fields asked delicately.

She nodded. "He's such a strong man. Mr. Teal . . . I thank God he was there."

"How long has this been happening with Mr. Ticknor, Miss Emory?" asked Fields.

Cecilia wept out the answer: "Three months." Almost since she had been hired. "But as God is my witness, I never wished to do it, Mr. Fields! You must believe me!"

Fields patted her hand and spoke paternally. "My dear Miss Emory, listen to me. Because you are an orphan, I will overlook this and permit you to retain your position."

She nodded appreciatively and threw her hands around Fields's neck.

Fields stood. "Where is he?" he asked Osgood. He was seething. This was a breach of loyalty of the worst kind.

"We have him in the next room waiting for you, Mr. Fields. He has denied her version of the story, I should tell you."

"If I know anything of human nature, that girl was perfectly pure, Osgood. Mr. Teal," Fields said, and turned to the shop boy. "Was everything Miss Emory said how you witnessed it?"

Teal answered at a snail's pace, his mouth working up and down in its habitual motion. "I was preparing to leave, sir. I saw Miss Emory struggling and asking Mr. Ticknor to leave her be. So I punched him until he stopped."

"Good boy, Teal," Fields said. "I won't forget your help."

Teal didn't know how to respond. "Sir, I must be at my other job in the morning. I am a caretaker at the College in the daytime."

"Oh?" Fields said.

"This job means the world to me," Teal added quickly. "If you ever require more from me, sir, please do tell me so."

"I want you to write out everything you saw and did here before you leave, Mr. Teal. In case the police become involved, we need a record," Fields said. He motioned for Osgood to give Teal some paper and a pen. "And when she calms down, let her write her story, too," Fields instructed his senior clerk. Teal struggled to write out a few letters. Fields realized he was only semiliterate, bordering on illiterate, and thought how odd it must be to work among books every night without such a basic power. "Mr. Teal," he said. "Let us have you dictate to Mr. Osgood so it will be official."

Teal gratefully agreed, handing back the paper.

It took Fields nearly five hours of questioning Samuel Ticknor to elicit the truth. Fields was a bit awed by how humbled Ticknor looked, his face having been pummeled by the shop boy. His nose actually looked to be off center. Ticknor's responses alternated between the vain and the shallow. He eventually admitted his adultery with Cecilia Emory and revealed that he had involved himself with another female secretary at the Corner as well.

"You'll leave Ticknor and Fields property at once and from this day never return!" Fields said.

"Ha! My father built this firm! He took you into his home when you were little more than a beggar! Without him, you would have no mansion, no wife like Anne Fields! It is my name on our spine, even above yours, Mr. Fields!"

"You have been the cause of ruin to two women, Samuel!" Fields said. "Not to mention the wreck of your wife's happiness and that of your poor mother. Your father would be more disgraced than I am!"

Samuel Ticknor was near tears. As he left, he cried out, "Mr. Fields, you shall hear my name again, I promise you that before God! If you had only taken me by the hand and introduced me to your social circle . . ." he trailed off for a moment before adding, "I was always counted a clever young man in society!"

A week passed without progress—a week without the discovery of any soldiers who might also be Dante scholars. Oscar Houghton sent a message to Fields after his inquiry telling him that no proof sheets were missing. Hopes were dimming. Nicholas Rey felt that he was being watched more closely at the station house, but he tried again with Willard Burndy. The trial had worn down the safecracker considerably. When he was not moving or talking, he looked lifeless.

"You will not make it through this without help," Rey said. "I know you're not guilty, but I know also that you were seen outside Talbot's house the day his safe was robbed. You can tell me why, or walk the ladder."

Burndy studied Rey, then nodded listlessly. "I did Talbot's safe. Not really, though. You won't believe it. You won't—I don't believe it myself! You see, some goosecap said he'd palm me two hundred if I taught him how to crack a particular safe. I thought it'd be an easy chore—and no chance of *me* getting pinched! Upon the honor of a gentleman, I didn't know the house belonged to no brother of the cloth! I didn't croak him! If I had, I wouldn't have forked over his money back to him!"

"Why'd you go to Talbot's house?"

"To case it. That goosecap seemed to know that Talbot wasn't home, so I peeked in to see the layout. I went in, just to see the stamp of safe." Burndy pleaded for empathy with a stupid smile. "No harm in that, right? It was a basic one, and it only took five minutes for me to tell him how to crack it. I drew it on a napkin of a tavern. I should've known the goosecap was cracked in the head. He told me he wanted only one thousand dollars—wouldn't take a copper more. Can you imagine that? Listen, moke, you can't tell I robbed the preacher, or I'll walk the ladder for sure! Whoever paid me to do the safe, *that's* the madman—that's who killed Talbot and Healey and Phineas Jennison!"

"Then tell me who paid you," Rey said calmly, "or you *will* hang, Mr. Burndy."

"It was at night, and I had been a little cup-shot, you know, from the Stackpole Tavern. It all seems so quick now, like I dreamt it and it only became truth afterwards. I couldn't really notice nothin' of his face, or at least I don't remember nothin'."

"You didn't see anything or you can't remember, Mr. Burndy?"

Burndy chewed at his lip. He said reluctantly, "There is one thing. He was one of you."

Rey waited. "A Negro?"

Burndy's pink eyes flamed and he seemed about to have a fit. "No! A Billy Yank. A veteran!" He tried to calm himself. "A soldier sitting right there in full uniform, like he was at Gettysburg swinging the flag!"

The soldiers'-aid homes in Boston were locally run, unofficial, and unadvertised, except through the word of mouth of the veterans who used them. Most homes stocked baskets of food two or three times a week to be dispersed to the soldiers. With six months passing since the war, City Hall was less and less willing to continue funding the homes. The better ones, usually aligned with a church, ambitiously strove to edify the former soldiers. In addition to food and clothing, sermons and instructional talks were offered.

Holmes and Lowell covered the southern quadrant of the city. They had engaged Pike, the cabman. Waiting outside the soldiers'-aid facilities, Pike would take a bite of a carrot, then give one to his old mares, then take another bite himself, keeping track of how many horse and human bites together would complete the average carrot. The boredom was not worth the fares paid. Besides, when Pike asked why they were traveling from one home to the next, the cabman—who had that shrewdness that came from living among horses—found that their false answers made him ill at ease. So Holmes and Lowell hired a one-horse coach, whose horse and driver would fall asleep every time the coach came to a stop.

The latest soldiers' home to receive their visit seemed to be one of the better-organized ones. It was housed in an empty Unitarian church that had been a casualty of the long battles with the Congregationalists. At this particular home, local soldiers were given tables to sit at and a warm meal to sup on at least four evenings a week. The supper having concluded shortly after Lowell and Holmes arrived, the soldiers were making their way into the church proper.

"Crowded," Lowell commented, leaning into the chapel, where the pews were being clogged with blue uniforms. "Let us sit in. Get off our feet at least."

"Upon my word, Jamey, I can't see how it can help us anymore. Perhaps we should head to the next one on the list."

"This *was* the next one. Ropes's list says the other is open only Wednesdays and Sundays."

Holmes watched as one soldier with only a stump for a leg was pushed in a wheelchair across the courtyard by a comrade. The latter was little more than a lad, with a mouth caved inward, his teeth having fallen out from scurvy. This was the side of the war that people could not learn from the reports of the officers or the letters of reporters. "What's the use of spurring an already beaten out horse, my dear Lowell? We are not Gideon watching his soldiers drink from the well. We can tell nothing by looking. We do not find Hamlet and Faust, right and wrong, the valor of men, by testing for albumin or examining fibers in a microscope. I cannot help feeling we must find a new course of action."

"You and Pike both," Lowell said, and shook his head sadly. "But together we will find our way. At the moment, Holmes, let us just decide whether we should remain or have the driver take us to another soldiers' home."

"You men are new today," interrupted a one-eyed soldier with tightly drawn, heavily pocked skin and a black clay pipe protruding from his mouth. Not having expected a conversation with a third party the astonished Holmes and Lowell were both at a loss for words and politely waited for each other to answer the speaker. The man was garbed in a full-dress uniform that had not seen a launderer since before the war, it appeared.

The soldier started making his way into the church and looked back only briefly to say, with some offense, "Beg your pardon. I just thought perhaps you fellows came in to see 'bout Dante."

For a moment, neither Lowell nor Holmes reacted. They both thought they had imagined the word he had uttered.

"Hold there, you!" Lowell cried, barely coherent in his excitement.

The two poets sprinted into the chapel, where they found little light. Facing a sea of uniforms, they could not pinpoint the unidentified Dantean.

"Down!" someone yelled angrily through cupped hands.

Holmes and Lowell groped for seats and positioned themselves on the aisles of separate pews and contorted themselves desperately to search the faces in the crowd. Holmes turned to the entrance in the event that the soldier tried to escape. Lowell's eyes scanned the dark stares and hollow expressions that filled the chapel and finally landed on the pocked skin and the single, shimmering eye of their interlocutor.

"I've found him," Lowell whispered. "Oh, I've done it, Wendell. I've found him! I've found our Lucifer!"

Holmes twisted, wheezing with anticipation. "I can't see him, Jamey!"

Several soldiers violently shushed the two intruders.

"There!" Lowell whispered, frustrated. "One, two . . . fourth row from the front!"

"Where?"

"There!"

"I thank you, my dear friends, for inviting me once again," a shaky voice interrupted them, floating down from the pulpit. "And now the punishments of Dante's Hell shall continue . . ."

Lowell and Holmes immediately turned their attention to the front of the stuffy, dark chapel. They looked on as their friend, old George Washington Greene, coughed feebly, adjusted his stance, and settled his arms to his sides at his lectern. His congregation was spellbound with expectation and loyalty, greedily waiting to reenter the gates of their inferno.

CANTICLE THREE

XV

"O PILGRIMS: Come now to the final circle of this blind prison that Dante must explore on his sinuous journey downward, on his fated journey to relieve mankind of all suffering!" George Washington Greene raised his arms wide above the compact lectern that stopped at his narrow bosom. "For Dante seeks nothing less than *that;* his personal fate is secondhand to the poem. It is humankind he shall lift up through his journey, and so *we* follow suit, arm in arm, from the fiery gates to the heavenly spheres as we cleanse this our nineteenth century of sin!

"Oh what a formidable task lay ahead of him in his unhappy tower in Verona, with the bitter salt of exile on his palate. Thinks he: How shall I sketch the bottom of the universe with this frail tongue? Thinks he: How shall I sing out my miraculous song? Yet Dante knows he must: to redeem his city, to redeem his nation, to redeem the future—and *us,* we who sit here in this reawakened chapel to revive the spirit of his majestic voice in a New World, we too are redeemable! He knows that in each generation there shall be those fortunate few who understand and see truly. His is a pen of fire with heart's blood as his only ink. O Dante, bringer of light! Happy are the voices of the mountains and the pines that shall forever repeat thy songs!"

Greene gulped down a deep lungful of air before narrating Dante's descent into the final round of Hell: a frozen lake of ice, Cocytus, slick as glass, with a thickness found not even on the river Charles in the dead of winter. Dante hears an angry voice flare up to him from this icy tundra. "Look how thou steppest!" cries the voice. "Take heed thou do not trample with thy feet the heads of us tired, miserable brothers!"

"Oh wherefore came these accusatory words to sting the ears of well-intentioned Dante? Looking down, the Poet sees, embedded in the frozen lake, heads sticking out from the ice, a congregation of dead shades—a thousand purple heads; sinners of the very basest nature known by the sons of Adam. What wrong is reserved for this frozen plain of Hell? Treachery, of course! And what is their punishment, their *contrapasso*, for the cold in their hearts? To be entombed wholly in ice: from the neck down—so that their eyes may forever view the miserable penalty called up by their wrongs."

Holmes and Lowell were overcome, hearts contorted in their throats. Lowell's beard hung low while Greene, glistening with vitality, described how Dante clutches the head of the berating sinner and demands his name, cruelly twisting out shocks of his hair by their roots. *Though thou strip off my hair, I will not tell thee who I am!* One of the other sinners unwittingly calls by name for his fellow shade to stop his galling shouts, much to Dante's satisfaction. He could now record the sinner's name for posterity.

Greene promised to reach bestial Lucifer—the worst of all Traitors and all sinners, the three-headed beast who is punisher and punished—in his next sermon. The energy that had charged through the old minister during the sermon drained rapidly when it was over, leaving only a pinwheel of color in his cheeks.

Lowell struggled against the crowd in the darkened chapel, parting soldiers mingling and squawking in the aisles. Holmes chased behind.

"Why, my dear friends!" Greene said cheerfully at the first sign of Lowell and Holmes. They shuttled Greene into a small chamber in the rear of the chapel, Holmes fastening the door. Greene took a seat on a board by a heating stove and held up his palms. "I daresay, fellows," he observed. "With this dreadful weather and a new cough, I shan't complain if we—"

Lowell roared, "Tell us everything directly, Greene!"

"Why, Mr. Lowell, I haven't the most remote notion what you are driving at," Greene said meekly, and glanced at Holmes.

"My dear Greene, what Lowell means . . ." But Dr. Holmes could not maintain his calm, either. "But what in the devil were you *doing* here, Greene?"

Greene looked hurt. "Well, you know, my dear Holmes, that I offer guest sermons at a number of churches around the city and in East Greenwich whenever I am asked and able. A sickbed is a dull place at best, and mine has grown anxious and painful in the last year, so I am more willing than ever when such requests arise."

Lowell interrupted. "We know of your guest preaching. But you were preaching *Dante* out there!"

"Ah, that! It is a quite harmless amusement, really. Preaching to these woebegone soldiers was so challenging an experience, rather different from any I had known. In speaking with the men the first weeks after the war, especially when Lincoln was so treacherously killed, I found them plagued, in great numbers, with urgency by worries of their own fate and of the workings of the afterlife. One afternoon—sometime in the late-summer weeks—feeling inspired by Longfellow's commitment to his translation, I introduced some Dantesque descriptions during my sermon and judged their effect rather successful. And so I began with general summaries of Dante's spiritual history and journey. At moments—forgive me. Look how I blush to confess to you—I fancied I could teach Dante myself and that these brave young men were my pupils."

"And Longfellow knew nothing of this?" Holmes asked.

"I wished to share the tidings of my modest experiment, but, well . . ." Greene's skin was pale as he fixed his gaze into the flaming porthole of the heating stove. "I suppose, dear friends, I was a trifle embarrassed to profess myself a teacher of Dante next to a man like Longfellow. Only, don't tell him so, if you please. It will only discomfit him, you know he doesn't like to think himself different . . ."

"This sermon just now, Greene," Lowell interrupted. "It was *entirely* made up of Dante's encounters with the Traitors."

"Yes, yes!" Greene said, rejuvenated by the reminder. "Isn't it marvelous, Lowell? Soon enough I discovered that expressing a canto or two in its entirety held the attention of the soldierly quarter quite better than a sermon of my own frail thoughts, and doing so served well to arm me for our Dante sessions the following week." Greene laughed with the nervous pride of a child who has reached some accomplishment unexpected by his elders. "When the Dante Club started *Inferno*, I began my current practice, preaching one of the cantos we were to translate in the next meeting of our club. I daresay I now feel quite prepared to take on this vociferous canto, for Longfellow has scheduled it for tomorrow! Normally, I would offer my sermon on Thursday afternoon, shortly before railroading back to Rhode Island."

"Every Thursday?" asked Holmes.

"There were times when I was confined to bed. And the weeks that Longfellow canceled our Dante sessions, alas, I had no heart to speak of Dante then," said Greene. "Then this last week, how wondrous! Longfellow has been translating at such a rapid, eager pace, I have stayed put in Boston and given a Dante sermon nearly every night for a week!"

Lowell lunged forward. "Mr. Greene! Review in your mind every moment of your experience here! Were any of the soldiers especially set on mastering the contents of your Dante sermons?"

Greene pushed himself to his feet and looked around him confusedly, as though he had suddenly forgotten their purpose. "Let me think. There were some twenty or thirty soldiers every session, understand, never all the same men. I've always wished I were better with faces. A number of them, now and again, did express admiration for my sermons. You must believe me—if I could aid you . . ."

"Greene, if you don't instantly . . ." Lowell began in a choking voice.

"Lowell please!" Holmes said, assuming Fields's usual role in taming his friend.

Lowell emitted a billowing exhale and waved Holmes forward.

Holmes began, "My dear Mr. Greene, you *will* aid us—tremendously, I know. Now, you must think fast for our benefit, dear friend, for Longfellow. Revisit all the soldiers you might have conversed with since starting this."

"Oh, hold." Greene's half-moon eyes opened unnaturally large. "Hold now. Yes, there was one *specific* inquiry directed at me by a soldier wishing to read Dante for himself."

"Yes! How did you reply?" Holmes asked, beaming.

"I asked whether the young man was at all familiar with foreign languages. He suggested he was the sharpest brand of reader since early boyhood but only of the English language, so I encouraged him to take up Italian. I noted that I was helping to complete the first American translation with Longfellow, for which we had a small club at the poet's home. He seemed quite enticed. So I urged him to look for news of the Ticknor and Fields publication early next year at his bookseller," Greene said with all the zeal of one of Fields's planted puffs in the gossip pages.

Holmes paused for a hopeful glance at Lowell, who urged him on. "This soldier," Holmes said slowly. "Might he have given you his name?" Greene shook his head. "Do you remember what he looked like, my dear Greene?"

"No, no, I'm terribly sorry."

"It's more important than you can imagine," Lowell entreated him.

"I have but the foggiest recollection of the exchange," Greene said, and closed his eyes. "I seem to remember he was rather tall, with a hay-colored mustache of the handlebar shape. And perhaps walked with a limp. But so many of them have become stumps of men. It was months ago, and I did not pay any special mind to the man at the time. As I say, I am not gifted at remembering faces—precisely why I've never written fiction, my friends. Fiction is all faces." Greene laughed, finding this last statement enlightening. But the distress on the faces of his companions sagged into heavy stares. "Gentlemen? Pray tell me, have I contributed to some sort of *problem?*"

As they carefully made their way outside through groups of veterans, Lowell helped Greene step up into the carriage. Holmes had to rouse the cabman and horse, and the driver turned his lethargic horse's head away from the old church.

In the meantime, from behind a dingy window of the soldiers'-aid home, the sight of the fleeing party was swallowed whole by the sentinel eyes of the man the Dante Club called Lucifer.

George Washington Greene was settled into a reclining armchair in the Authors' Room at the Corner. Nicholas Rey joined them. The questions teased every bit of information from Greene about his Dante sermons and the veterans who eagerly came to hear them each week. Then Lowell launched into a blunt chronicle of the Dante murders, to which Greene could hardly conjure a response.

As the details fell from Lowell's mouth, Greene felt his secret partnership with Dante gradually wrested away from him. The modest pulpit in the soldiers'-aid home facing his spellbound listeners; the special place where *Divine Comedy* stood in his library shelf in Rhode Island; the Wednesday nights seated before Longfellow's fireplace—all of these had seemed such permanent and perfect manifestations of Greene's dedication to the great poet. Yet, as with everything else that had once been satisfactory in Greene's life, all along there had been far more at hand than he could conceive. So much occurring independent of his knowledge and indifferent to his sanction.

"My dear Greene," Longfellow said gently. "You must not speak to anyone of Dante outside those in this room until these matters are resolved."

Greene managed to simulate a nod. His expression was of a man both useless and disabled, the face of a clock from which the hands had been torn. "And our Dante Club meeting that was planned for tomorrow?" he asked feebly.

Longfellow shook his head sadly.

Fields rang for a boy to escort Greene to his daughter's house. Longfellow started helping him into his overcoat.

"Never do that, my dear friend," Greene said. "A young man does not need it and an old one does not want it." He paused on the arm of the messenger boy as he stepped into the hall; he spoke but did not look back at the men in the room. "You could have told me what had happened, you know. Any one of you could have told me. I may not have the strongest . . . I do know I could have helped you."

They waited for the sound of Greene's footfalls to die in the hallway.

"If only we had told him," said Longfellow. "What a fool I was to envision a race against the translation!"

"Not so, Longfellow!" Fields said. "Think of what we now know: Greene preached his sermons on Thursday afternoons, directly before returning to Rhode Island. He would select a canto he wished to brush up on, choosing from the two or three cantos you had set as the agenda for the next translation session. Our blasted Lucifer heard the same punishment we were to sit down with—six days *before* our own group! And that left ample time for Lucifer to stage his own version of the *contrapasso* murder just a day or two before we transcribed it onto paper. So, from our limited vantage point, the whole farrago assumed the appearance of a race, of someone taunting us with the particulars of our own translation."

"What of the warning cut into Mr. Longfellow's window?" asked Rey.

"*La Mia Traduzione.*" Fields threw up his hands. "We were hasty to conclude it was the work of the murderer. Manning's damned jackals at the College would surely stoop so low as to try to frighten us off the translation."

Holmes turned to Rey, "Patrolman, does Willard Burndy possess anything that can help us from here?"

Rey answered, "Burndy says a soldier paid him for instruction in how to open Reverend Talbot's safe. Burndy, assuming it was easy profit with little risk, went to Talbot's house to scout the layout, where several witnesses happened to see him. After Talbot's murder, the detectives discovered the eyewitnesses, and with the help of Langdon Peaslee, Burndy's rival, they fixed their case against Burndy. Burndy is a lush and can barely remember any more of the killer than the fact of his soldier's uniform. I wouldn't trust his mind even for that if you hadn't discovered the source of the murderer's knowledge."

"Hang Burndy! Hang 'em all!" Lowell cried. "Can't you see, men? This is in our sights. We're so close on Lucifer's path that we can't help but step on his Achilles' heel. Think of it: The erratic pacing between murders now makes perfect sense. Lucifer was no Dante scholar after all—he was but a Dante parishioner. He could only kill after hearing Greene preach on a punishment. One week Greene preached Canto Eleven as his text—Virgil and Dante sitting on a wall to get accustomed to the stench of Hell, discussing Hell's structure with the coolness of two engineers—a canto that features no specific punishment, no murder. Greene then took ill the next week, didn't attend our club, didn't preach—no murder again."

"Yes, and Greene was ill once before that during our time translating *Inferno*, too." Longfellow turned a page in his notes. "And once after that. There was no murder in those periods, either."

Lowell continued, "And when we put a pause in our club meetings, when we first decided to investigate after Holmes's observation of Talbot's body, the killings stopped cold—because Greene had stopped! Until we had our 'respite' and decided to translate the Schismatics—sending Greene back to the pulpit and Phinny Jennison to his death!"

"The killer's putting the money under the Simoniac's head now comes into plain daylight, too," Longfellow said remorsefully. "That was always Mr. Greene's preferred interpretation. I should have noticed his readings of Dante in the particulars of the murders."

"Do not bring yourself down, Longfellow," urged Dr. Holmes. "The murders' details were such that only an expert Dantean would have known them. There was no way to have guessed Greene was their unwitting source."

"I'm afraid, however well-intentioned my reasoning," replied Longfellow, "that we've made a grave error. By our accelerating the frequency of our translation sessions, our adversary has now heard as much Dante from Greene in a week's time as he would over the span of a month."

"I say put Greene back in that chapel," Lowell insisted. "But this time we make him preach on something other than Dante. We watch the audience and wait for someone to become agitated, then we nab our Lucifer!"

"It is far too dangerous a game for Greene!" said Fields. "He is not up to the trick. Besides, that soldiers'-aid home is half-closed up, and the soldiers are probably dispersed throughout the city by now. We haven't time to plan anything of the kind. Lucifer could strike at any moment, against anyone who, in his distorted vision of the world, he believes has transgressed against him!"

"Yet he must have a reason for those beliefs, Fields," replied Holmes. "Insanity is often the logic of an accurate mind overtasked."

"We know now that the killer required at least two days' time, sometimes more, after hearing a sermon to prepare his murder," said Patrolman Rey. "Is there a chance we can predict potential targets now that you know the portions of Dante Mr. Greene has shared with the soldiers?"

Lowell said, "I fear not. For one thing, we have no experience by which to guess how Lucifer would react to this recent flurry of sermons as opposed to a single one. The canto of the Traitors we just heard would be most prominent in his thoughts, I suppose. But how could we possibly guess what 'Traitors' might haunt the mind of this lunatic?"

"If only Greene could better recall the man who approached him, who inquired about reading Dante for himself," Holmes said. "He wore a uniform, had a hay-colored handlebar mustache, and walked with a limp. Yet we know what physical strength was shown by the murderer in each of the killings, and what swiftness of foot—seen neither by man nor beast before or after the murders. Wouldn't a disabling injury render that unlikely?"

Lowell rose and headed for Holmes with an exaggerated limp. "Might your gait not turn soft as this, Wendell, if you wished to hide suspicions of your strength to the world?"

"No, we haven't seen any evidence of our killer hiding at all, only of our inability to see him. To think that Greene would have looked into the eyes of our demon!"

"Or into those of a thoughtful gentleman struck by the force of Dante," Longfellow suggested.

"It *was* remarkable to see how excitedly the soldiers anticipated hearing more Dante," Lowell admitted. "Dante's readers become students, his students zealots, and what begins as a taste becomes a religion. The homeless exile finds a home in a thousand grateful hearts."

A light rapping and a soft voice from the hall interrupted.

Fields shook his head in frustration. "Osgood, please manage it yourself for now!"

A folded paper skated in under the door. "Just a message, if you please, Mr. Fields."

Fields hesitated before opening the note. "It's Houghton's seal. 'Given your earlier request, I trust you would be interested to know that proofs from Mr. Longfellow's Dante translation appear to have indeed gone missing. Signed, H. O. H.' "

As the others fell silent, Rey inquired as to the context.

Fields explained: "When we mistakenly believed that the murders were racing our translation, Officer, I asked my printer, Mr. Houghton, to ensure that nobody had been tampering with Mr. Longfellow's proof sheets as they were being made and thus somehow anticipating our pattern of translation."

"Good God, Fields!" Lowell tore Houghton's note from Fields's hands. "Just when we thought Greene's sermons explained everything. This flips the whole thing over like a flapjack!"

Lowell, Fields, and Longfellow found Henry Oscar Houghton busy composing a threatening letter to a defaulting plate maker. A clerk announced them.

"You told me that none of the proofs were missing from the file room, Houghton!" Fields had not even removed his hat before he began to shout.

Houghton dismissed his clerk. "You're quite right, Mr. Fields. And those still haven't been disturbed," he explained. "But, you see, I deposit an extra set of all important plates and proofs in a strong vault downstairs, in precaution against the event of a fire—ever since Sudbury Street burned to the ground. I've always thought none of my boys use the vault. They have no call to—there certainly is not much of a market for stolen proof sheets, and my printer's devils would just as soon strike a game of pool as read a book. Who said, 'Though an angel shall write, still 'tis the *devils* must print?' I mean to have that engraved on a seal one day." Houghton covered his dignified chuckle under his hand.

"Thomas Moore," Lowell could not help answering, all-knowingly.

"Houghton," said Fields. "Pray show us where these other proofs are kept."

Houghton led Fields, Lowell, and Longfellow down a flight of narrow stairs and into the basement. At the end of a long corridor, the printer spun an easy combination into a roomy vault he had purchased from a defunct bank. "After I had checked on Mr. Longfellow's translation proofs in the file room and found them complete, I had a thought to check my security vault. And, lo! Several of Mr. Longfellow's early proofs for the *Inferno* portion of the translation have taken flight."

"When did they go missing?" asked Fields.

Houghton shrugged. "I do not enter these vaults very regularly, you understand. These proofs could have been gone for days—or months—without my noticing."

Longfellow located the bin labeled with his name and Lowell helped him sort through the *Divine Comedy* sheets. Several cantos of *Inferno* were gone.

Lowell whispered, "They seem to have been taken entirely higgledy-piggledy. Parts of Canto Three are gone, but that seems the only one stolen which also has a corresponding murder."

The printer horned in on the poets' space and cleared his throat.

"I could gather together everyone who would have access to my combination if you're so inclined. I'll get to the bottom of this. If I tell a boy to hang up my overcoat, I expect him to come back and tell me he has done it."

The printer's devils were running the presses, restoring foundry type to the cases and scrubbing away the ever-flowing lagoons of black ink when they heard the signal of Houghton's bell. They herded into the Riverside Press coffee room.

Houghton clapped his hands several times to silence the usual chatter. "Boys. Please, boys. A minor problem has been called to my attention. You surely recognize one of our guests, Mr. Longfellow of Cambridge. His works represent an important commercial and civic portion of our literary printings."

One of the boys, a red-haired rustic with a pale-yellow face soiled with ink, began squirming and casting nervous glances at Longfellow. Longfellow noticed this and signaled Lowell and Fields.

"It seems some proofs from my basement vault have been . . . mislaid, shall we say." Houghton had opened his mouth to continue when he caught the restless expression on the pale-yellow devil. Lowell arched his hand lightly on the agitated devil's shoulder. At the sensation of Lowell's touch, the devil toppled a colleague to the floor and darted away. Lowell gave immediate chase and rounded the corner in time to hear footsteps race down the back stairs.

The poet dashed to the front office and down the steep side stairs. He burst outside, cutting off the deserter as he ran along the riverbank. He threw a lusty tackle, but the devil eluded him, sliding down the frosty embankment and tumbling hard into the Charles River, where some boys were spearing eels. He smashed through the river's wrapper of ice.

Lowell took a spear from a protesting boy and fished out the ice-shocked devil by his water-logged apron, which was tangled in bladderworts and discarded horseshoes.

"Why did you steal those proofs, you blackguard?" cried Lowell.

"What'r'ya jawin' about? Away with you!" he said through chattering teeth.

"You'll tell me!" said Lowell, his lips and hands shaking almost as much as his captive's.

"Go stubble your red rag, ya shit ass!"

Lowell's cheeks flared. He dunked the boy by the hair into the river, the devil spitting and shouting into the chunks of ice. By this time, Houghton, Longfellow, and Fields—and a half-dozen hollering printer's devils from ages twelve to twenty-one—had squeezed out the front doors of the press to watch.

Longfellow tried to restrain Lowell.

"I sold the damned proofs, I did!" the devil yelled, gasping for air. Lowell raised him to his feet, holding his arm tight and keeping the spear at his back. The fisher boys had salvaged the captive's round gray cap and were trying it on for size. Breathing wildly, the devil blinked out painful ice water. "I'm sorry, Mr. Houghton. I never thought they'd be missed by nobody! I knew they were just extras!"

Houghton's face was tomato-red. "Into the press! Everyone back inside!" he yelled to the disappointed boys who had wandered outside.

Fields approached with patient authority. "Be honest, lad, and this'll come off better in the end. Tell us straightaway—to whom did you sell those sheets?"

"Some crank. Happy? Stopped me when I was leaving work one night, jawin' 'bout how he wanted me to heave out twenty or thirty pages or so of Mr. Longfellow's new work, any pages I could find, just enough so it wouldn't be missed. He kept edging me 'bout how I could put a few extra beans in my wallet."

"Blast your red whiskers! Who was he?" asked Lowell.

"A real swell—tall hat, dark greatcoat and cape, beard. After I yessed his plan, he palmed me. I never seen the pig-widgeon again."

"Then how did you get him the proofs?" asked Longfellow.

"They wasn't for him. He told me to deliver them to an address. I don't think it was his own house—well, that was just the sense from the way he talked. I don't remember what the street number was, but it ain't far from here. He said he'd get the proofs back to me so as I wouldn't feel no heat from Mr. Houghton, but the jackcove never came back."

"He knew Houghton by name?" Fields asked.

"Listen good, man," said Lowell. "We need to know exactly where you took those proofs."

"I told you," the shivering devil answered. "I don't remember no number!"

"You don't look that stupid to me!" Lowell said.

"Guess not! I'd remember easy enough if I went by the streets on my trotter, I would!"

Lowell smiled. "Excellent, because you're taking us there."

"Nah, I ain't turning stag! Not unless I keep my job!"

Houghton marched down the embankment. "Never, Mr. Colby! Choose to reap another's harvest and you'll soon sow on your own!"

"And you'll be hard-pressed for another job locked up in the blockhouse," added Lowell, who didn't exactly understand Houghton's axiom. "You're going to take us to the place you delivered those proofs you stole, Mr. Colby, or the police will take you there for us."

"Meet me back in a few hours, when night falls," the devil replied in proud defeat after considering his options. Lowell released Colby, who bolted off to thaw at Riverside Press's stove.

In the meantime, Nicholas Rey and Dr. Holmes had returned to the soldiers'-aid home where Greene had preached early that afternoon, but they found nobody who fit Greene's description of the Dante enthusiast. The chapel was not being prepared for its usual supper spread. An Irishman, bundled in a heavy blue coat, lethargically nailed boards over the windows.

"The home's been spending nigh all its money heating the stoves. The city hain't approved more funds for soldiers' aid, that's how I hear it. They say they gotta close up, at least for the winter months now. Doubt we'll see it reopen, 'tween us, sirs. These homes and their mangled men are too strong a reminder of the wrongs we've all done."

Rey and Holmes called on the manager of the home. The former church deacon seconded what the caretaker had told them: It was a function of the weather, he explained—they simply couldn't afford to heat the premises anymore. He told them there were no lists or registers maintained of the soldiers who made use of the facilities. It was a public charity, open to all in need, from all regiments and towns. And it wasn't just for the poorer lot of veterans, though that was one of the charity's stated purposes. Some of the men just needed to be around people who could understand them. The deacon knew some soldiers by name and a small number of those by regimental number.

"You might know the one we seek. It's a matter of absolute importance." Rey relayed the description George Washington Greene had given them.

The manager shook his head. "I'd be happy to write down the names of the gentlemen I *do* know for you. The soldiers act as though they're their own country sometimes. They know one another much better than we can know them."

Holmes wriggled back and forth in his chair while the deacon nibbled at the feather end of his pen with painstaking slowness.

Lowell was driving Fields's coach to the Riverside Press's gates. The red-haired printer's devil was sitting atop his old spotted mare. After cursing that they were putting his horse at risk for the distemper, which the board of health had warned was imminent after a review of stable conditions, Colby sped through small avenues and down unlit frozen pastures. The path was so circuitous and unsure that even Lowell, master of Cambridge since infancy, was disoriented and could only stay on course by listening for the pounding hooves ahead.

The devil pulled in rein at the backyard of a modest Colonial house, first going past and then turning his horse around.

"This house here—that's where I brought the proofs. Dropped them right under the back door, just as I was told to."

Lowell stopped the coach. "Whose house is this?"

"The rest is up to you birds!" Colby snarled, sandwiching his heels into his mare, who galloped away over the frozen ground.

Carrying a lantern, Fields led Lowell and Longfellow to the piazza at the rear of the house.

"No lamps lit inside," Lowell said, scraping frost from a window.

"Let's go around the front, take down the address, then return with Rey," Fields whispered. "That rogue Colby might be playing games with us. He's a thief, Lowell! He could have friends in there waiting to rob us."

Lowell slammed the brass knocker repeatedly. "The way this world goes for us lately, if we leave now, the house will have vanished by the morning."

"Fields is right. We must step lightly, my dear Lowell," Longfellow urged in a whisper.

"Hullo!" Lowell shouted, now pounding his fists on the door. "There's nobody here." Lowell kicked the door and was surprised that it swung open with ease. "You see? The stars are on our side tonight."

"Jamey, we can't just break in! What if this house belongs to our Lucifer? It is we who'll end up in the blockhouse!" Fields said.

"Then we'll make our introduction," Lowell said, taking the lantern from Fields.

Longfellow stayed outside to watch that the carriage was not spotted. Fields followed Lowell inside. The publisher shuddered at every creak and thud along their way through the dark, cold halls. The wind from the open back door sent the draperies fluttering in ghostly pirouettes. Some of the rooms were sparsely furnished; others were entirely bare. The house had the thick, tangible darkness that accumulates with disuse.

Lowell entered a well-appointed oval room with a chapel-like curved ceiling, then he heard Fields suddenly spit and scratch at his face and beard. Lowell drew the lantern's light in a wide arc. "Spiderwebs. Half formed." He placed the lantern on the center table of the library. "Nobody's lived here for some time."

"Or the person living here doesn't mind the company of insects."

Lowell paused to consider this. "Look around for anything that might tell us why that rogue would be paid to bring Longfellow's proofs *here.*"

Fields began to say something in response, but a garbled shout and heavy footfalls careened through the house. Lowell and Fields exchanged looks of horror, then scrambled for their lives.

"*Burglary!*" The side door into the library was flung open and a squat man in a wool dressing gown came charging in. "Burglary! Account for yourselves or I cry 'Burglary!' "

The man thrust his strong lantern forward, then paused in shock. He glared as much at the cut of their suits as their faces.

"Mr. Lowell? That you? And Mr. Fields?"

"Randridge?" cried Fields. "Randridge, the tailor?"

"Why, yes," Randridge answered shyly, shuffling his slippered feet.

Longfellow, having run inside, traced the commotion to the room.

"Mr. Longfellow?" Randridge fumbled off his sleeping cap.

"*You* live here, Randridge? What were you doing with those proofs?" Lowell demanded.

Randridge was bewildered. "Live here? Two houses down, Mr. Lowell. But I heard some noise, and thought to check on the house. I feared there was looting afoot. They haven't boxed up and removed everything. Haven't quite gotten to the library, you can see."

Lowell asked, "Who hasn't removed everything?"

"Why, his relatives, of course. Who else?"

Fields stepped back and waved his light over the bookshelves, his eyes doubling at the inordinate number of Bibles. There were at least thirty or forty. He dragged out the largest one.

Randridge said, "They've come from Maryland to clear out his belongings. His poor nephews were terribly unprepared for such a circumstance, I can tell you. And who wouldn't be? At all events, as I was saying, when I heard noises, I thought some fellers might be trying to make away with some souvenir—you know, for the sensation of it. Since the Irish began moving into the neighborhood . . . well, things have been missed."

Lowell knew exactly where Randridge lived in Cambridge. He was mentally galloping through the neighborhood, looking two houses in every direction with the frenzy of Paul Revere. He commanded his eyes to adjust to the dark room, to search out the dark portraits lining the wall for a familiar face.

"No peace these days, my friends, I can tell you that," the tailor continued with a sad lament. "Not even for the dead."

"The dead?" Lowell repeated.

"The *dead,*" whispered Fields, passing Lowell an unclasped Bible. Its inside cover was neatly inked over with a complete family ancestry, written in the hand of the house's late occupant, the Reverend Elisha Talbot.

XVI

University Hall, 8th October 1865

My dear Reverend Talbot,

I would like once more to emphasize the freedom you ought consider remains in your capable hands as to the language and form of the series. Mr. ________ has given us his assurances that he looks forward with great honor to printing it in four parts for his literary review, one of the chief and last competitors to Mr. Fields's *Atlantic Monthly* for the minds of the educated public. Only remember the most basic of guidelines to achieve the humble goals promoted by our Corporation in the present instance.

The first article should, employing your expert stroke on such matters, lay bare the poetry of Dante Alighieri on religious and moral grounds. The sequel ought find your doubtless inscrutable exposition of why such literary charlatanry the likes of Dante (and all alike foreign claptrap, increasingly encroaching on us) has no place on the bookshelves of upright American citizens, and why publishing houses with the "international influence" (as Mr. F. does frequently boast) of T., F. & Co. must be held responsible and must be submitted furthermore to the highest standards of social responsibility. The final two pieces of your series, dear Reverend, ought analyze Henry Wadsworth Longfellow's Dante translation and reprove this heretofore "national" poet for attempting to conscript an immoral and irreligious literature into American libraries. With careful planning as to highest impact, the first two articles would precede the release of Longfellow's translation by some months in order to arrange public sentiment in advance on our side; and the third and fourth would be released simultaneously with respect to the translation itself, with the aim of reducing sales among the socially conscious.

Of course, I needn't emphasize the moral zeal we trust and expect shall be found in your writing on these topics. Though I suspect you require no reminder of your own experience as a young scholar at our institution, but rather feel its weight each day on your soul as do we, it might do well to contrast the barbaric strain of foreign poetry embodied in Dante with the proven classical program championed by Harvard College for now some two hundred years. The gust of righteousness from your pen, dear Reverend Talbot, will serve as sufficient means to send Dante's unwanted steamer back to Italy and to the Pope who waits there, with victory in the name of *Christo et ecclesiae.*

I remain, ever Thine,

Augustus Manning

When the three scholars returned to Craigie House, they held four such letters, addressed to Elisha Talbot and headed by the emblazoned seal of Harvard, as well as a stack of Dante proof sheets—the ones missing from Riverside Press's security vault.

"Talbot was the ideal hack for them," said Fields. "A minister respected by all good Christians, an established critic of Catholics, and someone outside the Harvard faculty, so that he could give sugarplums to the College and sharpen his pens against us with the appearance of objectivity."

"And I suppose one needn't be an Ann Street fortune-teller to know the sum Talbot was awarded for his troubles," Holmes said.

"One thousand dollars," Rey said.

Longfellow nodded, showing them the letter to Talbot in which the amount was specified as payment. "We held it in our hands. One thousand dollars for miscellaneous 'expenses' related to the writing and research of the four articles. That money—we can now say it with certainty—cost Elisha Talbot his life."

"Then the killer knew the precise amount he wished to take from Talbot's safe," said Rey. "He knew the particulars of this arrangement, of this letter."

" 'Keep guard over your ill-gotten loot,' " Lowell recited, then added: "One thousand dollars was the bounty on Dante's head."

The first of Manning's four letters invited Talbot to come to University Hall to discuss the Corporation's proposal. The second letter outlined the content expected in each paper and forwarded the full payment, which had earlier been negotiated in person. Between the second and third letters, it seemed, Talbot had complained to his correspondent that no English translation of the *Divine Comedy* could be found at any Boston booksellers—apparently, the minister was trying to locate a British translation by the late Reverend H. F. Cary for the purposes of writing his critique. So Manning's third letter, which was really more of a note, promised Talbot he would procure an advance sample directly from Longfellow's translation.

Augustus Manning knew when he made this promise that the Dante Club would never hand over any proofs to him after the campaign he had already waged to derail them. So, the scholars surmised, the treasurer or one of his agents found a shady printer's devil, in the person of Colby, and bribed him to smuggle out pages of Longfellow's work.

Reason counseled where they would find answers to new questions regarding Manning's scheme: University Hall. But Lowell could not examine the files of the Harvard Corporation during the day, when the fellows hovered over their territory, and he lacked the means to do so at night. A rash of pranks and tampering had led to a complex system of locks and combinations to seal up the records.

Penetrating the fortress seemed a hopeless aim until Fields recalled someone who could do it for them. "Teal!"

"Who, Fields?" asked Holmes.

"My nighttime shop boy. During that ugly episode we endured with Sam Ticknor, he was the one to save poor Miss Emory. He mentioned that in addition to his several nights a week at the Corner, he is in the daytime employ of the College."

Lowell asked if Fields thought the shop boy would be willing to help.

"He is a loyal Ticknor and Fields man, isn't he?" Fields answered.

When the loyal Ticknor & Fields man stepped out of the Corner around eleven that night, he found, to his great surprise, J. T. Fields waiting out front. Within minutes the shop boy was seated in the publisher's chariot, where he was presented to his fellow passenger—Professor James Russell Lowell! How often had he pictured himself among such sterling men. Teal did not seem to know quite how to react to such rare treatment. He listened closely to their requests.

Once in Cambridge, he guided them through Harvard Yard, past the disapproving hum of the gas globes. He slowed to look over his shoulder several times, as though worried that his literary platoon might vanish as quickly as it had appeared.

"Come on. Move along, man. We're right behind you!" Lowell assured him.

Lowell twisted the ends of his mustache. He was less nervous about the prospect of someone from the College finding them on campus than about what they might find in the files of the Corporation. He reasoned that as professor, he would have a sensible pretext if caught at such a late hour by one of the busybody resident faculty—he had forgotten some lecture notes, he could explain. Fields's presence might seem less natural, but it could not be avoided, for he was needed to ensure the participation of the fretful shop boy, who did not seem much over twenty. Dan Teal had clean-shaven boyish cheeks, wide eyes, and a fine, almost feminine, mouth that constantly worked in a gnawing motion.

"Don't worry yourself at all, my dear Mr. Teal," Fields said, and took his arm as they started up the imposing stone staircase that led to the boardrooms and classrooms in University Hall. "We just need a peek at some papers and then shall be on our way, with nothing changed for the worse. You're doing a good thing."

"That is all I wish," Teal said sincerely.

"Good boy." Fields smiled.

Teal had to use a ring of keys—they had been entrusted to him—to negotiate the series of bolts and locks. Then, having gained entrance, Lowell and Fields lit candles packed in a case for the occasion and relocated the Corporation's books from a cabinet to the long table.

"Hold your peace," said Lowell to Fields when the publisher started to dismiss Teal. "Look at the number of volumes before us we must go through, Fields. Three would do it more efficiently than two."

Although he was nervous, Teal also seemed enthralled by their adventure. "Guess I can help, Mr. Fields. Anything at all," he offered. He looked on the mess of books in confusion. "That is, if you explain to me what it is you wish to find."

Fields began to do just that but, remembering Teal's wobbly attempt at writing, suspected his reading would be little better. "You've done more than your share and should have some sleep," he said. "But I shall call on you again if we need further assistance. Our united thanks, Mr. Teal. You shall not regret your faith in us."

In the uncertain light, Fields and Lowell read through every page of minutes of the Corporation's biweekly meetings. They came upon the occasional condemnation of Lowell's Dante class, sprinkled throughout more tedious university business. "No mention of that ghoul Simon Camp. Manning must have hired him on his own," said Lowell. Some things were too shady even for the Harvard Corporation.

After sorting through endless reams, Fields found what they were looking for: In October, four of the six members of the Corporation had eagerly sanctioned the idea of engaging the Reverend Elisha Talbot to pen critiques of the upcoming Dante translation, leaving the matter of "appropriate compensation for time and energies" to the discretion of the Treasury Committee—that is, to Augustus Manning.

Fields began pulling the records of the Harvard Board of Overseers, the twenty-person governing body, annually elected by the state legislature and one step removed from the Corporation. Speeding through the overseers' books, they found many mentions of Chief Justice Healey, a loyal member of the board of overseers even until his death.

From time to time, the Harvard Board of Overseers elected what it called advocates in order to thoroughly consider issues of particular importance or controversy. An overseer so anointed would offer a presentation to the full board, using the extent of his abilities of persuasion to argue the case for "conviction," as it were, while a counterpart overseer presented a contending basis for exoneration. The chosen overseer-advocate did not have to possess a personal belief in line with his side in the argument; indeed, the individual was to present a clear-thinking and fair evaluation to the board without influence of private prejudices.

In the Corporation's campaign against the various Dante-related activities by persons prominently affiliated with the university—that is, James Russell Lowell's Dante class, and the translation by Henry Wadsworth Longfellow with his purported "Dante Club"—the overseers agreed that advocates should be chosen to present both sides of the issue fairly. The board selected as the advocate for the *pro*-Dante position Chief Justice Artemus Prescott Healey, a thorough researcher and gifted analyst. Healey had never claimed himself a litterateur and so could evaluate the matter dispassionately.

It had been several years since the board had asked Healey to advocate a position. The idea of choosing sides in a venue outside the courtroom apparently made Chief Justice Healey uncomfortable, and he declined the board's request. Taken aback by his refusal, the board let the matter pass and did not follow through that day on the fate of Dante Alighieri.

The story of Healey's refusal occupied a mere two lines in the Corporation record books. Having understood its implications, Lowell was the first to speak:

"Longfellow was right," he whispered. "Healey wasn't Pontius Pilate."

Fields squinted over gold-framed glasses.

"The Neutral that Dante calls only the Great Refuser," Lowell explained. "The only shade Dante chooses to single out while crossing through Hell's antechamber. I've read him as Pontius Pilate, who washed his hands of deciding the fate of Christ—just as Healey washed his hands of Thomas Sims and the other fugitive slaves brought before his court. But Longfellow—nay, Longfellow and *Greene*!—always believed that the Great Refuser was Celestine, who turned away a position rather than a person. Celestine abdicated the papal throne conferred on him when the Catholic Church needed him most. That led to the rise of Boniface and ultimately to Dante's exile. Healey surrendered a position of great importance when he refused to argue on behalf of Dante. And now Dante's exiled again."

"I'm sorry, Lowell, but I shan't compare refusing the papacy to turning down a boardroom defense of Dante," Fields replied dismissively.

"But don't you see, Fields? We don't have to. Our murderer has."

They could hear cracking noises in the thick crust of ice outside University Hall. The sounds came closer.

Lowell ran to the window. "Hang it, a blasted tutor!"

"Are you sure?"

"Well no, I can't make out who it is . . . there's two of them . . ."

"Have they seen our light, Jamey?"

"I can't say—I can't say—clear out!"

Horatio Jennison's high-pitched, melodious voice rose above the sounds of his piano.

"'Fear no more the frown o' the great!
Thou art past the tyrant's stroke!
Care no more to clothe and eat!
To thee thy reed is as the oak!'"

It was one of his finer renditions of Shakespeare's song, but then his bell rang, a most unexpected interruption, for his four invited guests were already sitting around the parlor, enjoying his performance so thoroughly that they seemed on the verge of complete entrancement. Horatio Jennison had sent a note to James Russell Lowell two days ago, asking him to consider editing Phineas Jennison's journals and letters in memoriam—for Horatio had been named literary executor, and he would settle for nothing short of the best: Lowell was the founding editor of *The Atlantic Monthly* and now editor of *The North American Review*, and, along with all this, had been his uncle's close friend. But Horatio had not expected Lowell to simply appear at his door unceremoniously, and at a terribly late evening hour.

Horatio Jennison knew immediately that the idea presented in his note must have impressed Lowell, for the poet urgently requested, or rather demanded, Jennison's most recent journal volumes, and had even brought along James T. Fields to suggest his seriousness about publication.

"Mr. Lowell? Mr. Fields?" Horatio Jennison sprang to his front step when the two callers conveyed the journals, without further exchange, out the door and into their waiting carriage. "We will arrange the proper royalties from the publication, I trust?"

In those hours time became immaterial. Back at Craigie House, the scholars waded through the almost indecipherable scrawl of Phineas Jennison's most recent journal volumes. After the revelations surrounding Healey and Talbot, it was no surprise for the Danteans, intellectually speaking, that the "sins" of Jennison punished by Lucifer would revolve around Dante. But James Russell Lowell could not believe it—could not believe such a thing of his friend of so many years—until the evidence drowned his doubts.

Throughout the many volumes of his journal, Phineas Jennison expressed his burning desire to secure a spot on the board of the Harvard Corporation. There, mused the businessman, he would finally achieve the respect that had passed him by for not having attended Harvard, for not having come from a Boston family. To be a fellow meant to be welcomed into a world that had been locked away from him his whole life. And what otherwordly power Jennison seemed to find in the notion of holding sway over Boston's finest minds, just as he had over its commerce!

Some friendships would be strained—or sacrificed.

In the last months, on his many visits to University Hall—for he was a considerable financial patron of the College and often had business there—Jennison would privately entreat the fellows to prevent the teaching of such rubbish as was being advanced by Professor James Russell Lowell and that would soon be disseminated to the masses by Henry Wadsworth Longfellow. Jennison promised key members of the board of overseers his full financial support for a campaign to reorganize the Department of Living Languages. At the same time, Lowell recalled bitterly as he read the journals, Jennison had been urging Lowell to fight the escalating efforts of the Corporation to smother his activities.

Jennison's journals revealed that for over a year, he had toyed with plans to empty a seat on one of the university's governing boards. Building a controversy among the College's administrators would create casualties and resignations that would have to be filled. He was smoldering mad, after Judge Healey's death, when a businessman with half his worth and a quarter of his savvy was elected to the empty overseer seat—only because this other man was a Brahmin aristocrat by heritage, and an inconsequential Choate, of all things. Phineas Jennison knew the unspoken policy had been enforced by one person above all others: Dr. Augustus Manning.

At what exact point Jennison heard about Dr. Manning's consuming determination to emancipate the university from its connection to the Dante projects was unclear, but at that moment he found his opportunity to finally secure a seat in University Hall.

"There was never a jar between us," Lowell said sadly.

"Jennison spurred you on to fight the Corporation and spurred the Corporation to fight you. A battle would wear Manning down. Whatever the final outcome, seats would be emptied, and Jennison would look like a hero for having lent his support to the cause of the College. It was his objective all along," said Longfellow, trying to assure Lowell he had done nothing to lose Jennison's friendship.

"I cannot get it through my skull, Longfellow," Lowell said.

"He helped split you and the College, Lowell, and was split apart in return," Holmes said. "That was his *contrapasso*."

Holmes had appropriated Nicholas Rey's preoccupation with the scraps of paper found near Talbot's and Jennison's bodies, and they had sat together for hours sharing possible combinations. Holmes was now composing words or partial words with hand copies of Rey's letters. No doubt others had been left with the body of Chief Justice Healey as well but were taken away by the river breeze in the intervening days between the murder and discovery. Those missing letters would have completed whatever message the murderer wanted them to read, Holmes was certain. Without them, it was but a broken mosaic. *We cant die without it as im upon . . .*

Longfellow turned to a fresh page in their investigative journal. He drenched his pen in ink but sat staring ahead so long that the tip dried. He could not write down the necessary conclusion of all this: Lucifer had meted out his punishments for *their* sake—for the sake of the Dante Club.

The gated entrance to the Boston State House stood high on Beacon Hill; higher still was the copper dome capping it, with its short, sharp tower watching over the Boston Common like a lighthouse. Towering elms, stripped naked and whitened by the December frost, guarded the state's municipal center.

Governor John Andrew, his black curls coiling out from under a black silk hat, stood with all the dignity his pear shape would allow as he greeted politicians, local dignitaries, and uniformed soldiers with the same inattentive politician's smile. The governor's small, solid gold–framed spectacles were his only sign of material indulgence.

"Governor." Mayor Lincoln bowed slightly as he escorted Mrs. Lincoln up the steps to the entrance. "It looks to be the finest soldiers' gathering yet."

"Thank you, Mayor Lincoln. Mrs. Lincoln, welcome—please." Governor Andrew motioned them inside. "The company is more prestigious than ever."

"They're saying even Longfellow has been added to the list of attendees," Mayor Lincoln said, and passed a complimentary pat on the shoulder to Governor Andrew.

"It is a fine thing you do for these men, Governor, and we—the city, I mean—applaud you." Mrs. Lincoln held up her dress with a slight rustle as she took a queenly step into the foyer. Once inside, a low-hung mirror provided her and the other ladies a view of the nether regions of their dresses, in the event that the garment had repositioned itself inappropriately along the way to the reception; a husband was wholly useless for such purposes.

Mingling in the massive parlor of the mansion were seventy to eighty soldiers from five different companies, garbed splendidly in their full-dress uniforms and capes, alongside twenty or thirty guests. Many of the most active regiments being honored had only a small number of survivors. Although

Governor Andrew's counselors had urged that only the most upstanding representatives of the soldierly core be included at the gatherings—some soldiers, they remarked, had grown *troubled* since the war—Andrew had insisted that the soldiers should be feted for their service, not their level of society.

Governor Andrew walked through the center of the long parlor with a staccato march, enjoying a surge of self-importance as he surveyed the faces and felt the ringing of the names of those with whom it had been his good fortune to become familiar during the war years. More than once during those wrenching times, the Saturday Club had sent a cab to the State House and forcibly removed Andrew from his office for an evening of gaiety in Parker's hot rooms. All time had been separated into two epochs: before the war and after the war. In Boston, Andrew thought as he melted seamlessly into the white cravats and silk hats, the tinsel and gold lace of the officers, the conversations and compliments of old friends, we have survived.

Mr. George Washington Greene positioned himself across from a glowing marble statue that showed the Three Graces leaning delicately against one another, faces cold and angelic, eyes filled with calm indifference.

"How could a veteran from the soldiers'-aid home who heard Greene's sermons *also* know the minute details of our tension with Harvard?"

This question had been posed inside the Craigie House study. Answers were proposed, and they knew that to find this answer would mean to find a killer. One of the young men consumed by Greene's sermons could have had a father or uncle in the Harvard Corporation or the board of overseers who innocently related his stories over supper, not knowing the effect they might have in the shattered mind of someone occupying the next seat.

The scholars would have to determine exactly who was present at the various board meetings involving the roles of Healey, Talbot, and Jennison in the College's position against Dante; this list would be compared with the names and profiles of as many soldiers from the soldiers'-aid home as they could collect. They would require Mr. Teal's help once more to access the Corporation Room; Fields would coordinate the plan with his shop boy once the night workers arrived at the Corner.

In the meantime, Fields ordered Osgood to compile a list of all employees of Ticknor & Fields who had fought in the war, relying primarily on the

Directory of Massachusetts Regiments in the War of Rebellion. That evening, Nicholas Rey and the others would attend the governor's latest reception to honor Boston's soldiers.

Messrs. Longfellow, Lowell, and Holmes dispersed themselves through the crowded reception hall. Each of them kept a watchful eye on Mr. Greene, and, in casual pretext, interviewed many veterans, searching for the soldier Greene had described.

"One might think this was the back room of a tavern rather than the State House!" Lowell complained as he waved away some fugitive smoke.

"Why, Mr. Lowell, have you not bragged of smoking ten cigars in one day, and called the sensation a Muse?" Holmes chided.

"We never like the smell of our own vices in other people, Holmes. Ah, let's steer here for a drink or two," Lowell suggested.

Dr. Holmes's hands burrowed into the pockets of his moiré silk waistcoat; his words poured through him as through a sieve. "Every soldier I've spoken to either claims never to have met anyone remotely matching the description given by Greene or has seen a man *exactly* of that type just the other day but doesn't know his name or where I might find him. Perhaps Rey will have better luck."

"Dante, my dear Wendell, was a man of great personal dignity, and one secret of his dignity was that he was never in a hurry. You will never find him in an unseemly haste—an excellent rule for us to follow."

Holmes laughed skeptically. "And you've followed this rule?"

Lowell helped himself to a meditative sip of claret, then said thoughtfully, "Tell me, Holmes, have you ever had a Beatrice of your own?"

"Beg your pardon, Lowell?"

"A woman to have fired the awesome depths of your imagination."

"Why, my Amelia!"

Lowell bellowed with laughter. "Oh, Holmes! Did you never sow your tame oats? A wife cannot be your *Beatrice.* You may trust my advice, for in common with Petrarch, Dante, and Byron, I was desperately in love before I was ten years old. What pangs I have suffered my own heart only knows."

"How Fanny would enjoy such talk, Lowell!"

"Pshaw! Dante had his Gemma, who was the mother of his children but not the reach of his inspiration! You know how they met? Longfellow does not believe it, but Gemma Donati is the lady mentioned in Dante's *Vita Nuova,* who comforts Dante over the loss of Beatrice. You see that young woman?"

Holmes followed Lowell's gaze to a slender young maiden with raven hair, which was shining under the hall's brilliant chandeliers.

"I remember it still—1839, at Allston's Gallery. There was the most beautiful creature I had ever set eyes upon, not unlike that fair beauty enchanting her husband's friends over there in the corner. Her features were perfectly Jewish. She had a dark complexion, but one of those clear faces where every shade of feeling floats across like the shadow of a cloud across the grass. From my position in the room, the outline of her eyes entirely merged in the shadows of her brows and the darkness of her complexion, so that you only saw a glory undefined and mysterious. But such eyes! They almost made me tremble. That one vision of her seraphic loveliness gave me more poetry . . ."

"Was she intelligent?"

"Heavens, I don't know! She batted her lashes in my direction and I could not bring myself to say a word. There is only one way to go with flirtatious women, Wendell, and that is to run. Still, twenty-five years and more pass, yet I cannot banish her from my memory. I assure you we all have our own Beatrice, whether living near us or alive only in our mind."

Lowell stopped as Rey approached. "Officer Rey, the winds have shifted in our favor—I can tell as much. We are only fortunate to have you on our side."

"Your daughter must be thanked for that," Rey said.

"Mabel?" Lowell turned to him, aghast.

"She came to speak with me, to persuade me to assist you gentlemen."

"Mabel spoke with you in secret? Holmes, did you know of this?" Lowell demanded.

Holmes shook his head. "Not at all. We must toast her, though!"

"If you grow warm with her over it, Professor Lowell," Rey warned him with a serious upward lift of his jaw, "I shall have you arrested."

Lowell laughed heartily. "Incentive enough, Officer Rey! Now, do let us keep the pot boiling."

Rey nodded confidentially and continued across the room.

"Can you imagine that, Wendell? Mabel going behind my back like that, thinking she could change things!"

"She is a Lowell, my dear friend."

"Mr. Greene remains strong," Longfellow reported as he joined Lowell and Holmes. "But I am worried that—" Longfellow broke off. "Ah, here come Mrs. Lincoln and Governor Andrew."

Lowell rolled his eyes. Their station in society had proved bothersome for this evening's purposes, as handshakes and lively conversations with professors, ministers, politicos, and university officials distracted from their intended purpose.

"Mr. Longfellow."

Longfellow turned to his other side to find a trio of Beacon Hill society women.

"Why, good evening, ladies," Longfellow said.

"I was just speaking of you, sir, while on holiday in Buffalo," said the raven-haired beauty of the trinity.

"Is that so?" Longfellow asked.

"Indeed, with Miss Mary Frere. She speaks so tenderly of you, says you are a rare person. She had such wonderful times with you and your family at Nahant last summer, from the sound of it. And now I happen upon you here. How wonderful!"

"Oh? Well, how very kind of her to say that." Longfellow smiled, but then quickly adjusted his gaze away. "Now, where has Professor Lowell run to? Have you met him?"

Nearby, Lowell was loudly retelling one of his vintage anecdotes to a small audience. "Then Tennyson growled from his corner of the table: 'Yes, damn 'em. I'd like to take a knife and rip their guts up!' Being a true poet, King Alfred used no circumlocution—such as 'abdominal viscera'—for that part of the body!"

Lowell's hearers laughed and jested.

"If two men should try to look alike," Longfellow said, turning back to the three ladies, who stood with their ears glowing bright pink and their mouths helplessly open, "they could not do it better than Lord Tennyson and Professor Lovering of our university."

The raven-haired beauty beamed gratefully at Longfellow's swift flight away from Lowell's indecency.

"Why, isn't that something to think about?" she said.

When Oliver Wendell Holmes Junior received a note from his father that Dr. Holmes, too, would be attending the soldiers' banquet at the State House, he sighed, reread it, and then cursed. It was not a matter of minding his father's presence as much as a matter of others demanding for their entertainment that they account for each other's welfare. *How is dear old Dad? Still tinkering with his poems while he's at his teaching? Still tinkering with his teaching while at his poems? Is it true that the little doctor can speak ________ words every minute, Captain Holmes?* Why should he be bothered with questions on Dr. Holmes's favorite subject: Dr. Holmes.

In a crowd of other members of his regiment, Junior was now introduced to several Scottish gentlemen who were visiting as a delegation. At the enunciation of Junior's full name there was the usual rehearsal of questions regarding his parentage.

"Are you the son of Oliver Wendell Holmes?" a latecomer to the exchange, a Scot around Junior's age, asked after presenting himself as some sort of mythologist.

"Yes."

"Well, I don't like his books." The mythologist smiled and walked away.

In the silence that seemed to surround Junior, standing there alone amid the chatter, he felt abruptly angry at his father's omnipresence in the world and cursed him again. Did one want to spread his reputation so indiscriminately wide that worms of men, like the one Junior had just met, could judge you? Junior turned and saw Dr. Holmes on the edge of a circle, along with the governor, and James Lowell gesticulating in the center. Dr. Holmes was on his toes, mouth drifting open; he was lying in wait for a chance to barge in. Junior tried to skirt around the group to the other side of the hall.

"Wendy, that you?" Junior pretended not to hear, but the voice came again and Dr. Holmes pressed through some soldiers to reach him.

"Hello, Father."

"Why, Wendy, don't you wish to come and say hello to Lowell and Governor Andrew? Let me show you off in your dapper uniform! Oh, hold."

Junior noticed his father's eyes wander.

"That must be the Scottish coterie Andrew was talking about—over there, Junior. I should like to meet the young mythologist, Mr. Lang, and discuss some ideas I have about Orpheus fiddling Eurydice out of the infernal regions. Have you read anything of his, Wendy?"

Dr. Holmes took Junior's arm and pulled him toward the other side of the hall.

"No." Junior yanked his arm away hard to stop his father. Dr. Holmes looked at him, hurt. "I've only come to make an appearance for my regiment, Father. I must meet Minny at the Jameses' house. Please excuse me to your friends."

"Did you see us? We are a happy band of brothers, Wendy. More and more still as the years roar by us. My boy, enjoy your passage on the ship of youth, for it too easily grows lost at sea!"

"And, Father," Junior said, looking over his father's shoulder at the grinning mythologist. "I heard that dastard Lang talking down about Boston."

Holmes's expression turned solemn. "Did you? Then he is not worth our time, my boy."

"If you say so, Father. Tell me, are you still at work on that new novel?"

Holmes's smile sprang back at the interest intimated by Junior's question. "Indeed! Some other enterprises have taken up my time of late, but Fields promises it shall turn a penny when published. I shall have to leap into the Atlantic if it doesn't—I mean the original damp spot, not Fields's monthly."

"You shall invite the critics to assault you again," Junior said, hesitating to continue his thought. Suddenly, he wished to heaven he had been quick enough to run the wormy mythologist through with his dress sword. He promised himself he would read this Lang's work, knowing he would take satisfaction if it was poor stuff. "Perhaps I shall have a chance to read this one, though, Father, if some time appears."

"I'd like that very much, my boy," Holmes said quietly as Junior started out.

Rey had found one of the soldiers mentioned by the deacon of the soldiers'-aid home, a one-armed veteran who had just finished dancing with his wife.

"There were some who says to me," the soldier said proudly to Rey, "when they'd outfitted you boys, 'I ain't fighting a nigger war.' Oh, and wouldn't you know that made me red."

"Please, Lieutenant," said Rey. "This gentleman I've described to you—do you think you might have ever seen him at the soldiers'-aid home?"

"Certainly, certainly. Handlebar mustache, hay-colored. Always in uniform. Blight—that's his name. I'm absolutely certain of it, though not positively. Captain Dexter Blight. Sharp, always reading. Good an officer as ever broke bread, seems to me."

"Pray tell me, was he very interested in Mr. Greene's sermons?"

"Oh, sure liked 'em, the old rowdy! And wouldn't you know those sermons were some fresh air. So much bolder than anything I've heard. Oh sure. Cap liked 'em better'n anybody, seems to me!"

Rey could barely contain himself. "Do you know where I can find Captain Blight?"

The soldier plopped his stump into the palm of his only hand and paused. Then he threw his good arm around his wife. "Why, wouldn't you know, Mr. Officer, my pretty filly here must be your luck charm."

"Oh my stars, Lieutenant," she protested.

"I think I *do* know where you can see him," said the veteran. "Right ahead."

Captain Dexter Blight, of the 19th Massachusetts, wore an upside-down U mustache, hay-colored, just as Greene had described.

Rey's stare, lasting a long three seconds, was discreet but vigilant. He was surprised at the hunger, the curiosity he felt about every detail of the man's appearance.

"Patrolman Nicholas Rey? Now, isn't that you?" Governor Andrew looked up at Rey's intent face and ceremoniously extended his hand. "I wasn't told you were expected!"

"I hadn't planned on attending, Governor. But I'm afraid you must pardon me."

With that, Rey retreated into a throng of soldiers, and the governor who had appointed him to the Boston Police was left standing in a trance of disbelief.

His sudden presence, seemingly unnoticed by the others at the reception, eclipsed all other thoughts of the members of the Dante Club as they noticed him one by one. They consumed him with a collective stare. Could this man, seemingly mortal and ordinary, have overtaken Phineas Jennison and sliced him to pieces? His features were strong and brooding but otherwise unremarkable under his black felt hat and single-breasted dress tunic. Could this be him? The translator-*savant* who turned Dantean words into *action,* who had outdone them time and again?

Holmes excused himself from some admirers and rushed over to Lowell.

"That man . . ." Holmes whispered, filled with a sense of dread that something had gone wrong.

"I know," Lowell whispered back. "Rey has seen him, too."

"Should we have Greene approach him?" Holmes said. "There is something about that man. He does not seem . . ."

"Look!" said Lowell urgently.

At that moment, Captain Blight noticed George Washington Greene loitering alone. The soldier's prominent nostrils flared with interest. Greene, having forgotten himself amidst paintings and sculptures, continued his browsing as if at a weekend exhibition. Blight contemplated Greene for a moment, then took slow, uneven steps toward him.

Rey moved ahead to position himself closer, but when he turned to check on Blight, he found that Greene was in conversation with a book collector. Blight had crossed through the door instead.

"Hang it," Lowell cried. "He's leaving!"

The air was too still for clouds or snowfall. The wide-open sky showed off a moon so precisely halved that it appeared to have been sliced by a freshly honed blade.

Rey caught sight of a uniformed soldier in the Common. He was wobbling away with the support of an ivory cane.

"Captain!" Rey called out.

Dexter Blight swerved around and regarded his solicitor through hard, squinting eyes.

"Captain Blight."

"Who in the world are you?" His voice rang deep and bold.

"Nicholas Rey. I need to speak with you," said Rey, displaying his police badge. "Just for a moment."

Blight stabbed his cane into the ice, propelling himself faster than Rey would have thought possible. "I've nothing to say!"

Rey caught up and grabbed Blight by the arm.

"If you try to arrest me, I'll rip your damned guts out and scatter them over the Frog Pond!" Blight yelled.

Rey feared there had been a terrible mistake. This careless burst of anger, the uncontrolled emotion, belonged to the fearful, not the undaunted—not to the one they sought. Looking back at the State House, where the members of the Dante Club were hurrying down the steps, their faces lined with hope, Rey also saw the faces of the persons throughout Boston who had brought him to this pursuit. Chief Kurtz—with each death, his time growing shorter as the guardian of a city that was expanding too voraciously to accommodate all who wished to call it home. Ednah Healey—her expression fading in the dying light of her bedchamber, clinging to handfuls of her own flesh, waiting to be whole again. Sexton Gregg and Grifone Lonza: They were two more victims, not of the murderer, exactly, but of the insurmountable fear that created the murders.

Rey intensified his hold on the struggling Blight and met the wide, careful stare of Dr. Holmes, who seemingly shared all his doubts. Rey prayed to God there was still time.

Finally. Augustus Manning moaned as he answered the bell and let in his guest. "Shall we to the library?"

Smugly, Pliny Mead chose the most comfortable place to sit, in the center of the Mannings' molehair settee.

"I thank you for agreeing to meet at an evening hour, Mr. Mead, away from the College," Manning said.

"Well, sorry I'm late. Your secretary's message said this is about Professor Lowell. Our Dante class?"

Manning passed his hand over the bare ravine between his two cresting tufts of white hair. "Right, Mr. Mead. Pray, did you speak with Mr. Camp about the class?"

"Guess I did," said Mead. "For a few hours at that. He wanted to know just about everything I could tell him on Dante. He said he was asking on your account."

"He was indeed. Yet since then it doesn't seem he wishes to speak to me. I wonder why."

Mead crinkled his nose. "Now, how should I know your business, sir?"

"You shouldn't, my son, of course. But I thought perhaps you could help me nonetheless. I thought that we could marry our information and understand what he might have come upon that would prompt such a shift in his behavior."

Mead stared blandly, disenchanted by the fact that the meeting held little benefit or enjoyment for him. A box of pipes sat on the mantel. He cheered at the idea of smoking at the fireside of a Harvard fellow. "Those look A1, Dr. Manning."

Manning nodded pleasantly and prepared a pipe for his guest. "Here, unlike at our campus, we can smoke openly. We can speak openly as well, our words coming out as freely as our smoke. There are some other strange happenings of late, Mr. Mead, that I would like to bring into the light. A policeman came to see me and started asking questions about your Dante class, then stopped himself, as though he had wished to tell me something important but changed his mind."

Mead closed his eyes and puffed out luxuriously.

Augustus Manning had been patient enough. "I wonder, Mr. Mead, if you're aware what a dead slide your class ranking has taken presently."

Mead bolted upright, a grammar school child ready to be ferruled. "Sir, Dr. Manning, believe me it is not for any reason other—"

He interrupted. "I know, my dear boy. I know what happens. Professor Lowell's class last term—that is to blame. Your brothers have always been first scholars in their commencement classes. Haven't they?"

Bristling with humiliation and anger, the student looked away.

"Perhaps we can see to it that some adjustments are made to your class number to bring your standing more in line with your family honor."

Mead's emerald green eyes came to life. "Truly, sir?"

"Perhaps *I* shall have a smoke now." Manning grinned, rising from his chair and scrutinizing his beautiful pipes.

Pliny Mead's mind raced to find what it was Manning might be after to make such a proposition. He relived his meeting with Simon Camp moment by moment. The Pinkerton detective had been trying to collect negative facts about Dante to report to Dr. Manning and the Corporation, to boost their position against re-forming and opening the curriculum. In the second meeting, Camp had seemed excessively interested, now that Mead thought of it. But he did not know what the private detective could have been thinking. Nor did it stand to reason that Boston policemen would ask questions about Dante. Mead thought about recent public events, the insanity of violence and fear that had enveloped their city. Camp had seemed particularly interested in the punishment of the Simoniacs when Mead mentioned it in a long list of examples. Mead thought about the many rumors he had heard about Elisha Talbot's death; several, although details differed, involved the minister's charred feet. The *minister's* feet. Then there was poor Judge Healey, found naked and covered in . . .

Why, darn them all! Jennison too! Could it be? And if Lowell knew, wouldn't that explain his sudden cancellation of their Dante class without real explanation? Could Mead have unwittingly prompted Simon Camp to comprehend it all? Had Lowell concealed his knowledge from the College, from the city? He could be ruined for that! *Damn 'em!*

Mead sprang to his feet. "Dr. Manning, Dr. Manning!"

Manning succeeded in lighting a match, but then put it out, suddenly dropping his voice to a whisper. "Did you hear something from the entry?"

Mead listened, shook his head. "Mrs. Manning, sir?"

Manning hooked a long, crooked finger to his mouth. He glided from the parlor to the hallway.

After a moment, he returned to his guest. "My imagination," he said, locking eyes squarely with Mead. "I only want you to be assured that our privacy is complete. In my heart, I know that you will have something important to share tonight, Mr. Mead."

"I *might* indeed, Dr. Manning," taunted Mead, having organized his strategy in the time Manning had taken to prove their privacy. *Dante is a damned murderer, Dr. Manning. Oh yes, I might indeed share something.* "Let us talk about class rankings first," Mead said. "Then we can move on to Dante. Oh, I think what I have to say shall interest you greatly, Dr. Manning."

Manning beamed. "Why don't I fix some refreshment to accompany our pipes?"

"Sherry for me, if you please."

Manning brought over the requested stimulant, which Mead downed in a single gulp. "How about another, dear Auggie? We'll make a wet night of it."

Augustus Manning, hunching over his sideboard to prepare another drink, hoped for the student's sake that what he had to say was important.

He heard a loud thump, signifying, he knew without looking, that the boy had broken a precious object. Manning looked back over his shoulder with irritation. Pliny Mead was sprawled senseless on the settee, his arms hanging limply off either side.

Manning spun around, the decanter slipping out of his grasp. The administrator stared into the face of a uniformed soldier, a man he had seen almost daily along the corridors of University Hall. The soldier had a fixed stare and chewed sporadically; when his lips parted, soft white dots floated on his tongue. He spat and one of the white dots landed on the rug. Manning could not help but look; there seemed to be two letters printed on the wet bit of paper—*L* and *I*.

Manning rushed to the corner of the room, where a hunting rifle was posed decoratively on the wall. He climbed a chair to reach it, but then stuttered, "No. No."

Dan Teal plucked the gun away from Manning's trembling hands and pummeled his face with its butt in one effortless motion. Then he stood there and watched, watched as the Traitor, cold to the core of his heart, flailed and crumpled to the floor.

XVII

DR. HOLMES scrambled up the long staircase to the Authors' Room. "Hasn't Officer Rey come back?" he asked, panting.

Lowell's knitted eyebrows expressed his frustration.

"Well, perhaps Blight . . ." Holmes began. "Perhaps he does know something, and Rey will come with good tidings. What of your return visit to the University Hall records room?"

"I'm afraid we might not have one," Fields said, sighing into his beard.

"Why not?" Holmes asked.

Fields was silent.

"Mr. Teal has not shown himself this evening," Longfellow explained. "Perhaps he has taken ill," he added quickly.

"Not likely," Fields said, crestfallen. "The books show that young Teal hasn't missed a shift in four months. I've called some trouble down on the poor boy's head, Holmes. And after he volunteered his loyalty again and again."

"What folly . . ." Holmes began.

"Is it? I oughtn't have involved him! Manning might have found out that Teal helped us break in and had him arrested. Or that blasted Samuel Ticknor might have taken revenge on Teal for stopping his shameful games with Miss Emory. In the meantime, we've been talking with all my men who fought in the war. None admit to ever using a soldiers'-aid home, and none reveal anything remotely worth knowing."

Lowell paced back and forth with an extra long shuffle, inclining his head toward the cold window and glaring down at the dim landscape of snowbanks. "Rey believes Captain Blight was merely another soldier who enjoyed Greene's sermons. Blight is likely to tell Rey nothing of others, even after he's calmed himself—he may know nothing of the other soldiers at the home! And without Teal, we have no hope of breaking into the Corporation Room. Shan't we ever stop pumping at dry wells!"

A knock at the door brought in Osgood, who reported that two more employee-veterans were awaiting Fields in the cafeteria. The senior clerk had given him the names of all former soldiers in the employ of Ticknor & Fields. There were twelve men: Heath, Miller, Wilson, Collins, Holden, Sylvester, Rapp, Van Doren, Drayton, Flagg, King, and Kellar. One former employee, Samuel Ticknor, had been drafted but, after two weeks in uniform, had paid the mandated three hundred dollars to buy a substitute.

Predictable, thought Lowell, who said, "Fields, give me Teal's address and I will look for him myself. There's nothing we can do until Rey comes back, in any case. Holmes, will you come along?"

Fields instructed J. R. Osgood to remain in the clerks' quarters in case he was needed. Osgood threw himself into an easy chair with a tired sigh. To occupy his time, he selected a Harriet Beecher Stowe book from the nearest shelf, and when he opened it, he found that bits of paper, about the size of snowflakes, had been torn from the cover page, which was inscribed by Stowe to Fields. Osgood flipped through and found the same sacrilege had been committed on several pages. "How queer!"

Down at the stables, Lowell and Holmes discovered to their horror that Fields's mare was writhing on the ground, unable to move. Her companion looked on sadly and kicked at anyone who dared approach. The horse distemper had completely disabled public modes of transportation citywide, so the two poets were forced to trudge on foot.

The meticulously scrawled number on Dan Teal's employment form matched that of a modest house in the southern quarter of the city.

"Mrs. Teal?" Lowell pressed his hat to the careworn woman at the door. "My name is Mr. Lowell. And may I make you acquainted with Dr. Holmes."

"Mrs. *Galvin*," she said, and put a hand to her chest.

Lowell checked the number of the house against his paper. "There's someone boarding here named Teal?"

She looked at them with sad eyes. "I'm Harriet Galvin." She repeated this with slow elocution, as though her callers were children or simpletons. "I live here with my husband, and we'd take no boarders. I've never heard of this Mr. *Teal*, sir."

"Have you moved here recently, then?" asked Dr. Holmes.

"Five years now."

"More old wells," Lowell mumbled.

"Madam," Holmes said. "Would you kindly allow us a few moments inside to find our bearings?"

She led them inside and Lowell's attention was drawn immediately to a tintype portrait on the wall.

"Ah, might I trouble you for a glass of water, my dear?" Lowell asked.

When she left, he bolted to the framed portrait of a soldier, freshly suited in oversize army rags. "Daughter of Phoebus! That's him, Wendell! As I stand here, that's Dan Teal!"

It was. "He was in the army?" Holmes asked.

"He wasn't on any of Osgood's lists of soldiers that Fields has been interviewing!"

"And here's why. 'Second Lieutenant Benjamin Galvin,'" Holmes read the name engraved underneath. "Teal is an assumed name. Quickly, while she's busy." Holmes stole into the next cramped room, which was filled with wartime accoutrements, carefully arranged and displayed, but one object drew his attention immediately: a saber, dangling from the wall. Holmes felt a chill run through his bones and he called Lowell. The poet appeared and his whole body trembled at the sight.

Holmes waved away a circling gnat, which came right back.

"Forget the bug!" Lowell said, and smashed it dead.

Holmes delicately removed the weapon from the wall. "It is precisely the sort of blade . . . these were ornaments to our officers, reminders of the world's more civilized forms of combat. Wendell Junior has one and dandled it like a baby at that banquet . . . This blade might have mutilated Phineas Jennison."

"No. It's spotless," Lowell said, approaching the shining instrument cautiously.

Holmes ran a finger along the steel. "We cannot know with our naked eyes. Such carnage does not wash away lightly after only a few days, not in all Neptune's waters." Then his eyes rested on the blood smear on the wall, all that remained of the gnat.

When Mrs. Galvin returned with two glasses of water, she saw Dr. Holmes handling the sword and demanded that he stop. Holmes, ignoring her, marched through the entry and out the front door. She professed her outrage that they would come into her house to smuggle away her property and threatened to send for the police.

Lowell inserted himself between them and stalled. Holmes, hearing her protests in the recesses of his mind, stood on the front sidewalk and raised the heavy saber in front of him. A tiny gnat spun onto the blade like a chip of iron to a charged magnet. Then, within a blink, another appeared, and two more, and then three together in a mindless clump. After a few seconds had passed, an entire flock was scuttling and humming over the deep-set blood on the blade.

Lowell stopped in mid-sentence at the sight.

"Send for the others at once!" Holmes shouted.

Their frantic demands to see her husband alarmed Harriet Galvin. She slipped into a stunned silence watching Holmes and Lowell alternate gesticulations and explanations, like two buckets in a well, until a knock at the door suspended them. J. T. Fields presented himself, but Harriet fixated on the slender and leonine figure behind this plump and solicitous one. Framed by the silver whiteness of the sky, nothing was purer than his look of perfect calm. She raised a trembling hand as if to touch his beard and, indeed, as the poet followed Fields inside, her fingers brushed against his locks. He retreated a step. She pleaded that he come inside.

Lowell and Holmes looked at each other. "Perhaps she had not yet recognized us," Holmes whispered. Lowell agreed.

She tried her best to explain her wonderment: explained how she read Longfellow's poetry before going to sleep each night; how when her husband was bedridden from the war she would recite *Evangeline* aloud to him; and how the gently palpitating rhythms, the legend of faithful but uncompleted love, would soothe him even in his sleep—even now sometimes, she said sadly. She knew every word of "A Psalm of Life," and had taught her husband to read it as well; and whenever he left home, those verses were her only release from fear. But mostly her explanation came out as a repetition of the question "*Why*, Mr. Longfellow . . ." she pleaded again and again before giving in to heaving sobs.

Longfellow said softly, "Mrs. Galvin, we are in dire need of help that only you can provide. We must find your husband."

"These men seem to wish him harm," she said, meaning Lowell and Holmes. "I don't understand. Why would you . . . Why, Mr. Longfellow, how could *you* know Benjamin at all?"

"We haven't time to explain satisfactorily, I'm afraid," Longfellow said.

For the first time, she looked away from the poet. "Well, I don't know where he is, and I am ashamed for that. He hardly comes home anymore, and when he does, barely speaks. He's away days at a time."

"When was the last time you saw him?" Fields asked.

"He had been here briefly today, a few hours before you."

Fields pulled out his watch. "Where was he going from here?"

"He used to take care of me. I am a mere ghost to him now."

"Mrs. Galvin, this is a matter of . . ." Fields began.

Another knock. She dabbed her eyes with her handkerchief and smoothed her dress. "Surely another creditor come here to vex me."

As she passed into the hall, the group leaned toward one another with furious whispers.

Lowell said, "He's been gone a few hours, did you hear! And he's not at the Corner, we know that—there's no doubt what he'll do if we don't find him!"

"He could be anywhere in the city, though, Jamey!" Holmes replied. "And we still must return to the Corner to wait for Rey. What can we do on our own?"

"Something! Longfellow?" Lowell said.

"We haven't even a horse to travel with now . . ." Fields complained.

Lowell's attention snapped as he heard something from the front hall.

Longfellow studied him. "Lowell?"

"Lowell, are you listening?" Fields asked.

A barrage of words escaped from the front door.

"That voice," Lowell said, stunned. "That voice! *Listen!*"

"Teal?" Fields demanded. "She may be warning him to run, Lowell! We'll never find him!"

Lowell sprang into motion. He charged through the hall to the doorway, where a man's weary bloodshot glare awaited. The poet lunged forward with a cry of capture.

XVIII

LOWELL ENFOLDED THE MAN in his arms and dragged him into the house. "I have him!" Lowell cried. "I have him!"

"What are you doing?" Pietro Bachi screamed.

"Bachi! What are you doing here?" Longfellow said.

"How did you find me here? Tell your dog to take his hands from me, Signor Longfellow, or I shall see what manner of man he is!" Bachi snarled, jabbing his elbows futilely into his sturdy captor.

"Lowell," Longfellow said. "Let us speak with Signor Bachi privately." They ushered him into another room, where Lowell demanded that Bachi tell them his business.

"It is not with you," Bachi said. "I am going back to speak with the woman."

"Please, Signor Bachi," Longfellow said, shaking his head. "Dr. Holmes and Mr. Fields presently are asking her some questions."

Lowell continued, "What kind of plan have you concocted with Teal? Where is he? Don't play the deuce with me. You come back like a bad shilling whenever there's trouble."

Bachi pulled a sour face. "Who is Teal? I am the one who is owed answers for this sort of handling!"

"If he does not satisfy me at once, I shall carry him directly to the police and tell them everything!" Lowell said. "Haven't I known he was pulling the wool over our eyes all along, Longfellow?"

"Ha! Bring the police, do!" said Bachi. "They can help me collect! You wish to know my business? I've come for payment from that deadbeat rag in there." His thick Adam's apple rolled with the shame of his purpose. "Aye, you might guess I'm growing not a *little* tired of this tutoring line."

"Tutoring. You gave her lessons? In Italian?" Lowell asked.

"The husband," answered Bachi. "Only three sessions, some weeks ago—gratis, as far as he seems to think."

"But you returned to Italy!" Lowell said.

Bachi laughed wistfully. "If only, signore! The closest I have come was to see off my brother, Giuseppe. I am afraid I have, shall we say, adversarial parties that make my own return impossible, for many moons at least."

"You saw your brother off! What cheek!" Lowell exclaimed. "You were in a mad rush on a boat and were going to meet the steamer! And you were armed with a satchel full of bogus money—we saw it!"

"Now, see here!" Bachi said indignantly. "How could you know where I was that day?"

"Answer me!"

Bachi pointed accusingly at Lowell but then realized by the imprecision of his extended finger that he was queasy and rather drunk.

He felt a wave of nausea travel up his throat. He caught it and choked it back inside, then covered his mouth and belched. When he was able to speak again, his breath was noxious, but he was tamer. "I met the steamer, yes. But not with any money—queer or otherwise. I wish to Jove I had a bag of gold dropped on my head, *Professore.* I was there that day to give my manuscript to my brother, Giuseppe Bachi, who had agreed to escort it to Italy."

"Your manuscript?" asked Longfellow.

"A translation into English. Of Dante's *Inferno,* if you must know. I heard about your labor, Signor Longfellow, and of your precious Dante Club, and at that I must laugh! In this Yankee Athens, you men speak of creating a national voice for yourselves. You plead with your countrymen to revolt against the British command of libraries. But did you ever think I, Pietro Bachi, might well have something to contribute to your work? That as a son of Italy, as one who has been born of its history, its dissensions, its struggles against the heavy thumb of the Church, there might be something inimitable in my love for the liberty sought by Dante?" Bachi paused. "No, no. You never asked me to Craigie House. Was it the malicious talk of my being a drunkard? Was it my disgrace from the College? What freedom here in America? You happily send us away to your factories, your wars, to waste into oblivion. You watch our culture trampled, our languages squelched, your dress become ours. Then with smiling faces you rob our literature from our shelves. Pirates. Damned literary pirates, every one of you."

"We've seen more of Dante's heart than you can imagine," Lowell replied. "It is your people, your country that orphaned him, might I remind you!"

Longfellow motioned for Lowell to hold back, then said, "Signor Bachi, we observed you down at the harbor. Pray explain. Why were you sending this translation to Italy?"

"I had heard that Florence was planning to honor your version of *Inferno* in the year's final Dante Festival but that you had not yet finished your work and were in danger of missing the deadline. I had been translating Dante off and on for many years in my study, sometimes with the aid of old friends like Signor Lonza, when he was well enough. We thought, I suppose, that if we can show ourselves that Dante could be as alive in English as in Italian, we too could thrive in America. I had never considered seeing it published. But when poor Lonza died in the care of strangers, I knew nothing else but that our work must live. On the condition that I found a way to print it myself, my brother agreed to deliver my translation to a binder he knew in Rome and then take it to the Committee personally and plead our case. Well, I found a printer of gambling pamphlets and the like here in Boston to take the translation to press a week or so before Giuseppe was to leave—and for cheap. Wouldn't you know the idiot printer did not finish till the last minute, and probably wouldn't have finished at all had he not been in need of even my paltry coin. The rogue was in some sort of trouble for counterfeiting money for the use of local gamblers, and from what I understand, he was obliged to lock his doors in a hurry and lope.

"By the time I got to the piers, I had to beg some shady Charon at the wharf to row me out in a small boat to the *Anonimo.* After I dropped the manuscript aboard the steamer, I returned directly to shore. The whole matter amounted to nothing, you shall be happy to hear. The Committee was 'not at this time interested in further submissions to our festival.'" Bachi smirked at his own defeat.

"That's why the Committee chair sent you Dante's ashes!" Lowell turned to Longfellow. "To assure you that your translation's place in the festivities as the American representative would be secure!"

Longfellow thought for a moment and said, "The difficulties of Dante's text are so great that two or three independent renderings of it will be most acceptable to interested readers, my dear signore."

Bachi's hard face cracked. "Do understand. I have always held dear the trust that you showed by hiring me at the College, and I do not question the value of your poetry. If I have done anything to shame myself because of my situation—" He stopped suddenly. After a pause, he continued: "Exile leaves none but the dampest hope. I thought perhaps—only perhaps—there was an opening for me to make Dante alive in a New World with my translation. Then how differently they would think of me in Italy!"

"You." Lowell accused him suddenly. "*You* cut that threat into Longfellow's window to put a scare into us so Longfellow might stop the translation!"

Bachi flinched, pretending not to understand. He removed a black bottle from his coat and heaved it to his lips, as though his throat were just a funnel to somewhere far away. He trembled when he finished. "Do not think me a sot, *Professori.* I never drink more than is good for me, at least not in good company. The mischief is, what is a man to do all by himself in the dull hours of a New England winter?" His brow darkened. "Now. Are we through here? Or do you wish to fag me further over my disappointments?"

"Signore," said Longfellow. "We must know what you taught Mr. Galvin. He speaks and reads Italian now?"

Bachi threw his head back and laughed. "As little as you please! The man couldn't read English if Noah Webster were standing by his side! He always dressed in your American soldier's blue duds and gold buttons. He wanted Dante, Dante, Dante. It did not occur to him he must learn the language first. *Che stranezza!*"

"Did you lend him your translation?" Longfellow asked.

Bachi shook his head. "It was my hope to keep that enterprise entirely secret. I am sure we all know how your Mr. Fields reacts to any who try to rival his authors. In all events, I tried gratifying Signor Galvin's strange wishes. I suggested we conduct the introductory Italian lessons by reading the *Commedia* together, line by line. But it was like reading alongside a dumb beast. Then he wished me to give a *sermon* on Dante's Hell, but I refused on principle—if he wanted to engage me as a tutor, he must learn Italian."

"You told him you would not continue the lessons?" asked Lowell.

"That would have given me the greatest pleasure, *Professore.* But one day he stopped calling on me. I have not been able to find him since—and have still not been compensated."

"Signore," said Longfellow. "This is very important. Did Mr. Galvin ever speak of individuals in our own time, our own city, whom he envisioned in his understanding of Dante? You must consider whether he ever mentioned anyone at all. Perhaps persons connected in some way with the College who are interested in discrediting Dante."

Bachi shook his head. "He hardly spoke at all, Signor Longfellow, like a dumb ox. Is this something to do with the College's present campaign against your work?"

Lowell's attention perked up. "What do you know of it?"

"I warned you of it when you came to see me, signore," Bachi said. "I told you to take care of your Dante class, didn't I? Do you recall when you saw me on the College Yard some weeks before that? I had received a message to meet a gentleman for a confidential interview—oh, how convinced I was that the Harvard fellows wanted me to return to my post! Imagine my stupidity! In truth, that blasted rogue was on some assignment to prove Dante's *ill effects* on students, and wished me to assist."

"Simon Camp," Lowell said through clenched teeth.

"I almost punched his face in, I can tell you," Bachi reported.

"I wish to God you had, Signor Bachi," Lowell said, sharing a smile with him. "He yet may prove the ruin of Dante through all this. What did you reply to him?"

"How was I to respond? 'Go to the Devil' was all I could think to say. Here I am, barely able to buy my bread after so many years with the College, and who in the administration hires *that* jackass?"

Lowell snickered. "Who *else*? It was Dr. Mann—" He stopped suddenly and whirled around with a significant glance at Longfellow. "Dr. Manning."

Caroline Manning swept up broken glass. "Jane—mop!" She called out to the maid for the second time, sulking at the pool of sherry drying on the rug of her husband's library.

As Mrs. Manning made her way out of the room, a ring sounded at the door. She pulled back the curtain just an inch to see Henry Wadsworth Longfellow. Now, where was he coming from at this hour? She could hardly look at the poor man these last years the few times she saw him around Cambridge. She did not know how one could live through so much. How undefeatable he seemed. And here she was with a dustpan, looking positively like a housekeeper.

Mrs. Manning apologized: Dr. Manning was not at home. She explained that he had earlier been expecting a guest and had wished privacy. He and his guest must have gone for a walk, though she found this a bit queer in such ghastly weather. And they had left some broken glass in the library. "But you know how men *drink* sometimes," she added.

"Could they have taken the carriage out?" Longfellow asked.

Mrs. Manning said that the horse distemper would have precluded that: Dr. Manning had strictly forbidden even the brief removal of their horses. But she agreed to walk Longfellow to the barn.

"For Heaven's sake," she said when they found no trace of Dr. Manning's coach and horses. "Something is the matter, isn't it, Mr. Longfellow? For Heaven's sake," she repeated.

Longfellow did not answer.

"Has something happened to him? You must tell me at once!"

Longfellow's words came slowly. "You must remain at your house to wait. He'll return safely, Mrs. Manning. I promise." The Cambridge winds had grown blustery and painful to the skin.

"Dr. Manning," Fields said with his eyes downcast on Longfellow's rug twenty minutes later. After leaving the Galvin house, they had found Nicholas Rey, who had secured a police carriage and a healthy horse, which he used to drive them to Craigie House. "He has been our worst adversary from the beginning. Why didn't Teal take him long before this?"

Holmes stood leaning on Longfellow's desk. "*Because* he is the worst, my dear Fields. As Hell deepens, narrows, the sinners become more flagrant, more culpable—less repentant for what they have done. Until reaching Lucifer, who initiated all evil in the world. Healey, as the first to be punished, would have been hardly cognizant of his refusal at all—that is the nature of his 'sin,' which rests upon a lukewarm act."

Patrolman Rey stood tall in the center of the study. "Gentlemen, you must review the sermons given by Mr. Greene in the last week so we can discern where Teal would take Manning."

"Greene started this series of sermons with the Hypocrites," explained Lowell. "Then he went on to the Falsifiers, including Counterfeiters. Finally, in the sermon witnessed by me and Fields, he went to the Traitors."

Holmes said, "Manning was no Hypocrite—he was after Dante inside and out. And Traitors against Family have no bearing on this."

"Then we are left with the Falsifiers and the Traitors against One's Nation," said Longfellow.

"Manning did not engage in any real trickery," Lowell said. "He concealed from us his activities, true, but this was not his primary mode of aggression. Many of the shades in Dante's Hell have been guilty of cartloads of sins, but it is the sin that defines their actions which determines their fate in Hell. The Falsifiers must change one form to another to incur their *contrapasso*—like Sinon the Greek, who tricked the Trojans into welcoming the wooden horse."

"The Traitors against Nation undermine the good of one's people," Longfellow said. "We find them in the ninth circle—the lowest."

"Fighting our Dante projects, in this case," said Fields.

Holmes considered this. "That's it, isn't it? We've learned that Teal dresses in his uniform when involved in his Dantesque mode, whether he is studying Dante or preparing his murders. This shines light into the landscape of his mind: In his sickness, he swaps guarding the Union with guarding Dante."

Longfellow said, "And Teal would have witnessed Manning's schemes from his caretaker post in University Hall. For Teal, Manning is among the worst betrayers of the cause he now sets himself at war to protect. Teal has saved Manning for the end."

Nicholas Rey said, "What would be the punishment we'd be looking for?"

They all waited for Longfellow to answer. "The Traitors are placed wholly in ice, from the neck down, in 'a lake, that from the frost the semblance had of glass, and not of water.' "

Holmes groaned. "Every puddle in New England has frozen over in the last two weeks. Manning could be anywhere, and we have but one tired horse with which to search!"

Rey shook his head. "You gentlemen remain here in Cambridge and look for Teal and Manning. I shall drive to Boston to find help."

"What shall we do if we see Teal?" Holmes asked.

"Use this." Rey handed them his police rattle.

The four scholars began their patrol of the deserted banks of the Charles River, of Beaver Creek, near Elmwood, and of Fresh Pond. Looking out by the weak halos of gas lanterns, they were at such high mental alert that they barely noticed how indifferently the night passed without granting them the slightest advance. They wrapped themselves in multiple coats, not marking the frost collecting on their beards (or in Dr. Holmes's case, on his dense eyebrows and sideburns). How strange and silent the world seemed without the occasional clap of a horse's trot. It was a silence that seemed to stretch all the way across the North, interrupted only by the rude belches of bulging locomotives in the distance constantly transporting wares from one stop to the next.

Each Dantean imagined in great detail how at that *very moment* in time Patrolman Rey pursued Dan Teal through Boston, apprehending and shackling him in the name of the Commonwealth, how Teal would explain himself, rage, justify, but yield peaceably to justice, Iago-like never to speak of his acts again. They passed each other several times, Longfellow and Holmes and Lowell and Fields, offering encouragement as they circled the frozen waterways.

They began to talk—Dr. Holmes first, of course. But the others also comforted themselves with the exchange of hushed tones. They spoke about writing memorial verses, about new books, about political doings they had not been attuned to as of late; Holmes retold the story of the early years of his medical practice, when he had hung out a sign—THE SMALLEST FEVERS GRATEFULLY RECEIVED—before his window was smashed by drunkards.

"I've talked too much, haven't I?" Holmes shook his head in self-admonishment. "Longfellow, I wish I could make you talk more about yourself."

"No," Longfellow replied thoughtfully. "I believe I never do."

"I know you never do! But you confessed to me once." Holmes thought twice. "When you first met Fanny."

"No, I don't think I ever did."

They traded partners several times as though they were dancing; they traded conversations, too. Sometimes all four walked together and it seemed that their weight would crack the frozen earth below. Always they walked arm in arm, bracing each other.

It was a clear night, at least. The stars sat fixed in perfect order. They heard the hoof taps of the horse conveying Nicholas Rey, who was shrouded by the steam of the animal's breath. Each silently envisioned the sight of unrestrained achievement in the young man's striking countenance as he approached, but his face was steeled. No sightings of Teal or Augustus Manning, he reported. He had recruited a half-dozen other patrolmen to comb the length of the Charles River, but only four other horses could be secured from quarantine. Rey rode away with admonitions of care to the Fireside Poets, promising to continue his search into the morning.

Which of them suggested, at half-past three, to rest for a spell at Lowell's house? They spread out, two in the music room and two in the adjoining study, the rooms mirroring each other in their layout and with back-to-back hearths. Fanny Lowell was drawn downstairs by the puppy's anxious barks. She made tea for them, but Lowell explained nothing to her and only mumbled about the blasted distemper. She had been worried sick over his absence. That made them finally realize how late it was, and Lowell dispatched William, the hired man, to deliver messages to the others' houses. They settled on a thirty-minute lull at Elmwood—no longer—and drifted off at the two firesides.

At the hour of a motionless world, the warmth fell squarely on the side of Holmes's face. His entire body was so deeply fatigued that he hardly noticed when he found himself pulled to his feet again to tread softly along a narrow fence outside. The ice on the ground had begun to thaw rapidly with a sudden rise in temperature, and slush clotted the streams of water. The ground under his boots was set at a steep incline, and he felt himself crouch forward as though going uphill. He looked out on the Cambridge Common, where he could make out the Revolutionary War cannons coughing out billows of smoke and the massive Washington Elm that, with its thousand-branched fingertips reached in all directions. Holmes looked back and could see Longfellow gliding slowly toward him. Holmes motioned for him to hurry. He did not like Longfellow to be alone for too long. But a rumble drew the doctor's attention.

Two strawberry-specked horses with albino hooves were storming toward him, both hauling rickety wagons. Holmes cringed, falling to his knees; he gripped his ankles and looked up in time to see Fanny Longfellow—fiery blossoms flying from her loose hair and her wide bosom—at the reins of one of the horses, and Junior in secure control of the other, as though he had been riding from the day he was born. When the figures swept by either side of the little doctor, it did not seem possible to keep his balance, and he slipped into darkness.

• • •

Holmes pushed off from the armchair and stood up, his knees inches from the grate of the crackling wood fire. He looked up. The chandelier drops were rattling overhead. "What hour is it?" he asked when he realized he had been dreaming. Lowell's clock answered: fifteen minutes till six. Lowell, eyes peering open like a groggy child's, stirred in his easy chair. He asked if something was the matter. The bitterness inside his mouth made it difficult to pry open.

"Lowell, Lowell," Holmes said, pulling back all the curtains. "A pair of horses."

"What?"

"I think I heard a pair of horses outside. No, I'm fairly sure of it. They raced by your window only seconds ago, near as you please and speeding along. It was definitely two horses. Patrolman Rey has only one horse at present. Longfellow said that Teal stole two from Manning."

"We fell asleep," Lowell responded with alarm, blinking himself to life, seeing through the windows the light that had begun to break.

Lowell roused Longfellow and Fields, and then snatched his spyglass and flung his rifle over his shoulder. As they reached the door, Lowell saw Mabel, wrapped in her dressing gown, come into the front hall. He paused, expecting a reprimand, but she merely stood with a remote stare. Lowell reversed his course and embraced her hard. When he heard himself whisper "Thank you," she had already called out the same words.

"Now, you must be careful, Father. For Mother and for me."

Moving from the warmth into the frigid air outside brought on Holmes's asthma full force. Lowell ran ahead, following fresh hoof marks, as the other three maneuvered circumspectly through the stripped elms that reached naked branches for the heavens.

"Longfellow, my dear Longfellow . . ." Holmes was saying.

"Holmes?" the poet answered kindly.

Holmes could still see vividly dreamt fragments before his eyes, and he trembled to look at his friend. He was frightened that he might blurt out: *I just saw Fanny come for us, I did!* "We forgot the police rattle at your house, didn't we?"

Fields put a reassuring hand on the doctor's small shoulder. "An ounce of pluck just now is worth a king's ransom, my dear Wendell."

Up ahead, Lowell dropped to one knee. He scanned the pond ahead of them with his glass. His lips were trembling with fear. At first he thought he saw some boys ice fishing. But then, as he turned the spyglass, he could see the sallow face of his student Pliny Mead: only his face.

Mead's head was visible from a narrow opening cut into the lake of ice. The rest of his naked body was concealed by the ice water, under which his feet were bound. His teeth chattered violently. His tongue was curled up in the back of his mouth. Mead's bare arms were stretched forward on the ice and bound tightly by some rope, which extended from his wrists to Dr. Manning's carriage, which was hitched nearby. Mead, half-conscious, would have slipped down the hole to his death if not for this bondage. At the back of the parked carriage, Dan Teal, shiny in his military uniform, dipped his arms underneath another nude figure, lifted it, and started to walk over the treacherous ice. He carried the flaccid, white body of Augustus Manning, his beard hovering unnaturally over his sprout-thin chest, his legs and hips bound by rope, his body quivering as Teal crossed the slick pond.

Manning's nose was a dark ruby; a thick layer of dried brown blood had gathered beneath it. Teal slipped Manning feet first into another aperture in the frozen lake, about a foot away from Mead's. The shock of the freezing water pounded Manning to life; he splashed and groped madly. Teal now untied Pliny Mead's arms, so the only force that could possibly prevent the two naked men from sliding into their respective holes was a furious attempt, instinctually comprehended and instantaneously begun by both, to grasp each other's outstretched hands.

Teal stepped onto the embankment to watch them struggle, and then a gunshot rang out. It cracked the bark of a tree behind the murderer.

Lowell charged ahead, gripping his weapon and sliding wildly across the ice. "Teal!" he shouted. His rifle was poised for another shot. Longfellow, Holmes, and Fields all scrambled behind him.

Fields yelled, "Mr. Teal, you must stop this!"

Lowell could not believe what he saw over the barrel of his gun. Teal was remaining perfectly still.

"Shoot, Lowell, shoot!" Fields yelled.

Lowell always liked to take aim on hunting trips but never to fire. The sun now rose to a perfect height, unfurling over the vast crystalline surface.

For a moment the men were blinded by the reflection. By the time their eyes adjusted, Teal had vanished, the soft sounds of his running echoing in the woods. Lowell fired into the thicket.

Pliny Mead, shivering uncontrollably, went entirely limp, his head drooping against the ice and his body slowly sinking into the deadly water. Manning struggled to maintain a grip on the boy's slick arms, then his wrists, then his fingers, but the weight was too much. Mead sank down into the water. Dr. Holmes dived, sliding across the ice. He plunged both arms into the hole, catching Mead by the hair and ears, and pulling, pulling until he grabbed hold of his chest, and then pulling some more until he lay on top of the ice. Fields and Longfellow heaved Manning by the arms, sliding him to the surface before he could fall under. They untied his legs and feet.

Holmes heard the crack of a whip and looked up to see Lowell on the driver's box of the abandoned carriage. He urged the horses into the woods. Holmes jumped up and ran toward him. "Jamey, no!" Holmes cried. "We must get them into the warmth or they'll die!"

"Teal will escape, Holmes!" Lowell stopped the horses and stared at the pathetic figure of Augustus Manning, clumsily thrashing on the frozen pond like a fish yanked from water. Here was Dr. Manning nearly undone and Lowell could make himself feel nothing but sympathy. The ice bent under the weight of the Dante Club members and the would-be murder victims, and water bubbled up through new holes as they walked. Lowell bounded down from the carriage just as one of Longfellow's overshoes crashed through a weak strip of ice. Lowell was there to catch him.

Dr. Holmes stripped off his gloves and hat, then his overcoat and frock coat, and began piling them over Pliny Mead. "Wrap them up in everything you have! Cover their heads and necks!" He ripped off his cravat and tied it around the boy's neck. Then he kicked off his boots and his socks, slipping them onto Mead's feet. The others watched Holmes's dancing hands carefully and imitated him.

Manning tried to speak, but what emerged was a slurred humming, a faint song. He tried to raise his head from the ice but was entirely confused as Lowell forced his hat onto him.

Dr. Holmes shouted, "Make sure to keep them awake! If they fall asleep, we'll lose them!"

With difficulty, they carried the frigid bodies into the carriage. Lowell, stripped down to his shirtsleeves, returned to the driver's box. As instructed by Holmes, Longfellow and Fields rubbed the victims' necks and shoulders and raised their feet for circulation.

"Hurry, Lowell, hurry!" Holmes called out.

"We're moving as fast as we can manage, Wendell!"

Holmes had known at once that Mead had the worst of it. A terrible gash at the back of his head, presumably left there by Teal, was an ill ingredient to mix with the deadly exposure. He frantically jolted the boy's blood circulation on the short ride back to town. In spite of himself, Holmes heard echoing in his mind his poem he recited to his students to remind them how to treat their patients.

If the poor victim must be percussed,
Don't make an anvil of his aching bust;
(Doctors exist within a hundred miles
Who thump a thorax as they'd hammer piles;)
So of your questions: don't in mercy try
To pump your patient absolutely dry;
He's not a mollusk squirming on a dish,
You're not Agassiz, and he's not a fish.

Mead's body was so cold that it hurt him to touch it.

※

"The boy was lost before we arrived at Fresh Pond. There was no way to do more. You must believe that, my dear Holmes."

Dr. Holmes was sliding Longfellow's Tennyson inkwell back and forth between his fingers, ignoring Fields, his fingertips blackening with ink spots.

"And Augustus Manning owes you his life," said Lowell. "And me my hat," he added. "In all seriousness, Wendell, the man would be returned to the dust without you. Don't you see? We've thwarted Lucifer. We've plucked a man from the jaws of the Devil. We've *won* this time because you gave yourself completely, my dear Wendell."

The three Longfellow girls, dressed elaborately for outdoor play, knocked at the study door.

Alice was the first inside. "Papa, Trudy and all the other girls are sledding on the hill. Can't we go?"

Longfellow looked to his friends, who were fixed in armchairs all around the room. Fields shrugged.

"Other children will be there?" Longfellow asked.

"All of Cambridge!" announced Edith.

"Very well," said Longfellow, but then studied them as he was overcome with second thoughts. "Annie Allegra, perhaps you'll stay here with Miss Davie."

"Oh please, Papa! I have my new shoes to wear!" Annie kicked up her evidence.

"My dear Panzie," he said, smiling. "I promise just this once." The other two skipped out, and the little girl went into the hall to find her governess.

Nicholas Rey arrived in full-dress army uniform, with a blue coat and tunic. He reported that nothing had been found. But Sergeant Stoneweather had now raised several squads of men to search for Benjamin Galvin. "The board of health announced that the worst of the distemper has passed and is releasing several dozen horses from quarantine."

"Excellent! Then we'll get a team and start searching," said Lowell.

"Professor, gentlemen," Rey said as he sat down. "You men have discovered the identity of the murderer. You saved a life, and perhaps others we will never know."

"Only, it was because of us that they were in danger in the first place." Longfellow sighed.

"No, Mr. Longfellow. What Benjamin Galvin found in Dante he would have found elsewhere in his life. You have called down none of these horrors. But what you have accomplished in their shadow is undeniable. Still, you are fortunate to be safe after all this. You must let the police finish this now, for everyone's safety."

Holmes asked Rey why he was wearing his army uniform.

"Governor Andrew is holding another of his soldiers' banquets today at the State House. Clearly, Galvin has continued to wed himself to his service in the army. He might well appear."

"Officer, we don't know how he'll answer to having been stopped from this last murder," said Fields. "What if he tries again to enact the punishment of the Traitors? What if he returns to Manning?"

"We have patrolmen guarding the houses of all members of the Harvard Corporation and the overseers, including Dr. Manning. We're also stopping at every hotel for Simon Camp in case Galvin targets him as another Traitor against Dante. We have several men in Galvin's neighborhood, and we're watching his house closely."

Lowell walked to the window and looked down Longfellow's front walkway, where he saw a man in a heavy blue overcoat pass the gate and then return from the other direction. "You've a man here, too?" Lowell asked.

Rey nodded. "At each of your houses. From his choice of victims, it seems that Galvin believes himself to be your guardian. So he may think to consort with you about what to do after such a rapid turn of events. If he does, we'll take him in."

Lowell pitched his cigar to the fire. Suddenly his self-indulgence disgusted him. "Officer, I think this is a shabby piece of business. We can't just sit in this same room helplessly all day!"

"I don't suggest that you do, Professor Lowell," Rey replied. "Return to your own houses, spend time with your families. The duty of protecting this city is on me, gentlemen, but your presence is strongly missed elsewhere. Your life must begin to return to normal from this point on, Professor."

Lowell looked up, stunned. "But . . ."

Longfellow smiled. "A great part of the happiness of life consists not in fighting battles, my dear Lowell, but in avoiding them. A masterly retreat is in itself a victory."

Rey said, "Let us all meet here again this evening. With a little good fortune, I shall have happy tidings to report. Fair enough?"

The scholars conceded with mixed expressions of regret and great relief.

Patrolman Rey continued recruiting officers that afternoon; many of them had silently avoided Rey's path in the past out of prudence. But he had known who they were from afar. He knew instantly when a man looked at him simply as another man and not as a black or mulatto or nigger. His straight gaze into their eyes necessitated little additional persuasion.

He posted a patrolman at the front gardens of Dr. Manning's house. As Rey was speaking with the patrolman under a maple tree, Augustus Manning charged out from his side door.

"Yield!" Manning shouted, showing a pistol.

Rey turned. "We're police—police, Dr. Manning."

Manning shivered as though still locked in the ice. "I saw your army uniform through my window, Officer. I thought that madman . . ."

"You needn't worry," said Rey.

"You'll . . . you'll protect me?" Manning asked.

"Until it is no longer needed," said Rey. "This officer shall watch over your house. Well-armed."

The other patrolman unbuttoned his coat and showed his revolver.

Manning offered a frail nod of acceptance and extended his arm hesitantly, allowing the mulatto policeman to escort him inside.

Afterward, Rey drove his carriage to the Cambridge Bridge. He came into sight of a stopped coach blocking the way. Two men were hunched over one of the wheels. Rey steered to the side of the road and stepped down, walking to the stranded party to help. But as he reached them, the two men rose to their full height. Rey heard noises behind him and turned to see that another carriage had pulled behind his own. Two men in flowing overcoats emerged onto the street. The four men stood in a square around the mulatto policeman and remained motionless for nearly two minutes.

"Detectives. May I be of some help?" Rey asked.

"We thought we'd have a word with you at the station house, Rey," one of them said.

"I'm afraid I haven't time just now," Rey said.

"It's been brought to our attention that you're looking into a matter without proper authorization, sir," another said as he stepped forward.

"I don't believe that's your province, Detective Henshaw," said Rey after a pause.

The detective rubbed two fingers together. A detective moved closer to Rey menacingly.

Rey turned to him. "I am an officer of the law. If you strike me, you strike the Commonwealth."

The detective landed a fist in Rey's abdomen and then crashed another into his jaw. Rey doubled over, nestled in his coat collar. Blood spilled from his mouth as they dragged him into the back of their carriage.

Dr. Holmes sat in his big leather rocker, waiting to leave for their appointed meeting at Longfellow's. A partially opened blind threw a dim, religious light onto the table. Wendell Junior was rushing up to the second floor.

"Wendy, my boy," Holmes called after him. "Where are you going?"

Junior slowly backtracked down the stairs. "How are you, Father? Didn't see you."

"Can't you sit for a minute or two?"

Junior perched on the edge of a green rocker.

Dr. Holmes asked about law school. Junior answered perfunctorily, waiting for the usual barb about the law, but none came. He could never get under the skin of the law, Dr. Holmes said of himself, when he gave it a try after college. The second edition improves on the first, he supposed.

The calm clock dial counted out their silence in long seconds.

"You were never frightened, Wendy?" Dr. Holmes said into the silence. "In the war, I mean."

Junior peered at his father from under his dark brow, and grinned warmly. "It's rank folly, Dadkins, pulling a long mug every time one might fight or be killed. There's no poetry in a fight."

Dr. Holmes excused his son to go to his work. Junior nodded and resumed his trip upstairs.

Holmes had to be on his way to meet the others. He decided to take his grandfather's flintlock musket, which had last been used in the Revolutionary War. This was the only weapon Holmes allowed in his house, storing it as a piece of history in his basement.

The horsecars were still shut down. Drivers and conductors had tried to pull the cars by hand without success. The Metropolitan Railroad also attempted to use oxen to pull the cars, but their feet were too tender for the hard pavement. So Holmes traveled by foot, walking through the crooked streets of Beacon Hill, missing by only a few seconds Fields's carriage as the publisher drove to Holmes's house to see if he wanted a ride. The doctor took the West Bridge over the partially frozen Charles, through Gallows Hill. It was so cold that people were clapping their hands to their ears and hoisting their shoulders and running. Holmes's asthma made the walk feel twice as long as it was. He found himself passing the First Meeting House, the old Cambridge church of the Reverend Abiel Holmes. He slipped into the empty chapel and had a seat. The pews were the usual oblong ones, with a ledge before the parishioners to support hymn books. There was a lavish organ, something the Reverend Holmes never would have allowed.

Holmes's father had lost the church during a split in his congregation with members who wished to have Unitarian ministers as occasional guest preachers at their pulpit. The reverend had refused, and the small number of his remaining faithful moved with him to a new meetinghouse. The Unitarian chapels were all the fashion in those days, for there was shelter under the "new religion" from the doctrines of inborn sin and human helplessness propounded by Reverend Holmes and his more fire-eating brethren. It was in one of those churches that Dr. Holmes, too, had left behind his father's beliefs and found yet another kind of shelter, in reasoned religion rather than fear of God.

There was also shelter beneath the floorboards, thought Holmes, when the abolitionists were mixed in—at least, that was what Holmes had heard: Under many Unitarian chapels they dug tunnels to hide runaway Negroes when Chief Justice Healey's court upheld the Fugitive Slave Act and forced escaped Negroes into hiding. What would the Reverend Abiel Holmes have thought of that . . .

Holmes had returned to his father's old meetinghouse every summer for the Harvard commencement, where the ceremony was held. Wendell Junior, in the year of his college graduation, as class poet. Mrs. Holmes had cautioned Dr. Holmes not to add to the pressure on Junior by advising him or critiquing his poem. As Junior took his place, Dr. Holmes sat in the meetinghouse, the chapel that had been stripped away from his father, an unsteady smile fixed on his face. All eyes were on him, to see his reaction to his son's poem, written by Junior while he was drilling for the war his company would soon join. *Cedat armis toga,* thought Holmes—let the scholar's gown give way to the soldier's arms. Oliver Wendell Holmes, wheezing with nervousness as he watched Oliver Wendell Holmes Junior, wished that he might dive down into those fairy-tale tunnels supposedly running under the churches, for what use were those rabbit holes now that the Secesh traitors would be shown what to do with their slavery laws with bayonet and Enfield?

Holmes shot to attention in the empty pew. Why, the tunnels! That was how Lucifer had eluded all detection, even when the police had been out in full force! That was why the prostitute saw Teal disappear in the fog near a church! That was why the jittery sexton of Talbot's church had not seen the killer enter or leave! A chorus of hallelujahs lit up Dr. Holmes's soul. Lucifer does not walk or ride the cars while dragging Boston into Hell, Holmes cried to himself. He burrows!

※

Lowell anxiously departed Elmwood for their Craigie House rendezvous and was the first to greet Longfellow. Lowell did not notice, on the way, that the police guards in front of Elmwood and Craigie House were nowhere to be seen. Longfellow was just finishing reading a story to Annie Allegra. He excused her to the nursery.

Fields arrived soon after.

But twenty minutes passed without word of Oliver Wendell Holmes or Nicholas Rey.

"We shouldn't have left Rey's side," Lowell muttered into his mustache.

"I can't understand why Wendell wouldn't have come by now," said Fields nervously. "I stopped at his house on my way, and Mrs. Holmes said he had already departed."

"It hasn't been very long," said Longfellow, but his eyes did not move from his clock.

Lowell dropped his face into his hands. When he peered out between them, another ten minutes were gone. When he closed himself in again, he was suddenly hit by a chilling thought. He rushed to the window. "We must find Wendell at once!"

"What's wrong?" asked Fields, alarmed at the look of horror on Lowell's face.

"It's Wendell," Lowell said, "I called him a traitor at the Corner!"

Fields smiled gently. "That is long forgotten, my dear Lowell."

Lowell grabbed his publisher's coat sleeve for balance. "Don't you see? I had my row with Wendell at the Corner the day Jennison was found shredded, the night Holmes walked out from our project. Teal, or rather Galvin, was just coming down the hall. He must have been listening in on us the whole time, just as he would have done at Harvard's board meetings! I chased Holmes into the hall from the Authors' Room to yell after him—don't you *remember* what I said? Can't you hear the words still? *I told Holmes he was betraying the Dante Club.* I said he was a traitor!"

"Brace yourself, please," said Fields.

"Greene preached to Teal, and Teal followed up with murders. I condemned Wendell as a traitor: Teal was the vigilant audience for my little sermon!" cried Lowell. "Oh, my dear friend, I've done him in. I've murdered Wendell!"

Lowell rushed into the front hall for his coat.

"He'll be here any moment, I'm sure," said Longfellow. "Please, Lowell, let us wait for Officer Rey at least."

"No, I'm going to find Wendell right now!"

"But where do you mean to find him? And you can't go alone," said Longfellow. "We'll come."

"I'll go with Lowell," Fields said, gathering up the police rattle left by Rey and shaking it to show that it worked well. "I'm sure everything's fine. Longfellow, will you wait here for Wendell? We'll send the patrol officer to fetch Rey at once."

Longfellow nodded.

"Come then, Fields! Now!" roared Lowell, on the verge of crying.

Fields tried to keep up with Lowell as he ran down the front walkway to Brattle Street. There was no sign of anyone.

"Now, where in the deuce is that patrolman?" Fields asked. "The street looks entirely empty . . ."

A rustling noise sounded in the trees behind Longfellow's high fence. Lowell put a finger to his lips to signal Fields for quiet and crept closer to the sound, where he waited frozen in suspense.

A cat sprang into view at their feet and then raced off, dissolving into the darkness. Lowell let out a sigh of relief, but just then a man came hurtling down over the fence and struck a crashing blow to Lowell's head. Lowell collapsed all at once, like a sail whose mast had cracked in two; the poet's face was so inconceivably motionless on the ground as to be almost unrecognizable to Fields.

The publisher backed away, then looked up and met the gaze of Dan Teal. They moved in tandem, Fields backward and Teal forward in a curiously gentle dance.

"Mr. Teal, please." Fields's knees bent inward.

Teal stared impassively.

The publisher tripped over a fallen branch, then turned and launched into a clumsy run. He puffed his way down Brattle, faltering as he went, trying to call out, to scream, but only producing a rough, hoarse caw lost in the frigid winds shrieking in his ears. He looked back, then he drew the police rattle from his pocket. There was no longer any sign of his pursuer. As Fields turned to look over his other shoulder, he felt his arm being grabbed, and he was flung hard through the air. His body went tumbling to the street, the rattle slipping into the bushes with a soft jingle, soft as a bird's chirp.

Fields stretched his neck toward Craigie House with excruciating stiffness. A warm gaslight glow escaped Longfellow's study windows, and Fields seemed instantly to know the whole purpose of his assassin.

"Only, don't hurt Longfellow, Teal. He's left Massachusetts today—you'll see. I vow to you on my honor," Fields blubbered like a child.

"Have I not always done my duty?" The soldier raised his bludgeon high over his head and struck.

※

Reverend Elisha Talbot's successor had completed some meetings with deacons at the Second Unitarian Church of Cambridge several hours before Dr. Oliver Wendell Holmes, armed with his ancient musket and a kerosene lantern he had secured from a pawnshop, stepped into the church and sneaked into the underground vault. Holmes had debated with himself whether to share his theory with the others, but decided to confirm it first for himself. If Talbot's underground vault was indeed connected to an abandoned fugitive-slave tunnel, this could lead the police right to the killer. It would also explain how Lucifer had entered the burial vault in advance, murdered Talbot, and fled without witnesses. Dr. Holmes's intuition had launched the Dante Club into its murder inquiries, although it required the urging of Lowell to follow through; why shouldn't he be the one to point them to an end?

Holmes descended into the vault and fondled the walls of the tomb for any sign of an opening into another tunnel or chamber. He did not find the passageway with his searching hands but with the toes of his boot, which by sheer accident kicked into a hollow gap. Holmes bent down to examine it and found a narrow space. His compact body fit snugly into the hollow, and he dragged his lantern in after him. After he had spent some time on hands and knees, the height of the tunnel increased and Holmes could stand up quite comfortably. He would return at once to proper ground, he decided. Oh how the others would smile at his discovery. How swiftly their adversary would now see defeat! But the sharp turns and slopes of the labyrinth left the little doctor disoriented. He rested a hand on the long forestock of his musket, to feel safe, and had begun to regain his inner compass when a voice scattered all his senses.

"Dr. Holmes," said Teal.

XIX

BENJAMIN GALVIN enlisted at Massachusetts's first call for soldiers. At twenty-four, he had already considered himself a soldier for some time, having helped conduct fugitive slaves through the city's network of shelters, sanctuaries, and tunnels during the years before war officially came upon them. He was also among those volunteers who escorted anti-slavery speakers in and out of Faneuil Hall and other lyceums, serving as one of the human shields against rock-hurling, brick-tossing mobs.

Galvin, admittedly, was not political in the manner of other young men. He could not read the heavy broadsides and newspapers on whether this or that political scalawag should be voted out or how this or that party or state legislature had cried secession or conciliation. But he understood the stump speakers who declared that an enslaved race must be made free and the guilty parties submitted to rightful punishment. And Benjamin Galvin understood simply enough, too, that he might not return home to his new wife: If he did not come back holding the Stars and Stripes, the recruiters promised, he'd come back wrapped in it. Galvin had never been photographed before, and the one picture taken upon enlistment disappointed him. His cap and trousers appearing ill-fitting; his eyes seeming unaccountably frightened.

The earth was hot and dry when Company C of the 10th Regiment was sent from Boston to Springfield to Camp Brightwood. Dust clouds crusted the soldiers' new blue uniforms so completely as to make them the same dull gray color of the enemy's. The colonel asked if Benjamin Galvin wished to be the company adjutant and record casualty lists. Galvin explained that he could write out his alphabet but could not write or read correctly; he had tried learning many times, but the letters and marks got tangled up in the wrong direction in his head and crashed and turned into each other on the page. The colonel was surprised. Illiteracy was not at all unusual among the recruits, but Private Galvin always seemed to be in such deep thought, taking in everything with such big, quiet eyes and a completely still expression, that some of the men had called him Possum.

When they were encamped in Virginia, the first excitement came when a soldier from their ranks was found in the woods one day, shot in the head and bayoneted, maggots filling his head and mouth like a swarm of bees settling on their hive. It was said that the Rebels had sent one of their blacks over to kill a Yank for amusement. Captain Kingsley, a friend of the dead soldier's, made Galvin and the men swear no sympathy when the day came to whip the Secesh. It seemed they would never have the chance to engage in the combat all men itched for.

Galvin, though he had worked outdoors most of his life, had never seen the sorts of creeping things that filled this part of the country. The company adjutant, who woke an hour before bugle each morning to comb his thick hair and record lists of the sick and the dead, would let no one kill one of these crawling creatures; he cared for them like children even though Galvin saw, with his own eyes, four men from another company die from the white worms that infested their wounds. This happened while Company C marched to the next camp—nearer, it was rumored, to a live battleground.

Galvin had never imagined that death could come so easily to people around him. At Fair Oaks, in a single burst of noise and smoke, six men would lie dead before him, their eyes still staring as though with interest in what would come for the rest. It was not the number of dead but the number of men who survived that day that was a great wonder to Galvin, as it did not seem possible, or even right, for a man to live through. The inconceivable number of dead bodies and dead horses were collected together like cordwood and burned. Every time Galvin closed his eyes to sleep after that, he could hear shouts and explosions inside his spinning head, and could permanently smell the odor of ruined flesh.

One evening, returning to his tent with a ravenous pang, Galvin found a portion of his hardtack missing from his sack. One of his tentmates said he had seen the company chaplain take it. Galvin did not believe such wickedness possible, for all of them had the same gnawing hunger and same empty stomach. But it was hard to blame a man. When the company was marching through pouring rain or blazing heat, the rations inevitably diminished to only crackers infested with weevils, and not nearly enough of them, either. Worse than anything, a soldier could not stop for a night without "skirmishing," stripping off his clothes and digging out the bugs and ticks. The adjutant, who seemed to know about these things, said the way the insects got on them was when they stood still, so they should keep moving ahead always, always moving.

Wriggling creatures also populated the drinking water, a result of dead horses and rotten meat sometimes piled up into fords by soldiers. From malaria to dysentery, all maladies were known as camp fever, and the surgeon could not distinguish between the sick and the pretenders, and so usually thought it best to assume one belonged with the latter. Galvin once vomited eight times in one day, bringing up nothing but blood the final time. Every few minutes while he was waiting for the surgeon, who put him on quinine and opium, the surgeons would throw an arm or leg out the window of the makeshift hospital.

When they were encamped, there was always disease, but at least there were also books. The assistant surgeon collected the ones that were sent to the boys from home to keep in his tent, and he acted as librarian. Some of the books had illustrations that Galvin liked to look at, other times the adjutant or one of Galvin's tentmates would read a story or poem aloud. Galvin found in the assistant surgeon's library a shiny blue-and-gold copy of Longfellow's poetry. Galvin could not read the name on the cover, but recognized the engraved portrait on the frontispiece from one of his wife's books. Harriet Galvin always said that each of Longfellow's books found a way to light and happiness for its characters when they were faced with hopeless paths, like Evangeline and her beau, separated in their new country only to find each other when he was dying of fever and she was a nurse. Galvin imagined that was him and Harriet, and it reassured him as he watched men drop all around him.

When Benjamin Galvin first came from his aunt's farm to help the abolitionists in Boston after hearing a traveling lyceum speaker, he was knocked out by two hollering Irishmen who were trying to break up the abolitionist meeting. One of the organizers took Galvin home to recover, and Harriet, a daughter of this organizer, fell in love with the poor boy. She had never met anyone, even among her father's friends, so simply certain of the rightness and wrongness of things without a corrupting concern for politics or influence. "Sometimes I think you love your mission more than you can love other people," she said while they were courting, but he was too forthright to think of what he did as a mission.

She was heartbroken to hear from Galvin how his parents had died of the black fever when he was young. She taught him to write his alphabet by making him copy it out on slates; he already knew how to write his name. The day he decided to volunteer to fight the war, they married. She promised to teach him enough to read a whole book on his own when he returned from the war. That was why, she said, he must come back *alive.* Galvin would crawl under his blanket, lying on his hard board, thinking of her steady, musical voice.

When shelling began, some of the men would laugh uncontrollably or shriek as they fired, their faces blackened by the powder from tearing open cartridges with their teeth. Others would load and fire without aiming, and Galvin thought these men truly insane. The deafening cannons thundered across the earth so terribly that rabbits fled their holes, their little bodies trembling with fright as they hopped across the dead men sprawled all over the ground, which steamed with blood.

Survivors rarely had strength left to dig sufficient graves for their comrades, resulting in entire landscapes of protruding knees and arms and the tops of heads. The first rain would uncover all of it. Galvin watched his tentmates scribble letters home telling of their battles, and he wondered how they could put to words what they had seen and heard and felt, for it was beyond all words he had ever heard. According to one soldier, the arrival of support lines for their last battle, which had massacred nearly a third of their company, had been called off on the orders of a general who wished to embarrass General Burnside in hopes of securing his removal. The general later received a promotion.

"Is it possible?" Private Galvin demanded of a sergeant from another company.

"Two mules and another soldier killed," Sergeant LeRoy chuckled gruffly to the still-green private.

The campaign would prove only second in horrors and human flesh to Napoleon's Russian campaign, the bookish adjutant warned Benjamin Galvin sagaciously.

He did not like to ask others to write letters on his behalf like some of the other illiterates or semiliterates, so when Galvin would find dead Rebel soldiers with letters on them he would send them to Harriet in Boston so she might hear of the war firsthand. He would write out his name at the bottom so she would know where the letter came from, and he included a local flower petal or a distinctive leaf. He did not want to bother even the men who liked to write. They were so tired all the time. They were all so tired. Galvin could often tell by the slowed expressions of some men's faces before a battle—almost as though they were still asleep—who would surely not see the next morning.

"If I could only get home the Union can go to Hell," Galvin heard one officer say.

Galvin did not notice the diminishing rations that angered so many, because much of the time now he could not taste or smell or even hear his own voice. With food no longer particularly satisfying, Galvin began a habit of chewing pebbles, then scraps of paper torn from the assistant surgeon's dwindling traveling library and from Rebel letters, to keep his mouth warm and occupied. The scraps got smaller and smaller, to conserve what he could find.

One of their men who grew too lame on a march was left at camp, and was brought in two days later, murdered for his wallet. Galvin told everyone that the war was worse than Napoleon's Russian campaign. He was dosed with morphine and castor oil for diarrhea and the doctor gave him powders that made him dizzy and frustrated. He was down to a single pair of drawers, and the traveling sutlers who sold them from wagons asked $2.50 for a pair worth thirty cents. The sutler said he would not lower the price but might raise it if Galvin waited too long. Galvin wanted to bash the sutler's skull inside his head, but he didn't. He asked the adjutant to write a letter to Harriet Galvin asking her to send two pairs of heavy wool drawers. It was the only letter that was ever written for him during the war.

Pickaxes were needed to remove bodies fixed to the ground with ice. When the heat came again, Company C found a stubble field of unburied black bodies. Galvin marveled at so many blacks in the blue uniform, but then he realized what he was seeing: The bodies had been left in the August sun for a full day and were burned black by the heat and crawling with vermin. Men were dead in every conceivable position, and horses beyond count, many of them seeming to kneel genteelly on all fours, as though they were waiting for a child to saddle them.

Soon after, Galvin heard that some generals were returning escaped slaves to their masters and chattering with the slave masters like they were meeting for cards. *Could this be?* The war made no sense at all if it was not fought to better the slaves. On one march, Galvin saw a dead Negro whose ears had been nailed to a tree as punishment for attempted escape. His master had left him naked, knowing well how the voracious mosquitoes and flies would intercede.

Galvin couldn't understand the protests raised by Union soldiers when Massachusetts formed a Negro regiment. One Illinois regiment they came upon was threatening to desert as a group if Lincoln freed one more slave.

At a Negro revival Galvin had seen during the first months of the war, he listened to a prayer blessing the soldiers passing through the town: "De good Lord take dese 'ere mourners and shake 'em over Hell, but don't lieff 'em go."

And they sang:

> *"The Devil's mad and I am glad—Glory Hallelujah!*
> *He's lost a soul he thought he had—Glory Hallelujah!"*

"The Negroes have helped us, spied for us. They need our help as well," Galvin said.

"I'd rather see the Union dead than won by niggers!" a lieutenant in Galvin's company shouted in his face.

More than once, Galvin had seen a soldier take hold of a Negro wench fleeing her master and whisk her off into the woods to roaring cheers.

Food was gone on both sides of the battle lines. One morning, three Rebel soldiers were caught scavenging for food in the woods near their encampment. They looked nearly starved, jowls hanging out. With them was a deserter from Galvin's ranks. Captain Kingsley ordered Private Galvin to shoot the deserter dead. Galvin felt as though he would vomit blood if he tried to speak. "Without the proper ceremonies, Captain?" he finally said.

"We're marching for battle, Private. There's no time for a trial and no time to hang him, so you'll shoot him here! Ready . . . aim . . . fire!"

Galvin had seen a punishment for a private who had refused such an order. It was called "bucking and gagging," having one's hands tied over his knees with one bayonet lodged between his arms and legs and another tied in his mouth. The deserter, gaunt and empty, did not look particularly perturbed. "Shoot me, then."

"Private, now!" ordered the Captain. "You want your punishment with them?"

Galvin shot the man dead at point-blank range. The others ran the limp body through a dozen or so times with the blades of their bayonets. The captain recoiled, an icy glow in his eyes, and ordered Galvin to shoot the three Rebel prisoners on the spot. When Galvin hesitated, Captain Kingsley yanked him to one side by the arm.

"You're always watching, aren't you, Possum? You're always watching everyone like you know better what to do in your heart than we do. Well, now you'll do just what I say. Now you will, by thunder." All his teeth were bared as he spoke.

The three Rebels were lined up. After "Ready, aim, fire," Galvin shot each of them, by turn, in the head with his Enfield rifle. He could feel as little emotion, as he did so, as he could smell, taste, or hear. That same week, Galvin saw four Union soldiers, including two from his own company, molesting two young girls they had taken from a local town. Galvin told his superiors and, as an example, the four men were tied to a cannon wheel and had their backs beaten with a whip. Because Galvin had been the one to inform on them, he had to employ the whip.

At the next battle, Galvin didn't feel like he was fighting for one side or another, against one side or another. He was just battling. The whole world was battling and raging against itself, and the noises never ceased. He could barely make out Rebel from Yank, in any case. He had brushed against some poison leaf the day before and by nightfall his eyes were almost completely shut; the men laughed at this because, while others had their eyes shot out and heads split open, Benjamin Galvin had fought like a tiger and didn't get a scratch. One soldier, who was later put in an asylum, threatened to kill Galvin that day, pointing his rifle at Galvin's breastbone and warning him that if he didn't stop chewing that damned paper, he'd shoot him dead right then.

After Galvin's first war wound, a bullet to the chest, he was sent to be a guard at Fort Warren off Boston Harbor, where Rebel prisoners were being kept, until he could fully recover. There, prisoners with money purchased nicer rooms and better food, regardless of their levels of culpability or of how many men they had killed unjustly.

Harriet begged Benjamin not to go back to war, but he knew the men needed him. When he anxiously rejoined Company C in Virginia, there had been so many openings in the regiment from death and desertion that he was commissioned a second lieutenant.

He understood from newer recruits that rich boys back home were paying three hundred dollars to exempt themselves from service. Galvin boiled over with anger. He felt heart-wrenchingly weak, and he did not sleep for more than a few minutes a night. But he had to move: to keep moving. During the next battle, he dropped among the dead bodies and fell asleep thinking of those rich boys. The Rebels, poking through the dead that night and finding him, picked him up and took him to Libby Prison in Richmond. They let all the privates go because they were not important, but Galvin was a second lieutenant, so he spent four months at Libby. Galvin remembered only blurry images and some sounds from his time as a prisoner of war. It was as though he continued to sleep and dream the whole time.

When he was released to Boston, Benjamin Galvin was mustered out with the rest of his regiment in a big ceremony on the State House steps. Their tattered company flag was folded and given to the governor. Only two hundred of the original one thousand were alive. Galvin could not understand how the war could be considered done. They had not come close to meeting their cause. Slaves were freed, but the enemy had not changed its ways—had not been punished. Galvin was not political, but he knew that the blacks would have no peace in the South, slavery or no slavery, and he knew also what those who had not fought the war did not know: that the enemy was all around them at all times and had not surrendered at all. And never, never for a moment had the enemy been only the Southerners.

Galvin felt he now spoke in a different language that civilians could not understand. They could not even hear. Only fellow soldiers, who had been blasted by cannon and shell, had that capacity. In Boston, Galvin began to travel in bands with them. They looked haggard and exhausted, like the groups of stragglers they had seen in the woods. But these veterans, many of whom had lost jobs and families and talked about how they should have died in the war—at least their wives would get a pension—were on the prowl for money or pretty girls, and to get drunk and to raise Pluto. They no longer remembered to watch for the enemy and were blind just like the rest.

While Galvin was walking through the streets, he would often begin to feel that someone was following him closely. He would stop suddenly and spin around with a frightful look in his wide eyes, but the enemy would vanish into a corner or a crowd. *The Devil's mad and I am glad . . .*

He slept with an ax under his pillow most nights. During a thunderstorm, he woke up and threatened Harriet with a rifle, accusing her of being a Rebel spy. That same night, he stood in the yard in the rain in his full uniform, patrolling for hours. At other times, he would lock Harriet in a room and guard her, explaining that someone was trying to get her. She had to work for a launderer to pay their debts, and pressed him to see doctors. The doctor said he had "soldier's heart"—fast palpitations caused by battle exposure. She managed to convince him to go to a soldiers'-aid home, which, she understood from other wives, helped tend to troubled soldiers. When Benjamin Galvin heard George Washington Greene give a sermon at the soldiers'-aid home, he felt the first ray of light he could remember in a long time.

Greene spoke about a man far away, a man who understood, a man named Dante Alighieri. He was a former soldier, too, who had fallen victim to a great divide between the parties of his sullied city and had been commanded to journey through the afterlife so that he might put all mankind right. What an incredible ordering to life and death was witnessed there! No bloodshed in Hell was incidental, each person was divinely deserving of a precise punishment created by the love of God. What perfection came with each *contrapasso,* as the Reverend Greene called the punishments, matched with every sin of every man and woman on earth evermore until final judgment day!

Galvin understood how angry Dante became that the men of his city, friend and foe alike, knew only the material and physical, pleasure and money, and did not see the judgments that were rapidly at their heels. Benjamin Galvin could not pay close enough attention to Reverend Greene's weekly sermons and could not hear them half enough; could not get them out of his head. He felt two feet taller every time he walked out of that chapel.

The other soldiers seemed to enjoy the sermons as well, though he sensed they did not understand them the way he could. Galvin, lingering one afternoon after the sermon and staring at Reverend Greene, overheard a conversation between him and one of the soldiers.

"Mr. Greene, may I remark that I greatly liked your sermon today," said Captain Dexter Blight, who had a hay-tinted handlebar mustache and a strong limp. "Might I ask, sir—would I be able to read more about Dante's travels? Many of my nights are sleepless, and I have much time."

The old minister inquired whether the soldier could read Italian. "Well," said George Washington Greene after being answered in the negative, "you will find Dante's journey in English, in all the detail you wish, quite soon enough, my dear lad! You see, Mr. Longfellow of Cambridge is completing a translation—no, a *transformation*—into English by meeting each week with something of a cabinet council, a Dante *Club* he has formed, of which I humbly count myself a member. Look for the book next year at your bookseller, my good man, from the incomparable presses of Ticknor and Fields!"

Longfellow. Longfellow was involved with Dante. How right that seemed to Galvin, who had heard all his poems from Harriet's lips. Galvin said to a policeman in town, "Ticknor and Fields," and was directed to an enormous mansion on Tremont Street and Hamilton Place. The showroom was eighty feet long and thirty feet wide, with gleaming woodwork and carved columns and counters of western fir that shone under giant chandeliers. An elaborate archway at the far end of the showroom encased the finest samples of Ticknor & Fields editions, with spines of blue and gold and chocolate brown, and behind the arch a compartment displayed the latest numbers of the publishing house's periodicals. Galvin entered the showroom with a vague hope that Dante himself could be waiting for him. He stepped in reverentially, his hat doffed and his eyes closed.

The publishing house's new offices had opened only a few days before Benjamin Galvin walked in.

"Here answering the ad?" No response. "Excellent, excellent. Please fill this out. Nobody better in the business to work for than J. T. Fields. The man's a genius, a guardian angel of all authors, he is." This man identified himself as Spencer Clark, financial clerk of the firm.

Galvin accepted the paper and pen and stared widely, relocating the bit of paper he always carried in his mouth from one cheek to the other.

"You must give us a name for us to call you, son," said Clark. "Come on, then. Give us a name or I shall have to send you on your way."

Clark pointed to a line on the employment form, so Galvin put his pen there and wrote: "D-A-N-T-E-A-L." He paused. How was *Alighieri* spelled out? *Ala?-Ali?* Galvin sat wondering until the ink on his pen had dried. Clark, having been interrupted by someone across the room, cleared his throat loudly and snatched the paper.

"Ah, don't be shy, what have we got?" Clark squinted. "Dan Teal. Good boy." Clark sighed disappointedly. He knew the chap couldn't be a clerk with writing like that, but the house needed every hand it could find during this transition to the massive New Corner mansion. "Now, Daniel my lad, pray just tell us where you live and we can start you tonight as a shop boy, four nights a week. Mr. Osgood, he's the senior clerk, he'll show you the ropes before he leaves tonight. Oh, and congratulations, Teal. You've just begun your new life at Ticknor and Fields!"

"Dan Teal," the new employee said, repeating his new name over and over.

Teal thrilled to hear Dante discussed when passing the Authors' Room on the second floor as he rolled his cart of papers to be delivered from one room to another for the clerks to have when they arrived in the morning. The fragments of discussions he overheard were not like Reverend Greene's sermons, which spoke of the wonders of Dante's journey. He didn't hear many specifics about Dante at the Corner, and most nights Mr. Longfellow, Mr. Fields, and their Dante troop did not meet at all. Still, here at Ticknor & Fields were men somehow allied with Dante's survival—speaking of how they might go about protecting him.

Teal's head spun and he ran outside and vomited in the mall at the Common: Dante required protection! Teal listened in on the conversations of Mr. Fields and Longfellow and Lowell and Dr. Holmes and gathered that the Harvard College board was attacking Dante. Teal had heard around town that Harvard, too, was looking for new employees, since many of its regular workers had been killed or disabled in the war. The College handed Teal a day job. After a week of work, Teal managed to change his assignment from yard gardener to daytime caretaker in University Hall, for it was there, Teal learned by asking the other workmen, that the College boards made their all-important decisions.

At the soldiers'-aid home, Reverend Greene shifted from general discussions of Dante to more specific accounts of the pilgrim's journey. Circles separated his steps through Hell, each leading closer to the punishment of the great Lucifer, the possessor of all evil. In the anteroom of Hell, Greene guided Teal through the land of the Neutrals, where the Great Refuser, the worst offender there, could be found. The name of the Refuser, some pope, did not mean anything to Teal, but his having turned down a great and worthy position that could have ensured justice for millions made Teal burn with anger. Teal had heard through the walls of University Hall that Chief Justice Healey had point-blank refused an assigned position of great importance—a position that asked him to defend Dante.

Teal knew that the bookish adjutant from Company C had collected thousands of insects during their marches through the swampy, sticky states, and had sent them home in specially crafted crates so they would survive the trip to Boston. Teal purchased from him a box of deadly blowflies and maggots, along with a hive full of wasps, and followed Justice Healey from the courthouse to Wide Oaks, where he watched the judge say good-bye to his family.

The next morning, Teal entered the house through the back and cracked Healey's head open with the butt of his pistol. He removed the judge's clothes and stacked them neatly, for man's garments did not belong on this coward. He then carried Healey out back and released the maggots and insects onto the head wound. Teal also speared a blank flag into the sandy ground nearby, for under such a cautionary sign Dante found the Neutrals. He felt at once that he had joined Dante, that he entered the long and dangerous path of salvation among the lost people.

Teal was torn up inside when Greene missed a week at the soldiers'-aid home due to illness. But then Greene returned and preached on the Simoniacs. Teal had already been alarmed and panicked at the arrangement made between the Harvard Corporation and Reverend Talbot, which he had heard discussed on several occasions at University Hall. How could a preacher accept money to bury Dante from the public, sell the power of his office for a rotten one thousand dollars? But there was nothing to be done until he knew how it was to be punished.

Teal had once met a safecracker named Willard Burndy during his nights at back-alley public houses. Teal did not have trouble tracking Burndy down at one of these taverns, and though infuriated by Burndy's drunkenness, Dan Teal paid the thief to tell him how to steal one thousand dollars from Reverend Elisha Talbot's safe. Burndy talked and talked about how Langdon Peaslee was taking over all his streets anyway. What harm would it do to teach someone else how to open a simple safe?

Teal used the fugitive-slave tunnels to cross into the Second Unitarian Church, and he watched Reverend Talbot as he excitedly descended each afternoon into the underground vault. He counted Talbot's steps—*one, two, three*—to see how long it took him to cross to the stairs. He estimated Talbot's height and made a mark on the wall with chalk after the minister left. Then Teal dug a hole, precisely measured, so that Talbot's feet could be free in the air when he was buried headfirst, and he buried Talbot's dirty money beneath. Finally, on Sunday afternoon, he grabbed Talbot, took his lantern away, and poured the kerosene oil on his feet. After he punished Reverend Talbot, Dan Teal had a cloudy certainty that the Dante Club was proud of his work. He wondered when the weekly meetings were held at Mr. Longfellow's house, the meetings Reverend Greene had mentioned. Sundays, no doubt, Teal thought—the Sabbath.

Teal asked around Cambridge and easily found the big yellow Colonial. But looking into the window on the side of Longfellow's house, he did not see signs of any meeting taking place. In fact, there was a loud uproar from inside soon after Teal pressed his face against the window, for the moonlight had caught the buttons on his uniform and now glowed. Teal did not want to disturb the Dante Club if it was gathered, did not want to interrupt the guardians of Dante while they were on duty.

How bewildered Teal was when Greene again failed to show at his post at the soldiers'-aid home, this time without forwarding any excuse of illness! Teal asked at the public library where he might take lessons in the Italian language, for Greene's first suggestion to the other soldier had been to read the original in Italian. The librarian found a newspaper advertisement from a Mr. Pietro Bachi, and Teal called on Bachi to begin lessons. This instructor brought Teal a small armload of grammar books and exercises, mostly ones that he had written himself—these had nothing to do with Dante.

Bachi at one point offered to sell Teal a Venetian century edition of the *Divina Commedia.* Teal took the volume, bound in hard leather, in his hands, but had no interest in the book, regardless of how Bachi rambled on about its beauty. Again, this was not Dante. Fortunately, soon after this, Greene reappeared at the soldiers'-aid pulpit, and there came Dante's astounding entrance into the infernal pouch of the Schismatics.

Fate had spoken loud as cannon thunder to Dan Teal. He, too, had witnessed this unforgivable sin—splitting apart and causing schisms within groups—in the person of Phineas Jennison. Teal had heard him speaking of *protecting* Dante at the offices of Ticknor & Fields—urging the Dante Club to fight Harvard—but had also heard him *condemning* Dante at the offices of the Harvard Corporation, urging them to stop Longfellow and Lowell and Fields. And Teal led Jennison, by way of the fugitive-slave tunnels, to the Boston harbor, where he took him by the point of his saber. Jennison begged and cried and offered Teal money. Teal promised him justice and then cut him into pieces. He wrapped the wounds carefully. Teal never thought of what he was doing as killing, for punishment required a length of suffering, an imprisonment of sensation. This was what he found most assuring about Dante. None of the punishments witnessed were new. Teal had seen them all in large and small ways in his life in Boston and on the battlefields across their nation.

Teal knew that the Dante Club thrilled at the defeat of its enemies, for suddenly Reverend Greene offered a flurry of ecstatic sermons: Dante came upon a frozen lake of sinners, Traitors, among the worst sinners the journeyer discovers and announces. So were Augustus Manning and Pliny Mead sealed in ice as Teal watched in the morning light, clothed in his second lieutenant's dress uniform—just as a uniformed Teal had watched Artemus Healey, the Neutral, writhe naked under his blanket of insects and had watched Elisha Talbot, the Simoniac, squirm and kick his flaming feet, his damned money now a cushion under his head, and had watched Phineas Jennison quiver and shake as his body hung shredded and snipped.

But then came Lowell and Fields, and Holmes and Longfellow—and not to reward him! Lowell had fired his gun at Teal, and Mr. Fields had cried out for Lowell to shoot. Teal's heart ached. Teal had assumed that Longfellow, whom Harriet Galvin adored, and the other protectors who gathered at the Corner *embraced* the purpose of Dante. Now he understood that they did not know the true work needed from the Dante Club. There was so much to complete, so many circles to open in order to make Boston good. Teal thought of the scene at the Corner when Dr. Holmes fell into him—Lowell had followed from the Authors' Room, yelling, "You have betrayed the Dante Club, you've betrayed the Dante Club."

"Doctor," Teal said to him when they met in the slave tunnels. "Turn around now, Dr. Holmes. I was coming to see you."

Holmes turned so his back was facing the uniformed soldier. The muted blaze from the doctor's lantern shakily lit the long channel of the rocky abyss ahead.

"I guess *your* finding *me* is Fate," added Teal, and then ordered the doctor forward.

"Dear God, man," Holmes wheezed. "Where are we going?"

"To Longfellow."

XX

HOLMES WALKED. Though his view of the man had been brief, he knew him at once as Teal, one of the night creatures, as Fields called them, from the Corner: their Lucifer. Now he noticed, looking back, that the man's neck was as muscular as a prizefighter's, but his pale green eyes and almost feminine mouth seemed incongruously childlike and his feet, probably a result of hard marches, supported his body with the eager perpendicular posture of an adolescent. Teal—this mere boy—was their enemy and opposite. Dan Teal. *Dan Teal!* Oh, how could a wordsmith like Oliver Wendell Holmes have missed that brilliant stroke? DANTEAL . . . DANTE AL . . . ! And, oh, what a hollow sound was the memory of Lowell's booming voice at the Corner when Holmes had run into the killer in the hallway: "Holmes, you have betrayed the Dante Club!" Teal had been listening in, as he must have done at the Harvard offices too. With all the vengeance stored up by Dante.

If Holmes was slated for final judgment now, he would not bring Longfellow and the others into it. He stopped as the tunnel sloped downhill.

"I'll go no farther!" he announced, trying to shield himself with an artificially bold voice. "I shall do what you ask of me but will not involve Longfellow!"

Teal responded with a flat, sympathetic silence. "Two of your men must be punished. *You* must make Longfellow understand, Dr. Holmes."

Holmes realized that Teal did not want to punish him as a Traitor. Teal had come to the conclusion that the Dante Club was not on his side, that they had abandoned his cause. If Holmes *was* a traitor to the Dante Club, as Lowell had unwittingly announced to Teal, Holmes was friend to the *real* Dante Club: the one that Teal had invented in his mind—a silent association dedicated to carrying through Dante's punishments into Boston.

Holmes took out his handkerchief and brought it to his brow.

At the same moment, Teal latched a strong hand on to Holmes's elbow.

Holmes, against his own expectations, without forethought or plan, hurled Teal's hand away with such force that Teal was knocked into the rocky cavern wall. Then the little doctor launched into a flying run, gripping his lantern with both hands.

With laboring breath he scurried through the dark and winding tunnels, glancing behind him and hearing all kinds of noises, but there was no way to determine what came from inside his head and his heaving chest and what existed outside himself. His asthma was a chain attached to a ghost's leg, dragging him back. When he came upon some sort of underground cavity, he threw himself inside. There, he found an army-issue fur-lined sleeping bag and some scraps of a hard substance. Holmes cracked it with his teeth. Hard bread, the kind the soldiers had been forced to live on during the war: This was Teal's home. There was a fireplace made from sticks, and plates and a frying pan and a tin cup and a coffee boiler. Holmes was about to run off when he heard a rustle that made him jump. Raising his lantern, Holmes could see that farther back in the chamber, Lowell and Fields sat on the floor, their hands and legs tied, gags in their mouths. Lowell's beard slumped down into his chest and he was perfectly still.

Holmes tore the gags from his friends' mouths and tried to unsuccessfully untie their hands.

"Are you hurt?" Holmes said. "Lowell!" He shook Lowell's shoulders.

"He knocked us cold and brought us here," Fields replied. "Lowell was cursing and shouting at Teal when he was tying us up here—I told him to shut his blasted mouth!—and Teal knocked him out again. He's just unconscious," Fields added prayerfully. "Isn't he?"

"What did Teal want from you?" Holmes asked.

"Nothing! I don't know why we're alive or what he's doing!"

"That monster has something planned for Longfellow!"

"I hear him coming!" Fields cried. "Hurry, Holmes!"

Holmes's hands were trembling and dripping in sweat, and the knots were tied tight. He could barely see.

"No, go. You must go *now*!" Fields said.

"But another second . . ." His fingers slipped again from Fields's wrist.

"It'll be too late, Wendell," Fields said. "He'll be here. There's no time to free us, and we wouldn't be able to get Lowell anywhere like this. Get to Craigie House! Forget us now—you must save Longfellow!"

"I can't do this alone! Where's Rey?" Holmes cried.

Fields shook his head. "He never came, and all the patrolmen stationed at the houses are gone! They've been taken away! Longfellow's alone! Go!"

Holmes dived out of the chamber, running through the tunnels faster than he had ever run, until ahead he saw a distant spark of silver light. Then Fields's command grew in his mind: GO GO GO.

A detective unhurriedly descended the dank stairs to the basement of the Central Station. Groans and harsh curses could be heard through the bricked-up halls.

Nicholas Rey jumped up from the hard floor of the cell. "You can't do this! Innocent people are in danger, for God's sake!"

The detective shrugged. "You really do believe everything you dream up, don't you, moke?"

"Keep me in here if you like. But put those patrolmen back at those houses, please. I beg you. There is someone out there who will kill again. You know Burndy didn't murder Healey and the others! The murderer's still out there, and he's waiting to do it again! You can stop him!"

The detective looked interested in letting Rey try to persuade him. He tipped his head in thought. "I know Willard Burndy's a thief and a liar, that's what I know."

"Listen to me, please."

The detective gripped two bars and glared at Rey. "Peaslee warned us to keep an eye on you, that you wouldn't mind your business, that you wouldn't stay out of the way. I bet you hate being locked up with no way to do anything, nobody to help."

The detective took out his ring of keys and waved it with a smile. "Well, this day'll be a lesson to you. Won't it, moke?"

Henry Wadsworth Longfellow emitted a series of short, barely audible sighs as he stood at his writing desk in his study.

Annie Allegra had suggested any number of games they could play. But the only thing he could do was to stand at his desk with some Dante cantos and translate and translate, to lay down his burden and cross through that cathedral door. In there, the noises of the world retreated and became an indistinguishable roar and the words lived in eternal vitality. There, in the long aisles, the translator saw his Poet in the stretch of gloom and he strove to keep pace. The Poet's step is quiet and solemn. He is clothed in a long, flowing garment, and upon his head he wears a cap; on his feet are sandals. Through congregations of the dead, through hovering echoes flying from tomb to tomb, through lamentations below, Longfellow could hear the voice of the one who drove the Poet onward. She stood before them both, in the unapproachable, coaxing distance, an image, a projection with snow-white veil, garments as scarlet as any fire, and Longfellow felt the ice on the Poet's heart melt as the snow does on mountain heights: the Poet, who seeks the perfect pardon of perfect peace.

Annie Allegra looked all about the study for a lost paper box she needed to properly celebrate the birthday of one of her dolls. She came upon a newly opened letter from Mary Frere, of Auburn, New York. She asked whom it was from.

"Oh, Miss Frere," Annie said. "That's lovely! Will she be summering near us in Nahant this year? It is always so lovely to have her near, Father."

"I don't believe she will." Longfellow tried to offer a smile.

Annie was disappointed. "Perhaps the box is in the parlor closet," she said abruptly, and left to recruit her governess for help.

A knock struck the front door with an urgency that froze Longfellow. Then it came even harder, with demand. "Holmes." He heard himself exhale.

Annie Allegra, bored Annie Allegra, left her governess and cried out her claim to the door. She ran to the door and pulled it open. The chill from outside was enormous and embracing.

Annie started to say something, but Longfellow could sense from the study that she was frightened. He heard a mumbling voice that did not belong to any friend. He stepped into the hall and turned to face a soldier's full regalia.

"Send her away, Mr. Longfellow," Teal requested quietly.

Longfellow pulled Annie into the hall and knelt down. "Panzie, why not finish that part of your piece we talked about for *The Secret.*"

"Papa, the part? The interview—?"

"Yes, why not finish that part right away, Panzie, while I am engaged with this gentleman."

He tried to make her understand, his widened expression signaling "Go!" into her eyes, same as her mother's. She nodded slowly and hurried to the back of the house.

"You are needed, Mr. Longfellow. You are needed now." Teal chewed furiously, loudly spat out two scraps of paper onto Longfellow's rug, and then chewed some more. The supply of bits of paper in his mouth seemed inexhaustible.

Longfellow clumsily turned to look at him, and he understood at once the power that came from inhabiting violence.

Teal spoke again: "Mr. Lowell and Mr. Fields—they have betrayed you, they have betrayed Dante. You were there, too. You were there when Manning was to die, and you did nothing to help me. You are to punish them."

Teal put an army revolver into Longfellow's hands and the cold steel stung the soft hand of the poet, whose palms still had traces of a wound from years earlier. Longfellow had not held a gun since he was a child and had come home with tears in his eyes after his brother taught him how to shoot a robin.

Fanny had despised guns and war, and Longfellow thanked God that at least she did not see their son Charley run away to battle and return with a bullet having passed through his shoulder blade. For men, all that makes a soldier is the gay dress, she used to say, forgetting the weapons of murder that the dress conceals.

"Yes sir, you're going finally to learn to sit quiet and act like you're meant to, contraband." The detective had a laughing glimmer in his eyes.

"Why are you still here then?" Rey had his back facing the bars now.

The detective was embarrassed by the question. "To make sure you learn my lesson good, or I'll knock your teeth out, you hear?"

Rey turned slowly. "Remind me of that lesson."

The detective's face was red, and he leaned against the bars with a scowl. "To sit *quietly* for once in your life, moke, and let life to those who know best!"

Rey's gold-flecked eyes were sadly downcast. Then without allowing the rest of his body to betray his intentions, he shot out his arm and clamped his fingers around the detective's neck, smashing the man's forehead into the bars. With his other hand, he pried open the detective's hand for the ring of keys. Then he released the man, who now grasped at his throat to restore his breath. Rey opened the cell door, then searched the detective's coat and drew out a gun. Prisoners in surrounding cells cheered.

Rey ran up the stairs into the lobby.

"Rey, you're here?" Sergeant Stoneweather said. "Now, what's happening? I was stationed, just as you like and the detectives came around and told me you were ordering everyone off their posts! Where you been?"

"They locked me in the Tombs, Stoneweather! I need to get to Cambridge at once!" Rey said. Then he saw a little girl with her governess on the other side of the lobby. He rushed over and opened the iron gate separating the entrance area from the police offices.

"Please," Annie Allegra Longfellow was repeating as her governess tried to explain something to a confused policeman. "Please."

"Miss Longfellow," Rey said, crouching down next to her. "What is it?"

"Father needs your help, Officer Rey!" she cried.

A herd of detectives tore through the lobby. "There!" one shouted. He took Rey by the arm and threw him against a wall.

"Hold, you son of a bloody bitch!" Sergeant Stoneweather said, and cracked his billy club against the detective's back.

Stoneweather called out and several other uniformed officers ran in, but three detectives overpowered Nicholas Rey and caught both his arms, pulling him away as he struggled.

"No! Father needs you, Officer Rey!" Annie cried.

"Rey!" Stoneweather called out, but a chair came flying at him and a fist landed in his side.

Chief John Kurtz stormed in, his usual mustard coloring flushed purple. A porter carried three of his valises. "Worst damned train ride . . ." he began. "What in God's name!" he screamed to the whole lobby of policemen and detectives after he had assessed the situation. "Stoneweather?"

"They locked Rey up in the Tombs, Chief!" Stoneweather protested, blood streaming from his thick nose.

Rey said, "Chief, I need to get to Cambridge without delay!"

"Patrolman Rey . . ." Chief Kurtz said. "You're supposed to be involved in my . . ."

"Now, Chief! I must go!"

"Let him free!" Kurtz bellowed to the detectives, who withdrew from Rey. "Every damned one of you scoundrels in my office! This moment!"

Oliver Wendell Holmes constantly checked behind him for Teal. The way was clear. He had not been followed from the underground tunnels. "Longfellow . . . Longfellow," he repeated to himself as he passed through Cambridge.

Then in front of him he saw Teal leading Longfellow along the sidewalk. The poet was walking cautiously on the thinning snow.

Holmes was so afraid at that moment that there was only one thing he could do to stop himself from falling faint. He had to act with no hesitation. So he yelled at the top of his lungs: "Teal!" It was a shriek that could bring out the whole neighborhood.

Teal turned, completely alert.

Holmes took the musket from beneath his long coat and pointed it with trembling hands.

Teal did not seem to take note of the gun at all. His mouth stirred and he released a soaked orphan of the alphabet as he spat into the white blanket at his feet: *F.* "Mr. Longfellow, Dr. Holmes shall be your first," he said. "He shall be your first to punish for what you've done. He'll be our example to the world."

Teal lifted Longfellow's hand, in which he held the army revolver, and directed it at Holmes.

Holmes moved closer, his musket pointed at Teal. "Don't you move any further, Teal! I'll do this! I'll shoot you! Let Longfellow free and you can take me."

"This is punishment, Dr. Holmes. All of you who have abandoned God's justice must now meet your final sentence. Mr. Longfellow, on my command. Ready . . . aim . . ."

Holmes stepped forward solidly and raised his gun to the level of Teal's neck. There wasn't an ounce of fear in the man's face. He was a permanent soldier; there was no one left beneath. There were no choices left in him—only the incorrigible zeal to do right that had passed like a current through all humanity at one time or another, usually fizzling rapidly. Holmes shivered. He did not know whether he had sufficient reserves of that same zeal to stop Dan Teal from the destiny he had caught himself in.

"Fire, Mr. Longfellow," Teal said. "You'll fire now!" He put his hand on Longfellow's and wrapped his fingers around the poet's.

Swallowing hard, Holmes moved his musket away from Teal and pointed it directly at Longfellow.

Longfellow shook his head. Teal took a confused backward step, pulling his captive with him.

Holmes nodded firmly. "I'll shoot him down, Teal," he said.

"No." Teal moved his head in rapid motions.

"Yes I will, Teal! Then he'll not have had his punishment! He'll be dead—he'll be ashes!" Holmes yelled, aiming the musket higher, at Longfellow's head.

"No, you can't! He must take the others with him! This is not done!"

Holmes steadied the gun at Longfellow, whose eyes were tightly shut in horror. Teal shook his head rapidly and for a moment seemed about to scream. Then he turned as though someone were waiting behind him and then turned to his left and then his right, and finally ran, ran with fury away from the scene. Before he was too far down the street, a shot rang out, and then another ringing burst hung in the air, mixed with a dying cry.

Longfellow and Holmes could not help looking at the guns in their own hands. They followed the last sound. There on a bed of snow was Teal. Hot blood, cutting a rivulet through untouched white and unwilling snow, floated down from him. Two red spots gurgled in the man's army blouse. Holmes knelt down and his brilliant hands went to work, feeling for life.

Longfellow inched closer. "Holmes?"

Holmes's hands stopped.

Over Teal's body stood a crazy-eyed Augustus Manning, his body trembling, his teeth chattering and fingers shaking. Manning dropped his pistol into the snow at his feet. He motioned with his stiff beard back at his house and pointed.

He tried to string his thoughts together. It was several minutes before anything coherent emerged. "The patrolman guarding my house left a few hours ago! Then just now I heard shouting and saw him through my window," he said. "I saw *him*, his uniform . . . it all came to me, everything. He stripped my clothes, Mr. Longfellow, and, and . . . he tied me . . . took me without clothes . . ."

Longfellow offered a consoling hand, and Manning sobbed into the poet's shoulder as his wife came running outside.

A police carriage halted behind the small circle they formed around the body. Nicholas Rey had his revolver out as he rushed over. Another carriage followed, carrying Sergeant Stoneweather and two more policemen.

Longfellow took Rey's arm, his eyes bright and questioning.

"She's fine," Rey said before the poet could ask. "I have a patrolman watching her and her governess."

Longfellow nodded his gratitude. Holmes had grabbed a fence railing in front of Manning's house to catch his breath.

"Holmes, how wondrous! Perhaps you need to lie down inside," Longfellow said with giddiness and fear. "Why, you've done it! But how . . ."

"My dear Longfellow, I believe daylight will clear up all that lamplight has left doubtful," Holmes said. He led the policemen through town to the church and the underground tunnels to rescue Lowell and Fields.

XXI

"HOLD, HOLD, WAIT A MINUTE," spat out the Spanish Jew to his crafty mentor. "Then ain't that mean, Langdon, that *you'll* be the very last of the Boston Five?"

"Burndy wasn't one of the original five, my fair sheeny," answered Langdon Peaslee omnisciently. "The Five were, bless each one of their souls as they drop into Hell below—and mine own, too, when I join them—Randall, who's serving half-a-stretch in the Tombs; Dodge, who suffered from a nervous collapse and has retired out West; Turner, who was jammed by his ladybird of two and a quarter years—if that ain't a lesson to not hitch yourself I haven't heard one; and dear Simonds, holed up on the wharf side, too cup-shot to crack open a child's jug."

"Oh it's a shame. A shame," moaned one of the men in Peaslee's audience of four.

"Say again?" Peaslee raised a limber eyebrow in reproach.

"A shame to see him about to walk the ladder!" the cross-eyed thief continued. "Never met the man, no. But I've heard it said he was just about the best safecracker Boston's ever had! He could knock over a safe with a feather, says they!"

The other three listeners turned silent and, had they been standing rather than sitting at a table, might have shuffled their boots nervously on the rough shells littering the bar floor or wandered away at such a comment made to Langdon W. Peaslee. Under the circumstances, they took quiet swills of their drinks or absent drags on the unwrapped cigars that had been passed out by Peaslee.

The door to the tavern swung open and a fly propelled itself into the smoky black compartments that divided the barroom and buzzed around

Peaslee's table. A small number of the fly's brothers and sisters had survived the winter and a smaller number still had thrived in certain sections of the woods and forests of Massachusetts and would continue to do so, though Professor Louis Agassiz of Harvard, had he known, would have declared it preposterous. With a darting glance, Peaslee noticed the strange flaming red eyes and large bluish body. He swatted it away, and at the other end of the bar, some men made sport of chasing it.

Langdon Peaslee reached for his strong punch, the special drink of the house at the Stackpole Tavern. Peaslee did not have to adjust his position in his hardwood chair to reach the drink with his left hand, even though the chair was pushed out a fair distance from the table so that he could adequately address his crooked semicircle of apostles. Peaslee's arachnid arms allowed him to reach many things in life without the need to budge.

"Take my word for it, my good fellas, that our Mr. Burndy"—Peaslee hissed the name through the large gaps in his large teeth—"was merely the *loudest* safecracker the bean city's ever seen."

The audience accepted the defusing jest with a raising of their glasses and a peal of exaggerated laughter, fertilizing Peaslee's already excessive grin. The laughing Jew stopped cold with a strained glance over the rim of his glass.

"What is it, Yiddisher?" Peaslee twisted his neck to see a man standing over him. Without a word, the minor thieves and pickpockets around Peaslee rose and veered off to separate corners of the bar, leaving behind aimless clouds of stale smoke to add to the windowless bar's boiling atmosphere. Only the cross-eyed crook remained.

"Hike!" Peaslee hissed. The remaining cohort disappeared into the rest of the crowd.

"Now, now," Peaslee said, looking his visitor up and down. He snapped for the barmaid, barely garbed in a low-necked dress. "Hob or nob?" the safecracker asked with a shining grin.

Nicholas Rey dismissed the server pleasantly with a motion of his hand as he took a seat across from Peaslee.

"Oh come now, Patrolman. Blow a cloud then."

Rey refused the extended long-leaf cigar.

"What's with the Friday face? These are bully times!" Peaslee refreshed his grin. "See here, the fellas were about to adjourn to the back to buck the tiger. We have it every other night, you see. I'm sure they wouldn't mind you joining us. That is, unless you don't have enough beans for an ante."

"I thank you, Mr. Peaslee, but no," Rey said.

"Well." Peaslee put a finger to his lips, then leaned forward, as if to exchange a confidence. "Don't think, Patrolman," he began, "you haven't been shadowed. We know you were after some goose who tried to kill that Harvard mooseface Manning, someone you seem to believe had something to do with the other Burndy murders."

"That's right," Rey said.

"Well, fortunate for you, it didn't come out," Peaslee said. "You do know these are the fattest rewards since Lincoln was done in, and I won't be put in a hole for my bit. When Burndy walks the ladder, my quota'll be thick enough to choke a hog, as I told you, Rey old man. We're still watching."

"You've done Burndy in wrongly, but you don't have to watch for me, Mr. Peaslee. If I had the evidence to free Burndy, I would have brought it in already, whatever the consequences. And you wouldn't get the rest of your reward."

Peaslee raised his glass of punch thoughtfully at the mention of Burndy. "It's a nice story those lawyers make, 'bout Burndy hating Judge Healey for freeing too many slaves before the Fugitive Slave Act and quashing Talbot and Jennison for cheating him out of money. He's met his Waterloo, oh yes. And may he dance when he dies." He took a long sip, then became stern. "They say the governor's calling for the detective bureau dismantled after your row at the station, and that the aldermen are looking to replace old Kurtz and permanently demote you. I'd cap your luck, run while you can, my dear Lily White. You've made many enemies of late."

"I've made some friends, too, Mr. Peaslee," Rey said after a pause. "As I say, you don't have to worry about me. There's someone else, though. That's why I've come."

Peaslee's wiry brows pushed up his tan derby.

Rey turned around in his seat and looked at an awkwardly tall man sitting on a stool at the bar counter. "That man's been asking questions all around Boston. Seems he thinks there's some other explanation to the murders than what your side has presented. Willard Burndy had nothing to do with it, according to him. His questions could cost you the rest of your share of the reward, Mr. Peaslee—every cent."

"Dusty business. What do you suggest be done about it?" Peaslee asked.

Rey thought about it. "Were I in your position? I would convince him to take leave of Boston for a long while yet."

At the counter of the Stackpole bar, Simon Camp, the Pinkerton detective assigned to cover metropolitan Boston, reread the unsigned note that had been sent to him—by Patrolman Nicholas Rey—telling him to wait there at that time for an important rendezvous. From his stool, he was looking around with increasing frustration and anger at the crooks dancing with the cheap prostitutes. After ten minutes, he put some coins down and stood to get his coat.

"Now, where you loping off to so soon?" the Spanish Jew said as he grabbed his hand and shook.

"What?" Camp asked, throwing off the Jew's hand. "Who in the Lord's name are you swablers? Stand back before I grow warm."

"Dear stranger." Langdon Peaslee's grin was a mile wide as he pushed apart his comrades like the Red Sea and moved to stand in front of the Pinkerton detective. "I think it best you step into the back room and join us for some bucking the tiger. We'd hate to hear of visitors to our city ever growing lonely."

Days later, J. T. Fields was pacing an alleyway in Boston at the hour that Simon Camp had specified. He counted the coins in his chamois bag, ensuring that the hush money was all there. He was checking his pocket watch once again when he heard someone approach him. The publisher involuntarily held his breath and reminded himself to stay strong, then he hugged his bag to his chest and turned to face the mouth of the alley.

"Lowell?" Fields exhaled.

James Russell Lowell's head was wrapped in a black bandage. "Why, Fields, I . . . why are *you* . . ."

"See here, I was just . . ." Fields stammered.

"We agreed not to pay off Camp, to let him do as he would!" Lowell said when he noticed Fields's bag.

"So why have you come?" Fields demanded.

"Not to stoop to paying his price under the cover of darkness!" Lowell said. "Well, you know I don't have that sort of cash at hand, in all events. I'm not certain. Just to give him a large piece of my mind, I suppose. We couldn't let that devil drag Dante down without a fight. I mean . . ."

"Yes," Fields agreed. "But perhaps we shouldn't mention to Longfellow . . ."

Lowell nodded. "No, no, we shan't mention this to Longfellow."

Twenty minutes passed as they waited together. They watched the men on the street using staffs to light the lamps. "How has your head been feeling this week, my dear Lowell?"

"As if it were broken in two and awkwardly mended," he said, and laughed. "But Holmes says the soreness will be banished in a week or two more. Yours?"

"Better, much better. You've heard the tidings of Sam Ticknor?"

"That last-year's jackass?"

"Opening a publishing house with one of his wretched brothers—in New York! Wrote me that he'll run us out of business from Broadway. What would Bill Ticknor have thought of his sons trying to destroy the house with his own name, I wonder."

"Let those ghouls try! Oh, I shall write you my best poem yet this year—just for that, my dear Fields.

"You know," Lowell said after some more waiting, "I'd wager a pair of gloves that Camp has come to his senses and given up his little game. I think such a heavenly moon and quiet stars as these are enough to drive sin back to Hell again."

Fields lifted his bag, laughing at its weight. "Say, if that's right, why not use a little of this bundle for a late supper at Parker's?"

"With your money? What holds us back!" Lowell started walking ahead and Fields called after him to wait. Lowell didn't.

"Hold now! Poor obesity! My authors never wait for me," Fields grumbled. "They should have more respect for my fat!"

"You want to lose some girth, Fields?" Lowell called back. "Ten percent more to your authors, and I guarantee you'll have less fat to complain of!"

In the months to follow, a new crop of nickel crime magazines, loathed by J. T. Fields for their deteriorating influence on an eager public, reveled in the story of the minor Pinkerton detective Simon Camp, who, soon after fleeing

Boston following a long interview with Langdon W. Peaslee, was indicted by the attorney general for the attempted extortion of several top government officials over war secrets. For the three years preceding his conviction, Camp had pocketed tens of thousands of dollars by extorting persons involved in his cases. Allan Pinkerton refunded the fees of all his clients who had worked with Camp, although there was one, a Dr. Augustus Manning of Harvard, who could not be located, even by the country's foremost private detective agency.

Augustus Manning resigned from the Harvard Corporation and moved his family away from Boston. His wife said he had not spoken more than a few words at a time for months; some said he had moved to England, others heard he had gone to an island in unexplored seas. An ensuing shake-up in the Harvard administration precipitated the unexpected election of the newest overseer, Ralph Waldo Emerson, an idea hatched by the philosopher's publisher, J. T. Fields and endorsed by President Hill. Thus ended a twenty-year exile from Harvard for Mr. Emerson, and the poets of Cambridge and Boston were grateful to have one of their own inside the College boardroom.

A private printing of Henry Wadsworth Longfellow's translation of *Inferno* was produced before the close of 1865 and received gratefully by the Florentine Committee in time for the year's final commemoration of Dante's six-hundredth birthday. This raised expectations surrounding Longfellow's translation, which was heralded already as "choicely good" in the highest literary circles of Berlin, London, and Paris. Longfellow presented one advance edition to each member of his Dante Club, and to other friends. Though he didn't mention the subject very often, he forwarded the last one as an engagement present to London, where Mary Frere, a young lady of Auburn, New York, had moved to be near her fiancé. He was far too occupied, with his daughters and with a new full-length poem, to find her a better gift.

Your absence from Nahant will leave a gap like that made in the street when a house is pulled down. Longfellow noticed how Dantesque his figures of speech had become.

Charles Eliot Norton and William Dean Howells had returned from Europe in time to assist Longfellow in annotating his complete translation. The halo of their foreign adventures still on them, Howells and Norton promised their friends tales of Ruskin, Carlyle, Tennyson, and Browning: There were certain chronicles better relayed in person than by letter.

Lowell interrupted this sentiment with a hearty laugh.

"But aren't you interested, James?" asked Charles Eliot Norton.

"Our dear Norton," Holmes said, glossing Lowell's gaiety, "our dear Howells, it is *we*, though we have crossed no ocean, who had a voyage that could be contained in no mortal letter." Then Lowell swore Norton and Howells to eternal confidence.

When the Dante Club had to end their meetings, when their work was done, Holmes thought Longfellow might become uneasy. So Holmes volunteered Norton's Shady Hill estate to meet at on Saturday evenings. There they would discuss Norton's progressing translation of Dante's *La Vita Nuova*—"The New Life"—the story of Dante's love for Beatrice. Some nights their little circle was enlarged by Edward Sheldon, who began compiling a concordance of Dante's poems and minor writings, on his way, he hoped, to studying for a year or two in Italy.

Lowell had recently agreed to allow his daughter Mabel to travel to Italy as well, for a tour of six months. The Fieldses, who would depart by ship in the New Year to celebrate the passing of daily operations of the publishing firm to J. R. Osgood, would escort her.

In the meantime, Fields began arranging for a banquet at Boston's famous Union Club even before Houghton started printing Longfellow's *Divine Comedy of Dante Alighieri*, three volumes that reached the booksellers as the literary event of the season.

On the day of the banquet, Oliver Wendell Holmes spent the afternoon at Craigie House. George Washington Greene was in, too, from Rhode Island.

"Yes, yes," Holmes said to Greene of the great numbers his second novel had sold. "It is the individual readers who matter most, for in their eyes resides the worth of writing. Writing is not survival of the fittest but survival of the survivors. What are the critics? They do their best to cheapen me, to make me of no account—and if I cannot endure it, I deserve it all."

"You sound like Mr. Lowell these days," Greene said, laughing.

"I suppose I do."

With a shaky finger, Greene pulled his white cravat away from his baggy neck. "Just need some air, no doubt," he said while falling into a burst of coughing.

"If I could make you well, Mr. Greene, I believe I would turn physician again." Holmes went to see whether Longfellow might be ready.

"No, no, better not," whispered Greene. "Let us wait outside until he's finished."

Halfway down the front path, Holmes remarked, "I supposed I should have had enough, but do you believe, Mr. Greene, that I have begun rereading Dante's *Comedy*? I wonder, through all we experienced, you never doubted the value of our work. You never once thought something had been lost along the way?"

Greene's half-moon eyes closed. "You gentlemen, Dr. Holmes, always thought Dante's story the greatest fiction ever told. But I, I had always believed Dante made his journey. I had believed God had granted him that, and had granted poetry that."

"And now," Holmes said. "You still believe it was all true, don't you?"

"Oh, more than ever, Dr. Holmes." He smiled, looking back at the window of Longfellow's study. "More than ever."

The lamps turned low in Craigie House, Longfellow climbed the stairs, passing the Giotto portrait of Dante, who looked unfazed by his one useless, damaged eye. Longfellow thought that perhaps this eye was the future, but in the other would remain the beautiful mystery of Beatrice that set his life in motion. Longfellow listened to the prayers of his daughters, then watched Alice Mary tuck in her two younger sisters, Edith and little Annie Allegra, and their dolls, who had been taken with colds.

"But when will you be home, Papa?"

"Quite late, Edith. You'll all be asleep by then."

"Will they ask you to speak? Who else will be there?" Annie Allegra asked. "Tell us who else."

Longfellow brushed his beard with his hand. "Who have I said so far, my dear?"

"Not at all enough, Papa!" She removed her notebook from under the covers. "Mr. Lowell, Mr. Fields, Dr. Holmes, Mr. Norton, Mr. Howells . . ." Annie Allegra was preparing a book she called *A Little Person's Memories of Great People*, which she planned to publish with Ticknor & Fields, and had decided to start with a report on the Dante banquet.

"Ah, yes," Longfellow interrupted. "You may add to that Mr. Greene, your good friend Mr. Sheldon, and certainly Mr. Edwin Whipple, Fields's fine magazine critic."

Annie Allegra wrote as much as she could spell.

"I love you, my dear little girls," Longfellow said as he kissed each soft forehead. "I love you because you are my daughters. And Mama's daughters, and because she loved you. And loves you still."

The bright patches of the daughters' quilts expanded and dropped symphonically, and there he left them, secure in the infinite hush of the night. He looked out the window to the carriage house, where Fields's new carriage—it seemed he always had a new one—waited, the old bay horse, a veteran of the Union cavalry newly adopted by Fields, helping himself to water that had collected in a shallow ditch.

It was raining now, a night rain; a gentle, Christian rain. It must have been very inconvenient for J. T. Fields, driving from Boston to Cambridge only to go back to Boston again, but he had insisted.

Holmes and Greene had left a good space for Longfellow between them, on the seats across from Fields and Lowell. Longfellow, as he climbed up, hoped he would not be asked to speak in front of all the guests during the banquet, but if he were, he would thank his friends for bringing him along.

HISTORICAL NOTE

In 1865, Henry Wadsworth Longfellow, the first American poet to achieve true international acclaim, began a Dante translation club in his Cambridge, Massachusetts, home. The poets James Russell Lowell and Dr. Oliver Wendell Holmes, the historian George Washington Greene, and the publisher James T. Fields collaborated with Longfellow to complete the country's first full-length translation of Dante's *Divine Comedy*. The scholars withstood both literary conservatism, which protected the dominant position of Greek and Latin in academia, and cultural nativism, which sought to limit American literature to homegrown works, a movement stimulated but not always spearheaded by Ralph Waldo Emerson, a friend to Longfellow's circle. By 1881, Longfellow's original "Dante Club" had been formalized as the Dante Society of America, with Longfellow, Lowell, and Charles Eliot Norton as the organization's first three presidents.

Although prior to this movement some American intellectuals showed familiarity with Dante, gained mostly from British translations of the *Comedy*, the general public had remained more or less unexposed to Dante's poetry. The fact that an Italian text of the *Comedy* does not appear to have been printed in America until 1867, the same year Longfellow's translation was published, provides one reflection of the expansion of interest. In its portrayed interpretations of Dante, this novel attempts to remain historically faithful to its featured figures and their contemporaries rather than to our own accustomed readings.

The Dante Club, in some of its language and dialogue, incorporates and adapts portions of the poems, essays, novels, journals, and letters of the Dante Club members and those closest to them. My own visits to the Danteans' estates and their environs, as well as various city histories, maps, memoirs, and documents further assembled 1865 Boston, Cambridge, and Harvard University. Contemporary accounts, especially the literary memoirs of Annie Fields and William Dean Howells, imparted an indispensable direct window onto the daily lives of the group and find a voice in the narrative texture of the novel, where even passing characters are drawn, whenever possible, from historical personages that could have been present in the events narrated. The character of Pietro Bachi, Harvard's disgraced Italian instructor, actually represents a composite of Bachi and Antonio Gallenga, another early teacher of Italian in Boston. Two members of the Dante Club, Howells and Norton, greatly informed my perspective through their accounts of the group, although they find only brief occasion to appear in the present story.

The Dante-derived murders themselves have no counterpart in history, but police biographies and city records document a sharp rise in New England's murder rate immediately following the Civil War, as well as widespread corruption and underhanded partnerships between detectives and professional criminals. Nicholas Rey is a fictional character, but he faces the very real challenges of the first African-American policemen in the nineteenth century, many of whom were veterans of the Civil War and were of mixed racial backgrounds; an overview of their circumstances can be found in W. Marvin Dulaney's *Black Police in America*. Benjamin Galvin's war experience derives from the histories of the 10th and 13th Massachusetts regiments as well as firsthand accounts from other soldiers and from reporters. My exploration of Galvin's psychological state was especially guided by Eric Dean's recent study, *Shook over Hell*, which emphatically demonstrates the presence of post-traumatic stress disorder in Civil War veterans.

Though the intrigue that consumes the characters of the novel is entirely fictitious, one might note an undocumented anecdote from an early biography of the poet James Russell Lowell: On a certain Wednesday evening, it is said, a disquieted Fanny Lowell refused to allow her husband to walk down the street to Longfellow's Dante Club session until the poet had agreed to bring his hunting rifle along to the meeting, citing as her concern an unspecified crime wave that had reached Cambridge.

ACKNOWLEDGMENTS

This project has its origins in academic research providentially guided by Lino Pertile, Nick Lolordo, and Harvard's Department of English and American Literature. Tom Teicholz first challenged me to explore this unique moment in literary history further by constructing a fictional narrative.

The Dante Club's evolution from manuscript to novel depended most of all on two talented and inspirational professionals: my agent, Suzanne Gluck, whose extraordinary commitment, vision, and friendship quickly became as integral to the book as its characters; and my editor, Jon Karp, who immersed himself wholly in shaping and guiding the novel with patience, generosity, and respect.

In between origin and completion, there are many who contributed and are owed thanks. For their faith and ingenuity as readers and advisers: Julia Green, beside me without fail for every new idea and obstacle; Scott Weinger; my parents, Susan and Warren Pearl, and brother, Ian, for finding time and energy to help with all dimensions. Further thanks to readers Toby Ast, Peter Hawkins, Richard Hurowitz, Gene Koo, Julie Park, Cynthia Posillico, Lino, and Tom; and to counselors on various issues Lincoln Caplan, Leslie Falk, Micah Green, David Korzenik, and Keith Poliakoff. Thanks to Ann Godoff for staunch support; also at Random House, my appreciation to Janet Cooke, Todd Doughty, Janelle Duryea, Jake Greenberg, Ivan Held, Carole Lowenstein, Maria Massey, Libby McGuire, Tom Perry, Allison Saltzman, Carol Schneider, Evan Stone, and Veronica Windholz; David Ebershoff at Modern Library; Richard Abate, Ron Bernstein, Margaret Halton, Karen Kenyon, Betsy Robbins, and Caroline Sparrow at ICM; Karen Gerwin and Emily Nurkin at William Morris; and to Courtney Hodell, who fortified the project with zeal and her inventive perspective.

My research was bolstered by the Harvard and Yale libraries, Joan Nordell, J. Chesley Mathews, Jim Shea, and Neil and Angelica Rudenstine, who allowed me to study their home (formerly Elmwood) with Kim Tseko as guide. For outstanding help with forensic entomology, I extend thanks to Rob Hall, Neal Haskell, Boris Kondratieff, Daniel Maiello, Morten Starkeby, Jeffrey Wells, Ralph Williams, and to Mark Benecke in particular for his tutoring and creativity.

Special appreciation to the keepers of history at the Longfellow House, where we step into the rooms that once hosted the Dante Club, and to the Dante Society of America, the direct descendant of the Dante Club by virtue of legacy and spirit.